Death of a Serpent

Death
of a
Serpent

A Serafina Florio Mystery

Susan Russo Anederson

Conca d'Oro Publishing

ISBN: 978-0-9849726-1-6

Author's Website
www.susanrussoanderson.com
Give feedback on the book at:
gagasue@gmail.com

Printed and bound in the United States of America.

For Brittany, Tyler & Zach

Part One

October 7 - 22, 1866

Bella's Body

Sunday, October 7, 1866

*S*erafina Florio saw the soul leave its body, a shadow hovering over the corpse, sliding up the stucco before vanishing. "Poor woman," she muttered, and swallowed hard. She should have been used to death by now. After all, Sicily smothered in bodies; corpses rotted in the fields of war, swelled cholera pits, lined the streets after an uprising.

Hearing Rosa's sobs, she wrapped her arms around her friend while afternoon light freighted with the sea slashed the three figures.

The victim lay on the rear stoop facing upward, the coils of her chestnut hair undone, torso turned to the side and clothed in a traveling suit of fine wool detailed in velvet, not at all the costume of a prostitute. Where were her gloves, her hat, her reticule?

In a face so still, the mouth was a rictus of surprise. There was a cut in the center of her forehead and a dark stain seeped through the bodice on the left side. One arm was flung outward, fingers curled, as if in supplication or terror.

After crossing herself, Serafina lifted the poor woman's skirt just enough to reveal a layer of taffeta over several lace petticoats. The taffeta, she knew, was for effect: a woman wearing a stiff underskirt crinkled when she walked, inviting eyes to turn in her direction. Noticing that the hem was damp and that the dead woman's boots were caked in sand, she closed her eyes, breathed in deep, and smelled seaweed.

"My sweet girl!" Rosa slid her eyes to the ceiling and wailed.

Serafina handed her a clean linen. "You sent for Inspector

Colonna?"

Rosa nodded. "Dr. Loffredo, too. But stay with me." She rested her head on Serafina's shoulder. "Been here the longest, Bella," she said, weeping. "She sewed all our garments and such bold designs, too. We paid her, of course, and last week she told me she'd saved enough coins to follow her dream of dressmaking. Now she's dead."

As Serafina patted Rosa's black ringlets, she heard voices in the hall.

Swaying on splayed feet, Inspector Colonna lumbered in, holding his fedora, followed by two uniformed men and an artist. His good eye strayed to Rosa's décolleté. "The body, found when?"

Rosa glared at him. "This morning. My best girl lies here, snatched from life, the third one in three months."

Colonna opened his mouth to speak, but Dr. Loffredo appeared in the doorway carrying his satchel and accompanied by two hooded figures.

"Wait for my signal," the doctor said to the stretcher bearers. Loffredo's face, long and lean and noble, creased in a half smile as he greeted the two women, his eyes gravitating to Serafina.

The two policemen stood on the stoop near the dead woman while the artist sketched. Serafina bit the inside of her cheek as Colonna bent, butt out, to the body. After a moment he rose, motioned to his men and they followed him, slouching down the stairs, stopping first to speak with Rosa's caretaker, before beginning their walk around the house.

The inspector's gaze moved from Rosa, seated at her desk, to the bottle of grappa on a credenza behind her. He, Dr. Loffredo, and Serafina faced the madam.

Loffredo began. "Bella died by a single wound to the heart. There was very little bleeding, and death was instantaneous."

"Like the other two?" Serafina asked.

The doctor nodded. "All three victims, I believe, were killed by the same hand. Their wounds were almost identical. To be sure, the killer wields a deadly knife; his placement of the blade is exquisite—clean, deep, accurate."

Rosa pressed a linen to her mouth.

After watching as the black hoods bore the body away, Serafina lowered her gaze. She should be enjoying the day with her family, but how could she leave Rosa?

Loffredo continued. "All three bodies were moved, I'd say, at least three or four hours after death: *rigor mortis* was broken."

Pointing to the stoop outside Rosa's office door, Loffredo said, "All three bodies were found in that very same spot."

"Deliberate, I'd say," Serafina said.

"My dear, leave police business to us," Colonna said, playing with one end of his mustache.

Rosa eyed the inspector. "This time the viper bites my soul. Bella was a favorite, a friend, and her death is a shock, so I sent for Fina to give me comfort, but you could use her help." She narrowed her gaze. "You've had three months to catch this killer without success and you've no leads, no hope, no nothing."

Colonna's face mottled. "It could be the work of—"

"Never! It's not the work of Don Tigro. I pay him every month without fail." Rosa poured him a grappa. "Marsala?" she asked Loffredo and Serafina.

They shook their heads.

"The time of death?" Serafina asked.

The inspector downed his drink, opened his mouth to reply.

"If I might answer Donna Fina's question," Dr. Loffredo said. "I'd say very late last night or early this morning, sometime before first light, but that's a guess. I'm hoping the autopsy will tell me more."

"The mark on the forehead?" Serafina asked.

Loffredo shrugged. "A spiral of some sort, the same carving that appeared on the first two women, and before you ask, I couldn't guess its meaning."

"The calling card of a wild one," Rosa said.

"The bodies of the first two victims, had they been...?" Serafina's voice trailed off.

Loffredo shook his head. "No fresh bruises or other cuts on the bodies, other than the demon brand. No, there was no abuse of their flesh by their killer."

"How can you be certain?" Colonna asked. "We are dealing with fallen women, let us be clear."

"My dear inspector, leave the medical business to me."

After the inspector and doctor departed, Rosa said, "I must bear the news of Bella's death to her father. We'll take the carriage." 🐦

Breaking the News

Swaying on plush seats, Serafina was silent, looking out the window, marveling at the craggy hills, the sparkle of the sea. In August, after the killing of her women began, Rosa hired five more guards. They surrounded the coach, two of them still wearing their red shirts from Garibaldi's campaign, now faded after six years' wear.

As they picked up speed, Serafina swayed with the carriage. Her mind wandered far afield to the time of her mother's illness a few years ago, the news of her sister's and cousins' deaths that same week, and her feeling of overwhelming helplessness, gazing at caskets lining the piazza like fallen soldiers, many of them flimsy boxes slapped together. Nobles, merchants, peasants—no class escaped cholera, and after the condolences, the funerals, the prayers in the cemetery, came the agony of quarantine. The memory pitched her once again into that flat, dead landscape Giorgio called grief. Serafina didn't know what to call it, only wished it would go away. She stared out the window in an effort to dispel her mood, but with the scent of orange peel and lavender came the image of her dying mother. As distinctly as if she were alive and in the carriage with her, Serafina heard her speak.

"He's your half-brother. Are you listening?"

"No need to explain," Serafina said.

"Your father had been away for months in the north. And I? I was lonely."

"Pray with me." She wiped her mother's brow.

"A man from the next village knocked. Middle of the night," she rasped, her breathing labored. "He told me, 'Bourbon bastards brought me to your door. My sister's in labor. She cries out. Too hard to bear.'"

"You're having a fantasy," Serafina told her.

"He took me to his home. We rode like the wind. I saw the fields, smelled oranges in moonlight."

"Don't talk."

"A young girl, twelve, thirteen, lay on rumpled linen, a sharp smell of blood. Lying there, I thought, she's just a child. She was dead, her infant, stillborn." She stopped and breathed.

"Hush, my sweet." Serafina dried her mother's cheeks with a cloth. "No more bad thoughts. Think instead of the women you've saved, the infants you've birthed. The good times. My wedding day, remember?" Her mother's lips were blue. "And Papa took you in his arms and you danced. The guests clapped. How you loved Papa. You've had a dream, that's all, a bad dream."

She held her mother's hand.

"Hear me." Her breathing was ragged. "Afterward, the man and I sat in his kitchen. We wept together, found comfort in each other, became friends. More." She stopped for a time, her chest heaving for air. "I hid my condition, delivered the boy myself."

Bones clutched Serafina's arm. "Never told your papa. He was still away, teaching in Turin. He worked hard for us … loved me. I took the infant to Mother Concetta, God forgive me. Please forgive me."

"Nonsense, nothing to forgive. I love you, sweet Mama, forever."

"Remember him?" she asked. "Remember the boy with hair like ours? Concetta said the priest named him Tigro."

"No one else knows this?"

"She kept my secret."

Serafina heard again the sound of her mother's breath, like the wheezing of bellows. Then it stopped—she had used up all her words.

As the coach rolled and pitched, the image of her mother's last agony vaporized. Closing her eyes, Serafina made a conscious effort to forget her mother's deathbed secret, an hallucination, she was sure.

At the bend in the road, Serafina hung onto her seat, silent.

"Help me find the killer," Rosa said. "You're a wizard. You see how Colonna does nothing."

She was surprised by the madam's request, didn't know what to say. "Let me think. I need to spend more time with my family, my children."

Rosa sniffed into a wet handkerchief.

Serafina had never seen Rosa like this and they'd been close friends since forever, having met as children when Serafina's mother, summoned to the house for a birthing, brought her daughter along. 'Best way to learn midwifery,' her mother had explained. She could picture it in her mind—Rosa and Serafina helping with the cleanup, and afterward, sitting together at the long table while the robed women laughed or sat silent and ate their sauce.

She handed Rosa a fresh linen.

Ochre light filtered through palm fronds, the stillness in this fashionable Palermo neighborhood not unusual for a Sunday, as they walked the short distance to the home of Bella's mother and father, located on the top floor of a large building near La Vucciria. Rosa gestured to the Baldassare family business, a costume and tailor shop across the street, its doorways and windows shuttered as usual on a Sunday. When she glanced over, Serafina thought she saw movement behind a window on the second story, a flash of white. Bella's ghost?

A man in livery opened the door to the apartment building and ushered the two women inside. They ascended, the madam running up five flights like a mountain goat. After knocking several times on Baldassare's door, they waited. Waited some more. Serafina's stomach growled.

"Can't leave a note." Rosa fanned herself with a glove. "He lost all his sons in the war and the wife's caught in a spell. When he learns of his daughter's murder—oh, Madonna, the dread."

"We'll wait for him, of course. Perhaps he's running an errand, will return any minute."

Rosa's eyes welled up.

Bella's killing is too much for her. "We'll stand here a few moments," Serafina said, hugging Rosa, "and if there's no answer, we'll grab a bite down the street and return. There must be a taverna open in La Vucciria, or perhaps a vendor grilling *paneddi*. Aren't you hungry?"

Rosa repinned her hat and looked away.

Minutes passed. They knocked again and were about to leave when they heard a voice coming from inside the apartment.

"One moment!" There was a shuffle of slippered feet, the tumble of locks, and a tall man with a large head stood before them. "A thousand apologies. Maid's off today. Rosa!" Nittù Baldassare's voice boomed. His smile faded when he saw her face.

"I have bad news," Rosa said. "It's Bella."

In the center of the room, Bella's mother sat motionless facing the light, her mouth, a slash. Rosa planted a kiss on her forehead, whispered in her ear while Serafina held her withered hand for a moment longer before taking her seat. A marble bust of Garibaldi stood on a side table, and on the far wall, doors led to a patio with a magnificent view of Palermo, its domes gleaming in the afternoon light.

Serafina and Rosa sat across from Baldassare, his eyes focused inward. Through clenched teeth he said, "Find him!"

On the ride home Serafina again considered Rosa's request to find the murderer, even though her initial reaction had been to decline. Giorgio's death had been a sudden slap less than six months ago, and her children needed her now more than ever. Bad enough leaving them alone when she was called in the middle of the night to a birthing, but of course she must continue with midwifery—she had a commitment to the town, received a stipend, and they needed the coins. If she were engaged in finding the killer of Rosa's women, she'd be away from the little ones too much of the time, and when home, her mind would be forever wrestling with the mystery. She looked over at Rosa who was wrapped in grief and frowning out the window. Well, then, must not disturb, not now; Serafina would tell her later that she could not, must not, take up sleuthing.

The carriage slowed.

"What's that pounding I hear?" Rosa asked.

"Nothing. The wind."

They stopped.

She heard voices, laughter, roaring beasts, the crack of a whip, and squinted through clouds of dust to a long line of wagons.

The madam stuck her head out the window. Holding her hat firmly on her head with one hand, she called out to the driver. "Why have we stopped?"

"The circus blocks the road."

"Off the highway," someone shouted. "Let us pass!"

Serafina asked, "Can't the guards do something?"

"The guards are thick," Rosa said. "They're a show for bandits, otherwise of little use."

"Stay here." Serafina opened the door and climbed down.

The ringmaster was a ball of a man, short and round, clothed in the only garb she'd ever seen him wear—overalls, a tattered shirt stained with sweat, red tails, a balding top hat. He rolled over to Serafina.

"Eh, Donna Fina, haven't seen you since you was a tyke. Heard you married the apothecary. And you, a midwife, same as your mama, popping out babies like a hocus-pocus lady."

They hugged. She told him about Giorgio's death and the killings at Villa Rosa.

"Heard about the trouble at Rosa's. Word is, the red fox, he's in the coop." He leaned over, spat.

"Another woman killed today. We come from Palermo where we broke the news to her poor parents."

He chewed on the butt of his cigar. "Might as well camp here as anywheres," he said, motioning for his foreman and pointing dirty fingers to an open field. In minutes, mules began towing the wagons to one side of the road while performers and animals flooded the field trampling down the high grass and skirting the occasional clump of prickly pears. A group of knife throwers crowded around a tree where they were setting up a target. Acrobats tumbled. The cook began building a fire.

As Serafina waved goodbye, a clown in whiteface with a tuft of ginger hair stood in the ditch and stared at her, a knife handle sticking out of his belt. Running splayed fingers through her curls, she looked away, hearing the ghost of her mother ask again, 'Remember the boy with hair like ours?' ⌯

A Fair Foreigner

Monday October 8, 1866

*S*erafina decided to drive the long way to Rosa's, not wanting to navigate the Via Serpentina alone, the neighborhoods through which it snaked teeming with alleyways and crumbling fountains, infants wailing in one-room homes, young boys tossing knucklebones, and the smell of garbage heavy on the air.

She flicked the reins trying to hurry, but Largo kept to his own pace, skirting the piazza with its fountain and suppliant statue of St. Benedict, and was managing to maneuver through heavy traffic in the town's center when without warning, a begging monk stepped in front of her, his cart blocking her trap. She caught his eye, but he looked away, and that intrigued her.

Fair-haired and gloved, he wore a frayed cassock. Close to where he stood, white-haired women gathered around a street vendor blocking the monk's rapid movement—or was it his swaybacked beast moving like a snail, that slowed him?

"Whoa, Largo. This won't take long," she said. Largo's ears twitched. After hitching her trap to a post, she stepped into the throng surrounding the monk and shoved her way toward him, clanging money into his cup, knowing as she did so that she shouldn't have. 'Can't afford to help others, or we won't be able to help ourselves,' she heard Vicenzu's saying.

"We don't see many begging monks around here, not since the new government shackled us with more taxes," she said. "Did you have to wait long for your permit?"

He hunched a shoulder.

"You're from what abbey? It's not in Sicily, I take it." Something familiar about him, him and his crusty boots and no sandals. She sniffed the air and unusual odors assaulted her nose—a little seaweed, salt, the dung of foreign animals, all of them mingling about the monk who hadn't washed in a month or two, if that.

"Your *centesimi* will help many of the poor, dear lady. Grateful thanks to you, and may your family prosper. Don Roberto's my name. Remember me in your prayers." He brushed dust from his sleeve and seemed anxious to leave, but was momentarily prevented from going, wedged between another cart and a woman carrying a basket of vegetables.

Serafina persisted. "Where's your monastery?"

Glinting in the light, his eyes were ancient coins. "In one of God's neighborhoods far to the north of Naples, lady, but the people are too poor to buy our bread, so a number of us travel to raise funds. And now, good day to you."

She pursed her lips. Begging from Sicilians? Like squeezing wine from a stone. Took her *centesimi*, but didn't answer her questions, and what sort of monk wore boots instead of sandals? Shadows in his face she didn't trust. ✒

The Ride to Rosa's

The Duomo's bells clanged the angelus as she climbed back into the trap and flicked the reins. She waved to the baker whose fifth son she delivered last month, passed the expensive shops, the straw market, the open fields on the edge of town, but in her mind, she was with Giorgio as they rode in a coach and four, the air heavy with the scent of lavender. 'I'd give anything for a carriage this fine,' he said. She drifted to childhood, watched men clip trees, plant geraniums in great pots, scythe the grasses and wild broom. It was a time when her family kept a full complement of servants, but those days had disappeared.

It wasn't that Giorgio hadn't worked hard, not at all. As an apothecary, there was no one more respected, and his shop, run now by her son, Vicenzu, was busy, although more and more, the townspeople paid for their potions and medicinals with wheat or fish instead of coins. Because of crippling taxes, Carlo's school expenses, and maintaining a home for her family, lately she'd had trouble making ends meet.

Tilting her head she turned into Rosa's villa and signaled to the guard to unlock the gate. Serafina remembered a similar grill, this one on their hotel on the Via Sistina years ago and a merry footman who doffed his cap and beckoned to them with white gloves. Mustn't let the head wander, she could hear Giorgio warning her—in a blink, something might happen, and her eyes moistened at the memory. Oh, she knew his words by heart, pictured him, tall, spangled, scratching one ear, his finest frock coat stretched across his chest. 'And you're a woman traveling the streets alone; driving a trap, even in broad daylight, you must be wary, so keep the eyes fixed on your surroundings and remember, dreaming's bad for the bones.'

Rosa's front lawn was packed with men pruning shrubs, tending to her flowers and pools, her palm-lined drive. A high-class house on the outskirts of Oltramari, Villa Rosa, its gazebo and conservatory, backed onto the Tyrrhenian Sea and was shielded by cypress trees from its neighbors, the estates of British merchants who had first come to Sicily in the eighteenth century.

Inherited from her ancestors, Rosa's business had remained untouched for centuries by war and economic blight. Like her mother and grandmother, the madam had an eye for the main chance. During Garibaldi's campaign, she devised a scheme to remain open, charging his soldiers a special fee—five minutes, five *grani*—and after the war, she redecorated, hung paintings, raised fees. Velvet draped the windows; gilded overstuffed furniture sat on oriental carpets. And when the town installed gaslights around the train station and the promenade, Rosa had lines run into the villa and the nasty-smelling jets fastened to the walls in every room. Water ran in closets discreetly situated on all four floors. Unconventional, Rosa: she didn't keep a full complement of servants, but she had upstairs maids, downstairs maids, a cook, a laundress, a driver, stable hands, gardeners, and her most recent addition, guards.

The wheels of Serafina's trap whirred on the drive and Largo's ears pricked. "Rosa's stableboy spoils you," she said. "Apples and sea grass, is that what moves you?" When she flicked the reins this time, he trotted.

"La Signura isn't down yet," the maid told her.

"I'll walk around the grounds. I haven't seen the new conservatory she talks so much about."

"In the back, dear lady, toward the sea. I'll tell her you're here."

Serafina took the path around to the rear of the villa. The salty air prickled her skin and fat gulls flew in the distance, circling the shore. Ahead was an octagonal glass structure filled with plants and exotic birds. Taking care not to catch her skirt on the prickly pears, Serafina opened the door, sniffed the humid air, and decided she'd had enough, so she continued on toward the sea.

A sloping lawn led to large rocks surrounding a narrow path to the shore. As Serafina drew closer to the water, the wind blew sand in her face, whipping her skirts until she punched them down, expelling the trapped air. She squared her shoulders and stood for a moment, her face to the gale. Plunging ahead, she tripped, catching herself in time to avoid an ungainly fall and looking down, noticed her laces were untied. As she bent to fix them, she saw something peeking out of the tall grass on one side of the wooden stairs, a nest or cloth object, perhaps a purse. She reached out and grabbed it—Bella's hat.

Rosa sat behind her mahogany desk counting her coins and writing numbers in a book. Not dressed yet, the madam, but rouged and robed in her black negligee and robe, the one with the crimson silk tassels and matching slippers. Her office was in the back of the villa, dark-paneled with a stone hearth and a domed ceiling around which frescoed cupids flew. Hanging from its center was a crystal chandelier with over a hundred candles. Serafina knew this because she'd counted them once when waiting for the madam to appear.

One wall was lined with bookcases holding ledgers going back at least a hundred years, all of them fat with black ink. A marble bust of the Magdalene sat on Rosa's desk, head mantled, neck S-curved, lips parted in earthly delight, and on the outer wall, lead-glass windows faced the sea. This afternoon, bright sun played on the cliffs sloping down to the shore.

Rosa pointed to a chair inviting Serafina to sit. Colonna had paid her a visit yesterday, the madam told her. He asked Rosa how long Bella had worked here, when was the last time anyone had seen her, that sort of thing. "Not what you'd ask."

"How so?"

"Your questions are nasty barbs, make me furrow my brow and flip you a tart reply."

"Did he ask for a list of customers?"

"Don't keep lists, you know that." Rosa's face darkened.

"Bella was dressed for traveling, not for entertaining," Serafina said. "Did he ask where she'd been?"

Rosa shook her head. "And I couldn't tell him if he had asked.

Bella's different; she comes and goes as she pleases. All my girls do, come to that. I trust them; I must, or they don't work here."

"Bella came and went as she pleased, you mean," Serafina said, regretting the correction even as she spoke the words. Why must she always be so contrary?

Rosa frowned. "The inspector and his ample behind squirmed around in my chair, tossing his questions at me like an absent-minded butcher slicing a pig, and I could tell he wasn't listening to my replies so I poured him a grappa, watched him drink, watched him depart." She brushed her palms back and forth as if wiping away the crumbs. "He sees nothing, does nothing."

"I found this." Serafina held up the velvet hat, spilling sand on the madam's desk. Same color as the trim on Bella's suit, diamond shaped, with grosgrain ties and a feather. "Bella's?"

Rosa nodded, blinked.

The feather had a black oval design, an oculus, near its base, and there was a certain smugness to it, as if it saw everything on the earth, in the heavens, and under the sea. As if it were the eye of God.

"Where was it?" Rosa asked, then answered her own question. "Oh, outside somewhere." She waved a hand. "What does it matter?" Water brimmed on her lower lids.

Rubbing the plush of the hat, Serafina held it to her nose and smelled the sea, thinking that the madam didn't deserve to lose her business like this, one woman at a time. "It must have dropped when the killer carried the body up the stairs to the back stoop. I'm sure Colonna had his men comb the shore and scour the coves for her reticule and whatever else the police do to ferret out killers. They've been investigating these murders since when—Gemma was killed in July, no?"

Rosa nodded. "That's why I asked for your help yesterday."

Serafina shook her head. "Go to the commissioner. Ask him for a full report on Colonna's investigation thus far. Surely he'll oblige. He's a customer, isn't he?"

"None of your business, my customers." Rosa frowned.

Sometimes the madam's words masked her loving spirit. But she, Serafina, welcomed the barb as the harbinger of her friend's return from the isle of grief, although it was too soon, she knew, for the initial shock of Bella's death to end. It took Serafina over a month of sitting in her room after her mother's death for the restoration of her spirits to begin, and she knew that she'd never get over losing Giorgio.

Rosa stared at the coins on her desk. "Sorry, not myself today," she said and began counting a stack of gold lire, whispering the numbers to herself like a nun at her beads.

Serafina got up and hugged Rosa. "You'll feel better after you've dressed, and I'll go with you to visit the commissioner. Is tomorrow good for you?"

She shook her head. "The wake's tomorrow and the funeral's Wednesday. But Thursday?"

Serafina nodded.

"Will you come with me?"

"To the wake, of course. But won't it be here?"

"Think a bit—how could I hold it here? It's in the parlor adjacent to the embalmer's office where I held the other two. Used rarely, but my only choice. I won't have my girls forgotten." She dabbed her eyes.

"I'll see about getting away for the funeral," Serafina said.

"And you'll help me find the murderer?" Rosa asked.

Serafina gazed up at the flying cupids for a bit, thinking what to say. "I can't promise that. When the babies start coming, I must deliver, and my children come first, but they're in school today, everyone except Totò, of course, and today Renata takes him to the public gardens. If only he had children his age who lived near us—he's so lonely." She paused a moment, drummed her fingers on the chair. "But while I'm here, I could take a look in Bella's room," she said, angry with herself for giving in. She must not, simply must not become entangled in Rosa's web. After all, she had her children to consider. Her temples began to ache.

The madam's eyes sparkled. "You're a wizard!"

"I'm a midwife, not a detective."

"With the mind of a marvel," Rosa said.

Serafina shook her head and was silent.

"When we were young, you solved a riddle faster than a tuna

flips its tail. And I ask you, who solved the mystery of Scarpo's missing sheep?" Rosa asked.

"I did." Her forehead pounded.

Rosa peered up at her. "And who caught that flashy accountant skimming my profits?"

Serafina raised one eyebrow. "Handsome crook, that one. I remember your saying with that breathless, simpering voice of yours, 'Come into the office and feast your eyes, he looks like a Greek god.' You were so struck that you hated to see him leave."

"I kicked him out with relish the minute you discovered he was the one snatching my coins. I still don't know how you did it—you're so bad with numbers."

"Opened my eyes. Opened my mind. Spoke with Scarpo, your gardeners, the other servants. Kept detailed notes. Asked my mother's opinion. Had Beppe follow him and, of course, watched his clothes turn from shabby to silken and the shadows lengthen on his face."

"Too many words as usual, and your mother was dead at the time." Rosa shut her ledger, scooped up the coins, and threw them in the box. "But you're as good at birthing as your mama was, and if you can make a stubborn baby slip out of its womb and appear as if by magic, corner a wolf, uncover a thief, then you can do the same with the killer of my girls."

"Make truth slip out from wailing lungs for all to hear?" She chewed her lip. "Truth never slips out, not for me, not whole and breathing."

Rosa pulled the cord. "If it's clues you're after, Bella spent time in the new conservatory. Loved it, and you might make a visit."

"I tried but it's too gloomy in there—just poking my head inside was enough to frizz my curls."

Rosa smiled.

It was the first real smile Serafina had seen on her friend's face since the killings began.

Just then Tessa appeared, ran to Rosa, and threw her arms around her. Noticing Serafina, she walked over and hugged her and Serafina felt the sharp blades of her shoulders through the fabric of her dress.

"Grown since you last saw her," Rosa said.

For an instant the corners of Tessa's mouth moved upward.

Five years ago Rosa sent for Serafina: 'Bleeding, no baby, come at once.' Serafina slapped the reins and Largo knew enough to gallop. The trap careened around corners, nearly tipping onto Via Marsala, but Serafina was too late. The mother died—a messy, sad business—but she was able to save the infant. When health officials ordered Rosa to bring the baby to the orphanage, the madam refused. Money changed hands and Tessa remained with Rosa. Now the child adored her, and Rosa was a doting mother.

Serafina opened her bag. "I brought you some marzipan candies, my sweet." She handed them to Tessa, kissed her on both cheeks.

Embracing her friend, Serafina said, "We'll concentrate on Bella's life, the last one killed. She's left more for us to discover. I'd like to spend some time alone in her room."

"Tessa will show you the way, won't you, my girl?"

Bella's Room

*S*erafina smelled stale air and lye as Tessa led her to an object underneath one of the windows in Bella's room. Removing the draped muslin, she saw that it was a sewing machine attached to an oak table.

"Bella used this to make our dresses," Tessa said, her hand stroking the contraption. "'My magic,' she called it. She showed me how to turn the wheel and make stitches." Tessa opened the table's middle drawer, pulled out a piece of dark cloth with crude white stitching. "See? Bella was going to teach me how to thread the needle, too, but she died."

"My daughter, Giulia, has one of these. She tried to teach me once, but gave up. She said I haven't the patience." Serafina smiled and waited a moment. "Run along, now, Tessa. Tell Rosa I'll return soon with the key."

When Tessa had gone, Serafina touched the wheel and shut her eyes, trying to feel Bella's presence through the instrument that in life was her silent companion, but failing to get a sense of the poor woman, she told herself she'd dawdled long enough, told herself she'd head for home soon after she'd search the room carefully—she owed that much to her friend. She walked to the hearth swept clean of ashes and began to examine each object in the room, picking up a figurine on a nearby shelf, swiping the dust from a book cover. Seeing movement in the far corner of the room, she swung around, only to discover that the deception was caused by her own reflection distorted and mottled in a spotted mirror.

Even though the prostitute had been dead only a day, a film of dust lay over the room, on the mirror's gilt frame, on the chair below it, on the red silk bedcovers and pillowcases. Little wonder, she thought—someone had left a window open. Walking over to secure the shutters, she felt grit on the brocade draperies and on the windowsill, heard it grind underneath her boots.

She looked beyond the edge of land where foam and wind stirred the beasts of the deep and bracing herself against the sill, she let the elements blow full-throated against her face, listening to the incessant work of the sea. Why was a woman with such talent a prostitute? Doubtless money was a factor. Prostitutes, at least at Rosa's, earned far more than seamstresses. Where did she go two nights ago on the evening of her death? Whom did she meet on the night she was killed? Did she have enemies? Who were her customers? No doubt Rosa had a list of who was with whom and for how long—or at least she kept the information in her head—but, at least for now, when it came to customers' names, the madam's mouth was a sealed tomb. Serafina closed the shutters, pulled down the sash, and turned her attention back to the room.

Two large cabinets stood on the far wall, both of them unlocked. One held Bella's personal wardrobe, each item covered in muslin. Serafina leafed through these, one or two day dresses, several gowns, many a little too revealing, and smiled to herself, remembering how her children described her taste. What was the word Renata used—'bourgeois,' that was it. She held out a dress, examined the stitching. Although not a seamstress herself, Serafina knew expert finishing when she saw it. Again she pulled out a frock, looked at it, examined another and another, beginning to recognize Bella's strong gift, her sense of costume, a unique flair, and that's when she felt Bella's presence—the dead woman hung between her frocks, a specter not yet departed. Serafina stopped, letting the prostitute's spirit work its spell, feeling the strength of her talent.

Below the garments in neat rows were pairs of shoes crafted in fine leather, polished, buffed, and arranged below the matching garment. Serafina made a mental note to visit the shoemaker in town. Unless she had them fitted in Palermo, Bella may have been a good customer, and perhaps he saw her recently. Merchants sometimes knew a lot about their clients, when they were flush and when not, as well as their tastes and the company they kept.

In the second cabinet she found a shelf holding hats, a few of them wide-brimmed with feathers and pins, some made of straw, others of wool, one or two similar to the brown velvet she found on the beach, no doubt all fashioned by Bella. There were shelves with bolts of fabric, watered silks in all shades, a few garish colors, wools in gabardine, bombazine, cloth in a variety of textures, some finely woven, others thick, nubby, boiled. The bottom shelf held a basket stuffed with spools of thread, needles, jars of beads, and next to it was a stack of *Godey's Lady's Books*. She knew this name, *Godey's*. Giulia waited for her copy each month, disappointed when publication stopped during the war in America, so Serafina grabbed several, flipping through them, pausing at some of the colored plates.

She looked at her watch and felt pinched. How did she get herself into this? She wanted to continue helping Rosa, she must, but she must be home when her children returned from school for the noon meal.

Dust flew up her nose. She sneezed, stopped at a page with a creased corner, and peered through watery eyes at an article with drawings of Italian beadwork, embroidery, and church vestments—in a prostitute's bedroom, of all places. What were those swirling things carved in wood, etched onto a chalice, embroidered onto vestments? One snake-like creature wound itself around a holy book of some sort. Another drawing showed it slithering around a cross. She tried to read the words, but the article was written in English. No matter, she'd get Giulia or Vicenzu to translate.

She blew her nose and sat, her ballooning skirt forcing more dust into her face, and she coughed, wishing she had known Bella in life, someone who would rather have worked with her hands and mind than with her body, a woman who could have been a designer of high fashion, a creator of unique lines, expensive gowns for the nobility. Did all of Rosa's women have dreams like Bella's? She decided to take another look around. If she left by 11:30, she'd be home when her children arrived, and that thought, cold comfort as she examined her watch pin, gave her forty more minutes.

She opened the second cabinet again, feeling around in the dim light for something she may have missed and spied at the edge of her vision the ghost of something or other, a bundle perhaps, wedged between the stack of *Godey's* and the back of the cabinet. Pushing the *Godey's* aside, she saw what looked like letters neatly tied into two packets. She scooped them up, stuffed them into her pockets, and stopped, struck with another thought. If she were Bella, where would she hide valuables?

She looked behind the mirror and found nothing, no holes, no patching. She walked the floor listening for loose boards: there were none. Then she gazed at the bed. Of course! Why hadn't she thought of it before? After feeling underneath for a box or hole in the boards, she yanked off the linen, ran her hand over the top and sides of the mattress, but found nothing, wondering what Rosa would say when she saw the mess.

Serafina thought she'd have just enough muscle to flip the mattress, but try as she might, it wouldn't budge. Stuffed with the feathers of a thousand geese, oh, Madonna. Praying for more strength, she stopped to catch her breath, feeling sweat beginning to bead on her forehead, and with an upward thrust, she lifted the heavy contrivance, steadied it while it teetered on end for a moment before thudding against her body and pushing her backward, teetering until she righted herself. The heft of it had almost knocked her down and yet, perversely, it made her more determined to find whatever it was she sought. Taking ragged breaths as she mustered her strength, she felt drops of water running down the sides of her body and losing themselves in the folds of her corset. Again she flexed her arms. With one large grunt, she pushed. When it landed, the mattress shook the mirror on the wall, dislodging more dust.

She mopped her face, sat down, and stared for a moment, then felt every centimeter of the surface until her fingers found a neat square of stitching. After fishing around in the sewing basket for a scissors, she cut the thread and pulled out one little feathery book, an account ledger of some sort. She shoved it into her pocket, picked up the *Godey's* with the snaky designs, and stalked out of the room, closing the door behind her.

All that work for such a meager result. Perhaps reading Bella's letters would reveal more of the woman, something about her dreams, her friends, her enemies, that would help that lazy inspector find the mad killer of Rosa's women. ❧

Dates

"**W**hat did you find?"

"Not much. Any water?" she asked, wiping her face. Serafina dumped the letters, the *Godey's*, and the account book on Rosa's desk.

The madam stuffed the book down her front, reached for the bottle of mineral water, and poured a fresh glass. "You look worse than Scylla on a bad day. What have you been doing, luring young sailors to your lair?"

Serafina gulped the water, choked, and said, "That's better. Dust in the mouth from Bella's room."

"That clown, Colonna, didn't bother to search her room, and look what you've unearthed in a few minutes. And the most important discovery of all," she said, patting the book, now stuffed down her front. "This book belongs to Baldassare."

The madam was in a jovial mood. Time to strike. "I need the names of the customers who visited Bella on Saturday. One of them might know something, might even be the killer. Anyone come to mind?" She watched Rosa's face change to a wintry sunset.

"Bella had the evening off."

"On a Saturday, your busiest evening?"

"Bella was an exception to all the house rules. She asked for the weekend, left on Thursday, and probably went to Palermo to see the contessa—they were going to open a business of some sort."

Serafina raised her brows.

"Not that kind of business. Venturing into the dressmaking trade, the two of them."

Serafina opened the *Godey's* and showed Rosa the plates of the writhing serpent with their convoluted designs and strange vestments and the like. The madam looked at them a moment and shrugged.

Serafina untied the bundles of letters and fanned them out. Sunlight and shadows from the sea undulated on the envelopes. They crinkled at her touch. "From her father," Serafina said, indicating one. She picked up another and considered it. "But this address?" She tapped on the return address written in flowery script.

"From the contessa," Rosa said.

"I don't have time to read them now. I'd like to take these with me. They may tell us something we don't already know, but I doubt it. And the *Godey's*, I'll take that, too."

Rosa, Serafina could tell, was not concerned with letters or magazines or serpents, only that she, Serafina, was being raked into the search for the killer, and truth to tell, she felt herself drawn into the mystery, powerless to stop the pull of her own curiosity. Little wonder: the need for truth and justice in this instance was great. Officials did nothing and the dead women couldn't speak for themselves—they needed her voice. Well, she would continue searching for clues until she found enough evidence to reveal the villain, dump all of her findings into Colonna's lap, and compel him to act. Simple.

Serafina turned to leave, then asked, "The dates?"

"What dates?"

"The first two bodies—"

"What about them?"

"You discovered Bella on October 7th, but on what dates did you find the first two women?"

Muttering something about being late for dinner, Rosa retrieved a large leather-bound book from the shelf behind her desk, its ecru pages smelling of broom and albumen. Serafina walked around to get a better look.

Rosa leafed through the volume, each spread containing a month—seven columns across, with four or five rows down—the madam's scrawl filling many of the squares. Light from the sea swam over Rosa's face as she turned the pages, stopping at August. "The beginning." The square for August 7th contained one word, 'Gemma.'

"The day you found Gemma?"

Rosa nodded.

Serafina turned the page.

Rosa gestured to September 7th and Serafina saw the word, 'Nelli.'

"I opened the door, and there was our darling Nelli. The sight of her name dries my throat."

Without looking up, Rosa refilled their glasses and said, "October," gulping her water and caressing with a finger Bella's name written in the square for the seventh.

Serafina stared into space.

"Your mind's taking a walk." Rosa put on her spectacles and began flipping the pages back and forth. "Peasants are starving and you bite off a chunk of words and don't finish them. At least spit them out before you stare into space."

Serafina looked out to the sea, silent for a bit. "I was going to say that if you found each body on the seventh day of the month, it means the killer attacked on the sixth, or early on the seventh every time. Don't you see? It means if he kills again—and I believe he'll try, mark my words, he'll try—most likely he'll strike on the same date."

Rosa's face blanched.

Serafina continued. "There's a systematic ghoulishness about these murders, a wildness about this killer that we will never understand. He lusts not after flesh, but has the cunning of the wild, intent on one thing only—eliminating you and all your women and the business you think I know so little about. For lucre? I doubt it."

The madam's eyes were flaking embers but Serafina knew she had her attention.

"Why the mark carved into their foreheads?" she continued. "Why did each death occur between the sixth and the seventh of the month? We must discover how the victims' lives touched their killer's path. Why did these women need him? Agree to meet him? What did the three have in common, other than their profession and their address? How did they know him? Is he a customer who helped himself to all three? To others?" "Who is the one woman most likely to be his next victim?" ❧

The Apparition

Tuesday, October 9, 1866

*S*erafina's wardrobe wasn't extensive, never expensive, wouldn't do, not for a woman of her class. The dress she chose to wear, made of watered silk trimmed in velvet—black of course, she was in deep mourning for Giorgio—was designed and crafted by Giulia, her middle daughter, in a style dated by a year or two as did the other women in her class. For daytime, she wore a single petticoat, not too full in front, with an undergarment of unbleached silk ruffled at the collar. She fastened the ivory cameo her mother had given her and rouged her lips, the facial color and the brooch not strictly in keeping with widow's weeds, she realized, but some of these rules needed to be broken, and rang for Assunta to help with her hair.

"Not too busy, something simple," she told the domestic.

After Assunta left, she tied an embroidered net over her hair, similar to the one that Queen Maria Sofie might have worn. "Ready," she called out to the air in the room.

All at once there was a rattling at the window panes. The candles flickered, and Serafina felt the rush of air. A new smell, sharp, like shaved citrus and lavender, flooded the room and a cloud appeared. In a few seconds, it faded, and, in its place, a specter emerged, vaporous at first, almost invisible, a frescoed glaze upon the cushions of Giorgio's overstuffed chair. The phantom grew more distinct, taking on the shape of a woman, and Serafina saw her mother, Maddalena, crimson cheeked, skin moist, clothed in a gown of deep viridian. She'd forgotten how much like her own hair her mother's was, at least before hers started to fade.

Maddalena's head turned in Serafina's direction, but gazed through her, as if mesmerized by something beyond the room. Wrinkling her nose, she turned her attention to an object in her lap, a midwife's satchel. Her hands fiddled with the clasp, her lips moved, and she shook her head.

"Can't you say hello to your own daughter?" Serafina asked.

Hunching her shoulders, Maddalena plunged one arm into the bag, rattling objects inside, as if stirring old bones. "Carmela's gone and you do nothing. She's all alone, knows not of my death, nor of her father's. You must find her."

"But how?"

Maddalena stopped, lifted her head, wary and still, like a cat about to pounce. At the sound of footsteps in the hall, she vanished.

The doorknob turned and Serafina's youngest daughter poked her head into the room. Maria's arms were full of schoolbooks and musical scores and her spectacles slid down to the tip of her nose. Pushing them up, she said, "Are you coming? I'll be late for my lesson."

The Duomo's bells chimed the hour. Only seven o'clock and already Serafina's head ached. ✍

Numbers

Serafina and Maria traipsed across the piazza to the music store where Maria had a lesson each day before school. Opening the door, Serafina smelled sawdust and resin; she saw instruments hanging from the rafters, Minerva's cello standing in the corner, and the maestro in the corner playing his harpsichord.

"How lovely. Scarlatti?"

"Mozart." He continued to play as they talked.

"Isn't it lovely, my precious?"

Maria hunched her shoulders.

"If only our little genius here would play pieces with more melody. I tell her she can't go wrong with Scarlatti, but all she's interested in at the moment is Brahms—Brahms this, Brahms that, chords crash."

The maestro twisted his mouth and finished his sonata.

Maria clutched her books to her chest.

Serafina kissed her daughter goodbye and was reminding her to go to school directly after her lesson when Minerva entered the room, tapping a white cane in front of her.

Serafina pecked the maestra's cheeks. "I'd like your advice if I could steal some of your time while Maria takes her practice with the maestro."

"My studio—follow me."

Serafina could hear Maria's scales while she told Minerva about the investigation. "Dr. Loffredo is certain that Rosa's women were killed by the same man, and I'm convinced he's a wild creature who doesn't kill for pleasure or to sate his appetite," she said, "but the dates he's chosen to kill are significant in a way I don't understand.

He's killed one victim a month for three consecutive months, each murder occurring sometime on the sixth or seventh day."

Minerva frowned. "Not my field, numbers, but my brother is professor of mathematics and interested in the occult. I have an hour before my next lesson and will introduce you if you can drive me there—he lives on the edge of town."

Minerva's brother lived alone in a small house filled with books. Not a dish out of place, no dust on the floor. After greetings were exchanged, the reason for their visit explained, and refreshments declined, Minerva and Serafina sat.

The professor was a thin man who wore a white shirt, grey vest, and sat on a wooden chair while the women faced him on the edge of a horsehair sofa, Minerva bracing herself with her cane.

He had a slight lisp, the professor did, and Serafina had to strain to hear him. Reaching into her reticule, she pulled out her notebook and pencil and began writing as he spoke.

With curled fingers he combed his mustache, addressing the two women as if they were students in a large auditorium. "So," he said and paused.

Minerva said, "What? So what? Please continue."

"What I know of the numbers, six and seven, I'll tell you now. Or . . ."

Another pause.

"Or?" Minerva asked, her face a frown.

"If you prefer, you can read my book, *Numbers and Ecstasy.*

"Tell us please," both women said in unison.

"So, six is a perfect number," he said, looking first at his sister, then at Serafina.

"Get on with it," Minerva said.

"A perfect number is a whole number greater than zero. When you sum all of its factors, except for the number itself, you get that number."

After scribbling down what she thought he said, Serafina rubbed her forehead. "I take your word for it—six is a perfect number."

Minerva tried her hand at explaining her brother's words. "The factors of six are one, two, and three. When you add them, they make six, so six is a perfect number."

The professor continued. "Six is followed by twenty-eight, then four-hundred ninety-six, followed by—"

"Somehow I don't think the killer is a mathematician," Serafina said, "and I trust I won't need to know all the perfect numbers."

"Agreed. Not too many murderers are interested in the genius of Euclid," Gasparo said, straightening his vest.

Minerva nodded.

He said, "Now we come to the number, seven. According to the Greeks, it contains perfection, being the sum of the sides of an isosceles triangle and a square. The Romans, on the other hand, thought the number contained everything since it is the sum of four, the four corners of the earth, and three, a symbol of the divine."

Serafina thanked the professor. She and Minerva were about to depart when he stopped them. "Perhaps your killer is caught in the web of numerology, for sometimes the mad will act according to the heavens. For instance, the full moon which pulls the tides also holds captive their emotions, and thinking the spirits call to them, they are powerless not to carry out their deeds under its influence."

Serafina shook her head. "No full moon last Saturday, I would have remembered."

They were halfway home when Minerva said, "Trouble ahead, I hear it. Can we take another road?"

Serafina was aware only of a faint blowing in the distance, like the whisper of air through fronds. "Children playing?" she asked.

"Not children. Something else."

As they drew closer, Serafina peered down the street and saw what must be causing the commotion, a knot of onlookers forming around something. She slowed. An accident? A dodgy vendor? Voices grew louder. Shoving and pushing began, a few fists were thrown and dust clouded her view, but at one point the throng parted and she could see a disheveled creature standing next to a swaybacked mule and a weather-beaten cart. The man was arguing with several others, if anything, angrier than himself.

"Poor man. Living rough, I suspect," Serafina said.

Minerva stared into the crowd, nodding, as if seeing. "Up to no good, by the sound of it."

Serafina's only choices were to muscle past the crowd or to trust in Largo's sense of direction. Deciding on the latter, she turned the trap and headed into a maze of narrow streets, letting him take the trap through one twisted road after another.

"I hope you know where you're going," she said to the mule.

Largo brayed, increased his speed, and in a few moments, Serafina could see the piazza and the music shop. Drawing up to the door, he thanked her friend, kissed her on both cheeks, and helped her inside. 🙾

Dr. Loffredo

*W*ho else but Dr. Loffredo would sit at his desk with his breakfast served on fine china by a maid dressed in black with a white apron, a table linen tucked into the collar to protect his boiled shirt?

Pulling at his napkin, he came around to kiss Serafina's hand. So gentle his touch and understanding of women, and with eyes that would melt Scylla. He was tall with not a hint of paunch, his clothes from the best tailors in Palermo. She remembered their university days together, heady times, when class differences didn't matter and bedroom walls echoed with daring talk of revolution. A pity she had loved her Giorgio so much.

He held the back of her chair. "Latté, my dear?"

"Don't worry about me. Eat your breakfast while you tell me the results of the autopsy."

"Too early in the day to talk of murder." He rang the bell.

She ignored his remark. "Rosa asked me to investigate the deaths of her women."

His gaze was tender. "But you're a midwife."

She raised her shoulders, palms out. "I can't sit by while her business is destroyed—she's my best friend, and Colonna does nothing."

"The police have their hands full."

The maid entered, balancing a tray and silver coffee service. She swept up the remains of his breakfast, shot Serafina a look, and left. Loffredo poured espresso and steaming milk, passing a cup to Serafina.

She said, "You've heard the rumors."

"Don Tigro?" Loffredo sipped his caffè.

"Doesn't make sense. Not to me. You?"

He shook his head. "Not the don's kind of killing, unless, of course, Rosa's not telling us everything."

"She doesn't hold things back from me." Serafina paused. "Well, almost nothing."

He reached over and touched her hand.

"Spent time this morning combing through Bella's room. I uncovered some information, nothing that gave me answers, only more questions." Serafina's gaze swept his face. She savored her first sip of latté, breathing in the cocoa, the caffè, and the steam. "To tell you the truth, I'm intrigued. Horrified, yes, but also fascinated by the prospect of sleuthing." She looked into his eyes. "Of late, my practice has been slow. Most families do their own birthing when coins are scarce, and not so many tips from grateful fathers."

"Is it hard for you with Giorgio gone?" he asked.

Her face colored. She couldn't tell Loffredo money was tight, wouldn't do. "Oh, that. We're fine. No worries there."

Loffredo swiped his mouth with fresh linen. "Be careful, Fina."

"You know me."

"Too well. Yes, you're a wizard, but sometimes it takes more than magic to right the world's wrongs."

"But I have to try."

"Perhaps, but I couldn't bear to think of your meeting the same fate as those women." Loffredo crossed his legs. "This killer knows what he's doing."

"He?"

"Well, I don't know for sure." He ran two fingers down a perfect pleat. "A knife has been the weapon of choice for female murderers for centuries. It takes great skill to wield a deadly blade, but not great strength, and judging from the wounds on the three victims, the knife was razor-sharp. Double-edged, a stiletto. A vigorous woman could have killed Rosa's women, but with these murders, I'm inclined to suspect a man, even though ..." He paused.

"Even though what?" she asked.

"There was no indication that this prostitute had been sexually violated either before or after death," Loffredo said. "No bruising."

And the other two?"

He shook his head. "None, but I still think the killer is male."

"You said *rigor mortis* had been broken?"

"Yes. Although Bella's right arm defied gravity, there was evidence that the body was moved sometime after death."

"So that means the murderer could have left the scene and returned for the corpse?"

He nodded.

But why? Did he need to perform ritualistic acts after killing, or did he wait for help to arrive? Aloud, she said, "Did the autopsy tell you anything more?"

"It corroborated what seemed apparent when I examined initially: the wound to the heart was mortal. No food in the small intestines, so Bella died at least eight hours after eating. Assuming she ate a light supper at the normal hour, say, anywhere between four and six o'clock, death occurred very late on the sixth or early on the seventh." ꜟ

The Embalmer

A round man with fish lips and protruding eyes, the embalmer wore a green apron over striped pants and stood in the doorway of his shop smelling like vinegar and hair oil and sucking on a cigar. He blinked several times in response to Serafina's greeting, nodding his head as she told him that Rosa had asked her to find the killer of her women, and if he wouldn't mind, she'd like to speak with him about the mark on all three of the dead prostitute's foreheads. "I saw it on Bella's brow when Rosa found her Sunday morning, but wanted to talk to you before the wake this evening."

He gave her a pursed smile, more visible in his eyes than on his mouth.

She continued. "Dr. Loffredo told me Rosa's women died from a single stab to the heart, the wounds, identical on all three women," she said, "and that each had a similar cut on the forehead, a signature, he thought, that must have been signed by the murderer."

"Just so. Almost finished dressing the body, but the face is not yet fixed. Would you like to see her?"

Did she want to see Bella's body again? Not really, but she followed him inside.

The embalmer stuck the butt of his cigar between his lips and led the way to his workroom in the basement. Lifting her skirts, Serafina picked her way down a stairwell wide enough to hoist a casket. The smell was like the distillation of death, and she heard the scurrying of claws, the swish of tails, perhaps a lizard slithering away.

As he held the door, he beckoned her inside a room with a long table. On it was a body covered with a sheet, and by its side, an oil lamp, vials, powders, and a magnifier. He lifted the cloth covering the corpse, revealing the dead woman's head and neck.

It was Bella, all right, her face like a wax parody of itself, but the chestnut hair was still full of life. Rude to stare and probe without observing at least a moment of silence, so Serafina, feeling the coldness of the grave seeping into her from the corpse, closed her eyes and asked the saints to lead the poor woman into paradise. Then she bent to the body, and through the glass, studied the mark on the prostitute's forehead.

"All three carvings were the same, but this one is … artistic, you might say," he said, esteem for the killer's mastery with a blade evident in his voice and eyes.

"How so?"

He pointed a nicotine-stained fingernail at Bella's forehead. "This one has more detail than the other two. The top of the coil has a faint mark, here, like the tongue of a snake."

Serafina peered through the glass again and saw what he meant, the distinctive V-shape at the end of a serpent's tongue. "Made by a very small knife, I'd say."

He nodded. "A scalpel."

His shoe ground the butt of his cigar, and he motioned her upstairs and into his office, a room cluttered with papers, books, and the dusty contraptions of his trade. A diploma from the Capuchin catacombs in Palermo hung above his desk, and in one corner, casket lids stood on end.

Looking around the room, Serafina felt something deep and complex run through her. The thought, or whatever it was, disturbed her stomach.

Blinking several times, the embalmer offered her a chair and held out a plate of sweets. "Caffè, *dolci*?"

She shook her head and swallowed. "One more question if I may."

"For you, dearest lady, what you wish."

"At the other two wakes, were there any mourners you didn't recognize? Anyone whose demeanor was strange, who seemed, what to say, not properly distraught or otherwise out of place?"

He bit into a cookie and let his watery gaze drift. "Not many attended. Rosa asked me to do my best work, and I did." He paused, taking another bite, spewing crumbs onto his apron. "But now that you mention it, yes, there was a man who was unusual, and before you ask, no, he was not from around here, at least not anyone I recognized. To Gemma's mourning he came with leather face and seeping eyes."

"Seeping eyes?"

"The eyes were disconnected from the mouth, you see. They teared, but not from grief."

Nodding, she scribbled his words into her notebook.

"Carried a cane, unusual for one his age. Not old, not young, he stayed away from the other visitors."

"How so?"

"He came alone, stood in a back corner until it was time for the closing prayers from the priest, then he walked to Gemma's casket, scowling and shaking his head. I watched as he raised his fists and cursed the corpse. Caused a stir among the other visitors, and we were about to escort him out of the room when he disappeared, vanished into the air, as if we had imagined him. Searched for him outside, up and down the street and around the piazza, but couldn't find him."

Serafina rose, thanked him for his time, and told him how much she admired his ability. "I'm sure you'll fashion Bella into a sleeping angel for the viewing tonight."

"Yes, dear lady." He shook his head. "Who or what did she see the instant before her death? By the look on her face, it was the scaly Satan himself." ❧

The Wake

A tribute to the artistic powers of the embalmer,
the corpse lay as if sleeping while the males in
her family took turns standing alongside the bier.
Candles flanked the open casket and flickered in wall sconces.

Accompanied by her son, Vicenzu, Serafina made her way to the
front of the parlor to pay her respects, afterward stepping to the
back of the room and watching as a stream of mourners filed to
the front. Most of the men wore frock coats, carried silk hats and
gloves. The women, corseted, clutched their children, whispered in
their ears, and led them to the front to say their farewells.

Parting this sea of black, Nittù Baldassare wheeled his wife
into the room. A gaggle of women flocked to her, in their lead,
a dramatic, willowy figure in a flowing black gown, thick with
rouge and French perfume. Sobbing and flailing her arms about,
she hugged Bella's mother. Such a display—surely not one of Rosa's
girls.

Younger mourners gathered in a far corner of the room while
Rosa played the part of hostess, moving in measured grace among
them and making introductions. Family members and Baldassare
business associates greeted one another. Serafina heard the talk of
wakes and funerals, knew this jargon by heart, she'd been to so
many of these gatherings. Smiling, nodding, Serafina listened to
snatches of the conversations: "I'm the cousin twice removed …
how can the father continue … alone now, except for his wife and
she, poor soul … the harvest, another desolation … on her father's
side … her hair? No, the heir … such a swagger."

Someone tapped her on the shoulder.

"You don't recognize me?" the man, a younger version of Bella's father, intruded. Her eyes rested on his armband. "It's me—Falco!" He stretched out his arms to embrace her.

Serafina shook her head, confused for a moment until all at once, the years tumbled away. How could she forget him?

He pointed to the casket. "My niece. Her father is my brother." Clearing his throat, he said, "Such a pity, he lost all of his sons in the war and now, he loses Bella, his favorite child, despite her recent … peccadillos. I run the business with my sons."

Serafina drummed a fist back and forth on her thigh, remembering their affair. Brief, torrid, best forgotten. Betrothed to Giorgio at the time, she had betrayed his love and had gotten what she deserved.

"Ravishing, still, Serafina." His eyes couldn't help it. They devoured her. "You are Rosa's friend, no?

She smiled.

"Give her this message," Falco said. "Tell her that Nittù and I, we want to help her catch the killer. Tell her to call on us." He kissed her hand, gazed into her eyes, a look that once had the power to melt. "Rosa told me about your husband. My deep …" But he was interrupted by someone who caught his eye. Following his gaze, she saw who it was, a lithe creature, one of Rosa's prostitutes, waving to him. He took his leave with a nod and, she was sure, not another thought for her.

"That tall man with the chestnut curls, I saw him kiss your hand. Who is he?" Vicenzu asked, pulling Serafina aside while Bella's father talked to Rosa and Falco cavorted with the young woman.

"Later," she said.

"He's got quite a way with Rosa's women—must know all of them," Vicenzu said.

Before she left, Serafina gave Rosa a double kiss goodbye, and out of the corner of her eye, saw Falco and a young redhead in the back of the room acting like love birds in a nest of rooks. She chewed her lip. Hadn't changed, Falco.

Serafina took her leave, walking out of the parlor the same way she'd entered, on the arm of her son. As they passed Falco's group, the redhead waved. ✒

Bella's Letters

Wednesday, October 10, 1866

*S*erafina chose to read Bella's letters in her father's study, hoping they'd contain information of value—not just addresses and facts, but something of the character of the writers, and more importantly, a glimpse into Bella's life.

In addition to those from Baldassare, there was correspondence from a woman, a noblewoman, judging from the seal and the fine grade of parchment, and considering the loopy script and garish color of ink, written by the woman Serafina had seen at the wake last night, Bella's contessa friend. The return address contained a number on the Piazzetta del Garraffo, which, if Serafina remembered correctly, was close to Baldassare's shop.

She arranged the letters by sender, sorted them by date with the oldest on top, and settled in for a good read.

The father's spanned a decade, a long time in a prostitute's career. The oldest contained short bursts of news along with commands for his daughter's return—nothing of the man in them, only announcements of life and death. In an early letter her father wrote,

> *Your brothers are dead, all of them. Lost in a despicable battle on the outskirts of Milazzo. One day, one bridge, four brothers dead among eight-hundred others. Your mother's mind, too heavy with grief, is a sinking ship. You must come home.*

In his middle correspondence, Serafina noticed a shift in the man's regard for his daughter. Gradually, his anger and disbelief changed to resignation. Those were the longest letters, containing news of this cousin, that marriage, a feast, a play they'd attended. He told Bella about their customers, their orders, the relative ease of obtaining cotton "now that the war in America is over." Serafina began to get a sense of Baldassare, laughed at his humor, smiled at his words of endearment.

In his last letters, it was apparent that father and daughter had been meeting, and that the reason for his change toward her was Bella's decision to leave an occupation he loathed. Serafina read these letters a second and third time, was struck by the frequency of words like 'love,' 'sweet,' 'tender,' phrases such as 'your joyous face.' He seemed filled with his plans for the future, and he signed all of these, 'Your loving father, Nittù.'

The contessa's were fewer. They alluded to Bella's plans with phrases like, 'I go to Paris next month to visit Worth & Bobergh,' and 'I trust the *monzù* will honor his intention to let me visit his great house,' and 'My trip proved all that I hoped it would and more. I cannot wait to talk. We have so much to prepare.' It was clear that the two women were engaged in an economic venture. Bella's need for capital explained her work at Rosa's and supported the madam's contention that the prostitute planned to quit the house.

Serafina wrote a summary of what she'd learned from the letters—character impressions of Baldassare, Bella, and the contessa, plus a corroboration of what she'd already known—but the letters yielded no fresh information, no leads. She fingered her cameo, lost to her surroundings. ❧

The Brazen Serpent

"Giulia, sweetness, I need you to look at something," Serafina said, waving the magazine and entering the kitchen.

Her middle daughter, the one born with a needle and thread, took the *Godey's* from Serafina and made a face. "Where did you get this?"

"From Rosa. Tell me what the words say."

Giulia hunched over the pictures, scanning the type with her fingers. "It's about a church in the north, their vestments and cups and such. And," her finger paused over a phrase, "they talk about a bronze serpent. I didn't know Rosa embroidered."

"You'd be surprised what Rosa gets into. By the way, who's been using Papa's English dictionary?"

Giulia's smile lit her face.

"You're so industrious, my designer of high fashion. Just remember to put his books back when you've finished with them—I noticed some of his shelves were disordered."

Giulia nodded.

Serafina kissed her daughter's forehead.

Bronze serpents? 'Cups and such'? Serafina needed more information, so she decided to visit the Duomo's priests.

As she hitched her trap to a post near the rectory, Serafina caught the scent of warm bread and waved to the baker. She saw a group of children on their way to school, some running, others skipping or walking backward. The streets were full of people heading to the straw market and to the more expensive shops facing the piazza. Mules with jingling headgear pulled painted carts. Greeting a peasant whose thirteenth child she delivered last week, Serafina stormed up the rectory's stoop, misjudging the depth of the last step, and snagging the hem of her skirt.

While she waited for the priest, Serafina ran a palm over her scuffed boots, wiping her hand on the side of her dress. She was sick of wearing black, certain she could grieve for her husband just as well in a fine watered silk of alizarin crimson or jade.

"I'm investigating three murders. Perhaps you can help," she said to the priest. She handed him the *Godey's Lady's Book*, opened to a colored plate of the brazen serpent on a cross. "What can you tell me about these drawings?"

He glanced at the pictures, stabbing a finger at one. "I know nothing about these, except that they're very beautiful, especially this chalice—we could use one like it." He put a hand to his lips and considered. "But we have a visiting priest, a scholar, and he might know." He rang the bell.

Soon a tall man entered, tonsured, wearing a hooded cassock. A large set of rosary beads hung from his belt. Serafina wondered what possessed monks to wear sandals, especially when their feet were, like his, big and yellow and purple-toed.

After introductions and a brief explanation of her murder investigation, she asked, "What can you tell me about the symbols on these pages?"

He examined the plates. "The brazen serpent. Where did you get these?"

"In the room of a seamstress, one of the victims," she said.

"Beautiful, this magazine. I'd like to study it some more. May I?"

"Not mine to lend, I'm afraid," she said, and continued. "Each of the murdered women had a spiral carved into her forehead, similar to this," she said, tapping the embroidery detail of a serpent. "Their marks were spirals of some sort, starting from the bridge of the nose and winding to the top of the forehead."

He shrugged. "But the brazen serpent is a symbol of salvation, not of destruction, of eternal life, not death. It appears in some form in most cultures, like Michelangelo's fresco on the ceiling of the Sistine Chapel, the one with the Israelites and the brazen serpent."

In her mind, she was with Giorgio on their honeymoon in Rome, what, some twenty years ago, and he was explaining the meaning of one of those writhing depictions on a frescoed ceiling, probably the same chapel mentioned by the monk. Was it the fresco with Moses and his staff? Probably, and she wished she'd paid more attention, but more than that, she wanted to rest her head on her husband's shoulder instead of listening to Fra Yellow Feet.

The priest shook his head. "The carvings you saw on the dead women were something else entirely, the markings made by a deranged soul."

Serafina didn't think so. She considered telling him about the serpent's tongue she saw on Bella's embalmed body, but rejected the idea.

"I need to know more about the plates in this *Godey's*. The magazine belonged to one of the murdered women. Odd that she would have such a publication in her possession, but there it is, and I'd like to find out why." Serafina showed him the crease in the page. "You see, the bent corner indicates to me that she read the article, perhaps even studied it, referred to it from time to time, but at least she was curious enough to mark its place. Before he died, I would have asked my husband about the brazen serpent. He knew everything." Serafina blinked hard. "But now I must ask others, and since you're a church scholar, I've come to you."

He ran the end of his crucifix back and forth through his beard and began. "In the Book of Numbers we find the reference to a bronze serpent, a powerful creature who drew his strength from the God of Moses and saved the Israelites from a plague of fiery serpents. The symbol of the brazen serpent continues in the New Testament where it is linked to Christ. St. John said, 'As Moses lifted up the serpent in the wilderness, even so must the Son of Man be lifted up, that whoever believes in Him should not perish but have eternal life.'"

Her head swam as she tried to digest his words. "I've never seen vestments like these in Oltramari, not that I pay close attention to what priests wear in church."

He shook his head. "You won't see them here, only in churches where they practice the Ambrosian Rite. They use the image of a serpent winding itself around a cross as the symbol of a healer, and their chalices are carved with it, their vestments embroidered with designs like these, their croziers bearing the brazen serpent. It is a symbol of Christ, and has nothing to do with murder, I'm afraid."

"Not in the keep of a sane man, but this killer does not murder for pleasure or for coins. He's a lunatic, bent on twisting meaning to suit his own ends, and his mind is riddled with phantoms."

In the Conservatory

Thursday, October 11, 1866

The madam wasn't available, the maid told her, so Serafina headed outside, glad for the prickly sea air on her skin and the warmth of the sun. She followed the path to the conservatory and opened the door, a humid blast hitting her face and tightening her curls, but there was a bench underneath a dwarf palm where she could sit for a moment and look out at the park. A parrot squawked. Another large-winged creature flew over to a wide palm tree and perched on one of its fronds.

"Interesting," a voice said. "Your hair, I mean."

"I didn't hear you enter," Serafina said, a bit startled by the woman who was clothed in a low-cut ultramarine day dress, the costume of an expensive prostitute. Petticoats crinkled when she sat beside Serafina, and her hair was perfectly coiffed. Serafina remembered her, the redhead from the wake.

"Gioconda's my name," she said.

"Don't tell me your parents named you after a painting."

"Oh no, it's the name I took when I started working for Rosa, and I never knew my parents."

Serafina wanted to ask her how she knew Falco but the prostitute continued. "Don't use our real names, mostly. Well, some of the girls do—Carmela, for instance. She said her father named her, and that was good enough for her, she'd stick with it."

Serafina's feet were ice. Perhaps she misheard the woman. She needed to focus. "Carmela?"

"Bit of a thing," the redhead said. "Here about three, four years ago. Had hair just like yours—ginger, I'd call the color. Yes, like a stale carrot, you might say. The same hair, I said to myself. As I said, I saw you from the path, just your head with the same color hair, tight curls and all. Matter of fact, that's why I came in here. I said to myself, Carmela's back."

"Who?"

"Carmela, a girl who used to work here. I thought you were Carmela."

Odd, Rosa would have told her if Carmela had knocked on her door. She must be talking about another Carmela. Doubtless, that was it—such a common name, Carmela. Serafina gazed out to sea and tried to slow her breathing but the air felt like a horsehair blanket pressing down on her and her legs began to move in that uncontrollable way they sometimes had. She stood and straightened her skirt, then sat back down again. "This girl with hair like mine, when was she here?"

Gioconda pressed her lips together and rolled her eyes. She seemed to be thinking. "Three, four years ago. Didn't last long, mind. Before we knew it, she was gone—took up with a soldier or guard, one of those, soon after she arrived."

"Did you know her well?" Her hair was wet. Her face, burning. She must calm her breathing.

The woman shook her head. "Nope, kept herself to herself. Don't get me wrong, she was friendly, not snooty like some round here I could name, I'll tell you, but particular, you might say, as to how she spent her time. Smart. When she wasn't working, well, she, I don't know, walked on the shore a lot, tended to flowers and the like. Loved the blooms."

"Do you know where she was born?"

"Well, why would I know that? But let me think." The woman wrapped a curl around her finger and for a moment assumed a faraway look. "Not far from here, if I remember correctly."

"Yes?"

"Right, I remember once, early spring it was, gorgeous day, and Scarpo and Turi—this was a long time ago, mind you, before the madness started—they used to take us on drives, and we'd all pile in the carriage, some of us in the rumbler, all fixed up, waving and shouting and sticking our arms out the window, none too delicate, mind, and Turi, he'd drive fast round the statue, the one with the sunken eyes. Well, this one time, Carmela, she asked Turi to stop and she started to cry because she said it was close to her home and she had half a mind to get out, just get out and walk, saying as how she could walk to her house from the sunken-eyed statue."

"What town was that?"

"Oltramari, of course."

Serafina felt her stomach churn. Her daughter worked at Rosa's, and the madam—who she thought was a friend, who knew that she, Serafina, and Giorgio were wretched about Carmela's flight—that same madam, that *strega*, that erstwhile friend, never bothered to tell her.

She swallowed. "Anything else you remember about Carmela?"

"That's about it. Said she had a twin brother that she missed and was thinking of writing to him, but if the mother found out, she wouldn't like it. But she was smart to leave, Carmela. Money's good and Rosa, she's fair, always jolly and such, and the pay's more than double what it is in Palermo, I tell you, but now, well, it's not a good time, not good at all." Gioconda stopped. "Is something wrong? You look like you've seen a specter!"

Serafina closed her eyes, but could not stop the spinning. "The damp air unsettles my stomach. What did you mean by 'now, no good'?"

"Well, you never know who's going to creep round the corner, do you, stab you in the heart? Some of the girls, the careless ones, are getting knifed, I can tell you."

"Are any of Carmela's friends still here?"

"Gusti. Want me to get her?"

Serafina sat in the conservatory, gathering her strength. She'd heard enough of this horrid tale and wanted to get out. Didn't care if she ever saw Rosa again. What a ... what a *fiend* she'd turned out to be! But when Serafina stood, she found to her surprise that her knees were wobbly and she was shaking, so she thumped back down on the bench, one hand caressing the fronds of a fern that had brushed up against her as if in sympathy, thinking that she would wait a few minutes until her breathing returned to normal. By then, the shock of hearing a name she'd nearly succeeded in forgetting would pass, the rapid coursing of her blood would still, and the usual colors of the day would once again take hold. She was deep in her thoughts when the conservatory door opened and she heard slippered steps upon the granite, the whispering of silk.

"Gusti said she'd be down in a minute." Tall and blonde, this prostitute, and she spoke with a northern accent. "She's dressing, you know, but perhaps I can help? I'm Lola." She smiled at Serafina, crouching a little in front of her, and clowning into her face. "Oh yes, I see it, too. Gioconda was right, you *do* look just like Carmela only much taller and, you know, well … if Carmela wants to know how she's going to look when she's … mature, all she need do is gaze at you."

"Carmela doesn't want to see me, not today, not tomorrow, not ever." By this time, Serafina's skin was clammy and her curls were claws tearing at her scalp, but the prostitute's smile was engaging, and she was making an effort to be friendly. Despite her mood, Serafina had to smile. She realized at once why the madam liked her. "You knew Carmela?" Serafina asked.

"Not very well. We didn't talk that much. Liked one another, we did. Bit of a thing, Carmela, but she had her opinions. Not friendly to me." The prostitute brushed a curl from her face. "Do you mind?"

Serafina shook her head, making room for her on the bench.

She sat. "Probably jealous. Most of the girls are when they first meet me, and Carmela wasn't here all that long—a year, maybe more."

Serafina's toes were ice. "She worked here? Like you? I mean, she wasn't a maid or a laundress?"

Lola nodded. "Worked like me. Not very good at first, but those of us with experience and flair, we helped her." She retrieved a cigarette holder wedged down her front, and from her pocket, drew out paper and tobacco and began rolling a weed. "I suppose you want to know about the murders?"

Most definitely, she did not. "Not interested in the madam or her murders; I'm a midwife, not a sleuth, but I'd like to know for certain if the person who looks so much like me, according to Gioconda, is indeed my daughter."

"Well, her name is Carmela, and she was here for a year, maybe more, and she looks exactly like you." She puffed and looked away, blowing out a thin stream of smoke. "Same eyes, a surprising shade of jade, I'd say, but she doesn't have your wrinkles or crooked nose."

Serafina felt her cheeks crimson, but she wasn't about to show this saucy tart that she was getting to her. "Rosa's told me a little about you. She said you were from Enna. How long have you been here?"

"From Enna?" Lola smiled, removing a piece of tobacco from her tongue. "Rosa invents histories for me, a new one every day. Been here five or six years, and I'm sure she's told you all about me. You're good friends; you must discuss everything."

"We discuss only what Rosa wants me to hear, and that's precious little. She molds the truth into a pleasant fantasy that skips and changes direction, but to be fair, she's always spoken highly of you. I'm curious, your accent is not Sicilian."

She took the last puff and lingered over it, crushing the ember. "Born in Lombardy, in the hills, and I was born poor. My father was a shepherd."

"How was it you traveled all the way to Sicily?" Serafina asked.

Lola looked out the window, not at the rocks or sea, but at something half-formed inside her, like the shard of a memory or at what she was willing to reveal. "You wouldn't understand."

"Perhaps not. It's hard for me to understand why a woman would want your profession. The work is hard, no?"

The prostitute hesitated, and while she did, Serafina peered at her. Like the heavens with changeable winds, clouds whisked past Lola's face, stormy, billowy, luminous, foreboding.

"Tell me, dear lady, have you ever delivered a child and then removed that child from his mother?"

"Several times. Women die giving birth."

She frowned. "Not that kind of removal."

"Taken the child from its mother you mean?" Serafina asked.

The prostitute nodded.

"Never. I would never do such a thing, no, despite the state and their horrid laws. They say that if the mother is a criminal or otherwise unfit, the child should be given to a foundling hospital, but that's talk from Turin. Some women, one or two, perhaps, don't want their children, but even in those cases, I wouldn't take the child from the mother except in rare cases, say, if the mother were a raving one and threatened harm, and thank the Madonna, I've not run into that mother, not yet. Not Sicilian to take a child from its mother—it's against our blood, just not done."

Lola rubbed an eyelash. "I wish you'd been my midwife." As Serafina watched, her eyes, which had been clear pools, blurred with water.

Serafina put her arm around the prostitute's shoulders. "And the father?"

Different shadows clouded Lola's face. "A man of learning. He wanted his child raised by the monks, so they took him from me."

Serafina shook her head. "How did you happen to meet him?"

"After my mother died, my father brought us to the orphanage. All right for a while, being a changeling, until the mother superior died. Not so good after that, so I left." Lola seemed lost in her mind for a long moment before continuing. "I found work at the university."

"Teaching?"

She shook her head. "I cleaned the lecture halls, the library, the offices. Good, honest labor for a few cents a month. Backbreaking, not like this profession, mind, but hard, all the same. One day I opened the door to a professor's office." She worried her lip.

"And?"

"He was at his desk reading some papers when I came upon him. Quite by accident, you must understand, and I was about to scurry away, like we were told to do when we entered a room that wasn't empty. I can feel it now, the door knob in my grip, the heft of the pail in my other hand. I should have gone—oh, why didn't I—but he said, 'No, need, do continue.' He talked to me as I scrubbed, speaking to me as if I were a real person. Fascinating his words were, too, about the oceans and the rivers of the world, the wars, the ebb and flow of ideas, of men who would be kings, of revolutions in the mind, and upheaval in the streets. The following week I returned, and he was at his desk, as if he had been waiting for me. We talked again. That's the way it began. Nine months later, I gave birth to his son."

"How old were you?"

She looked away. "Thirteen."

Serafina took a breath.

"Unless you've had a child taken from your arms, you'll never understand, never. I walked until I came to a land that looked foreign to me. I wanted a new life, don't you see, so for a time, I stayed with a family near Naples. They fed me, gave me work, but something happened—too long ago to matter—and I left. Fishermen brought me to this island, far away from anything I'd known. I worked in Palermo, but the girls talk, you know, and Villa Rosa, well, it has a reputation. I was fifteen when I knocked on Rosa's door."

Lola's face cleared. She brushed her skirts. "But you have to make your life, don't you? You have to heave the past, just chuck it out and move on. My good fortune finding Rosa. Bad times right now for her, and if I can help in any way, please let me know."

"You can help me right now. Tell Gusti I'll talk to her another time."

The Fight

"**W**as my daughter here?"

The madam looked up from her ledger, still whispering numbers. "What are you talking about?"

"You know what I'm talking about. Carmela, was she here?" Rosa frowned.

"Say something. Did my daughter come here four years ago? Did you let her in? She worked here? You didn't tell me?"

"Where did you hear that?"

"Never mind, answer my question—did my daughter work here as a prostitute?"

Rosa's attention finally snagged itself on the question, her face, pale. "Fina, that was long ago. She stayed only a few months. The night she arrived, she told me had no roof over her head and you made her leave."

This madam, this so-called friend was rousing Serafina's anger. Despicable creature, no wonder she was so fond of her secrets—taking in children and accusing the mother of making them leave. "I made her leave? Not on your life. Giorgio and I told her she had to finish school. Women of our class do, you know."

A fury possessed the madam. "Women of your class? Putting on airs, is it?" Fists in her armpits she cocked her elbows and strutted with her torso like a short Napoleon. "'Women of our class!' Well, women of my class never talk to our children the way you talked to her. Mean, snarly words you used to your flesh and blood. I'm Sicilian and proud of it, not pretend noble. They're nasty to their offspring, shipping them away to school barely weaned, not returning for years. We love our children, and you should be ashamed!"

"What would you know about children?" Serafina asked.

"*Strega!*" She stabbed the air with a finger. "I fought for my child. Is she my flesh and blood? No, but I'm the mother, she's mine, part of me, she's in my heart and mind always."

"I take it back."

Silence.

"I take back the part about Tessa, but you believed my daughter's story and never asked for my side. Worse, you took her in to work in your … your cheap little bordello and never came to me. Never told me, even though I came running whenever you summoned, dropping everything in the middle of the night, caring for your prostitutes as if they were my own clients. I saved them after they'd taken the *strega's* evil draughts to rid themselves of their baby; saved them when they hid their condition underneath tight corsets. And all the time, Carmela was right here, under your roof working on her back and not a word out of your lips about her. A child came to your door, not yet fifteen, and you took her in!"

"Take this handkerchief and sit down. I hate it when you cry."

"Keep your damn linen! Running around with boys, Carmela. When I saw her in the public gardens with that soldier, half undressed, I became incensed, yes. Mad. Wild. Perhaps I used words."

The madam snorted. "Perhaps?"

"You know nothing, you shrew. Carmela found school 'boring.' Said she knew more than the teachers. 'Only children attend' and 'I'm a woman now.' We insisted she finish school, Giorgio and I. She refused. We told her, 'Follow our rules while you live under our roof,' never suspecting, never dreaming that she'd leave. She packed."

"Did you try to stop her?"

"Of course we tried! Giorgio and I pleaded with her, so did Carlo. But no, she left, running down the steps one horrific night and I haven't seen her since."

"You looked for her?"

"What a question to ask!" Serafina slammed a palm on the desk. "Of course we did. And she was here, right under our noses, and you didn't tell me!"

"Not here long."

"Over a year."

"Who said?"

"Gioconda."

"What does she know?"

"Lola, too."

The madam was silent.

"Carmela doesn't know about the deaths of her grandmother and her father. You had the chance to send for me when she knocked on your door, and what did you do?" Serafina knew she was repeating herself, but she had to get the words out, had to force them through her teeth, feeling their weight, say them again and again before they choked her. "You saw a child with skin as soft as a petal. You saw coins, the coins you think I know nothing about, and you never told me. You groomed her, ate off her earnings. You slut!" Serafina slowed her breathing. "You never told me. Fine. You can get yourself another detective. You can find yourself another friend." ✒

The Discovery

Tuesday, October 16, 1866

The next few days were a blur. When she wasn't delivering babies, Serafina helped her children with their schoolwork, accompanied Renata to market, went with Maria to her lessons, or watched Giulia sew their garments. Evenings, she spent in her mother's room on the third floor where she read, thought, frowned up at the stars.

Despite her best attempts to banish it from her mind, Serafina could not forget her horrid behavior the other day after Vicenzu berated her for spending too much money on fabric. He showed her the ledger, and her face flushed. While he chattered on about red ink, Renata clattered in the kitchen. It was all too much, what with the domestic shuffling back and forth, and Maria playing her scales, and Totò racing around the room like a wild specter. Something inside her snapped. "Enough!" she yelled, slamming a platter to the floor. Shards of porcelain flew all over the kitchen, and she saw fear, real fear, in her children's faces. It must never happen again, never.

The following morning she traipsed around the Duomo and piazza, climbed up to the promenade, and wound down to the sea. Gulls cried as she sat on the edge of the arena between the remains of two Greek pillars, breathing in the salt air, glimpsing porcelain explode in her mind, watching fishermen leaving with the tide. In the distance a steamer plowed the waves.

She decided to walk on. Where she was headed, she did not know, maybe as far away as Cefalù, maybe farther. Stopping a moment, she turned toward the sea, visoring her eyes. That was it, she wanted to be on that steamer unfurling its sails. As she walked, the stones bit into her boots. The wind tore at her clothes, but she continued, past a platoon of boats heading out to claim their catch, past the cove on the edge of town, past citrus groves now picked clean of fruit. And still she walked as if motion would kill the lump in her throat, sinking her shoes into the soft soil, one step after another, on and on until her limbs hurt and her vision blurred. Soon she came to steep rocks jutting out almost to the water's edge. Straight above her and some thirty meters from the edge stood a decrepit building, its lawns replaced by sand and clumps of grass, its gate rusted, its shutters askew. Guardian Angel Orphanage read the sign, Mother Concetta's domain. As Serafina stood there staring up, she heard laughter, carefree, guileless. She smiled.

Something glinting near the rocks broke the moment. She plodded over to whatever it was, lost or perhaps discarded in sea grass, and picked it up—a reticule, brown velvet, with a gold chain and clasp. Inside she found Bella's identity card, a fifty lire gold piece, a pair of yellow gloves, a rosary. She kissed the cross, dumped the articles back in the bag, and headed for home.

Shutting the gate behind her she saw the caretaker perched on a ladder pruning the bougainvillea, his shoulders blading in and out as he cut. When Serafina waved to him, her skirt snagged on a prickly pear, and, yanking to free the silk, she pulled another thread. Her hem, still wet from the sea, puckered now, but no bother, she'd blame it on the goat and Giulia would fix it in a blink. Near the cactus bloomed the geranium her great-grandmother had planted, one of her mother's favorites because of its acrid stench, its stem now the size of a man's thigh. Serafina smelled its sourness, the bitter-sweetness of the soil. The stone angel over the lintel smiled down at her. She glared back. Her stomach growled.

"Too early in the morning for you. Where did you go?" Renata asked.

"Took a walk."

"What happened to your skirt?"

Before Serafina could reply, Giulia said, "The goat again."

In the parlor, Maria played her scales or one of those Brahms pieces, Serafina couldn't tell which.

"Vicenzu?"

"Left early for the shop."

"While you were gone, Rosa came in her shiny carriage," Renata said. "First time she's come to the house since Papa died."

Serafina shrugged, listening as Maria transitioned to Scarlatti.

"She brought us these," Renata said, holding up a silver tray piled with *dolci*.

Serafina said nothing. "Beppe!" she called.

When he appeared Serafina handed him the reticule and said, "Take this to Inspector Colonna. Tell him I found it on the shore. It belongs to one of Rosa's deceased." 🖋

Reconciliation

Sunday, October 21, 1866

From her room, Serafina saw the madam's carriage pulling into the drive, so she grabbed a book, ran up the steps to the third floor, shut the door, pulled the drapes, and turning up the wick of the lamp, curled up in her mother's favorite chair to read.

"Donna Fina! La Signura to see you," Assunta rasped.

Serafina pictured the domestic's lips on the other side of the keyhole. "Put her in the parlor. Tell her I'll be down in a while; tell her there's something I must finish first, and if she wants to wait, fine, but it will be a long time, a very long time, before I'm free to greet guests."

Serafina shivered. She flipped around in the pages of *Moby Dick*, attempting to get beyond the first sentence, but she found the story boring, the English words, difficult. Setting down the heavy book, she ranged over the floor, sat down with the whale again and, turning to the middle, was having another go at the story when the sound of a knock interrupted her.

Her daughter entered. "Rosa's downstairs in the parlor."

"So?"

"She's your oldest friend," Renata said. "What happened between you two?"

"I'll be down after I finish this book."

"She doesn't look well. She's lost weight and her face is drawn."

"Tell her I need to finish. Perhaps she doesn't need to know I'm reading. Tell her I'm straightening Giorgio's papers. If she wants to wait, I'll be down, but I don't know when."

"I can't imagine what words were exchanged, but—"

"She crossed the boundaries of friendship." Serafina continued to read, but the words swam together.

Renata sat on the corner of the bed. "It's going to take you a year to finish that book, especially with Giulia not here to translate every other word."

"Nonsense, I do quite well in English."

Silence.

"Rosa helped us during the war. Saved the apothecary shop, Papa said."

"Since that time she's hurt us, I'll tell you that much. The disturbance between us has to do with your older sister. I'll say no more, but what she did was despicable."

"She doesn't look well. Her gait is slow, her color, pallid."

"A fantasy she creates." Serafina saw her daughter frown.

"She's your friend, Mama, no matter what she's done. Besides, it looks like she's aged fifteen years."

Serafina rose. She should have chosen a more interesting book.

Rosa stood when Serafina entered the parlor.

Renata served them caffè and brought Rosa a special tray of *dolci*, but the madam declined.

Serafina heard soft notes coming from the parlor. "Maria's piano," she said.

Rosa nodded. "Lovely."

They listened to the music, a slow movement, melodic, hopeful. Their eyes did not meet.

Rosa hung her head. "So sorry that I didn't call you when Carmela knocked on my door. I was wrong. Scarpo hired two more guards, and on his orders, they begin to search for her."

Serafina pressed her lips together and looked down at her hands. "Nothing more you can say or do, no more words about Carmela."

The music stopped, and a moment of silence took over the room.

"The commissioner, that prancing hippo, accused me of not wetting the don's beak."

"He said that?" Serafina asked.

She nodded. "He simpered around the room." Rosa moved her torso from side to side, crooking her elbows and swaying in imitation.

Serafina sent her a slow smile. She had missed the madam's view of the world.

"A day after I met with the commissioner, who comes around but the inspector. Waddled in holding Bella's purse. He found it on the shore, he said, that and a pair of yellow gloves."

"Along with a rosary, fifty lire, and Bella's identity card," Serafina said. "Inside the purse. I was the one who found them near the cove and had Beppe bring them to Colonna."

"That fat inspector!" Rosa twisted her handkerchief. "What will I do? Whatever we know about the killings, we know because of you." She looked at Serafina and her eyes were hungry.

Serafina chewed her lip.

Silence.

She told Rosa about visiting the embalmer, the carving of the winding snake-like creature on Bella's forehead, and what she'd discovered from talking to the priests about the brazen serpent.

The madam put a hand to her chest. "Brazen serpent?" Frowning, she seemed to regard the air in the room. "There was a girl from the north who talked about the end of the world. My girls loved to listen to her fantasy. 'At the end of the world, the serpent will hiss.'" Rosa made a long hissing sound, imitating the prostitute. "How her eyes looked when she hissed! Such a lovely fantasy, but the girl is long gone."

"When did she leave?"

"I sent her away. Not popular with the customers. Three, maybe four years ago. She didn't last long."

"Her name?"

"Hilaria, she called herself."

"Do you know where she is now?"

The madam shook her head. "Nor if she still uses that name."

Serafina said, "There was a reason why you found the bodies on the seventh day of each month." She told Rosa what she'd learned from the professor about the perfection of six, the fullness of seven, but she could tell that the madam was only half listening. ✒

Serafina Decides

"Don't wait up for me. One of Rosa's women must be in a difficult way." Serafina studied the pale skin beneath her children's eyes. "Come here, all of you, and give me a kiss goodnight. Renata, Vicenzu, you are in charge. Maria and Giulia, don't forget your studies. Who will help Totò brush his teeth? Thank you, Maria."

"Do you have to go?" Totò asked.

"Shhh!" someone said.

As she entered Rosa's office, Serafina sensed a brighter mood. Glancing at the bust of Mary Magdalene on the desk, she kissed her friend on both cheeks, and sank into a chair.

"The earth cools and the babies are busy—so many to deliver." Serafina removed her gloves and rubbed her hands. "First it was Graziella. Her children arrive with big heads, and she's such a small woman. The peasants have been at it, too, Crocifisa and Maruzzedda, both of them at once. Ran back and forth from one home to the other. No sleep." She paused. "And now another one? Which prostitute needs me?"

Gowned for the evening in deep aubergine, Rosa poured the marsala, handed a glass to Serafina. "No birth tonight, only death." She flattened a page in her ledger.

"But your visit with the commissioner helped, didn't it?"

Rosa shrugged. "Colonna came again today, the visit due to his thirst, not to give me any news. He told me I must have more

70

patience." Her eyes blazed, and she slammed the desk. "As if the murders happened yesterday! Three months, and he's done nothing." She shook her head, and the madam's curls caught the candlelight. "But what more can I say to him? I need to be on his good side—he certifies the house—so I swallow my words and pour him another grappa." Rosa twisted linen back and forth in her hands. "That's why I sent for you. No more dawdling, Fina. We've had words, lately, my fault, but for the sake of our friendship, I need you to find the killer before another girl is murdered."

Silence, except for the wind outside and the spitting of logs. Rosa wiped her eyes.

Turning to the hearth, Serafina remembered the casket of the first victim as it journeyed to the grave in August heat, the procession engulfed in a cloud of dust, the smell of death and the sweat of mourners thick around the jostling bier. After Rosa found the second prostitute's body, *Giornale di Sicilia* featured a story about the two murders, listing their ghoulish similarities, lamenting the increase in violence.

But two weeks had passed since they found Bella's body, and there were no words in the papers, no prayers from the priests, although the gossip had begun in the straw market and behind merchants' shutters. A growing hum in the air, it flew to the far corners of the piazza where wizened crones scattered their words like bits of straw. Even Vicenzu voiced it one evening by the fire, sticking his head above the top of his apothecary catalogue long enough to say, "Rosa forgot to wet Don Tigro's beak." But Serafina knew better—not the don's style, these killings.

She walked to the window, stared into the dark. Tall and high-breasted, Serafina, proud of her figure, even after having seven children, but she had to admit it—a corset laced with care tucked her in at the waist and lifted the start of sagging flesh. Each year the lines on her face multiplied and deepened. Too well she knew that monster, Time, crouched ahead, ready to pounce. She pictured Bella's face and the remains of those three women lying in the ground, their murders unsolved. Are the rest of Rosa's prostitutes in danger? Rosa, too? Carmela?

She fought to catch her breath and sat down. "You and I will find the killer, we must."

Rosa's eyes sparkled.

"Tell me about the dead women," Serafina said.

"First I must discuss the sauce with cook. She needs to know how much to make—we have big appetites scheduled this evening." Rosa whisked around the desk, kissed Serafina on both cheeks, and bustled out of the room.

In her wake, Serafina marveled at the swift change in her friend. This was the Rosa she knew, and while Serafina's mind whirred and her feet froze, while her stomach churned and her heart raced, Rosa, her burden lifted by Serafina's involvement, went about the business of her house with energetic focus. In the madam's eyes, it was almost as if the killer had been caught and awaited trial. Was Rosa's a faith buttressed by her financial success or was it the other way round?

Remembering that her children were alone and that it was getting late, she rubbed her arms, smelling citrus and lavender. Turning around in her seat, she swept the room with her eyes until her sight was arrested by a cloud growing more distinct, encompassing the chair in the corner, and in a blink, her mother appeared, young, gowned in velvet.

"You busy yourself by toying with a riddle while your children sit at home? And have you found Carmela?"

"The guards and Scarpo search for her."

"The guards are dim."

She'd had it with her mother, nagging her even after the old ghost's death. "Carmela's the one who left us. You were the one who spoiled her."

Maddalena's nose wrinkled. Serafina knew it signaled a storm.

"Stop blaming others. Who's the mother, you or Rosa? Find your daughter."

"Look at me: two, three hours of sleep a night, and I don't know what to do first. The babies arrive and I must attend, you know that. Giorgio's death has been a financial devastation for us, but Rosa needs me, too, and most of all, my children need me."

"Say that last line again."

Serafina shook her head, squeezing her eyes shut and crossing her arms.

"Stubborn, just like your father. Listen to yourself. 'My children need me.' And who is Carmela, a stranger? Your child left, and you, the mother, heap shame on Rosa's head for taking her in, yet you, the mother, do nothing to find her. Shame on you. Yes, the guards can help, but you must find her first."

"As usual, you make no sense: if I find Carmela first, then why would the guards also need to find her?"

"You must find her first in here," Maddalena said, pointing to her heart. Lifting her chin, the apparition must have heard footfalls in the hall. With a spurt of fire, the vision disappeared, and Serafina sat alone and hunched, arms wrapped around herself in a cold room, wishing she were sitting by the fire reading Totò his bedtime story.

The door opened, and Rosa returned, licking her fingers, her skirts swaying above stiffened hoops. "You look like a startled ewe. Did you scare yourself, or do you dawdle while I do all the work?"

Remembering the look on Maddalena's face before she vanished, and wondering whether she'd dreamt the vision of the specter or if her mother had taken up a permanent haunt in her mind, Serafina asked if the guards were able to locate Carmela.

Rosa sat. "They're still searching, canvassing the other brothels in town. If they don't find her, they'll go to Palermo, but Carmela could be anywhere."

Silence, except for the wind outside.

"You've asked the women she knew? Gusti? Gioconda? Lola?"

"Of course, and my friends in the trade. No one's seen her or heard from her, not that they're telling me, at any rate."

Serafina looked beyond Rosa to the windows. There was only so much she could do—after all, Carmela was eighteen now—and she felt like pushing all thoughts of her back down into the bottom of her mind where they'd been hidden and out of her reckoning for the past four years, but she said, "Tell me when Carmela was here. No fantasy, just the dates."

"She came here in July 1862, left in August 1863, and I've had no word from her since then."

"She could be anywhere, or not," and having said those words,

Serafina felt a flash of something hot and sharp and scattered attacking her. Her cheeks burned; her armpits moistened. Better not to think of Carmela, no, not to think of her at all, or her mother, for that matter; best to let all thoughts of them fly away like birds. Otherwise, she'd get nothing done, and the rest of her children would suffer. Serafina rose, opened a window, waiting for her heart to calm and her lungs to fill before she fastened the sash and returned to sit in front of Rosa.

"Getting back to the murdered women …" Serafina reached into her reticule for her notebook. "I want to hear where they were born, their talents outside the bedroom, their families, their friends, their enemies, troublesome customers, where they went on their free evenings. I want to interview everyone who was in the house or who should have been here at the time of the murders. I want details, anything that comes to mind no matter how small—a new shadow on the wall, a different scent in the air, an unsettled light in someone's eyes."

So the madam told her about Gemma, the first woman murdered, a country girl from Enna who seldom laughed, but who earned more than any of the others. "Given a five lire gold piece by one of Garibaldi's generals," Rosa said, and continued, describing Nelli, the second prostitute killed. "A natural in the kitchen, she helped cook make the *caponata*, but she was slow to learn all the ins and outs of the trade, so clever Lola became a sister to her, showed her artistic twists."

Serafina scribbled. "Lola. Tell me about her."

"You met her the other day."

"But I want to hear what you have to say about her. The more you talk, the more pieces of the puzzle I can fit together, and the greater our chance of finding the killer."

Rosa nodded. "Lola appeared in the doorway one day, homeless and in rags, with whip marks on her back, but from the moment she started, she was one of my best. She has style, can do anything with her hands when she wants to—trusses up our hair, carved the sign on the gatepost, draws our likenesses. She'll do anything to lift the mood, a real actress." Rosa was silent a moment. "Where was I with Nelli?"

Serafina read from her notes. "'So clever Lola became a sister to her.'"

"Under Lola's care, Nelli changed. She got repeats and became popular, especially with the priests, but now I've lost her." Rosa's voice grew wispy. "Last month it was Bella ... but you know about her."

Serafina nodded, picturing Falco surrounded by a group of Rosa's prostitutes at Bella's wake, his arms around one while he flirted with the others, but decided to save him for later.

"Bella had dreams," Rosa said, and her jeweled fingers caught the candlelight. "She'd saved enough to buy her own dress shop, and was about to give notice, she told me as much." Rosa paused, cocking her head to one side. "Close to thirty and getting sour, but customers still asked for her, and she couldn't refuse."

"And you were the one who found all the bodies?" Serafina's pencil finished scratching.

Rosa nodded. "By the door leading to the sea."

The two women were silent. Again, Serafina heard the call of the wind. "Do your women go out at night after work?"

Rosa shrugged. "I don't ask them questions, I trust them and they take pride in their work. Every morning I give them their portion of the take. If they receive tips, they share them with me, unless they're trinkets—those they keep. They want to know who earned the most. The best girls clamor for a spot here, or at least they did. Now, who knows what will happen, although I still have a steady stream of knocks at the door. My house is unrivaled."

"No doubt. The grounds are beautiful."

"And the girls are free to graze. They go down and bathe in the sea, walk on the shore, some of them—Carmela, for one. Good exercise, climbing up and down the rocks." Rosa smiled.

Serafina rubbed her forehead. "Scarpo and his men watch the doors?"

She nodded. "Don Tigro's men are useless. They lurk in the shadows with their filthy clothes and flat eyes and I won't let them near my house."

"Do you keep a list?"

"Of what?" Rosa asked, feigning innocence and pouring herself another marsala. She offered the bottle, but Serafina declined.

"You know what I mean, a list of customers."

"Fina, please understand, it would ruin me if word got out that I kept a list—this is a respectable house." She gulped her drink, tapped the side of her nose and whispered, "But I know most of the men and if I don't, Scarpo knows who they are. Some of them come to the door in costume—priests and council officials, mostly, and we pretend not to recognize them. The police commissioner, for instance, he wears a wig." She paused. "Don't write that down."

"Have you entertained strangers recently?"

"Admit a stranger? Never. Unless he has a recommendation from someone we trust, a member of the city council, for instance, that's different."

"So you reject?"

"All the time."

"We'll make a list of the rejected in the last few months," Serafina said.

Rosa pulled the cord.

"Get Scarpo," she said to the maid.

Candlelight reflected from the surface of Scarpo's bumpy pate. He reminded Serafina of a cabbage wearing red suspenders. The butt of a revolver stuck out of his belt and a shepherd's knife hung from the other side. After bowing to Rosa, he nodded to Serafina, and arranged himself in the chair facing the madam.

"Rosa tells me you turn men away all the time. Can you describe any of them?"

He pulled on his braces, directing his gaze toward Rosa. "There is one who keeps coming back, a stranger with a funny smell. Pigheaded, too. Wears a brown cloak and hat."

Serafina asked, "Same man? You're sure?"

He nodded

"When did you last see him?"

Scarpo was silent a moment. "Middle of last week, I think it was when I waited for him to finish his business with the smith. I thought to myself, that smell, it's the same creature who comes around here and every time he shows up, I need to tell him to leave.

No girls for you tonight or ever, I tell him, but still he returns."

"Anything else that's odd about him?"

He thought a moment before replying. "He wears gloves when it's not cold."

"That's one," Rosa said.

Serafina ran a hand through her curls and wrote down Scarpo's description of the gloved stranger. When finished, she frowned at the page.

"What is it?" Rosa asked.

Serafina told them about the begging monk she'd seen last week. "Smelled of foreign lands and told me that he was from a monastery north of Naples. Didn't like my questions."

Scarpo shook his head. "Not a monk, my stranger, and he wasn't begging. Not the same man."

Serafina considered his words, wrote something in her notebook, but said no more about the brown-cloaked foreigner. "I want to know about all of the others you've told to leave, and anything else unusual that comes into your head—men walking outside or in the back, someone sneaking in the shadows, anyone who picked a fight or followed you into the center of town."

He shrugged. "Well, there's another, he limps, one of Don Tigro's men. Keeps asking for a turn, and you told me, 'Nothing on the house,' Signura. You know the one I mean."

Rosa nodded. "A snake. Of course, good work, Scarpo. Put him down."

Serafina added him to the list.

Scarpo continued, describing a few first time customers who, because the prostitutes did not like their demands, were not allowed to return. When he'd finished, Serafina had a list of seven suspects.

"What about Falco? He's your client. Has he ever given you trouble?"

"Who?" Rosa asked. "I've no client named Falco."

"But I saw him at the wake with a few of your prostitutes—two in particular, Gioconda and someone else, a blonde, I think it may have been Lola, but I'm not sure. The rest of your women were gathered round them, forming a tight, cozy group, and they all knew one another."

Rosa shook her head and looked at Scarpo who said he didn't remember him. "So there. You're mistaken. He's not my customer."

Serafina rolled her eyes.

Scarpo considered, shook his head, and stood. "Getting late, Signura."

After he'd gone, Rosa said, "You've no sense of time, of right and wrong. Scarpo—"

"I don't have a sense of right and wrong? What about your sense of right and wrong when my daughter came to you?"

"We've been over this before. She needed—"

"Don't *you* tell me what she needed. She needed her mother. She needed her family. She needed sense knocked into her." She stopped, gazed into the air, shaking her head. Would Carmela always be between them, the ruin of a friendship? "Thinking about Carmela makes me slow, broody, unable to act, and I have so much to do."

Rosa bent to Serafina, handing her a linen. "Forgive me. More marsala?"

Serafina shook her head and blew her nose.

Breaking the silence, Rosa said, "Take all the time you need. Only …"

"Only what?"

Rosa bit her lip. "Only, nothing."

"What?"

"Only mind the hour."

Serafina considered the list. "Two of these descriptions, the brown-cloaked stranger and the one who limps—I have a feeling about these men. And there's another." Serafina brought up Falco's name.

"Again? I told you, he's not a customer."

"Whether or not you admit to it, I saw him at the wake. He was about to kiss my hand when someone, a beauty, tapped him on the shoulder and he was off like a cat hunting prey."

"But he's not a customer," Rosa said.

"Then how does he know your women?"

"You're dreaming."

Serafina shook her head. She let time pass, then told Rosa about her affair with him. "It was years ago. We were both in school. I stopped studying, so infatuated I was with him."

"Let me understand, you had a flirtation with him years ago; he's the one who stopped it, and that's why you think he's a customer?" Rosa's eyes twinkled.

Serafina narrowed her eyes, leaned over the madam's desk so that their faces almost touched. "He's a customer, confess it."

The madam shook her head.

"I saw him cooing with your women."

"Maybe he's a fast worker."

"Behind my back, he was dating other women, and he was betrothed besides, but I never knew it," Serafina said.

The madam shrugged. "Like half the men I know."

"But there was something about him, about the way it ended."

"Tell me," Rosa said.

"I saw him kissing another woman. He was in disguise, wearing a wig."

"That's good." Rosa grinned. "And you remember this from school? Tell me more of the story."

Serafina touched her temples. "And when I called out his name, he stopped kissing the little vixen, turned to me, doffed his cap, and bowed."

Rosa laughed so hard she cried.

Serafina frowned. "Handy with a blade, Falco, and a passable actor, too, but he plays to the cheap seats."

Rosa wiped her eyes. "Better than *dolci*, that story. So add him to the list if you want, but circle Brown Cloak and Limping Cobra."

"And don't forget, he's Bella's uncle, and he may well have gained from her death."

Now the madam was alert. "How?"

"She was the last living child of the oldest living Baldassare, no?"

Rosa's eyes widened. "Now that you mention it, his face is familiar. He may have been a guest once or twice. We must question him and Bella's father, too."

Serafina wiped her face with a linen. Why was this so hard? "As soon as I've finished talking to everyone here, we'll meet with the Baldassare brothers. Perhaps we can see Bella's contessa friend as well."

"You mean travel to Palermo?"

Serafina nodded. "We'll leave early, take the train to Bagheria, then a cab to Palermo. More reliable than the roads, and faster. Renata can come with us and shop in La Vucciria while we talk to Bella's father. Bring Tessa. Has she ever seen Palermo?"

Rosa was quiet, considering.

"You need to show her the world. Renata will mind her while we do our work. Meet us at the station tomorrow at seven."

Rosa nodded.

"Now I want to speak to your women, Scarpo and his men, the cook, the laundress, the maids. I'll use your office. I might have to return, but I'd like to start this evening." 🙋

Scarpo

ullen creatures with hooded eyes, the first few women Serafina interviewed entered the room one at a time, bathed but not yet dressed for the evening. Like parrots, each one said the same thing. No, the prostitutes had no trouble with their customers. No, they'd seen no one suspicious, not around here, not in the straw market, not in the piazza. And the maids barely remembered Gemma, Nelli or Bella. At the time of the prostitutes' deaths, they saw, heard, felt nothing unusual. She was beginning to despair of learning anything when Scarpo entered.

"Cold in here," he said. As he carried wood over to the hearth, his hobnailed boots shook the walls. Serafina watched the muscles of his upper arm pump while he stoked the embers and added another log to the grate. If Rosa were out of the way, would he gain or lose? Mentally she added him to her list of key suspects—the brown cloak, the limping man, Falco, Scarpo.

She asked him if he had time for a few questions.

Nodding, he sat in the chair she'd pulled up in front of the desk, displacing the air as he settled himself, and rippling the flame in Rosa's lamp. Serafina heard the new log crack as it fed the fire.

"What can you tell me about the women who died?"

"Meaning what? I'm a busy man. My son helps me when he's not in school but look here, look there." He made large, circular gestures. "A lot for me, this house. I manage the gardeners, supervise the guards—and they're a sorry lot, the guards. I work all the time, but let me think about the women who died." He pitched forward, squirming to the edge of the chair, and bowed his head.

Silence.

Hadn't he heard her question? "The first one to die, Gemma. In

August. I remember her funeral," Serafina said. "Can you tell me about her?"

Again he made no reply.

A mysterious man, this Scarpo, strutting around like King Bumma in a pair of braces. He played the strong man, yet, like a child hiding in the corner, she thought he longed for discovery. Serafina spoke again, and this time her voice softened the room. "I think I met your son last week—a handsome boy. He looks just like you, but with hair. He helped Beppe with our trap and must have a way with mules because Largo seemed unusually calm on the way home."

He gave her a down-from-under look and his smile, slow to spread, lit his face. "Arcangelo will be sixteen next month, the same age I was when I started helping my father here." He dug into his pocket, fished out a dirty yellow bandanna. "The sudden heat you know," he said, wiping his forehead. He took small swipes at his eyes. "The wife's been gone three years." He stared at the floor. "Good in the morning, baking bread for Rosa. I came home for dinner, and the table was bare. She, the wife, was curled up on the floor. Cholera." His body sagged. "Only me and Arcangelo now. He works like a man and La Signura knows it."

"So you know this house," she said.

"All of it." He looked at her, this time in control of his eyes.

"That's why I need to talk to you. If something were strange, you'd know."

"Yes, I know when Don Tigro's men trample one blade of grass."

"That's what they're saying in town."

"What?"

"That Don Tigro is behind the killing because he wants Rosa's business." Her eyes scrutinized his face for any change of expression.

His answer was quick. "Never. We pay him every month, and I take extra care of his men." He tapped the side of his nose with a callused finger, squared his shoulders, and said, "Don't tell La Signura about the extra. Besides, against their honor for the don's men to kill a woman for nothing. Kill Gemma, Nelli, Bella? Why would they? We're not like the *strega* who owned a store some years ago and refused to pay—you know the one I mean."

"The one who sold fruit and vegetables in town? Her daughter was shot, wasn't she?"

"Yes, the daughter shot, they say, by the don's men after she was used, you know how. But the old woman had a nasty mouth and didn't pay. We knew it, too. La Signura, she pays Don Tigro's men. I make sure of it."

"Thank you for your help." She meant it as a dismissal, but he didn't move.

Instead, he stared at the patterns on the rug. "One thing I noticed, but it's probably nothing."

"Tell me anyway."

"I need to find the words," he said.

"Take your time, and they'll come."

"Well, something in the air—more sound this summer, yes, and more movement during the day." He twisted his mustache. "And the women got dressed earlier, a lot of going out in the afternoon. There's always been more movement in spring and summer, but this year?—oh, the comings, the goings! Bella for instance, she took trips to Palermo, stayed for a few days. Gemma, I think, was in and out. Starting in June, maybe. The weather was hot, I know, because I remember seeing her leave while we were scything the field in back—Rosa likes it trimmed and a path cleared to the sea—and I can see them now, as I speak, going in and out, in and out." He waved his arms back and forth. "Yes, and in August, just before La Signura found Gemma's body, Arcangelo stopped in the middle of cutting and told me, 'Got to drive Gemma to town. Then I'll come back.' Yes, and he did, too, and we finished before evening."

"Did he tell you where he went?"

He shook his head. "Gemma was all dressed up, he told me."

"I'd like to talk to the rest of your men, then to Arcangelo. He saw something that may be important. Get them for me, please, Scarpo."

Soon, eight men stood before her, boots, aprons, bowed heads— one driver, two gardeners, five guards. Their squat fingers were hooked into their belts or squeezed onto their straw hats. No, they saw nothing, they told her, speaking in a dialect she barely understood, all the while giving her reverent stares. Let's face it: they barely spoke. She was sure that if they knew something, they were not about to tell her. She'd have to rely on Scarpo and Arcangelo.

Arcangelo

"Don't look at me like I'm from the heavens. I've got a son a little older than you, although I think you're taller, probably stronger. His nose always in a book, my Vicenzu, especially after the accident, and he loves his numbers."

"Numbers?"

"You know, you add them, subtract them, make them tell whatever story you want. Vicenzu keeps the ledgers for the apothecary shop."

"Ledgers?"

"Yes. He tells me I spend too much money. Do you believe it?"

Arcangelo pulled at his sleeves.

Serafina waited.

"One day, I'll be a doctor of animals, and your mule, dear lady, needs new shoes. Wrong, not to shoe a mule, not for these roads."

"I'll tell Carlo, my oldest son. He's supposed to tend to things like that." She circled her hand in the air. "A mother doesn't know about these things."

"My mother did, but she died."

She waited a few moments. Softly she said, "So did mine, last year." Serafina paused. "Terrible disease, cholera. One day she was fine, the next day, dead. I miss her, and I'm a grown woman with children of my own, but I still need her. I talk to her, and she answers, usually with words I don't like." She saw her dead mother's smile, her wrinkled nose. "Sometimes she still scolds me."

Arcangelo looked up and furrowed his brows. His ears were red. His eyes might have been wet.

She continued. "My mama told me once that she'd never leave

me, and I believed her, but she did leave. She lied, and there are no answers and no smiles for that. Anyway," she blew her nose, "I have a few questions to ask, and your father said you might be able to answer them. He told me you drove Gemma to town in August on the day before she died. Can you tell me about it?"

"Of course, dear lady."

"Call me Donna Fina, everyone does."

"Of course, Donna Fina. I drove Gemma because she asked me to."

"Where?"

"To the blacksmith's, close to the stables. She told me, 'My uncle meets me.'"

"Did you see him, the uncle, I mean?"

He nodded. "He wore a hat. I remember thinking at the time, it's cool for August, but still hot, and I wondered why the uncle wore a fedora in summer. Dark, the color, and he dressed in a heavy jacket of some sort, as if it were winter."

"Can you describe it?"

"Dark brown or grey, like a monk's cape, but without the hood. His back was to me and hunched over, his cape, all bunched in the back. Tall, I think. But I didn't say hello. I helped Gemma out of the carriage and said goodbye to her. He took her hand or beckoned to her or something." Arcangelo's face worked to remember. "He had a small mule and cart with him. The mule was old and worn. I could tell just by looking at him, he was not cared for by one who loves animals. For one thing, he wasn't shod. But I had to get back to help Papa—scything time—so I left."

"Of course. Give me a minute to write down what you've just said."

When she finished, she read it back to him. "A man, tall, in wintry clothes, wearing a fedora and a short jacket or cape. Mule and cart. Clothes bunched in the back. You mean like a hunchback?"

"Yes, that's it. Like Quasimodo."

She smiled. "My son liked the book, too. Would you recognize him if you saw him again?"

He frowned. "Perhaps the clothes and his shape, but I didn't see his face. His dress was foreign, at least not from around here, and he took Gemma's case and put it in his cart." He paused, looking up at the ceiling. "Now I remember something else: when he reached for the case, I saw that he wore gloves. This was in the heat of August."

She wrote down what he said, read it back to him, then said, "Some men wear them when they work or drive."

Arcangelo laughed. "Not around here. Kept his head down. Didn't greet me or look at me, as if he were afraid or slippery. If I saw the hat again and the cape—"

"Cape or jacket?"

"Cape. Like Fra Berto wears in the winter, only without a hood."

"The color?"

"Me? Colors?" He pulled at his cuffs. "I'm no good with colors, but I'd say darker than the color of your dress, lighter than my pantaloons. Grey, green, brown, blue—they all look the same to me."

"What did he wear on his feet?"

Arcangelo shrugged. "Shoes?"

"Shoes or sandals or you didn't notice?"

"Didn't notice."

"And the day, do you remember? Do you know your days of the week?"

He laughed. "Of course I know the days of the week." He looked up at the ceiling, one eye closed, rubbing the fuzzy stubble on his chin. "It was the day after Sunday." He winked.

She laughed. "Last time I considered, Monday followed Sunday."

"I remember it was Monday because we don't work on Sundays, so we sleep late, and I remember thinking as I drove away from the stable, five more days until I can sleep late again."

Serafina counted on her fingers. "Six more days."

He rocked his hand back and forth, two fingers pinched. "Depends on how you look at life, my mother would say."

Wise for someone his age. She liked this young man. "If you see him again, please tell me right away. You know where I live?"

He nodded.

"Ring the bell by the gate, day or night, doesn't matter. We're used to being awakened. I'm a midwife, you see, and babies love to arrive at night, just when they think everyone's asleep. Tell me right away. It's important."

He said he would and rose from his chair. Standing before her, he held his cap. She heard excitement in his voice, saw it in that bent-toward-her way he held his torso.

"You think I may have seen the killer?" His eyes looked straight into hers.

"Yes. I think you did, but tell no one. I can count on you? It's important."

"Don't worry." He screwed his thumb and forefinger on tightly-closed lips, bowed, walked to the door, said, "And don't feel bad, I talk to my mother, too."

After Arcangelo left, Serafina sat still for a moment, lost in thought.

Rosalia

"Rosalia, named after the saint," the prostitute said, "the one in a cave high in the mountains. When I was old enough, my mother shoved me out the door. Not enough coins for my keep. Told me I needed to make my way in the world. All done with me," she said.

Not yet sixteen, Serafina guessed, younger than Giulia. She cursed Rosa for taking in children.

"Are you going to catch the killer? Please, before he kills all of us. The others tell me he's a ghost. Comes in the middle of the night."

"Nonsense. He's flesh and blood, this killer. We'll catch him. But we must put our heads together. That's why I called for you. What do you know about the women who were murdered?"

Rosalia drew in her lower lip, but said nothing.

Serafina heard the wheeze of gas jets.

"Tell me the first thing that comes into your head. I'll decide if it's important."

Minutes passed. Serafina waited for the shell to crack.

"One thing about Gemma, she changed before she died."

"How so?"

The young prostitute picked at a blemish on her cheek. Serafina wanted to push the girl's fingers away from her face. Instead, she sat on her hands and waited. Why couldn't she behave this way with her own children?

"Stopped talking to me, all at once, Gemma." Rosalia snapped her fingers. She narrowed her eyes. "Maybe I said something she didn't like? Maybe I asked too many questions? Yes, that's it, too many questions ... maybe."

"Did you ask her why she stopped talking to you?"

"Yes." A wash of color began on the girl's shoulders. It crawled up her neck and filled her face the way dawn sometimes floods the world.

"And?" Serafina asked.

"She said she could no longer be my friend."

"Did she, now."

"Said I needed to be saved, she'd show me the way."

"And you said?" Serafina wrote in her book.

"Nothing. Slammed the door in her face!" Rosalia was solemn. Serafina raised her brows.

"Wouldn't you? Brushed me away like a customer shaking off the last dregs of me. All done, they say, before they leave."

"But you can't think you caused Gemma's distance. She removed you from her mind because of some disturbance inside *her* head, not yours."

"They all leave—Carmela, the same. She was a girl, here for a while, older than me. Knew the names of flowers. A miracle with the gardens. We'd talk after the men left, sometimes until morning. But one day she was gone, too. No goodbye, no nothing." Rosalia's eyes began to swim. "One day, one day, I'll show them all. They'll be sorry."

Serafina took deep breaths. Walking over to the girl, she had the sensation of falling, but she stroked Rosalia's cheek and took her in her arms. While she sobbed, the candlelight played tricks, and for an instant, Serafina held her child, Carmela, the first-born twin, soft as the inside of a goat's ear, Giorgio said, but she shoved the memory away, punched it down deep until it couldn't hurt anymore.

*L*ola sailed into the room. Sapphires sparkled on her fingers—and pearls, she dripped pearls. They wound around her neck in long ropes, dangled from her ears, reflecting opalescent light from tiered bracelets. Her gown of watered silk was cut low in the front with a lace surround, pleated in the French manner. She seemed somehow different from the last time Serafina had seen her, that day in the conservatory, almost a different person—more, how to say it, more mature. But no, that wasn't it at all, not at all: harder. Over her bodice she wore a fitted mauve jacket of boiled wool, a feathered boa draped around her shoulders. Her golden hair was trussed with tortoise combs, around which curls were carefully coiled, and wedged into her cleavage was her ivory cigarette holder.

She sat. "Rosa told me you wanted to see me." Her voice was expensive. Reaching for her cigarettes, she stuck one into the holder, and swung a leg over the arm of the chair, revealing a taffeta underskirt, lace petticoats, and black crocheted stockings. On her feet were satin shoes.

"My first customer is in the parlor now. Impatient." Lola blew smoke from rouged lips. "A dignitary." Inhaled. Exhaled. "Can't spare much time, but I want to help." One propped-up leg arced back and forth.

"I don't care if he's the king of Savoy. He'll have to wait."

She slid her leg off the arm and crossed it at the knee. As she rearranged herself, Lola's eyes roamed over Serafina's shape.

Serafina had a set of questions she asked each prostitute: did you know Gemma? Nelli? Bella? If yes, for how long? Who were her friends? Did she confide in you? When was the last time you saw her? Did you notice anything strange or new, a change shortly before she died? A new customer? And while the prostitute answered this barrage, Serafina made notes of her facial expression, choice of words, accent, gestures, what she said, what she didn't say, how she walked, the cut of her gown, the color and style of her hair, her scent, her jewels.

Lola was no exception. She answered with a shrug of one shoulder or a slight shake of her head. Amused by the spectacle, Serafina kept up her battery of questions long enough to study this new side of Lola. When she'd taken her measure, Serafina asked, "What do you know that you're not telling me?"

Lola's mask dropped. "Forgive me. I'm about to work, you see, and this is a pose I use. If you'd ever done what we do, you'd understand. I want to help you find this killer. I doubt you'll catch him—he's clever—but I owe it to them, to my friends, to the women who died, and most especially to Bella. She taught me, you see, and I am indebted to her, and to La Signura."

"Taught you what? Rosa told me you were the teacher here."

"Bella taught me costume and artifice, the skills necessary in my line of ... " She stopped.

Serafina waited for her to continue.

"The skills each woman must have in order to be captivating."

Serafina nodded.

"As I say, I'm here to answer all of your questions, and I think I may have information of interest."

"That would be?" Serafina arched one brow, her pencil poised.

The prostitute considered her cigarette. Leaning over, she crushed it with a ferocity that surprised Serafina. Small bits of paper and tobacco lay in and out of the ashtray as if a miniature cannon had laid waste to that part of the desk.

"The evening before she died, Nelli said she was going to meet a man outside of town who would change her life."

"Did she name this mysterious man or say where she would meet him?"

Lola shook her head. She nestled the cigarette holder back into its place, crossed her legs again, and said, "I assumed that if she'd go with this mysterious stranger, we'd never see her again."

"Did you see him?"

"No."

"Any idea who he is?"

"No. We used to be friends, Nelli and I, until she stopped confiding in me. She'd grown secretive before she died. I guess I wasn't good enough for her." She looked down at her hands, now folded in her lap.

"When did you first notice the change?"

"I think some of it was good," she said, waving her boa and licking her lips.

"Answer the question."

"Can't remember."

"Some of *what* was good?" Serafina asked.

Lola shrugged. "You know, the ..."

"The what? Don't waste my time."

She faced Serafina. "The separation was good, especially for her. She used to follow me everywhere, except of course when I was with a client. Her hanging on my every word became too much for me. Rosa asked me to look after her when she came to the house, and truth to tell, at first she needed me. I taught her everything, don't you see. She became adept at our profession."

"Adept?"

Lola stopped talking. She reached into her fringed bag, pulled out a pot of rouge and applied color to her lips, pressing them together before she continued. It seemed to Serafina that this version of Lola, the working Lola, did not expend more energy than was necessary. Ever. Serafina guessed that trains ran or not, according to Lola's schedule; customers were satisfied or not, according to Lola's mood, but no matter what, they paid for the privilege of being with her for what, ten or fifteen minutes, and considered themselves lucky.

The prostitute continued, "You may not believe it, but our profession demands great skill: how to please a taxing customer, how to control a difficult one, how to move in interesting ways to please the flaccid, the shy, the pompous, even with the final customer of the evening, even with the lethargic, the rowdy, the toothless." She played with a lock of hair, winding and unwinding it around a finger.

"You taught all this to Nelli?"

"She was a child, inexperienced when she first arrived. Rosa asked me to look after her, and I did. I can never refuse La Signura. I show the new ones how to dress, how to make up the face. I even take them to Palermo, show them where to buy rouge, how to make undergarments more interesting, how to curl locks, set hair, brush it to make it shine. I sense when the mood in the house is heavy or there has been a fight between two or three, and I become a clown to make us all happy again. If you'd had my childhood, you'd understand. I learned, growing up in a cruel world, that you make your own happiness by making others happy. La Signura confides in me, asks me for special favors. She values my talents. So, yes, I try to teach the new ones all the tricksy shortcuts." Lola primped the back of her cascading locks. "Most of the girls here are from the country. Peasants. They don't understand."

"And you? You told me you're from the north?"

"Yes."

"You must miss it."

She looked long at Serafina before answering. When she spoke, she almost spat the words. "Like I told you, they took my child; they took my life; I left."

Serafina was silent, trying to generate warmth in her feet by working them back and forth on the madam's soft carpet. For an instant she could see the other Lola, the bittersweet woman she met the other day. That Lola flickered again in the prostitute's eyes, but on command, she disappeared, replaced by one mask or another that Lola tried on at will.

And truth to tell, wouldn't she, Serafina, be the same as Lola, had she been forced into or chosen to work in this profession? What would she be like had she, as a child, recoiling from, but all the same, been forced to give a grown man his pleasure, not knowing what it was she was doing, making herself afterward forget, coping alone with the nightmares, having promised never, ever to confess what it was she'd done? What would Serafina do if she, as a child, didn't understand what was happening to her body for nine months, stuffed down the mortal fear of it, shocked by the sickness, the agony, the blood of childbirth? What would she do if her child had been taken from her arms? And for a second, she imaged all her children, waif-like, crowded together and shivering in a barren room without her.

While Lola waited for her to finish the interview, Serafina massaged her temples. Had these interviews produced anything, other than confusion and doubt? Did she know the truth about any of the prostitutes she'd interviewed? Could she trust that any of them were telling her the truth, showing her their real selves—how they felt, what they thought, what they knew about the deaths of Gemma, Nelli, Bella? And what about the madam? Was she living in a fantasy? Whatever, she was clear on one thing: she, Serafina, was no closer to solving these murders than she'd been when she looked into the face of the dead Bella over two weeks ago. Was she wasting her time and doing a disservice to her children?

Serafina cleared her throat. "So why this sudden change in Nelli's attitude, her coldness toward you?" she asked.

Lola sat straighter and frowned. "I'm not sure. Maybe it was jealousy, but whatever it was, suddenly, Nelli turned. When she'd see me coming toward her, she'd walk the other way. And she began keeping herself to herself, going out alone. Saturday afternoons mostly. I think she went out the day before she died."

"She must have done. Did you see her leave?"

The prostitute hesitated before shaking her head. "No. I feel useless, as though I haven't given you much help so far, but I can only tell you what I know."

Serafina came back to her earlier question. "Rosa found Nelli's body in September. Can you tell me when you first noticed a change in her?"

"Like I said before, I can't remember, really." Lola rubbed an eyelash. "But, well, I think it might have been, yes, it was late in March, close to Easter. Yes. I asked if she'd like to go with me to Palermo the Saturday before the procession of palms. 'Other plans,' she said and didn't explain. Explain? She barely looked at me. Yes, that was the first I noticed her coolness."

A tap at the door.

"Ah, time to go."

"I may have more questions. Tomorrow or the next day, I might have to call you back."

"Of course. Whatever you wish." She ambled toward the door, her boa trailing behind, and with a backward glance, sent Serafina a dazzling smile. ❧

Formusa

*S*he hadn't seen the cook in what, twenty-five years, so after the kisses, after the tears for poor dead Donna Maddalena, the two sat facing each other at the long chestnut table.

Formusa poured the coffee.

"My husband, too, we lost him. His death, hard on the children."

The cook rose, cupped Serafina's cheeks in her hands, and Serafina felt flour on her face, smelled sweet cocoa, almonds, the zest of Formusa's sauce—a gift.

"I've missed this room."

"Biscotti?" The cook stared at her with octopus eyes.

Serafina rolled her hand from side to side. "Your pastry, always so tempting, but no, thank you. Do you have some time for me tonight?"

"La Signura, she says you have questions. Bad, the times, for the house."

"That's why I've come to you, Formusa. Tell me what you know, what you've seen, anything that comes to mind about Gemma, Nelli, Bella, or any of the other women in Rosa's house. Anything at all, even if you think it's not important."

The cook rubbed her hands on her apron and sat, unmoving.

She knew something, Serafina could tell, by the woman's stillness. A burnt piece of log dropped from the grate, sending a puff of ashes into the flames. Serafina waited.

Presently, Formusa slid her eyes from side to side. "Nelli told me not to tell."

Serafina said, "A secret?"

The cook nodded.

"Nelli's secret?"

Nodded again.

"Do you think it would help us to know it?"

The cook lifted her hands. "Maybe."

After a few moments, Serafina ran a finger back and forth on the smooth tabletop. "If it—the secret, that is—if it happened shortly before Nelli died, and if we knew this secret, our knowledge might save all of us."

The cook drew in her lower lip. She looked down at the table and was silent.

"Nelli's dead now. You know what Donna Maddalena used to say about the dead?"

Formusa smiled. "The dead have a lot to tell us."

"And so do you. What you know may help us survive."

Silence.

Serafina waited while Formusa's cheeks worked up and down. Nothing came out of the mouth, not for a while. More than a while.

"So, I begin," cook said.

This was followed by more silence.

"Rosa told me you taught Nelli how to make your sauce."

"Nelli, good with the soup. Not good with the pastry."

Serafina waited for more words.

"Always wanting to cook, that one."

"It's all right. Nelli's gone now. You can tell the secret."

"Nelli had coins, a lot of them. One day, she told me to hide them because they weren't safe in her room. She told me not to tell anyone. I didn't, of course, not until now. Don't know why, didn't ask why she brought them to me." Formusa got up, rolled from side to side to some bins on a shelf above the large black stove. She opened one, lumbered back to the table and showed it to Serafina. It was empty.

Formusa sat back down and continued. "Every night, Nelli came in here, and I sat by the fire. She opened the tin, put in the coins. I heard them drop." The cook stopped, smiled at Serafina.

"When did she start keeping her coins with you?"

Formusa nodded. "Two, three years ago."

"Where are they now?"

"One day, maybe two weeks before she died, she said to me, I cannot cook for you today, Formusa." The cook made fat floury gestures. "Bah, I don't care if she doesn't cook. I showed her how to cook because she wanted to learn, that's all. And Nelli took the tin, dumped it here." Formusa pressed the red pad of her forefinger on the table. "She lined up the coins and counted them." Formusa gave a toothless whisper, "Into her pocket they went. Not all, some. She left."

For a while Formusa sat still. Then she bobbed her head up and down. "Yes, it's true. Believe it?"

"Of course."

"Again, the night before La Signura found Nelli's body, Nelli came here. In a hurry, face red. No counting this time. She dumped all the coins into her pocket, kissed me goodbye, and ran out the back." She brushed her palms together. "That was the end. No more coins, no more Nelli."

"Did you tell Rosa?"

She shook her head. "She said to tell no one."

"You said Nelli ran out the back. Where?" Serafina asked.

She took a candle, gave one to Serafina, and padded to the other end of the kitchen.

Serafina followed. "The back stairs, I'd forgotten about them."

The candle in Serafina's hand shuddered from the wind seeping through the door. She heard the howling, held her candle higher. Even in the dark she could see steps leading to a landing and, branching off from this platform, two separate sets of stairs. She turned to Formusa. "This way goes to the back and the sea."

Formusa nodded.

Serafina pointed to a closed door on the other side of the landing. "Beyond that door, the back stairs to the bedrooms?"

She nodded, shivering.

Another blast of wind almost extinguished Serafina's flame. Without words, they walked back to the kitchen where, stooping, Serafina kissed Formusa on both cheeks, holding her close, grateful, she told her, for her help. It was the first solid thread she'd gotten that evening relating directly to the murders. ✎

Gusti

"My name is Gusti, short for Julia Augusta. Named myself after an ancient Roman queen, or goddess—one of those."

Underneath that stained robe of hers, she had breasts like mountain peaks. Must be wearing all the jewelry she owned, ropes of pearl and gold, jingly bracelets, a silver rosary, rings on all her fingers.

Serafina began by asking the usual questions.

The remnants of sweetened figs whiskered her lips. Gusti swept them off with the back of her hand, settled in the chair. "I didn't know any of the dead women, poor dears, not well, at least. I don't know what I can tell you. Don't know who'd want to kill them. Of course, I was busy on the days they died, I'm always busy."

"When was the last time you saw Bella?"

"Oh my, they've all been dead for such a long time. But when was it that I last saw her?" She looked up at the ceiling, drummed her fingers on one knee. "I remember now—it was in the station here in Oltramari. Yes, that was it." She slapped her knee. "I was going to Palermo, she was returning, it must have been, oh, two or three months ago, in the spring. She was getting off the train and I was waiting on the next platform. All of a sudden Bella came out of the car, packages and all in her hand. No suitcase. I yelled, 'Bella!' We waved to each other, and she disappeared into the crowd. That's the last time I saw her alive. I love to ride the train, don't you? The clack of the wheels, the rhythm of the car, it lulls me to sleep. The conductors are so nice to me, and the passengers you meet, oh, la, some of the men, stunning. I love the ride, I tell you."

Serafina laughed. "And that was the last time?"

"Alive? Oh, you mean, you mean, oh yes, I went to Bella's wake and all. Sad. She was the one I felt closest to. I mean, of the ones who died. Not like a sister, mind you, like Carmela and I, we were almost like sisters, but close enough, Bella and I. Even though we both kept to ourselves and all."

The air was heavy with cheap perfume. Serafina felt queasy. "And what about Gemma and Nelli? Do you remember the last time you saw either of them?"

Gusti shook her head. "We lead our own lives. We come and go here at Rosa's. Rosa wants us to be more like a family, 'my girls' and all, you know how she talks." The prostitute adjusted herself in the chair. "You and Rosa are friends, yes?"

Serafina nodded.

"But we are none of us friends here, not like you and Rosa. Oh wait, you must mean, maybe a few girls were friends with the dead ones, but not me, I wasn't one of them. I avoid most of the girls. Hard to trust. Well, except for Carmela."

"They told me you were friends with … her."

"And you're her mother. They told me. Hair the same. Skin, maybe the same. Eyes, definitely. Younger than me. Little bit of a thing, Carmela. Short. Bouncy. Fun to be with, Carmela. Loved flowers and the sea and walking. Could walk the legs off a sailor, that one."

Serafina rubbed her forehead. "When did she leave?"

The prostitute considered. "Left with a soldier, I don't know, about two, three years ago. Said she knew him. From before and all."

"Do you know where she is now?"

Gusti held her lower lip. "My friend, Carmela. Told me she didn't want anyone to … no one in the family must know where she was. Not Rosa. Said Rosa knew her mother. Sad and all, but she's my friend, and she made me promise. Not in danger. Happy."

Serafina felt tears prickle. "We haven't heard anything from her. At least now I know she's alive. When you write to her again, would you tell her that we need to talk to her? We have some family news for her, not good, but she must know."

Gusti nodded.

Serafina blew her nose. She was silent for a moment, blinking. She thought of what her children would say when they heard that Carmela was alive and happy. First bit of good news since their father died. They'd be thrilled, of course, all of them except Totò who didn't remember Carmela, and Maria—who could guess what her response would be to anything? She must write to Carlo. *Satisfied, Mama?* Not that she needed to, not that she'd ever forget, the words were seared into her brain, but all the same, Serafina wrote what Gusti had said Carmela—not in danger, happy—in her notebook, word for word.

The prostitute continued. "And then there was that big girl, came here about the same time as Carmela. Thought I could trust her, but I was wrong. She didn't last long, I tell you. La Signura got rid of her, presto." Gusti reached into her pocket for a handkerchief and wiped her forehead. "And what was that big one's name? It'll come to me. Her arms, can see them now, arms like a gunner's. Wait. Yes, Eugenia, that's her name. Had a laugh like a mule. Anyway, the three of us were friends, I mean, not all together, not like the three musketeers and all, but I was friendly with Carmela and I was friendly with Eugenia. Until, you know, the bad things happened with her. But now they're both gone. Like the wind, one hour it blows over Oltramari, and by that very afternoon, would you believe, it's in Enna. Well, after what's been happening in this house, I keep myself to myself, I do."

Serafina thought that Gusti's words flew like bullets but in different directions at once. She asked, "This Eugenia, you say she didn't last long. Do you know why?"

Gusti shrugged, then thought better of it, pulled her chair closer to Serafina and whispered, "My customers, generous, always giving me pearls, stones, gold bracelets. Rosa lets us keep those. Couple of us had things stolen. I got scared. We talked about it one day in town. When we got back, someone went to Rosa, and boom, Eugenia was gone. After that, well, you can't be too careful." She fingered her pearls and waited for Serafina to stop writing.

"Did you ever see Gemma, Nelli, Bella together? Were they friends?"

Gusti paused to consider before she responded. "Well, Bella

and Gemma, I used to see them talking together. Not a lot. Maybe Lola with them, too. Lola with Nelli of course. The four of them together? I might have done; I think they used to sit together. Well, no, oh you mean, because Lola was with Rosalia a lot. Poor little thing. Not robust in the head, Rosalia. Hard to figure out, that one. Like that wind I told you about, only, blowing this way one day, that way the next. As I said, I keep to myself." Gusti shivered. "Once or twice we'd all go to town, a bunch of us, not often, you know, order a caffè at Boffo's, sit and watch everyone in the piazza and make jokes. And they maybe would sit together, but no, come to think on it, they weren't together a lot. More like Lola with Nelli until they had a to-do, then Rosalia with Lola."

"Bella went with you to town?"

"No, Bella was different, more like me and Carmela, only quieter. Not so bouncy. Getting on, Bella. Lots of talent, too. She kept to herself unless she was sewing for someone. Well, of course, you know, Bella made our clothes, the ones for special occasions. Bella was usually sewing for someone. Except for when she wasn't."

"Rosalia?"

"Hard to figure, but as I said, dim. Given over a little too much to tales and all. Miracles and the like. But one time when we were in town, all of us, like I said, one of the times Turi drove us, we piled in the carriage, a few of us on the rumble, we went to the sea near the cove. Carmela was still here. She and I, we took a walk on the shore and as we were coming back we saw Rosalia. Beating her fists on the pebbles, she was. In a state, the little minx, like a bleating lamb, her dress a shambles, her blonde hair all messed. Saw Eugenia bending over her, Lola looking out to sea, Prudenza off a ways, waving at us to hurry, the others with their arms crossed tight to their chests or letting the wind blow their skirts, ribbons flying, all of them laughing. Well, Carmela and I, we got there and I took one look at Rosalia and stooped close, don't you know, and told her to pick herself up and stop the bawling."

"What did she do?"

"Obeyed. I found out that if you talk to her serious and all, she'd stop her little girl acting."

Serafina held up her hand. "Wait." She flicked pages back and forth and her fingers flew as she wrote down the jumble of Gusti's words.

"Does any of that make sense? Oh, I don't know, how do you expect me to remember everything? Really, I'm busy all the time, truly busy. Hard work, this. Pays well if you keep up a steady stream. In and out, that's how I like them—no lolling about. But still, it's unending. And I have the most vigorous customers. Hard to take notice of the other girls when you work as steady as me. I'll write to Carmela tonight or tomorrow, if there's time." She tightened the belt of her robe.

"Have you seen any strangers hanging about lately, I mean, from the time of their deaths?"

"Strangers? How would I know?" She heaved her chest, looked around the room.

"What about visitors? Any of the women have visitors? Gemma? Nelli? Bella?"

"Visitors? You mean, not customers?"

Serafina nodded.

She shook her head and picked at a fingernail. "Wait, now. Bella, she had a visitor. Not a customer, I can tell you." Gusti turned around, and for a second or two stared at the blackness outside the window, as if she saw someone. A customer? Another prostitute? "Brrr, too cold tonight to talk."

"Should I send for some coffee?"

Gusti hugged herself. "Not enough time. We'll be done soon, won't we?"

"You were saying, about Bella's visitor?"

"An old woman called on Bella. Used to come once or twice a week. Funny creature, that's how I remember her—not her mother."

"How do you know?"

"Didn't look at all like Bella. And from a different class. Carried herself like a snooty duchess or something. All bends and bumps and angles, that one. Hair tied up in an old rag, but her clothes were gorgeous and oh, la, the jewelry. Really. Usually had bundles of clothes with her, perhaps for Bella to mend? And one time I saw her all gussied, almost didn't recognize her. Dressed herself up she did. Had a stunning frock on, all fringes and beads and feathers. Flowing. And, oh, the furs. Quite the figure she had, too, for an old cow. All made up with rouge and white powder and all."

"Strange company Bella kept," Serafina said.

Gusti hunched forward. "Maybe Bella was her seamstress. Helped all of us with our sewing and, as I say, made a gown for Gemma. Made lots of frocks for Rosa, for Tessa, too. Rosa paid her well, but Rosa, you know, can afford it. Don't mistake me, I love Rosa. Knows how to treat us. Leaves us alone. Knows how to put some of the bossy ones in their place, I can tell you. But she favors some of the girls, too. I'm not one of them. Rosa wants us all to be close, like a family, and we're not like that, no." The prostitute looked down, whisked a bit of dust off her shoulder. "And I've got an honest mouth. If I don't trust someone, I say so, and to her face. But talk like that, well, Rosa doesn't want to hear." ✐

Gioconda

"**I** have a few more questions if you don't mind. In particular there's something I've been meaning to ask you. At Bella's wake I saw you with a gentleman."

Gioconda laughed. She was dressed in indigo damask, full skirts, gold stars embroidered on the bodice. A matching scarf draped her shoulders. "Which one?"

"Tall, chestnut curls. Wore black of course, frock coat, cravat, armband."

The redhead drew a blank.

"Struts a bit," Serafina said.

"Oh, why didn't you say so? You must mean Falco. Not exactly a gentleman, I'll wager."

Serafina nodded. "How do you know him?"

"Same way everyone does." Gioconda winked. "Bella's uncle, at least that's what Bella called him. Met him through her."

"How?"

"In the parlor of course. I think he was with her father."

"And you've known him for how long?"

"Oh, la, couple of years, I'd guess."

"Your customer?"

"I'm not the only one. Helps himself."

"Does he know all the women?"

"Just a few of us. The select, you might say. On his last visit, he was with a couple of the girls in the parlor, chatting and such, having a gay old time. Likes to be surrounded by what he calls 'the choicest meats.'"

Serafina's brows furrowed. Rosa didn't bother to tell her about Eugenia. Now Falco. *Rosa keeps secrets from herself.* ✒

Not Much Time

After Gioconda left, Serafina sat alone in Rosa's office. Laughter drifted in from the parlor, faint squeals and the rocking of springs from the floors above. No doubt Rosa would shoo her away soon, but until she did, Serafina had time to think about what she'd learned. She tried to picture Carmela, wondering what she looked like now and how she'd changed, but thoughts of her daughter plunged Serafina's mood from bright into dark, and she felt herself being dragged down to a place she had no time for, so once again, she forced Carmela out of her mind.

She'd gotten more information about the most important suspect—she called him "the monk"—first, from Scarpo, strengthened by Arcangelo who saw someone fitting the same description with Gemma on the day she disappeared. Despite what Scarpo avowed, Serafina believed he was the same man she'd seen begging in the piazza, perhaps wearing the disguise of a monk, remembering the roughness of his habit, his gloves, his boots, although she reminded herself that Sicily was full of such strange-looking creatures.

And another suspect, Eugenia, had emerged, a prostitute who took personal belongings from the other women. Nelli's fear of being robbed made sense in light of Gusti's revelation, and she reminded herself that the buxom prostitute took the trouble of wearing all her jewels to the interview, declining to leave them unattended in her room. Just like the madam not to tell her about trouble and thieving in her house.

Three strands wove in and out of her mind. The first was a sense of foreboding. Everyone in the house carried the burden of fear,

Rosa, Scarpo and his men, the prostitutes, Formusa, even that actress, Lola, poor woman. The whole lot of them squirmed in their seats, cast a backward glance, as if death lurked around the next corner, ready to surprise. The second thread: a sense of upheaval and change. What was once a house of laughter and friendship had become a hospice of silence and mistrust. And third, Serafina's certainty that some or all of the prostitutes, and of course Rosa herself, that *grande dame* of secrecy, hid information from her, but only because the madam hid it from herself.

There were moments this evening when she felt sure she glimpsed the killer's presence—in the glint in Scarpo's eyes, in the wisps of Rosalia's hair, in the shadows on Lola's face. But now she saw these as illusory, a reflection of fear, and she felt the distance she must travel. She needed to find this killer before he struck again, and the madam wasn't helping.

Too many parts of the tapestry needed mending before the real picture would emerge. For he was a wily killer, this one, eluding detection by donning masks, taking on shapes that flipped faster than a tuna's tail. And yet there must be something, some truth that held the key, a clue that, for now, lay beyond her ken. Who or what caused the change in Rosa's house? How could she peel away the madam's layers of secrets? She forgot her surroundings, cocked her head to one side and swirled the liquid in her glass.

Only when the wick in her oil lamp began to sputter, Serafina went in search of Rosa.

"What's this I hear about Falco and the women? And this time, don't deny it."

Rosa nodded. "He's harmless."

"Harmless? He's a viper and he's been here in your house. A customer who helps himself, according to Gioconda, who had financial motive for killing his niece." As she talked, Serafina wrote so quickly in her book that she nearly tore the page. "We will never find this killer if you keep the truth inside your head."

There was a deep silence between them. It spread throughout the room. Even the wind outside seemed to still.

Rosa hung her head. "Circle him on your list, but he's a charmer."

Serafina shook her head, stared into space. Either Rosa wanted her to investigate or she did not. What would it take for Serafina to open her friend's eyes, to make Rosa realize that truth about those closest to us was the most difficult to see? She flipped through her notebook for a minute. "Judging from what Scarpo and the women told me, things changed here a few months before the murders began."

Rosa nodded slowly, blinking. She twisted her handkerchief. "For instance?"

"The comings, the goings. The friendships stopped. Confidences dried up. Gemma and Nelli became secretive. There is a pattern that emerges before each death."

"Now you're losing me."

"Well, then, tell me about Eugenia."

Rosa bit her lip. "Why dig her up? She's ancient history, has nothing to do with the murders."

"A woman comes to this house and steals from your other women, causes pain and mistrust. She could be your killer, or a link to him, and you think she's not important? If you want to get yourself another wizard, just keep up with your secrecy, your grand fantasy that everything is sweet and loving around here, because it's not. I need your help. If I ask you about customers, I want an answer, not a withholding, and until these murders are solved, everything that's happened in this house and all of the people passing through it are relevant to the investigation."

Rosa ran a hand around the edges of her blotter. "You're right. I don't know what comes over me sometimes. I must, I don't know … I hide the truth from myself."

Serafina nodded slowly and waited for Rosa to begin.

"Eugenia knocked on the door, all sparkles, and with muscles like a sinewy mule. Looking at her, at her high cheekbones, her long limbs, those powerful eyes, that thick head of shining hair, her youth, I could see her at work: one effortless, glorious toss after another, and I'll admit it, I could hear the ca-chink of my coffers. She said she came from Palermo and named a fancy house, so I opened the door to her. Time passed. We prospered. But one day, Gusti came to me and complained of pearls missing. Your Carmela, too, said she was missing a bag and some slippers. I didn't want to hear their stories. I admit it—I made a mistake." Rosa squirmed a little in the chair. "But when Lola told me about some clothes she was missing, an expensive petticoat she used to wear on special occasions, I became suspicious. I sent for Eugenia, and I told her to get out. The thieving stopped."

"And you didn't tell Colonna?"

Rosa shook her head. "We take care of these things ourselves," she said, wiping her hands back and forth. "I went to see Secunda. You don't know her. She runs a house in Palermo, and we're friends, not like you and me, but all the same, friends, associates, I guess." Rosa stared at the oil lamp on her desk. "She made sure Eugenia never worked again." As if to wipe the stain from her hands, Rosa ran them up and down her boned bodice, picked up her glass and downed her wine.

"You mean you had her killed?"

"Don't be silly. Of course not. Together, Secunda and I spread the word about her thievery."

"Where is she now?" Serafina asked.

Rosa shook her head. "Scarpo knows, I think. Remind me to ask him."

She told Rosa about Arcangelo's ride to the stables with Gemma on the evening she disappeared, his description of Gemma's uncle as a hooded figure. "I think the three of us—Scarpo, Arcangelo, and I—saw the same man, even though Scarpo doesn't think so. We, the three of us, noticed that he wore gloves even when it was warm."

Rosa crossed herself. "Marsala?"

Serafina shook her head.

She filled her glass and plunked back down in her chair. "Add Eugenia to your list, below Falco's name." She gazed into the fire. "You and Scarpo and Arcangelo saw the killer, disguised, of course, and the spider crawls up my spine, but at least now we seem to be getting somewhere."

The beech log crackled. High notes, low notes, all were eaten alive by a clean flame. Serafina felt its heat on her face, and she relaxed, feeling how good it was to sit across from Rosa, her oldest friend on a cold evening by a warm fire.

"One of the last prostitutes I interviewed, Gusti, the one with the swollen chest? She knows where Carmela is. Wouldn't tell me."

Rosa frowned and started for the door.

"Sit. I don't blame her. Carmela made her promise not to tell her family, and Gusti is her friend and cannot break a promise. I admire her for that, but it gave me hope. Carmela must be near, I feel it, and Gusti said she was happy."

"I'll get it out of her. I have my ways."

"Don't. Not yet. We'll give the guards another week," Serafina said. "Gusti also mentioned seeing Bella at the train station. Said she had a female visitor."

"A what? Oh, a real visitor, you mean. The contessa. Francesca Grinaldi. With luck, we'll see her in Palermo tomorrow. I'll dispatch one of the guards with a note."

"Gusti described her as 'all bends and bumps and angles.' Called her 'an old woman.'"

Rosa smiled. "To my girls, anyone over thirty is old."

"Don't forget, the early train. It leaves at seven, more or less. I'll meet you at the station, fifteen before the hour."

"Barbaric, the hour, but as you wish."

A knock and the door opened. A maid said, "The baron."

"Time to go." Turning to the domestic, Rosa said, "Get Turi and Scarpo." And to Serafina, "They can take you home in the carriage."

"I came with Beppe in the trap. The fresh air will clear my head."

"Then fetch Arcangelo," Rosa said to the maid.

The domestic nodded, closed the door.

"After dark, you need two men to protect you. Arcangelo can ride behind, keep his eyes on you. Tell him to return at first light."

They kissed each other on both cheeks.

"Oh, and I almost forgot." Serafina turned back.

"You are impossible, standing there, tapping your chin like a potentate! You're always late, take way too much time, and say far too many words. They cling to you, your words, like maggots on the dead."

Serafina smiled. She had missed her friend, and now, finally, Rosa was back. "Ask Scarpo to go to the blacksmith's tomorrow. Tell him Donna Fina wants to know if anyone rented a stall between mid-July and August 6th. I want names and dates. All the names, all the dates. And swear the smith to secrecy: he is to tell no one."

Rosa nodded.

Serafina told her what Formusa said about Nelli's coins.

"The most important detail of all, and you almost forget to tell me."

"Because if I told you about coins in the beginning, you wouldn't hear anything else."

Rosa wagged her finger. "Mark my words, think on it well: money is at the root of these crimes. I know it, I know it." She twisted her fingers. "The killer promises them something for a big fee. He takes their coins and kills them. At the heart is lucre."

"That may be a part of it. Falco, for instance, gains by Bella's death."

Rosa nodded.

"But that's not all, not the most important part. There's a systematic ghoulishness about these murders, a madness about the killer that lust for money will never explain. He has the cunning of a wild one, intent on one thing only—eliminating you and all your prostitutes and the business you think I know so little about."

Rosa wrung her handkerchief. "I know, but ..."

Looking at her friend, Serafina realized how hard this was on Rosa, how far she'd come in her realization of the evil surrounding her, and how far she needed to go. In agony, the poor woman, Rosa was as pale as a sheet in the sun except for two spots of riotous color on her cheeks, and Serafina hated to hurt her friend, but she had to say it. "But what? No more 'buts.' Why the mark branded on their foreheads? Why did each death occur between the sixth and the seventh of the month? We must discover how the victims' lives touched this killer. Why did these women need him? Agree to meet him? What did the three women have in common, other than their profession and their address? Is the killer someone who helped himself to all three?"

"Never!"

"Rosa, listen to yourself. Falco is a customer. He's on the list."

The madam stood at the door trembling and staring at something inside. "You're right, I know you are, but I can't quite believe him capable of such evil, or for that matter, any of my other customers, or any of my girls."

"Then be prepared to bury more women." 🕊

The Ride Home

On their way home, mist obscured the moon, but Serafina saw thousands of stars, perhaps millions. Brilliant tonight, the world. Letting her body follow the sway and swing of the trap, she peered into the ether, high up into that mighty interstellar darkness, not opaque but not quite transparent; where space went beyond itself to somewhere lighter, bluer, farther up than she or it or any star had ever traveled; where past and future were finished and truth existed, pure, whole, untouched. What would Rosa say if she could hear these thoughts? Serafina saw the face her friend would make. She smiled, and giving herself over to the ride, bumped on, bending with the curve in the road.

She felt an excitement, a tingling in her toes, in the vigorous beating of her heart. Life had changed and she was brand new. Or perhaps it was her quest to find the killer of Rosa's women, a calling she was always meant to follow. No matter the reason, she began viewing her surroundings for the first time. "Look at the glittering heavens, Beppe. The big star, see it?"

His brows furrowed. His cheeks moved in and out as he poked a dirty finger at the sky. "That one?"

"*La Puddara*, a good friend. It never moves. Walk toward the star, you'll pass through the rough neighborhoods and come upon the sea. Walk away from it, you'll come back to the center of town. Keep going, you bump into the Madonie or a wheat field, one of those, it depends. Shepherds and fishermen know how to work *La Puddara* better than I. Talk to them, they'll teach you all the ins and outs, or maybe Giulia has a book about the polar star. Ask her." As she spoke, the wind took her breath, the night air stung her nose. She thought of her children's laughter, the way her sweet

Giorgio used to warm their bed.

"Tomorrow night, too?"

"Yes, and the night after that, and after that, in a string of nights as far and as wide as the mind can imagine. The power of *La Puddara* is forever—when it chooses to appear, that is. Learn how to use this star and it'll keep you on the right path. Admit it, you're lost half the time in this part of town."

He lifted one corner of his mouth.

Beppe, what would she do without him? Two years ago, she received a letter from the head of the orphanage. 'Finished with schooling, Beppe, too old to stay here,' the nun had written, 'but no one wants him.' So he came to live with Serafina's family. They fed and clothed him, gave him a room of his own and a stipend. In exchange, he ran errands for the house, accompanied Serafina to and from her midwife's work. To most, he seemed a simpleton, but she knew better. Oh, his brain was a little sluggish at times, but his fists were not, a fact which endeared him to her children. That, and his height—he towered above most men, including her own boys, and, more to the point, over the town's troublemakers, of which there seemed to be more and more. The lot of them, cowards all, looked away when Beppe passed. "An estimated 25,000 deserters," her son, Carlo, had told her. Many of them gathered in the piazza each day, and by night, they lurked in the shadows of unlit streets.

Beppe quickened Largo's pace, and Serafina shivered despite wearing her thick winter cape. They passed the market stalls shuddering in the wind, the stables, the blacksmith, the houses of the artisans, dark and small, standing like battered sentinels on the edge of town. Serafina heard bawdy laughter coming from somewhere, the angry voices of a man and woman arguing, the howling of a mad dog. Turning around, she saw Arcangelo on his mule riding a few paces behind. A black cat skirted in front of Largo's hooves and shone its yellow eyes at Serafina, the feline's belly close to the ground, a rodent's tail and claws wriggling between clamped teeth. Serafina smelled wet laundry, cheap wine, human waste.

Closer to town, they passed the former abbey flying the tricolor. Ever since the government muscled it away from the monks, soldiers marched back and forth in front of it, lean and tall, handsome in their uniforms, tight in all the right places, and she'd looked. Her cheeks warmed at the thought. She could live with that change and, she admitted, was grateful for the show of strength, glad when the Bourbon rulers slinked off her land. Good riddance: ugly, self-righteous pigs, every last one.

Except for the queen. Stately, beautiful, stubborn, Maria Sofie held out in Gaeta surrounded by all of Savoy's troops, soldiers and cannon stacked against her as high as the peaks of Monte Pellegrino. Yet she refused to surrender, stood her ground while the king, her husband, cowered in the closet. Defeated, the queen, still my queen, she'd said one day to Giorgio who replied, "While she ruled, Maria Sophie cared not a jot for Sicilians." But Serafina had no plans to remove her picture from its place of honor in the parlor.

Beppe snapped the reins. Again and again he touched his back, twirled his head left and right, looked up at the heavens searching for the star. His Phrygian cap crimped the tops of his ears as he turned onto a side street, their usual shortcut.

Not far from home, now, but Serafina couldn't see a light anywhere, except for their lantern, and a small beacon behind them, Arcangelo's torch. It was dark ahead, and Beppe paid too much attention to that star. And she, wishing she hadn't mentioned *La Puddara*, not at all, thought that Largo was going too fast, probably sensing the end of the journey, when one of their wheels rolled over a large stone.

The trap canted to one side, as if suspended, creaking on two wheels for ever so long, it seemed. Beppe slid into her. Serafina hung onto the iron railing, biting her lip and trying with all her might to push Beppe back, but it was seconds before the trap righted itself.

Largo halted. In the distance, Serafina heard a mandolin, the melody unrecognizable. In the dark, something moved toward them. The shimmering of an ancient shade? Whatever it was, the form grew more distinct in the glow of the trap's lantern, a shadow running toward them. The shadow took on a weathered hat with straggly ends of matted hair whipping out as he ran. He had a beard and legs that looked stretched, they were so long. But he didn't turn, he ran straight toward them, no doubt mistaking them for someone else.

Later, she remembered the sight of his bare feet slapping the cobbles, his tattered shirt and pantaloons, the knife handle sticking out of his belt. Lips formed words, indistinct. An accent? Funny, he held the pistol with both hands. Unsteady. Too much wine, perhaps? Before she could duck, he fired, hitting the trap's lamp. Blackness.

Serafina heard another shot, more shouting, metal clattering on stone.

Afterward, she recalled the set of the stranger's mouth, a taut red band, remembered flaming shards exploding around them like fireworks at the end of a *festa*.

"Stop or I shoot!" Arcangelo yelled, framed in the light from his torch. He dismounted. His revolver pointed at the attacker who sunk to his knees, begging for his life.

Beppe jumped down to join Arcangelo. As they stared at the man, probably a deserter or some such unfortunate living rough, he wrested the gun from Arcangelo's hands, swiped it across Beppe's jaw, and ran.

"Quick," she heard Beppe shout, "let's get him!"

"Let him go!" Serafina said. She handed Beppe a cloth to dab the blood from his lip.

"But my revolver," Arcangelo said, stretching the cuffs of his sleeves.

"Do as I say. You're both going to run after him and leave me alone in the dark with no gun, a frightened mule, and the Madonna knows how many of the bandit's comrades lurking in the shadows?"

A Quick, Sure Stab

"Why do you weep?" asked the monk, gesturing freely. "Look around. The air is sweet for November, and this spot is a pleasant respite from the strife of daily toil. Birds sing and flowers bloom. Dry your eyes and take joy in the simple beauty of nature." He stretched his arm to indicate the public gardens surrounding them.

Through a stuffy nose, she said, "Better leave. I've no money for the likes of you."

"I'm not begging for coins, my child." The monk made the sign of the cross over the young woman. "May your heart flood with the peace of the brazen serpent." He sat back and began reading his holy book.

They were both silent for several minutes before she asked, "What kind of a monk are you?"

He smiled. "From the north. We practice an ancient rite, one that bequeaths peace beyond understanding."

"Not for the likes of me." Her smile was lopsided.

"I know what you do, and believe me, forgiveness is yours if you ask and perpetual absolution if you so desire, but only for a select few."

She shook her head. "You don't understand. I must continue with my work or my family starves. Yesterday, my brother took the money I gave him, but said it wasn't enough. It'll be my fault, he said, if my family can't stay together. I need to earn more, but La Signura won't raise my fee."

The monk was silent. "Tell me about your brother."

She shrugged. "What is there to say?" She told the monk that she sent money home with one of her siblings who came to call

117

each month. She cannot earn more.

"And your family, where are they?"

"Enna." She began to relax.

"My work needs many hands," the monk said. "I could use yours, and they would fill with gold."

"Not interested," she said, rising.

"Easy work. Information, that's all I need," the monk said. "For you, enough prayers to last a lifetime. I need recruits for my life's work, the work of the brazen serpent."

When the voices told me to begin, I left, like you. Careful, now, I am so careful. The last one, smooth, the blade like the serpent's razor, the flesh like jelly. I sharpened it beforehand, you see. A quick, sure stab, and she stilled. The carving, perfect. This time there were no screams. The voices do not drown them out. They howl when the moon is black. I cannot abide their ringing. You'd be proud of me, I follow the will of the serpent, my work has begun. Early days yet, but I will triumph, and then I will go back soon to rescue my helpless one. He has sticks instead of arms. In the grave they told me, but they are wrong—he is alive and visits me in my dreams. I know he lives. Perhaps he is with you.

In dreams, too, lurks the wizard. She was so near to me that I saw the fear in her face. I could have triumphed—one quick pull of the trigger, a sure shot to her heart—but the moment was inauspicious. Righteous and sacred, the voices say, telling me to wait for the totality, the perfect number containing the fullness of the earth and of the heavens. Next time, and there will be a next time, now that I have help, I will not fail. So precious to herself she is, the wizard, but she will be no more, and with her demise, the harlot's house will collapse, and the work of the serpent will kiss the land. The voices demand it. Blood washes blood, they sing in my ears, a honeyed melody, a cloak for dreaming. And they heal me, they tell me I cannot fail. ✒

Part Two

October 23 - November 4, 1866

The Train Station

*S*erafina thought there would be a few passengers at the station, but when she and Renata arrived, she saw a long line of carts waiting at the front door to discharge passengers. Inside, wiry men wearing collarless shirts and carrying knapsacks stood together smoking cigarettes and talking fast. They'd take the train to the harbor, board a steamer bound for one of the Americas, and work long hours, sending money home each week before returning in a year or two.

But this time, Serafina also saw whole families, large clumps of them, each person with a cloth bundle by their side. It looked like they had all their belongings with them. Peasants, Serafina knew from their dress and inflection, or as Loffredo would say, "people of the soil," thin, with leathery faces and dreams in their eyes.

A voice cut through the crowd. "Feeeeena! Where aaaarrre you?"

"Here, Rosa!" Serafina watched the swarm of people part for her. Her face purpled and she scurried toward Serafina, rearranging her load of packages from one hand to the other, and clutching her hat. Tessa clung to Rosa's skirts, skipping to keep up.

"Finally!" Serafina pecked Rosa on both cheeks, bending to kiss Tessa whose hair was in ringlets. She wore a silk dress of red and green plaid reaching to mid-calf, the bodice cut deep to reveal a linen blouse with ruffled collar and tiny pearl buttons. Her petticoat had rows of lace near the tops of cordovan boots.

"What a pretty dress!" Serafina said.

"Bella made it for her," Rosa said.

"Let me take some of these packages. Oh, this one smells delicious. What did you bring?"

"Gifts for Bella's father and for that Grinaldi woman, and cook fixed a box of food for the train. It's heavy, can you manage?" She looked down at Tessa. "Sorry I said those words to you, my sweet girl. Pity, we couldn't find your bracelet." The madam fanned herself and whispered something into her daughter's ear while Tessa, her face pointing straight ahead and her expression immobile, gazed at the crowded station and listened. She gave Rosa a swift peck on the cheek when she'd finished.

In front of them, two boys began a tug of war over a wooden toy. The older boy yanked it from the younger one's grip. He fell, cracking his knee on the stone floor, and began to bawl. Motes of dust erupted into the light streaming from high windows. Seeing blood, the mother wailed, and people closed around the scene, fluttering and waving arms.

Serafina brushed dust from her cape. "Who knew there'd be so many people at this early hour? Let's find Renata. She's buying the tickets."

Rosa peered ahead, shaking her head. "How can you find anyone in this crowd?"

"There she is—over there!" Serafina gestured to the front of the line where her daughter was handing money through the bars of a window. Holding hands, the three of them walked over to Renata who managed to collect the tickets, peck Rosa's cheeks, and introduce herself to Tessa. They squeezed over to an empty space next to a large window. Looking out, they saw hundreds on the platform, talking, bustling, calling to one another, the men in vests and caps and starched shirts, most of the women in homespun skirts and Garibaldi blouses, their children fat with layers of clothing.

"We'll never get on the train," Serafina said. "We'd better go home and ask Carlo or Vicenzu to drive us to La Vucciria."

"Better yet, we'll drive ourselves," Renata said.

"Not on your life." Rosa repinned her hat. "I'm brave, but not foolhardy, and I've given my driver the day off because we planned to take the train." She shot Serafina a look. "We'll take a later one."

"Perhaps there's someone outside who knows when the crowd will thin. Hold hands. We'll have to force our way to the door," Serafina said.

The three women arranged themselves around Tessa and pushed their way forward, making progress toward the platform until a man with an infant in his arms blocked their way.

Serafina smelled dirty diaper. The baby began to cry, and the man tried to calm him, but the infant's yowls became more strident.

Rosa held a linen to her nose.

The man looked up at Serafina and Renata. "Please, dearest ladies, can you help?"

"Let me have a look." Rosa elbowed her, but Serafina continued reaching for the infant.

The man, dressed in a clean but threadbare suit, handed him to Serafina.

"There, there." Serafina rocked him. Renata bent close to see the child's face, then pulled away.

"You got us out of our beds at such an hour to watch you hold this crying baby? Give the child back to his father."

"About a month old, I'd say. Didn't deliver him, or I'd remember the shape of his head." She smoothed the infant's brows with two fingers, stroked his ears, and felt his silky hair. The baby made sucking noises and slept. "Hungry for his mother's milk. Where is she?"

The man's brow furrowed. "My wife, she comes soon. Now she makes a final look over the house, because today we take the boat. Leaving for good." He strained upward, trying to see beyond the crowd. "One moment, I think I see her. Yes, dear ladies, wait one moment—she's getting off the cart now." Smiling, he stretched and waved and turned back to them. "Be right back."

"You see, Rosa, no harm done. The mother's here."

"And all of Palermo will walk on the other side of the street when they smell you coming." Rosa looked at her watch. It's after seven thirty. Where's the train? We should have been on the platform by now. Oh, Fina," she said, stomping her foot, "you'll be the death of me! How do you stand this mother of yours?"

Renata shrugged. "Whatever she wants, we do."

"Not all of you," Rosa said. "Some of you leave."

Renata's eyes widened and she put a finger to her lips.

By this time the waiting room was dangerously overcrowded. The man, barely visible, continued yelling for his wife. After they watched him disappear out the door, Serafina, Rosa and Renata stood motionless, hemmed in by the press of people while the baby slept in Serafina's arms.

Renata stood on tiptoe, intent on finding him. "There he is! Let's follow him." Slowly, they pushed their way to the door and opened it, accosted by the warmth of the morning, the air fresh and weighted with the smell of lavender, as if it were early spring instead of November. The man was nowhere in sight. The crowd outside the waiting room swelled.

"The mother must be frantic by now. Any moment she'll appear, flailing her arms and shrieking. Let's see if we can get through these people," Renata said.

Rosa muttered, "Oldest trick in the book and the wizard falls for it."

"Excuse us," Serafina said, glaring at Rosa, and at the same time elbowing her way through a small opening. With the infant now whimpering, she tripped on someone's bag, catching herself before falling. As the contents of the bag flew out over the floor, the owner blocked their way, yelling in dialect.

"Someone's life is strewn before you, and what do you do—step on it!" Rosa said.

Serafina felt her jaws tighten. "You fat cow, you pushed me." Her movements were sharp, she knew, and she felt her blood coming to the boil, but could not control it. Something about this infant and the missing father was not right, she knew, should have known it from the first sight of him and his yowling son.

"Enough, both of you." Tears pooled in Renata's eyes. She and Tessa bent down to help the woman. Renata murmured something to her. The woman looked up at Renata and smiled, closed up the bag, and scurried off.

Renata stood. "You two, act your age!"

Serafina and Rosa looked at each other. Rosa made a face at the infant. Serafina laughed.

"This way, everyone." Renata led them outside, jamming through the throng to the platform, and Serafina told them to look around for a short man wearing a cap. Rosa couldn't resist one of her remarks—something about all men being short and wearing caps—and Serafina was about to correct her when steam and smoke engulfed them, and the train pulled into the station, wheezing to a stop, the blast of its whistle piercing Serafina's ears. Peasants muscled their way ahead of them to the edge of the platform.

Spying a porter, Serafina pulled his sleeve. "Excuse me, but can you help me find the parents of this baby? I agreed to hold him while the father went to looked for—"

"—his wife and sister who went home for one last look?" the porter asked.

"Oh, thank the Madonna! See, Rosa? You were wrong about him—he told this agent to look out for us!"

The porter's face was twisted. "You won't find him here."

Serafina said, "No, you don't understand—"

But the man had disappeared.

Train officials helped the last of the passengers squeeze onto the cars. One signed to the engineer, and the doors closed. People hung out of open windows, waved handkerchiefs, cried, blessed the air, and Serafina saw passengers standing in aisles, wedging themselves between cars, sitting on the roofs. Near them, a fight started and the crowd around them swayed, the sounds of bones cracking and men shouting swallowed by a belch of steam. The world stilled for an instant, and slowly, the wheels began to turn as the throng cheered, cried, blew kisses, and waved handkerchiefs.

Serafina stood on the platform unmoving even after the last car had disappeared behind San Calogero, anger crowding disbelief. Her face paled and her hands were stiff. The baby slept. Tessa gazed up at the infant. Serafina turned to Rosa. "I'm so sorry, my true friend. Of all people, I should have known."

"No matter." Rosa waved bad words away, hugged Serafina and the baby.

"Follow us." Renata and Tessa navigated the way to a conductor selling tickets. Tugging his sleeve, Renata said, "Can you tell me the time of the next train to Palermo? We couldn't board this one—too crowded. May I exchange these?"

The conductor peered at the three women and consulted the filigree dials of a large watch. "In an hour fifteen."

"And after that?" Renata asked.

He bent to scratch an ankle. "Well, there's one at eleven, one at—"

"Four round trips on the eleven o'clock, please."

"Make them first class and give the tickets to me," Rosa said. She held out coins.

His mouth worked as he studied Rosa.

Taking Tessa's hand, she said over her shoulder, "We'll meet you here at ten fifty. Don't be late." ✒

The Orphanage

other Concetta entered the room, stooped, shorter, and more wrinkled than Serafina remembered, but her eyes were the same. Serafina explained the baby in her arms. Without a word the old nun rang the bell, and in a few moments, a child of about six appeared, wearing a resized dress. Pushing strands of hair away from her face, she stood, still and solemn, before the nun.

"You are in charge of our newest orphan. One, get him fresh clothes and another diaper. Two, give him a bath. Three, give him to Grandma Colletti—he needs milk. Four, find him a place to sleep. After he wakes up, Dr. Loffredo will need to see him. Get him."

"No vacant cribs, Mother."

"Improvise, child. Put two infants in one crib until the carpenter can make another."

The child nodded.

"And Ave?"

"Yes, Mother."

"Before you do your improvising, sit down and put your boots on the correct feet."

She sat.

"One more thing."

"Yes, Mother."

"When you remove his diaper, be careful of the burr. Put some salve on the wound."

Throwing a smile over her shoulder, the child disappeared with the wet bundle.

"Second baby from the train station this month."

"I thought they left them on your doorstep," Serafina said.

She nodded, adjusting her wimple. "The unmarried do. But a mother who is leaving for a strange land with the rest of her family, afraid for the life of her newborn during the voyage, or too poor to care for another hungry mouth? She doesn't make her decision to leave her baby until the last minute. I can't imagine the depth of her pain. The husband, or someone else in the family, convinces her it would be better for the child if the mother left him behind, so a family member, usually the father, takes the infant to the train station and finds an unsuspecting passenger." She pointed a gnarled finger at Serafina. "Someone like you, for instance—your clothes give you away. The story they tell is the same—the man asks for help calming the baby, says that the mother is coming any minute, then disappears. It's an old trick played on the naive."

Serafina's cheeks burned.

"The orphanage is full. We need money to pay the wet nurse, to feed them when they're older, to clothe and to teach them, but God provides."

"And if not?" Renata asked.

"And if not, I go to Palermo and visit the archbishop. The coffers open."

Serafina pursed her lips. "How can a mother abandon her infant like that?"

The nun's eyes hardened. "Terrible to abandon a child at any age, no matter what that child has done, don't you think?"

Serafina breathed in and out. In her mind she heard the sound of Carmela's feet running down the stairs, saw Carlo speeding after his twin, returning hours later, admitting that he couldn't persuade her to return, "Too stubborn, too much like you," she heard Carlo say again, over and over she saw him spitting on the ground before her feet, saw Giorgio lifting him by the collar and slapping his face. The reverie fading, she pulled her head up sharply and put a hand to her cheek. She must say something to this nun, but what? From somewhere outside, she heard feet thudding, youngsters shouting.

"No running, children!" a voice said.

Renata pointed to the door, forming an 'O' with her mouth.

Serafina's hand flew to her heart. She gripped her chair.

"Your child is here, you know," the old nun said. "Came to us in the spring."

"I ... we didn't know." Serafina felt the knot in her stomach return.

"Of course not. She pleaded with me not to tell you."

"But we've been looking for her," Serafina said. She paused before continuing, wiping her brow with a linen. "To be fair at first only her father, Carlo, and Renata were searching. I ..." She heard the heavy beat of her heart, felt the blood in her ears, couldn't stop her sight from blurring.

Mother Concetta said nothing.

"Does she know about the death of her grandmother?"

The nun looked at her hands. "She came here after Maddalena's death. I knew they were close, but I couldn't bring myself to tell your daughter about her death, no. Each time I began talking about her family, she wanted nothing to do with the conversation."

"Her father?"

She shook her head. "She doesn't know of her father's death, either, but a voice tells me I was wrong not to tell her."

Serafina stared at the nun's bowed head. Perhaps she wasn't such an iron heart. "Does the voice have a wrinkled nose?"

Concetta smiled.

"When can we see her?" Renata asked.

Serafina said, "Call her now."

Concetta shook her head. "I'd like to prepare her for your visit. The meeting might be too much of a shock in her condition."

A hand flew to Serafina's mouth. "What's wrong with her?"

"No cause for alarm, but sit down, please." ❧

The Train to Bagheria

The air smelled like burnt oil as they rocked back and forth on plush seats, while outside their window, the world softened and the train spit steam. Serafina and Renata sat on one side facing Rosa and Tessa. Rosa swayed this way and that, hanging onto her hat for most of the ride.

When Renata told her about the orphanage and their conversation with Mother Concetta, the madam was full of questions about Carmela.

"We haven't seen her yet," Renata said. "Tomorrow the whole family goes. We've gotten permission to take Giulia and Maria out of school for the day."

Serafina said nothing. Thinking of tomorrow made her stomach queasy.

Rosa and Renata exchanged a look. Tessa played with her doll.

Serafina stared out the window, vowing not to be distracted from her work, not today. Towns dotted the hills next to orange groves and olive trees. In the distance, she spotted a peasant leading a pair of oxen. On the other side of the car, there was an abrupt drop to the sea.

No one spoke until Renata opened Rosa's basket of bread and figs, not a meal but a snack before dinner. If they had enough time after the interviews, they'd eat a little something in La Vucciria—*paneddi* and *babbaluci* washed down with a house wine. Later they'd buy *cannoli* from the convent of St. Dominic.

Serafina told Rosa about her brush with the deserter.

Rosa clutched her chest. "Anything to do with the murders?"

Serafina shook her head. "I don't think so. A deserter living rough, my guess."

Renata said, "If it weren't for Arcangelo, who knows what would have happened. We have you to thank for lending him to us."

Serafina changed the subject. "Who do you think is the killer of your women?"

"In front of Tessa?" Renata asked.

Rosa batted the air and said with her mouth full of cookies, "My Tessa knows everything, don't you?"

Tessa nodded.

"Would you like a cookie?" Renata asked.

Tessa shook her head.

Rosa swallowed and looked at Serafina. "Why would we be sitting here if I knew the answer to your question?"

"But you must have some idea."

"Not really. Oh, I've had my share of hunches, but they all fly away."

"After Gemma died, who did you think might be the killer?"

Rosa considered, gritting a pin between her teeth while she readjusted her hat. "At first I thought it must be a relative or someone from the past. Or Gemma's mourner."

"Say again?" Serafina asked.

She repinned and said, "There was an odd mourner who came to Gemma's wake."

Serafina consulted her notes. "The embalmer told me about him."

"A man came up to the casket, raised his fist, and cursed the corpse." Rosa wiped her forehead. "Gave me the creeps."

"A customer?"

She shook her head, scowling at Serafina. "I thought he might be the killer, so I told Colonna about him. Of course, the inspector was in the room at the time. I watched his face while he did nothing. Later, I asked him to find the mourner, but guess what happened?"

"He did nothing?" Serafina asked.

"Oh, I had the guards search for an angry father, a jealous suitor, but they found no one. After Nelli's murder, I abandoned all thoughts of the mysterious mourner. The two, Gemma and Nelli, were from different towns, had no relatives in common, no friends together, so I gave up trying. And with Bella's death, I've been … not myself, out of sorts."

"You trust Scarpo?"

The question had its intended effect: it stunned Rosa who reddened and narrowed her eyes, shooting Serafina a look. "Scarpo, the killer? Utter nonsense. What are you saying?"

"All I'm saying is that we need to look at everyone around us with new eyes."

"Your mind is filled with wild thoughts. It's little wonder you can't keep your daughter at home."

"Where was he, Scarpo, around the time of the murders?" Serafina continued. "The afternoon, the evening, the night before you found the bodies?"

"My house, of course. Scarpo doesn't leave unless he has an errand in town. At night he's always there. The house would fall without him. Who'd see to the guards, call the time, collect the money, throw out the scruffy ones, scare off the bandits?"

"What was the first thing you did after you saw Gemma's body?"

"Screamed, of course, and ... and what did I do? I pulled the cord? I don't remember, I must have done. People poured in from all around, upstairs, the front parlors. All the girls were around me, I think, and Scarpo. Arcangelo ran for Colonna."

"Any of the women missing? Away? On a day off?"

The madam considered. "Bella was the only one. She had the week off. All the others were at the house, but if one of them were gone, what would that mean? Nothing. These killings are the work of a wild devil with a thirst for my coins."

"But he could have had help from inside," Renata said.

"For instance, Eugenia, the thief," Serafina said, casting a glance at the madam. "And several of the women said the house has changed."

Rosa nodded. Tears formed in her lower lids. "You're right. The house is different now, strange. The girls are silent or they whisper in the halls. We used to be so lovely, so droll, before the killing started. Just like a family."

"You mean before Eugenia came," Serafina said.

"You mean like a family during good times," Renata said, "because families can be silent and untrusting, too, when something bad happens."

Serafina shot her a look. "Enough Renata. Let's stay fixed on these killings, nothing else. I know what you're up to, you and Carlo, but not here, not now."

Renata and Rosa looked at each other.

"If you die, does Scarpo gain?"

"You always have a way to make me squirm. Why ask such questions?"

Serafina watched the color spread over her friend's cheek and waited.

"Who'd gain from my death?—Tessa, of course. I fooled them, those greasy officials. They said I couldn't adopt her, being a woman without a husband, but I have a smart lawyer who knows all the ins and outs." Rosa twirled her hands in the air. "Struts around the courts like a silky black rooster. Expensive, but he knows the laws of adoption and inheritance and how to make them work for me." Rosa folded her hands. "Tessa inherits my estate, all of it, I'm afraid to disappoint you."

Serafina chewed the inside of her cheek. "Didn't you need a husband?"

"I bought one. A hefty charge, but my lawyer took care of it."

"You're married?"

"Was. Deceased, the spouse." Rosa made an elaborate gesture with her hands. "No need for you to know all the details; I'm not sure I understand them myself. Either he was dead before we were married, or I'd been married for longer than I realized when he died, but shortly after the ceremony, Tessa was legally adopted."

Renata passed the basket of food, and Rosa reached for several cookies, a slice of cheese, and a fig. They all ate something, even Serafina.

A conductor with a purple nose opened the door to their compartment, offering drinks from his beverage trolley. The three women asked for caffè which he poured from a dented tin pot. Steeped for days, it seemed to Serafina, but it was wet and washed down their food. With a flourish, the man handed Tessa an orange drink.

After he left, they were silent for a while. Serafina picked at her food and stared at the passing scenery, swaying back and forth, lulled by the movement. Presently she said, "I want to talk about this figure in brown that Scarpo described, the one lurking about your house."

She told them about her encounter with the begging monk in the piazza shortly after Bella died. "He smelled like a thousand foreign sheep, wore gloves and boots and called himself Don Roberto. Even though Scarpo thinks not, I'm convinced he's the same man he saw at the blacksmith's, the same one Arcangelo saw posing as Gemma's uncle when he drove her to the stables to meet him the evening before you found her body. It was the last time she was seen alive, except by her killer, of course."

Rosa's face colored. She reached across and stroked Tessa's cheek.

Serafina read aloud from her notes. "'A man, tall, in wintry clothes,' that's the way Arcangelo described Gemma's uncle."

Rosa smiled. "Arcangelo is bad with his colors."

wears brown and smells funny, not from around here.' And something else about their descriptions, something odd, the detail that convinces me it's the same man: both Scarpo and Arcangelo say the man was wearing gloves and the weather was warm."

"Gloves in August?" Rosa asked. "Surely he's got something to hide, like a hand with six fingers or a missing thumb." She was silent for a moment and Serafina could see the wheels of the madam's mind churning. She nodded slowly. "The man in mocha, he's our killer. Forget the others."

"Speaking of forgetting, did you remember to ask Scarpo to talk to the smith? Did you ask him to get Eugenia's address?"

Rosa shook her head.

The four munched their food while the train slowly rounded a corner.

Breaking the silence, Serafina said, "Whoever he is, he plans on killing again. And soon."

"Not while we're eating—what's wrong with you?" Rosa asked.

Tessa tapped a finger on Rosa's sleeve. "Once I saw a man in brown talking to Gemma and Nelli in the piazza. Bella, too. They called him 'the monk.'"

Serafina looked at Rosa who said, "First I've heard Tessa talking of a monk."

"And your women never spoke of him?"

"Never, not to me at any rate."

Serafina looked at Tessa. "Have you seen this monk since then?"

Tessa nodded. "Sometimes in the morning when I buy bread, I see him in the piazza."

Rosa's face blanched.

Serafina wrote down Tessa's information in her book and stared out the window for the rest of the journey. Soon, the train blasted steam and slowed, chugging into Bagheria, the end of the line, where they would hire a cab to Palermo.

"Who do you think will be the next to die?" Serafina asked. "Any of your women seem different, more secretive or quieter? Need to visit relatives? Go out more often now? Change their disposition?"

"Changed? We're all changed! And there will be no 'next time.'" Rosa's eyes narrowed. "We'll stop this madman before he strikes again."

"We're here," Renata said, looking out the window.

The train lurched to a stop, and Serafina reached for Rosa's heavy package. "Hurry, we must queue up to get off the train. Tessa, take Renata's hand. We'll meet beneath the statue of St. Dominic between two and half past. That should give us enough time to meet with Bella's father, Falco, and the contessa."

"The contessa?" Renata asked.

"Bella's friend. They were going into business together. Keeps a dress shop not far from the Baldassare shop."

"Why didn't you take Giulia with us? She'd love to see a dressmaker's studio, especially one in Palermo. She dreams of making gowns in Paris."

Serafina put her hand on her heart and glanced out the window at a line of peasants bound for the wharves. "Giulia's a child. Let her grow up first."

"She's sixteen, but you're afraid of losing her, like you've lost Carmela. I know you. If Giulia leaves, you're wondering who will sew our clothes."

"You're still children, all of you. Even you—seventeen is nothing. Living with your family, all of us together in this uncertain hour—savor it."

"All of us together? Not all of us," Renata muttered, as they filed off the train. ⚬

Brothers

"I don't know what I can tell you of Bella, but I'll try." Nittù Baldassare straightened his cravat and led them through the kitchen where a cook was preparing food. Serafina watched as the woman slid a long-handled spatula into the deep interior of an oven and fished out bread, oiled and steaming, crackling at the edges.

Rosa breathed audibly. "Heavenly, the smells—oregano, tomato, pesto, basil."

They walked down a long hallway into Baldassare's study washed in tawny gold. Serafina smelled tobacco, leather, the mustiness of old books. In the middle of the room was a carved mahogany desk piled with papers, and on the wall behind it, shelves stuffed with books. Not a mote of dust anywhere. Several large volumes lay open on the desk, some containing plates of women's gowns, others with drawings of men in uniform. Underneath the window was a long table heaped with rolls of fabric. Swatches of brocades, silks and wools spilled onto the carpet. In front of Baldassare's desk were two chairs covered in damask. He invited Serafina and Rosa to sit.

Serafina took out her notebook and pencil. "Tell me about yourself."

He passed a hand over his eyes. "Born into a trade that has served me well. Inherited my father's shop. Across the piazza. You noticed it?"

They nodded.

"Built up that business with these," Baldassare said, holding up his hands. "I got the idea to specialize in uniforms—Bourbon, Redshirt, monk, didn't matter—and my wife and I made a good life. My sons attended university, and they were about to take over the business when Garibaldi landed at Marsala."

Serafina waited for Nittù Baldassare to continue, knowing he must tell his own tragedy many times before he could believe it.

As he spoke, his voice grew soft, and a line of color moved up his cheeks. "My sons followed him. The oldest wrote telling me it would be over soon. He was right. When the messenger came with the news, I'll never forget it." He pushed himself away from the desk, loosened his cravat. In a few moments, he continued, talking more to himself than to his guests. "Killed in one battle, all five of them. In a moment, in the blink of an eye, our world vanished." He waved a hand toward the living room. "You saw what the news did to my poor Addolorata."

Rosa began to speak, but Serafina sent her a daggered look.

"And, so, to Bella. When she was born, she was betrothed to Pirandello's youngest son. You know the family? They own a shop on Piazza San Domenico, tailors who make fortunes with every stitch."

Rosa nodded.

Baldassare pointed to his books and swatches. "But when she came of age, Bella told us she didn't want marriage, not to Pirandello, not to anyone. Instead, she left, and she broke our hearts." He looked at Rosa. "Her mother would have been devastated had she known about Bella's life with you. When I heard what she was doing, I couldn't believe it. Now, when I think of it ..." He stopped, and the room seemed to still.

"You must have been wild with anger," Serafina said.

"I disowned her." He cradled his head. "She wrote to me. At first I threw her letters into the fire, but she persisted, every week for several years. Suddenly, she stopped writing, and I became worried."

Serafina looked at Rosa. The moment stretched beyond the four walls and the apartment building. His mood seemed to blanket the streets of Palermo.

"In time, we reconciled." He rubbed his forehead. "I can't remember how or why, but we did." He rubbed his eyes. "Such plans she had—to earn enough to open a business of her own, 'twice as grand as Pirandello's,' she told me, 'at first, serving only the aristocracy, and then, the wives of wealthy merchants. I'll make the name of Baldassare as famous for high fashion as the House of Worth. Women from all over the world will flock to our door.'" His smile was wistful. "She took my dreams, blew them up higher than Monte Pellegrino. For that kind of enterprise she needed money, far more than she'd inherit from me—and she'd have gotten everything with my death."

Rosa sat without speaking. Serafina wrote in her notebook.

He frowned. "Finally, after all these years, I understood her. I began to see my daughter as if she were a son."

Rosa squirmed in her seat.

He looked at her. "You were generous, she told me. Earned good money working for you—far more than she could make being a seamstress, even in Paris. Oh, they asked for her, those fancy designers. La Contessa would have arranged it. Would have given Bella experience, prestige, but not the capital she needed for the control she wanted, and not as an equal."

Rosa said, "Bella used to say to me, 'You want a dress? We'll find the right fabric,' she'd tell me. And she charged me for her time, the fabric, beads, the thread, the needles. She was a saver, your girl."

Nittù Baldassare grinned. "She thought of everything, that one, everything. Even had a scheme for salvation. So clever, my daughter."

Serafina stopped writing.

Rosa's eyes widened. "Do I know about this, Nittù?"

He shook his head. "The last time she visited—July, it was—she told me it wouldn't be long. She'd given her money to La Grinaldi and was ready to move back into town. 'Just some unfinished business,' she said." He shook his head before continuing. "She told me that she'd met a monk who offered salvation. Permanent absolution, even for one such as herself."

Silence. Serafina looked up, even as her pencil continued scratching. There it was, and she marveled at it—the information she needed, the glittering jewel in the queen's headpiece. Now they were getting somewhere. When she finished writing, she looked at Rosa.

"Don't give me the evil eye—the first I've heard of this scheme. But there's our monk again, right in the middle of it."

"I never saw her again." He looked at the floor.

Serafina heard the faint noise of traffic and a dove cooing to its mate. Minutes passed. Through clenched teeth, Nittù Baldassare turned to Serafina and said, "Bring her killer to me. I'll take care of him." He stood up, brandishing a fist, his face florid. "Flailing is too good for him, but I will find something worthy of this beast." He sat, sinking into himself.

"Can you tell me anything about this monk?" Serafina asked. "Where did Bella meet him? Was it here in Palermo or Oltramari?"

He shrugged.

"Is there anyone who'd know? Bella's contessa friend?"

"She might," he said. "But she's in Paris at the moment, I think."

A maid announced the afternoon meal.

Standing before the vestibule's mirror, Rosa patted her curls, straightened her hat while Serafina fastened her cape.

Rosa put a hand to her mouth, "Something for you, almost forgot." She dug into her front. "Bella's record of account at *Banco di Sicilia*." She kissed him on both cheeks.

Serafina asked, "Who inherits your business, now that Bella's gone?"

Rosa's eyes widened and Baldassare, surprised at the question, it seemed, took his time answering.

"My brother. Last month after Bella died—" His voice cracked.

Rosa clasped his hand. "Slowly, Nittù."

He continued. "After Bella died, I changed the will. The lawyer took care of it. My brother inherits the business."

Rosa raised her brows.

"I'd like to talk to him," Serafina said.

"Falco, it's Nittù!" Baldassare called out, opening the door.

When they entered, Serafina smelled wool and something else—perhaps sizing used on fabric—that made her eyes smart. She waited a bit, at first seeing a room filled with fantastic-looking silhouettes, weird presences, like a stage set for a dream. But as the objects took on familiar shapes, headless bodies became models wearing uniforms or clerical garb. On one wall, shelves held spools of thread, braids, buttons, bric-a-brac. On the opposite wall, rolls of fabric leaned against a tall chest. Serafina walked over to it. She reached out to examine one of the small carvings sitting on top of the chest. Smiling to herself, she put it back: Falco's clay figures.

Baldassare pointed to a dress uniform worn by Joachim Murat, an ostrich-feathered hat sitting on its shoulders. Another mannequin sported a red Garibaldi shirt beneath a leather jerkin. Others were draped in grey or blue homespun—for soldiers in America, Nittù told them. Several figures wore monastic scapulae and hoods. Neat and well-ordered, the room, almost a museum.

Serafina wiped her eyes. Presently she heard footsteps. A door opened and Falco entered, stroking his mustache with a table napkin.

"This woman with eyes like the sea—she investigates the killing of Bella and wants to meet you," Nittù said.

"We've met," Falco said, not taking his eyes from her face.

"Good. While you two get caught up, I'll take Rosa over to the shelves. There's some silk I'd like to show her."

Serafina stood still. Such an actor, Falco. In school he imitated teachers, mimicking the priests, her father, her mother, Giorgio, his fiancée, but she never would forget his callous heart: he betrayed her ardor with casual abandon.

"We've just finished our dinner," he said, gesturing with the hand still clutching his napkin, "and the domestic cleans the kitchen, but perhaps she can make us some tea. If you'll wait—"

Serafina shook her head. "This won't take long. What I need to know is, where you were the evening of October 6th, almost a month ago."

He smirked. "You're serious? This is me, your old Falco!" He shook his head and crossed his arms. "The evening of October 6th, around the time of Bella's murder? Preposterous!"

She felt her face burn. Oh Madonna, how she hated this. But she persisted, a small atonement for her betrayal of Giorgio so many years ago.

"Think I had something to do with my cousin's death, do you? Shame forever on my soul." He signed himself. "I don't know where I was on October 6th."

"A Saturday evening."

"Probably at home here with my family." He pointed to the stairs. "Yes. With my family. Of course, where else would I be?"

"The shop would be open until when, seven or eight on a Saturday evening? As the proprietor you'd keep a record of sales and appointments with customers for fittings. Documents written in your hand on that date, any fittings you may have had—especially for late in the day—they'd confirm your whereabouts, at least until the shop closed Saturday evening. And if you'd also supply evidence of your location Sunday morning, it would let me eliminate you as a suspect in Bella's death."

"Preposterous. It is I, Falco. We made love in the blossoming days of our life, and you question me like this?"

Serafina pressed her lips together before she spoke. "Death is ugly. It demands an accounting of us all. I need to know where you were at the time of the murders. I need to place everyone who was close to Bella, including Rosa herself."

He continued hugging himself with his arms, rocking back and forth. After a few moments of maintaining this pose, he spoke. "I keep the current month's calendar and bills of sale in a drawer in my desk. Would you like to see them?"

She shook her head.

"At the end of the month, I transfer this information to a ledger, and keep the ledgers of past months locked in cabinets in the attic. Now, if you've finished, I've no more time left for you."

"No, I'm not finished, not at all. You wanted Bella's killer found. At her wake, you offered to help. Well, I'm finding him." She stopped for a moment, piercing him with her gaze before she continued. "I'm sure you'll be ready with October's books and any bills of sale you may have for the sixth of that month by, shall we say, sixteen hundred hours tomorrow? I'll send someone who can attest to having seen them."

Eager for Home

Serafina heard blasts of steam each time the train slowed, lurching forward and crashing against the seat with each grind of the wheels. She chewed her cheek. She wished she could have spoken with the contessa, one of the last people who saw Bella alive, but the woman was still in Paris, according to her secretary, not expected to return until after *Li Morti*. Serafina made an appointment to see her on November 4, the earliest available opening on the contessa's calendar, hoping that by talking to her, she'd discover the whereabouts of Bella's monk. Absent the contessa, she must ask some of Rosa's prostitutes—Gioconda or Gusti, for instance—who might know how to locate him.

Tessa slept, rocking sideways when the train gathered speed and banked inward, her head pillowed by Rosa's shawl. To Serafina's right, hills cast long shadows over fields and citrus groves. A pair of oxen plowed the earth. On her left fishermen mended their nets, the spars of their boats bobbing in the setting sun.

She tried to sleep, but saw scarlet through closed eyelids. Rearranging herself, she glanced into the aisle and caught Rosa and Renata standing near the door of their compartment in animated conversation. She closed her eyes again and was able to drift.

"Is your mind stuck?" Rosa asked, shaking her. "Halfway home. We need to talk."

Serafina stared out the window until Rosa, now seated next to her, nudged her foot.

"I'm awake, just thinking."

They discussed what they'd learned about Bella's desire for salvation.

"Significant new information," Serafina said.

Rosa agreed.

Serafina yawned, paged through her notebook. "A few of the women mentioned salvation when I talked to them yesterday. According to Rosalia, Gemma told her, 'I can no longer be your friend because you are not saved.'"

"That explains the fight they had shortly before I found Gemma's body. Slamming doors, crying, the two of them not speaking, it upset the whole house."

"Quite hurt, Rosalia," Serafina said.

Rosa's eyes were like transparent marbles as she considered, and for a time they were silent while they swayed with the train.

Serafina said, "I wonder if it was this 'permanent salvation' that Bella's father talked about. Did Gemma find the same monk? Is he the killer?" She turned a few pages, then quoted Baldassare talking about his daughter, 'She thought of everything, that one, everything. She even had a scheme for salvation. So clever, my daughter.' And don't forget the rosary in her reticule," Serafina said. "And most of all, the carvings on their foreheads?" Was that the sign of permanent salvation, at least in a wild one's ken? She was quiet for a time, trying to remember what the scholarly priest told her about the brazen serpent. "That reminds me, now that we've found Carmela, I'd like to borrow two of your guards. I want them to search the shore with me. There may be other clues I've overlooked."

"Colonna said they searched and found nothing."

Serafina sent Rosa a withering look. "They found nothing, but not because they searched, but because they did not." She glanced out the window, not at anything in particular, and anyway, the scenery was blurred by this time. "Doubtless it's this monk who convinced them they must pay for a unique type of salvation. And Nelli paid for something, too."

"Nelli?" Rosa asked.

"Don't tell me you don't remember Formusa's account of Nelli's secret—how she kept her coins with the cook until she needed them? Scooped them up the night she disappeared?"

"Of course I remember. I told you, these murders are all about lucre."

"We don't know about Gemma's wish for salvation, only that she was going someplace with someone whom she called her uncle," Serafina said.

"Arcangelo's wintry-clothed man."

"Yes. The monk," they said in unison.

"Duping the weak out of their hard-earned coins," Serafina said. "We all long for salvation, but it's given to us at birth or baptism or confession, one of those," Serafina said.

Tessa stirred in her sleep, her head now in Renata's lap.

Serafina said, "I think Scarpo, Arcangelo, Tessa and I, we all saw the killer."

"Stop the blabbering. Too many words."

The train chugged on. Serafina closed her eyes, rolling with the motion of the clacking wheels. Then she said, "And I think that the three women were lured someplace by a man disguised as a monk, duped into following him by his promise of salvation, and after he took their coins, he killed them."

"Wonder how much they paid him?" Rosa asked and was silent for a time until she asked about Falco.

Serafina looked down at her hands. She felt her face redden, and her heart began to pump great quantities of blood. She swallowed, pushing down whatever demon it was who rose to frighten her. "Don't trust him. I asked him where he was on the night Bella was killed, and he claims he doesn't remember."

"I'm sorry I didn't see Falco for what he was," the madam said, in a rare moment of insight.

Serafina was silent for a while, savoring the madam's words and the struggle she must have waged with herself to say them.

"He had special privilege, you know. Came and went as he pleased. A charmer, but no more charmers in my house," the madam said.

Serafina patted her friend's knee. "We all see what we want to see." The train began to slow. "But I'll need to send Arcangelo and Beppe tomorrow for evidence of where Falco was, if he can produce it."

"Should give him enough time to concoct something," Rosa said.

Serafina shifted in her seat. "We must keep half an eye on him. He gains the most by Bella's death."

Rosa sat up. "Perhaps he'll gain from Gemma's and Nelli's deaths too."

"How so?"

"Each death weakens me, don't you see?"

"Each death weakens us all." Serafina couldn't resist saying it. "But go on, I interrupted."

The madam gave her a look. "Another one, and the reputation of my house is in ruins. If Falco schemes to take my business from me, then that explains why he's killed the other two as well as Bella. Falco gains from multiple sources, and he is our main suspect."

Serafina stared out the window.

Rosa hugged herself a moment longer and—so like her friend who had little time for dread or sorrow before she moved on—the madam's fear seemed to have fled and she stretched. Tessa and Renata slept. The train plowed through the late dusk.

Serafina examined her watch pin. "We arrive in Oltramari soon."

Renata rubbed her eyes and sat up, looking at Rosa. "Please let Tessa stay with us tonight. We'll drive her back tomorrow afternoon—"

"Out of the question, Tessa stays with me."

Hearing her name, Tessa sat up.

"But this is your busy evening. Tessa will be left alone."

They were silent, until Tessa saw her home town approaching. "Our piazza!" she shouted. Jumping up and down, she looked from one woman to the other.

Rosa bent to whisper in her ear. Tessa smiled and nodded. "This once, Tessa stays with you. Bring her home tomorrow afternoon."

In the west, the sky was lapis lazuli, the clouds, rimmed in gold. They walked through the gardens in front of the station to a taxi stand, hoping to find a cab to take them home. Gas lamps glowed in the gathering dusk, and their pungent odor mingled with the richness of the soil.

Traffic was brisk this evening on the roads circling the station. Carts, carriages, and traps moved in all directions, the din of their wheels on the cobblestones like the rumble of thunder. *Carabinieri* stood on platforms blowing ineffective whistles at the snarl. Peasants rode bareback. Large baskets hung on either side of their beasts. One mule sat in the middle of the road and refused to budge. Hat in hand, the driver pleaded with the animal.

Serafina had to walk fast to keep up with Rosa. Renata and Tessa followed behind.

"Oh, the air, how sweet, almost like spring. I can smell the scent of loam," Serafina said, her eyes sweeping the traffic to find an empty cab.

"Not loam—sand and rocks, our soil," Rosa said.

"Our house has rich earth. My ancestors brought it with them from the fields to make fertile gardens. The city did the same when they built the station. Giorgio told me."

"Such fantasy! All I smell is the foulness of the train on me, like a thousand mules passing wind, and I feel the grit of the day." Rosa buried her nose in one of her sleeves and made a face.

Tessa skipped to keep up, holding Renata's hand.

"Impossible. You can't agree with me, can you? You haven't changed. You were the same as a child. Always seeing the bleak, never the poetic. I remember helping my mother deliver difficult babies, and, afterward, you refused to listen to my joyful words of life and birth. When will you grow up?"

Rosa laughed. "I built my business, didn't I, but not by thinking deep thoughts, and I must bathe and perfume before our guests arrive. The fine weather and the end of the *festa*, good for the trade. I feel a full house coming on tonight!" Rosa rubbed her hands together. There was a bounce in her step, caprice in her soul. Was this the same woman who could barely move when they got off the train in Palermo?

"Hurry, too slow, you're like an old woman." Rosa churned the air with her gestures. She never stopped long to wonder or to ask why, with her flinty mind and scorn for fantasy. Her haunches strained the seams of her dress as they flexed forward. Yes, Serafina had to admire Rosa. When the war came and the apothecary was closed along with all the other shops around the piazza, Rosa's brain kept Serafina's family from starving. Did her house close? Not at all. Clever Rosa prospered with the ebb and flow of history. Except for now—she could be ruined by the murders of her women—and it was Serafina's turn to help. She'd crush this killer. She must. Her fingernails bit into her palms.

"Look who's coming. It's Beppe and Arcangelo!" Serafina hallooed, waving her arms. "Our luck, Rosa, let it last." She crossed herself.

Beppe rolled to a stop, jumped down and bowed, almost touching his leggings. "Vicenzu was worried. He asked me to come and wait for you." Arcangelo tipped his hat, a rifle slung underneath one arm.

The four of them piled into the cab, Rosa grunting as she reached for the footplate, but bouncing up and into the carriage as if she were a trapeze artist. Serafina heard the click of the door, the crack of the whip, and the carriage lurched forward.

"Beppe!" Rosa hung her head out the window, holding onto her hat, now skewed to the side of her head, curls and feathers blowing in the air. "Take me home first. They need me. The week before a holiday, you know." 🖋

Weeping Madonna

Wednesday, October 24, 1866

The whole family sat together on the sofa, younger children piled on top of older laps. Horsehair tufted from a hole in one of the cushions.

"You touched me," Maria said.

"Did not!" Totò held his finger out, almost, but not quite touching Maria's arm.

"Did so! Get away!"

"Did not!"

"Enough!"

"But he's rolling his train on my leg!"

"Totò!" Serafina looked up at the crucifix. She heard children's voices. They grew louder.

"Can I go outside and play?" Totò asked.

"It's raining," Giulia said.

"But they're outside. See?" He pointed to the window. A line of children marched up the walk. "Can I?"

"No."

"Anyway, they're orphans." Maria pushed up her spectacles.

"So?"

"Orphans can do anything they want. They live here," Maria said. "And tell him not to roll his toy on me ever again."

"On the rug, Totò," Renata said.

"And be quiet." Vicenzu brushed lint from his lapels. "She should be here soon. We're early, as usual." He shot a glance at Serafina.

They waited.

Totò made the sound of a steam engine. Water dribbled from his mouth. The steam engine grew louder.

"I could be practicing," Maria said.

"You'd be in school if you weren't here," Vicenzu said. "Count to a thousand."

"Don't waste my time."

"Maria, no more," Renata said.

The door opened and Carmela entered. She was older, shorter than Serafina remembered, hair the same, skin, iridescent, eyes like the sea, stomach distended. She smelled like neroli oil and powder.

Renata, Vicenzu, Giulia rushed to her. They hugged. They kissed. They laughed, hugged again.

"Where's Carlo? Papa?"

Serafina's eyes gazed at her daughter's waist. "Carlo's at school. He'll be home next week for *Li Morti*."

Her children stood aside while Serafina hugged Carmela. Her daughter felt stiff.

"Sit down, my precious," Serafina said, wiping her eyes. I have harsh news. Someone hand your sister a towel."

"A towel?"

They laughed.

"Handkerchief. You know what I mean."

They laughed again.

Renata and Giulia sat on the sofa with Carmela. Vicenzu pulled up the chair for Serafina.

"Something bad?"

She held her daughter's hands. They were callused. "About six months ago, your papa was in the shop. He collapsed." Serafina tried to control herself, but couldn't. "Vicenzu ... tell her, tell the rest."

"I was in the back of the store," he said. "I heard a crash. Papa was on the floor. I held him. He tried, but couldn't talk. Closed his eyes. A customer ran to Dr. Loffredo. Mama was delivering. He was still breathing, Loffredo said. They rushed him to hospital, but he ..." Vicenzu stopped. "Died."

Renata and Giulia held Carmela. No one spoke.

After she dried her eyes, Carmela stared at Serafina. Her daughter looked like a weeping Madonna.

"There's more," Serafina said, stroking Carmela's cheek. She told her about Maddalena's death.

Carmela's voice was thick. "Achille went away, but left me this." She pointed to her middle. "I feel nothing for him. Nothing. The baby is all I need." Tears gave the lie to her words. "I'm happy here. The children need me."

Serafina offered Carmela a clean handkerchief, touched a lock of her daughter's hair. "Come home, Carmela."

"Please," Renata and Giulia said.

Carmela shook her head.

"We've kept your room the same, all your clothes," Serafina said.

"Please. We need ..." Again Vicenzu lost his words.

Maria bit her lip.

"Can't you say anything, Maria?" Renata asked.

Maria held Serafina's skirt, said nothing.

"She was only four when Carmela ..." Serafina's voice faded. "Perhaps she doesn't remember—"

"I do." Maria waved an arm at Totò. "He doesn't."

"See my steam engine?"

Carmela grabbed Maria and Totò and held them.

"I'll fix your dresses. The waists, I mean," Giulia said.

Carmela smiled.

"Do you live here?" Totò asked. "Can you play outside whenever you want?"

"Come home with us," Serafina said again. "We've borrowed Rosa's big carriage. We'll fit, but you'll need to hold Totò on your lap."

Totò stuck his tongue out at Maria. "She can play with my train. You can't."

Carmela looked at her lap. "I need some time."

The door opened and Ave Maria entered. She stared at Totò while she clomped over to Carmela.

"Innocenza is screaming and won't stop. We need you," she said.

Carmela rose, kissed her siblings.

Serafina held her arms out, but Carmela looked at the ground and hurried away. ✒

Falco's Alibi

"*Y*ou made it." Serafina pulled them inside. "We were going to wait for you but the children were too hungry." She wiped her mouth with her napkin. "Eat with us, we haven't finished."

Assunta shuffled back and forth from the kitchen to the table, setting two additional places and heaping their plates with food. The others looked up from their meal and smiled. Vicenzu slapped Beppe on the back, shook hands with Arcangelo. He poured the wine.

"Finish eating while Assunta and I put the children to bed, then tell us your story of Falco," Serafina said, gathering Totò and Tessa. Assunta followed her. "You are excused, too, Maria. Study your score if you want, but in your room."

"At eighteen-hundred hours on October 6, Falco Baldassare was fitting a bishop for a new set of clothes, a cassock, a cape, several shirts," Arcangelo said.

"Which bishop?" Serafina asked. "Palermo is loaded with them."

Beppe said, "Bishop Antonio Ricci. He lives off Piazza Sant'Andrea on the Via Roma. That's what took us so long. Arcangelo said we must confirm the appointment Falco showed us in his ledger."

Arcangelo said, "Took us a while to find the bishop's apartment, even longer for his secretary to answer the bell, but he confirmed the appointment, all right, even opened the bishop's calendar and showed it to us."

"We asked how long he was there. No record, the secretary told us," Beppe said. "But he said the fitting would have taken no more than an hour to an hour and a half, unless, of course, there were problems or other circumstances, say, if the bishop was late for the appointment, or the cape had to be reworked."

Arcangelo said, "So Falco Baldassare's whereabouts are accounted for."

"The best we can hope for, from that slippery eel," Serafina said. "We rode here from Palermo, Rosa and I, in less than two hours, and we had a few delays, so he could have left in a carriage after the fitting, arrived in Oltramari by what, eight o'clock at the latest? Dined with his niece then did her in. Just like him. Not ruled out, Falco Baldassare, not by a long shot. He'd still have plenty of time to do the deed and return to Palermo."

"And the others, did he kill them, too?" Vicenzu asked. "Doesn't make sense."

"Agreed, unless … Her eyes glazed. Her voice trailed off.

"Unless what?" Renata asked.

She shook herself. "Unless he hankers for Rosa's business, or he and the monk are in some sort of league."

"More wine?" Vicenzu asked.

Arcangelo declined. "Time for me to go home. School tomorrow." He tugged a sleeve.

An Altercation

Thursday, October 25, 1866

Serafina opened her bedroom window, shielding her eyes against a tepid sun. Streets surrounding the piazza were filled with people on foot or in carts pulled by mules, heading home for the noon meal. The smell of roasting pork wafted from a plume of smoke. Her stomach growled.

Mingling with children's laughter were shouts coming from somewhere down the street. Leaning out, she saw the rope seller yelling into a stranger's face, a peddler with a worn mule harnessed to a weathered cart. Had Serafina seen him before? She thought not. A few men stopped and pointed.

The argument became physical when the peddler shoved the rope seller. More men gathered. The rope seller delivered blows to the neck and face of the stranger, who, poor man, mustn't have been taught how to defend himself. He bled from the nose. The crowd thickened. Two men stepped in and tried to stop the fight. The rope seller swung at one of them and missed. The peddler struck the rope seller, but it was the punch of a weakling, the effect, comic to some in the crowd who laughed.

Serafina blinked. The fighting spread like fire in a summer wind. Soon she couldn't tell who did what, but saw a fist hit a face, a spray of blood, a kicking shoe, a cloud of roiling dust.

Bells clanged. Swords flashed. Pistols fired in the air. *Carabinieri* charged into view. As fast as it formed, the crowd vanished. No more dust. No more peddler. No more cart or mule.

Peace restored, the rope seller limped back to his customary corner and, grunting, sat.

Serafina stared a moment longer before closing the window.

From his seat on a pile of hemp, the roper worked a piece of twine like swift fingers braiding hair. He was wiry, the rope seller, with a patch over his eye. He had the odor of straw, hemp, and old newspaper. She wondered how old he was. Probably over sixty, ancient, but young enough to protect himself from the fists of the stranger with the weathered cart.

"Donna Fina, some twine? Got rope, all kinds, all sizes, thick as your arm for mooring ships, or scented, for tying up delicates."

"Out my window today I saw a fight." She watched the crowd of emotions march across his face—fear, resentment, disbelief, male pride, humor.

"Stole my hemp, he did."

"Today?"

He nodded. "Another time, too. See, when my cat talks to me, I know there's trouble. Today, for what reason I don't know, the creature gets up from his morning nap, stretches, looks me in the face and talks. Like Beelzebub, he sounds."

As if on cue, a thick, gray shorthair appeared and began a stream of plaintive meows like the speech of a rackety geezer.

"See? Say hello to Donna Fina," he said to the cat.

The mouser sat, folding his front paws underneath a massive chest and blinked his moon eyes.

"Aren't you going to say something?" he asked.

The cat was silent.

"So I go outside. And what do I spy? I find a man dressed in rags, he was, peering at some anchor line, feeling the netting, holding a roll of three-strand twisted in his hands. He thinks I'm not wise to him, see, so he asks me questions, how much for this reel, for that twine, the cost for a small piece of hawser, of solid braid. I growl the prices, and all the time Bumma, he meows. When he drives away, I glimpse a piece of rope snaking down the back of his cart. My rope. I know my rope. Today, see, my Bumma again he stretches, talks to me, so I go out, sit in the corner, cap over my eye, wary, feigning sleep. I see the same one leaving with the rope in his hands, and I decide to teach him a lesson."

"The color of his hair?" she asked.

He shook his head. "Dunno."

"You didn't notice or he had no hair or he wore a cap?" she asked.

He shrugged. "You saw him fighting," he said.

Chagrined, she admitted she didn't notice his hair. "Wore a cap, he must have. A stranger, I haven't seen him before," she said. She must be more focused. She may have seen a significant bit of information, but, instead, part of her mind was elsewhere.

"Me neither. Except for the other day when Bumma announced him. Not from around here, I think not. His mule, broken down, like his cart. A bandit, or a deserter. Up to no good."

The Shoemaker

"Shoes fit for walking on clouds? Leather from Florence?"

She smiled. "No shoes today."

"Caffè?"

She shook her head.

The shoemaker, who spoke more with his hands than with his mouth, was dressed in a shirt and tie, striped pants, green apron. His shoes shone like the glass on his storefront. As her eyes swept the shop, Serafina saw rows of men's boots arranged along one wall. Closer to the front stood women's and children's shoes in various colors and styles, all finely crafted. Rodolfo must have contacts throughout Italy. His family dealt in leather for centuries.

"I'm looking for information."

He guided her to a chair.

Serafina told him that she was investigating the deaths of Rosa's prostitutes and that the other night, she'd spent some time in the room of one of the deceased. "I saw many shoes in her cabinet, of such high quality, I was sure you'd created them. Her name was Bella."

He nodded, thought a moment before speaking. "Good customer. Had to have the very best. Particular. Came in with a piece of fabric, pointed to a color, and said 'Match this.' When I told her I'd have to buy the leather, have it tanned, possibly make a trip to Palermo, even to Naples, she said she didn't mind the time or the cost."

"How often did she shop here?"

"Not sure—every month? Could look through my receipts if it's important. Coming here for years, Bella."

"Alone?"

"At first. Dressed like a *puttana*, but expensive, you know." He drew large curves in the air. "Said shoes mirrored the soul. Paid cash. Lots. I'll miss her. And brought me a new customer, too, from Palermo. Last year or two, they came in together. Another one with means. Sorry Bella died. A woman, I don't ask questions where she gets her money, where anyone gets the money. Better not to know." He cupped his chin and was silent for a moment. "Hard to feed a family these days, I don't need to tell you."

"The other customer. Can you give me his name and address?"

"*Her* name. Sour, that one. Nose in the air. Thinks she's a queen. When I first measured her feet, she told me I was wrong, but I insisted. In the end I had to show her: I squeezed her into the size she said was hers, and that convinced her. Wanted everything made, delivered to a Palermo address."

"May I have it?"

He walked over to the counter, opened a green ledger, and riffled through the pages, scratching one bushy eyebrow.

While she waited, Serafina looked out the window and saw clotted traffic in the piazza. Two carts had collided, their back wheels interlocked. Feathers spun in the air and a jumble of garments—capes, wigs, bits of clothes—had fallen onto the cobbles. The driver swooped them off the ground and shoved them back into his wagon, all the while yelling and gesturing. A crowd watched, growing until two tight-pantalooned soldiers appeared. *Presto*, everyone scattered. As she looked at the cart commotion, a black carriage drawn by a matched pair whisked directly in front of the window, its red wheels purring.

"Ah, yes, I have it here. A moment while I write it for you."

Serafina stuffed the address into her handbag and stepped outside. Hugging her cape, she visored her eyes, peered toward the piazza, and saw the red-wheeled carriage return. It circled the statue, its spokes whirring, the horses straining. Pedestrians scurried out of its way.

When it halted in front of her, bits of straw and clods of earth flew into her face. She glimpsed a blur of silk sitting inside. Brushing dust from the folds of her dress, Serafina muttered something about the vulgarity of the nobility, watching while the driver opened the door and a foot emerge sheathed in calfskin, saw a slice of white silk stocking and a few layers of petticoat peek out from under a skirt of watered silk. The woman was clothed in the latest fashion at this early hour. Must be bone-breaking work for the maid.

A familiar voice called her name. Serafina squinted into the light as the woman approached, reeking of Roget & Gallet, and wearing a day dress with an indefinite waist. And that hairdo—she must have a French maid.

"Serafina? What luck," the woman said. "First, my deep sorrow for your loss."

"Elisabetta! I didn't recognize you. Sun in my eyes, you know." They embraced. "I never saw it coming, Giorgio's death. How could I be so blind?" Serafina asked. Her eyes swam.

The two women discussed Giorgio, his illness, and her family's sudden loss.

Changing the subject, Serafina asked, "How are your boys. They must be, what, nineteen?"

"Almost grown, both in university. Franco studies business, Vito, the law. So fortunate I found you. Went to your home just now looking for you. The magnificence coming from your kitchen! I thought it must be your cuisine."

"My daughter, Renata. Born cooking, that one," Serafina said.

"Oh, my, if she's available for Christmas parties, I'll tell my friends."

Serafina felt her cheeks burn. "Her schedule's heavy through the holidays, a pity."

"Such a sweet girl. She resembles you, your eyes and height, your smile, yes she does. She gave me a plate of *ossa da mordere*. I've eaten two already. Delicious! She thought you'd be back for the noon meal."

"Baking early for *Li Morti*," Serafina said. Her mind ranged over the years. They'd known each other, she and Elisabetta, since childhood. Her mother, Maddalena, had—what to call it—a special relationship with the orphanage where Elisabetta and Tigro grew up. Inseparable, those two. Even as a child, Elisabetta watched over Tigro until he left suddenly. Broke her heart.

After Serafina went away to school, she lost touch until much later when it was time to deliver Elisabetta's twins. But she'd heard the stories, how Tigro returned one day, stole Elisabetta during the night. She remembered how the couple showed up in Oltramari a year later, stood in front of the priest to pledge their vows with the Duomo's bells pealing and the incense smoking, the candles blazing, the choir singing; Tigro, his teeth sparkling, his pockets bulging with coins; Elisabetta, her face radiant, her belly distended. *The poor woman, she adores him.*

Aloud she said, "Tell me, are you feeling well?"

"I'm with child. That's why I called on you, and I wondered if—"

"But of course. Certainly, my dear. You don't have a midwife that lives closer?" She could hear delivery coins rattle in her purse.

"No one I trust," Elisabetta said.

"Perhaps I can call on you in a few days? Tomorrow I have a chore and I expect to be busy with deliveries next week. Unfortunate, but—"

"A week from Saturday I'll be home all day. If you arrive, say, early afternoon, after dinner? Bring your girls. Stay for tea—love to see them. But now you need to be home, and I'm to meet Tigro and the boys, so I won't keep you. Gianni, help me into the coach."

"Saturday, November 3?" Serafina asked.

"Perfect."

The women kissed on both cheeks.

A clubfooted man with serpentine eyes jumped down from his perch, scratched himself, limped over to where the women stood. He held Elisabetta's elbow while she stepped into the carriage. After he closed the door, he stood with crossed arms, spat tobacco, and stared at Serafina.

Her eyes met his without flinching. Then she let her gaze roam from his face down to his feet, pausing to take in the uneven height of his shoes, traveling slowly, ever so slowly up his leg, to his thigh, to his not much of anything, up to the curved knife in his belt, to the ragged scar on his left cheek, and ending with the wildness in his eyes.

After the women said their goodbyes, Serafina wondered if that limping cobra could be murdering Rosa's women for pleasure or for knife practice, with or without orders from the don. ❧

No More Carmela

They sat, the three of them on the sofa and waited. Bright sunlight filtered through a slit in the drapery, revealing the shabbiness of the furniture and the cleanliness of the wooden floors.

In a low voice, Serafina said to Giulia, "How your sister can live here and not long to return home is outside my ken."

Giulia looked at her hands. Vicenzu straightened his vest.

They waited.

"I thought you might like to wear some of your dresses for a change," Serafina said.

Carmela did not look at Serafina. "I was a child when I left," she said. She looked at Giulia and Vicenzu, and she grinned.

"But I've redesigned them," Giulia said. "I've let out the waists, removed the lace. The fabric, still very good."

"Vicenzu, open the trunk so your sister can see."

"A bribe?" Carmela winked at Vicenzu. She gave him a peck on the cheek.

"See?" Giulia asked, and she held up a rose watered silk. Giulia's work was so fine that it took a practiced eye lurking around the seams to see a change.

"Try it on. See what you think," Serafina said.

Carmela felt the fabric, and her eyes began to water. She shook her head. "Not right for the orphanage."

"We want you to come home," Serafina said.

"Carlo still in school?" Carmela asked.

"He comes home at the end of the week for *Li Morti*."

"You'll have to take the trunk back. The dresses are too fine to wear here."

Silence.

Serafina said, "Vicenzu, Giulia, take the trunk outside and wait for me in the carriage."

After the door closed, Carmela said, "Why do you surround yourself with your other children? Are you trying to hide from what I might say to you?"

Serafina's cheeks flamed, and she felt her pulse quicken. She had returned too soon. Should have waited until Carlo was home. The wardrobe was an excuse, she knew. She begged Giulia to redesign the dresses and her daughter had worked furiously these past two days, even skipping school yesterday—all with Serafina's blessing, of course—and the scheme hadn't worked. Her throat swelled.

She was silent for a while, then said, "In the past, we haven't worked well together."

Carmela said nothing but stared at the wall, immobile.

Serafina could hear children playing outside.

"Never did anything well together," Carmela said. "From the moment I was born, there was another one to occupy your thoughts. All I heard was, 'Carlo this, Carlo that.' Never talked to me like you talked to him. When you were tender with him, you were cross with me. You never considered me as his equal. I hated you for it, hated you." Her voice rose. "You are haughty, heartless, and you use your children. Just use us! Look at Renata. She does all your cooking. Giulia sews all your clothes. I'll wager she worked day and night fixing those dresses for me!" Carmela's lips trembled.

Serafina heard laughter. It seemed so far away. Like a hideous dawn, her failure as a mother loomed before her. Her eyes ached. Her ears rang. She needed Giorgio by her side. He knew how to make everything right. Where was he now? He'd jilted her by his death, same as running away: what difference did it make? What would he say to Carmela?

"So flighty you were, enamored of boys and men, and, yes, in love with yourself, but not interested at all in finding your own specialness. Hard to handle. Not at all like Carlo, no, worse than a stubborn mule. Even though you were more mature, had more brains, more fire than he, yet you were a terrible student. You didn't care a jot about anyone but yourself!"

"Too much like you," Carmela said.

Serafina's face burned. She sat next to her daughter, touched her hand, but Carmela jerked it away and would not look at her. Had she, Serafina, been an unknown, a wretched one living rough on the streets, Carmela would have shown her more regard.

Enough. I've had enough. No more, Carmela. 🐦

Carlo's Return

Wednesday, October 31, 1866

Serafina entered the kitchen, scooped a few olives from the barrel, and popped them into her mouth. "What's for dinner, Renata, my good sweetness?"

"Chopped eggplant with melted goat cheese on garlic bread, swordfish and broccoli with charred pig over a hot green salad," Renata said.

Carlo rattled his paper. "Asking about dinner when we haven't eaten breakfast yet?"

"You're home early my disheveled doctor. Skipped out on your exams?"

He rose to greet Serafina. "Renata wrote to me about Carmela so I came a few days early. Stubborn, my sister. Perhaps I can help her to see."

"I've tried, believe me. She has no time for me. Visit as much as you like, but I'm finished. No more talk of Carmela." She felt the prickle of tears, and swiped them from her eyes.

"But you can't just—" He stopped when Renata put a finger to her lips.

Carlo buried his face again in his *Giornale di Sicilia*. "Where've you been so early in the morning?" he asked.

"None of your business. You think just because you're a big shot, the world owes you an explanation." She swatted his newspaper. Then kissed him, hugged him a little longer than usual.

"You smell like the sea, Mama."

"And you, like the cadaver room, and your hair needs a

trimming. Poor Gloria."

"Assunta is doing his laundry. He brought at least a month's worth with him." Renata rolled her eyes. "And since you ask, Mama takes long walks in the morning."

"Alone?" Carlo asked.

"Perfectly safe. The ne'er-do-wells are sleeping, and I walk no farther than the cove. Well, not too much farther than the edge of town."

Silence.

"Where's Vicenzu?"

Renata scraped crumbs from the table. "Left early for the shop. He's expecting the arrival of some supplies. After breakfast, I'm going to Sabatini's for honey. Might buy some figs if they look good."

Giulia and Maria sat on the other side of the kitchen, both of them busy. Serafina smiled, watching Giulia's finger moving underneath a string of English words as she read her *Godey's*. Maria studied a sheet of music. They ran to kiss her when Serafina called to them.

Chewing a piece of bread she stole from Carlo's plate, Serafina said, "Giulia, I have an assignment for you, but later. Maria, my lamb, a new piece of music?"

"Brahms. All the rage in Europe, Donna Minerva says."

"I know, but you're too young for that darkness. Stick to Scarlatti."

"But ... "

"I'm teasing. But a little lightness would be good for us today. Merriment, please." She looked at her watch pin.

"I fixed the hem of your wool dress," Giulia said. "Hung it back in your closet."

"Done before I even asked." She kissed Giulia's head.

"Graziella had her baby last night, I heard," Renata said.

"A boy with excellent lungs." Serafina reached into her reticule, handed over the money. "From the proud father."

She wiped the corners of her mouth with forefinger and thumb, and sighed, "I thought Maria would be the midwife, but she was born for music, Giulia for costuming, you for cuisine. No matter, we must each follow our own specialness. Too bad your papa died before we could have made one more girl."

Renata set her mother's breakfast on the table, and Serafina sat. She took a bite of breakfast and closed her eyes. "The orange sauce, delicious. Makes me crazy, such bitterness smashing into sweetness, the smell of almonds and oranges mixed in with the aroma of your caffè—divine, your *biancomangiare*. I feel springtime invade November." She twirled her spoon.

Carlo reached for part of Serafina's bread but she slapped his hand.

"Not yet November," he corrected.

"Make sure we have enough cream and eggs for tomorrow's breakfast. Sabatini's honey, you say? Get a big jar. I need to eat well. Rosa's guards and I have business."

Carlo folded his paper. "What sort of business? Better yet; don't tell us, it's too early to hear about your treacheries."

"We search the lower part of town and shore for clues to the killing of Rosa's women."

Her children stared at her as if she had spoken in a different tongue. She looked from one to the other. Then the dawn: the loss of their father was raw, her efforts at comedy, another one of her failures. "Not to worry," she said, softly. "The wild one hasn't been invented who can rid the world of me."

Giulia's finger began moving again on the page of her magazine. Maria buried her head in her music, humming a strange melody.

The domestic entered, carrying Totò. When he saw Serafina, he reached out to her.

"See how he adores me?" she asked Carlo.

"Wait a few years," he said.

She got up and walked over to her youngest son, arms outstretched. "Renata, some breakfast for our little prince, and warm milk with bits of chocolate. He needs to eat, grow tall like his brother, don't you, my honey bee, but without his fat mouth." She planted his face with kisses. "And your specialness, my little man, what is it? Never mind, you'll know it soon enough." ❧

Li Morti

Friday, November 2, 1866

After the noon meal, Serafina snipped flowers from the old geranium. Blowing her family a kiss, she left for the cemetery, telling her children she'd meet them there later.

In contrast to the vermilion blossoms she clutched, the November light flattened the world on this, the *festa* of *Li Morti*. Events would begin with a procession of actors from the cemetery gates, winding through town and down the Via Serpentina to the arena near the sea. There they'd stage a play, usually a farce of recent events and public figures. But as Serafina passed through the public gardens and the piazza, her attention was far from the festivities. She seemed not to notice the old soldiers, the roughs with vacant stares and missing limbs, a newcomer in need of a bath lurking near the rope seller's store. Like the spokes of a carriage wheel spinning around its hub, her brain whirled round and round a half-formed picture of the murderer.

Who could he be, this killer? He was mad, of course, but clever at hiding his wild torment, someone whom all three victims knew and trusted. Eugenia? At this stage, she couldn't rule her out, but believed, along with Loffredo, that the killer was male, his soul caught in a spell. Like Falco, he was a customer who had helped himself to all three women. Was Rosa keeping information from her, more than what she, Serafina, hadn't already wrenched from the madam's mouth? Probably. Her customers tended to be wealthy with impeccable stature, but she knew a public persona was often a chimera and reputation, a mask. She shivered. That mysterious monk-like figure who picked up Gemma was their best lead. He was probably the same monk she saw in the piazza several days ago. Was he Falco costumed as a monk, or someone else, someone, like the scholarly monk she'd met at the rectory, who had knowledge of the brazen serpent. And what if this killer monk had an inside accomplice, one of Rosa's precious girls or perhaps Scarpo? Was there enough time to catch him before he struck again? Three or four more days, that's all she had, and if he discovered she knew about him, what then? Murder them all in their sleep? Her family too?

She'd heard about Allan Pinkerton and his agency, had read about London's Scotland Yard, their brilliant successes as well as their failures, quick-witted men who uncovered master villains in a flash. They lived for detection, foiled assassination attempts, spotted a pickpocket by the way he walks. She was so new at this. Her breathing was too rapid so she stopped a moment, leaning against a cypress. Did she have the skills necessary to solve these murders? What would happen if she failed? Continuing on her way, she stumbled on a stone. Even the cobbles seemed to be testing her. It was as if the air itself held the answers she could not fathom. And then there was that other voice, the one telling her she should be at home, taking care of her children. Was she being fair to them? And what if she was killed? How would her children fend without her?

"Very well," her mother's voice interrupted, "Do nothing. Be a coward. Add to the chaos around you. Or open the window, let justice fill the room, and make mocking thoughts fly away."

Serafina heard the creak of metal as she opened the cemetery gates, the crunch of her steps on the gritty path. Stately larch trees lined her way. A bird sang to its mate. Iridescent marble figures— kneeling angels and weeping Madonnas—glared at her in the half-light.

She felt it again, the press of her soul against her stomach. That stone angel over there, did it breathe? It was *Ci Morti* after all, and there were bound to be other mourners in the cemetery paying respects to their loved ones, yet she saw no one else as she continued down the path toward the family's graves. Stroking the flowers in her hand, she remembered the wryness of her mother's smile. If only she could image her, if only she'd appear, it would afford her some peace.

Stopping first at Giorgio's grave, she prayed, wept, and left some of the geraniums at his headstone. At Maddalena's grave, Serafina saw them at once. They lay next to the marker, another spray of geraniums identical to hers. Without thinking she knelt, mixed her flowers in with the others, and retied the twine as quickly as she could. She tried to conjure down Maddalena's face, squeezing her eyelids shut, the better to see inside to her soul and the spirit life surrounding all living things, waiting several minutes in vain, so whispering a hasty prayer, she left, certain that a pair of eyes watched her as she hurried away. She ran splayed fingers through tangled curls. Shed the shell of fear, a voice inside proclaimed, like the snake does its skin. "Enough," she said aloud. She squared her shoulders and seeing them waiting for her in the distance, she waved to her children.

"Look!" Totò pointed to skeletons peeking from behind a praying angel. Other costumed players emerged from mausoleums, assembled near the cemetery's gates. As usual, the king and queen of the dead began the parade. The queen, in snaky wig and blackened teeth, smiled at them. Scores of players wore military costumes, some dressed as Napoleon, Murat or King Bumma. A faded Redshirt stumbled toward them, stopping and staring at Serafina. Hands on hips, she fixed him with her eyes until, with a boozy whimper, he vanished, and they joined the procession. Decorated carts carried ghosts, skeletons, and lidless coffins with monks lying in repose. Onlookers roared when, green-faced, one sat up. A bloodshot eye sprang from his forehead. Spectators threw flowers as they marched through the piazza, snaked into the older section of town, scrambled down to the arena. Last night when she and Beppe drove through this neighborhood, the road was choked with rubbish. They must have cleared it early this morning, but, Serafina stepped with care, mindful of the lingering turmoil from last month's uprising.

Ahead, someone dropped a bottle from the roof. She heard glass breaking, shouting, shrill whistles. The parade stopped. Uniformed men shoved past her. Serafina held her breath, but the disturbance ended quickly, and they moved on.

Vendors selling sausage, rice balls, sweetened figs, mulberry, blueberry, and orange ices lined the road near the entrance to the arena. Even though Renata packed food for them, Totò wanted some of everything he saw. Serafina obliged. "An ice, my little precious? Would you like another? One of these figs maybe?"

"Watch the coins," Vicenzu said.

"Quiet, Mr. Money. It's *Li Morti*, after all, and this is your brother's first."

"Tomorrow we starve, is that it?"

She didn't answer at first, balancing Totò on one hip. "You're right. From now on I'll take care, but I have a plan. We'll talk about it after I find the killer of Rosa's women."

"You joke. Look no further than the royal box." He gestured toward plush seats in the center of the arena. "There's your killer."

She followed his gaze, saw men in top hats, women in billowing skirts, sable capes, feathered hats. Perched in the center of the box sat a shock of red hair. While Tigro cultivated puffed-up nobles, his wife sat between their two sons, lost. Serafina waved to her. Elisabetta fluttered back an anxious linen. Serafina noticed that Giulia, too, waved to someone.

"That baroness with the important nose, she wears your dress? What a gorgeous frock. Surpasses all the rest. Such haunches she has, yet she barely fills the top."

"Not my design," Giulia said. "I let out the waist, that's all."

"Maria, hold my hand, my precious lovely. We don't want to lose you—who would play Brahms for us?"

Maria pushed up her spectacles. A clown in whiteface with gamy breath smiled close to her nose, and Maria cringed, waving the foulness away.

The throng mashed them, and they stood for hours, it seemed, immobile, then lurched forward, only to wait some more. Someone stepped on Serafina's foot. Again they advanced.

Carlo was missing, she realized. She asked Vicenzu who said, "He went off with friends after you left for the cemetery. Told me he'd try to find us here, but if not, he'd be back in time for supper."

The wind off the sea muffled the laughter and calls of the crowd. Black clouds massed, and Serafina could feel her curls pull in the dampness. Vicenzu limped ahead to scout for seats. When he found them, he waved his crutch back and forth in the blowing air.

Serafina navigated the first step. "Come on, girls, let's all stay together." She tripped, caught herself just in time. There it was again, that sharpness to her movements. She missed Giorgio. As soon as they settled, Renata passed the basket of food, Vicenzu, the wine, Giulia the fruit juice for Totò. He drank it as if he hadn't drunk all day.

Maria puckered her lips. "I'm too old for this. I should be home."

"You're eight. Now watch the stage and be quiet," Giulia said.

Vicenzu told Maria she sounded like a prima donna.

The audience shouted for the show to begin.

Clowns rolled out of entryways onto the stage. Actors dressed as straw men hit one another with sticks. Priests cavorted with female clowns. Led by the ringmaster whose coattails swelled like red sails, the circus performers entered. There were fire eaters and fat ladies, painted elephants, and brown bears. Acrobats tumbled, jumping high through hoops of fire.

Totò whispered to Serafina who picked him up and, lifting her skirts, made her way down the steps. Renata elbowed Vicenzu, who swooped Totò from Serafina's arms. When they got to the water closets, he took Totò inside.

"It's been a long time," a familiar voice said, and Don Tigro, appearing from out of nowhere, tilted his head and flashed a smile. "About Giorgio, my condolences."

Startled, she turned around, took a moment to compose herself, and thanked him.

"You visit Betta tomorrow."

She nodded.

"Bringing your children?"

His teeth, she noticed, were perfect. Not inherited from her side of the family—her mother must have been delirious in the last moments of her life. *A burden you've given me, Mama.* "Perhaps my daughter, Giulia who'd like to see Elisabetta's gowns. From Paris, no?"

"I don't pay attention to those things. Maria comes with you?"

Maria, Serafina wondered, why he asked about her.

As if reading her thoughts, he said, "One afternoon last year, the most exquisite Brahms came from the maestro's workshop as I passed by, so I stopped. 'Maria Florio, a prodigy,' he said, and I haven't forgotten the sound of her piano. If you bring her, she can play Betta's concert grand." He touched his hat and melted into the crowd as Totò slammed into her, hiding in her skirts. She gave him a hasty peck on the cheek.

"Didn't you hear me?" Vicenzu asked.

"What? Oh, of course, dear."

They ascended.

Carlo reached for Totò.

"You're back with us!" Serafina said.

Vicenzu smacked his forehead. "I just told you he was here. Watch your mind or we'll be orphans."

Carlo slid over and gave his mother a kiss.

"You." She pinched his ear. "I haven't seen you this whole visit, probably pestering poor Gloria."

"In Prizzi with her family."

"Then why so scarce? No, I don't want to know—my ears are too delicate, but now I'm happy, I have my whole family with me."

"Not your whole family," Carlo said.

She was silent a moment in the sudden heat. "Not here, wrong time," she said.

Carlo shot her a jagged look. "When's the right time? If you won't talk about Carmela—"

"You have your boots on backwards: it is she, Carmela, who won't look at me. Believe me, I've tried. Too painful, I tell you, but you wouldn't understand, so no more. I don't want to hear her name, not today, not ever. That's it." She pointed to the stage. "Oh, Totò, look at the clowns!"

Red-faced, Carlo rose and straightened his coat, storming down the steps and disappearing into the crowd.

Serafina blinked at a watery stage. Totò started to cry. Vicenzu took him. Looking down, Serafina rubbed her forehead. Maria, Giulia, and Renata looked at one another. Minutes passed.

Renata said, "I think I see blue sky."

"You always say that," Maria said, pushing up her spectacles.

"No, Renata's right. It seems sunnier. Well, at least the clouds are beginning to lift, what do you say, my best player of Brahms?"

Maria shook her head. "No more Brahms. I'll play Scarlatti so Mama will be happy and not worry about Carmela."

Again, silence.

The family, those that remained, watched the rest of the performance with unwavering attention. At the finale, they clapped with the others when clowns dressed as Redshirts rolled onto the stage and, with a flourish, handcuffed players dressed as King Bumma and his ratty son. Whistles blew, crackers popped.

The crowd streamed out of the arena under a sky streaked with crimson.

The Message

"Yes?" Vicenzu stood in the doorway.

"My name is Arcangelo," the young man said, taking off his cap and holding it with both hands. "I work for Rosa. You know her?"

"Of course. And you saved my mother's life the other night. A thousand thanks. Come in, please." He smiled.

"Oh, you are—"

"Her son. One of them. Grateful to you." Looking over at Carlo, Vicenzu said, "Come here and meet the fellow who saved Mama."

Arcangelo rocked a little from side to side. "Rosa asked me to bring Donna Fina. She begs her, please, to come right away. Is she here?"

"So. Arcangelo, is it?" Carlo said.

They shook hands.

Arcangelo nodded. Rocked. Pulled at the cuffs of his sleeves.

"Make yourself at home," Vicenzu said. "We'll get her in a minute, but you'll have to wait. She stepped out to do some walking quite early, so she's not finished with her formal dressing, if you know what I mean. And I believe she'll need to eat something before she leaves, knowing my mother as I do," he said. "Unless, of course, it's a baby coming into the world. That's not the reason you're here, is it?"

Arcangelo shook his head.

Carlo straightened his coat, brought out a key from his pocket and opened the door to the grandfather clock. "Go on, we're listening." Carlo said, beginning to wind the clock.

Arcangelo swallowed. "I'm to tell only Donna Fina. La Signura said to hurry. Please, dear sirs."

Vicenzu put a hand on Arcangelo's shoulder. "Sit for a moment." He pointed to the great room and hearth where logs crackled.

"Yes," Carlo said. "Join the family. Have something to eat, something to drink. Best to take the day on a full stomach."

Arcangelo sat on the edge of a chair in the far corner of the room, holding his hat and peering into the flames. Not once, but a couple of times, he had to stop himself from biting his lip and covering his hands with the sleeves of his jacket.

Vicenzu whispered something to a young woman wearing an apron. She left the room. He and Carlo sat back down at the table and continued eating their breakfast. Across from them a girl sewed. Both men crammed in large bites of omelet, *biancomangiare*, and bread smeared with orange marmalade while they read the paper and drank caffè. In between bites, they talked to one another in low tones.

The woman in the apron returned, stood at the stove, spooning food onto plates while an old lady in carpet slippers shuffled from the table to the stove and back again, serving and clearing with a steady rhythm. Arcangelo smelled toast, citrus, and eggs.

The young woman approached. "My name is Renata," she said. She smiled. "My mother will be down shortly. In the meantime, won't you have some caffè and something to eat? We are all grateful to you for saving her the other night." She introduced him to the others in the room.

"Caffè only, and you are too kind."

"Assunta, caffè, please, for our visitor."

Three children entered.

"Tessa, what are you doing here?" Arcangelo asked.

"She's our guest," Maria said. "Who are you?" She straightened her spectacles.

Tessa said, "That's Arcangelo. He lives with Scarpo. They help us. Arcangelo fixed Uno's leg yesterday."

"Who is Uno?" Totò asked.

"One of our mules—who else?" Tessa said.

"Oh." He reached for a strand of her hair and pulled it.

"Ow!" Tessa twisted around to grab him, but Totò ran away, laughing. Tessa chased him around the table while Giulia sewed on, ate, and talked to Vicenzu and Carlo.

Assunta shuffled over with caffè for Arcangelo. In one motion, he gulped the hot liquid and handed back the cup.

Tessa stopped in front of Arcangelo. "Why are you here—to take me home?"

Arcangelo shook his head. He was about to explain when, pinning a brooch to the front of her dress, Serafina entered. Her hair was undone and she hadn't yet painted her face. Her children stopped talking and stood up.

Totò ran to her and pulled on her skirts.

She bent and kissed him. "My beautiful boy, good morning. Did you eat something?"

He nodded. "They did, too," he said, pointing a finger at Maria and Tessa, "but Tessa didn't finish it all."

Maria and Tessa looked up at her. Serafina gave a kiss to both. "Maria, show Tessa your piano. Play something soft." The three children ran into the parlor.

She turned to face Arcangelo. "Lovely to see you again."

He bowed. "La Signura asks that you come, please, at once. I don't like to say more." He circled the room with his arm.

Serafina said, "Another—"

"Yes."

Arcangelo kept nodding like a broken jack-in-the-box. The clock struck the hour. "But it's not time yet. It's only Sunday. It cannot be, not yet. We have until Tuesday."

No one spoke.

Serafina closed her eyes. Her feet were cold. "Renata and Vicenzu, stay with the children while I go to Rosa's. Carlo, come with me."

He walked to her side. "And forgive my rudeness to you yesterday. It's just that—"

"Enough!" Renata said.

The room stopped.

Serafina put her arm around his waist and pecked his cheek.

"You'll be a great help." Turning to Arcangelo she said, "Did Rosa call the police?"

He shrugged.

"Vicenzu, get Beppe. Tell him to go to Colonna and ask the inspector to come to Rosa's right away." She blew him a kiss.

Vicenzu smiled, hobbled to the back door yelling Beppe's name.

She took a step, combing fingers through her hair. She could hear a sonata coming from the parlor, the music flowing, timeless. "Tessa stays with us today. And Giulia, were you able to finish—"

"All done, Mama." After she cut a thread and stuck the needle back into her pin cushion, Giulia stood and held the cape out for her mother to see.

"Oh, Giulia, my quiet precious, look at those gorgeous braids."

"The way you wanted them, 'gold braids, just like the queen's.'" Giulia grinned.

"Thank you." She turned to the domestic. "Assunta, help me with my hair."

"I know my way, thank you," Serafina said to the maid who opened the door for them. She led her son past several small parlors, their doors open to reveal wine-stained glasses, ash trays spilling over onto tables, plates with crumbs and dried bits of food. A gentleman's top hat, cane, and silk scarf lay on one chair. Chiaroscuro paintings hung from the walls. She smelled cigar butts and stale sex. "Saturday morning," she whiffed. "Time to open the shutters and clean."

"Typical smells for a brothel," Carlo said.

"I won't ask how you know," she said, buttoning her lips with thumb and forefinger.

Carlo knocked on Rosa's door. No answer.

After a slight hesitation, Serafina opened it. "This way," she told Carlo, pointing to a back door on the far wall.

"Rosa keeps her own books, I see," Carlo said, glancing at shelves of ledgers. A fire burned in the hearth. "Beech. I can tell by the color of the flames."

"How do you know?"

"Papa taught me. Look at the flame, a white light. Listen to how softly it crackles. Gives good heat, too. Beech logs burn cleaner than any of the others, he told me. We used to burn beech, but now, they're too expensive, Vicenzu told me."

"Bah, Vicenzu, tighter than bark."

"Rosa must be doing well, despite all the murders."

"Born with a vigorous business sense. Not a dreamer like me."

"She'll need to close her house or find a way to placate the don if these murders don't stop."

"What makes you think the don is behind these murders? Rosa pays him each month, and without fail, she tells me."

"But—"

"Not the work of the don. You'll see in a minute when you examine the body with me."

"I'm a student, not a medical examiner, I can't—"

"Haven't talked about these murders with you. You're away at school most of the time, but they don't seem like the work of bandits, more like the work of a wild man." She told him the characteristics, the timing, the autopsy results for the three victims. "When bandits kill, it's different, and they're not so precise about the date. How could they be? They don't even read. No, these murders are not the work of bandits or a lustful killer."

"Trying to convince me or yourself?

Silence. She felt her stomach doing flips and tried to wriggle her toes, but they weren't working at the moment.

Carlo said, "He's called 'mafia,' Don Tigro."

"Says who?"

"Worse than the bandits. A fair wind blows for them since Unification. Last year the prefect gave a speech talking about the mafia—a new kind of threat, he said, clandestine, with complex rules of initiation and belonging. They talk a lot about 'honor,' call their organizations 'families,' each family run by a boss and his deputies. They run it just like a business, collecting their protection money from—"

"From us. I know all about them, Carlo. You don't have to lecture me like I'm a—"

"And do you know who Don Tigro is? Do you?"

At this question, she stopped, looked at her son who regarded her with that goading persistence of his, standing there, waiting for her reply. If he only knew Maddalena's secret, he wouldn't be so smug, and she was tempted to tell him just to shut him up, but how could she reveal her mother's dying words uttered in a state of delirium, and ... of course, that's it: Maddalena's last story was the fantasy of a dying woman.

Carlo continued. "Known in Palermo as the capo of Oltramari. Peasants adore him. The large landholders support him, or else."

"I know all about Don Tigro and his kind." Her temples throbbed.

He raised an eyebrow. "I doubt it. You're a woman, but anyway, how could you fight them?"

Serafina said, "These murders are not the work of the mafia or the bandits. And another point I need to make." She wagged her finger at him. "If the land is strewn with dead bodies, as our land has been for centuries, does that excuse another dead body? Do we bury our dead and forget them and try to stay out of harm's way? Do we hide in the house and not hunger for truth? Cave into the bandits and the mafia and an inept government? No, we find the murderer and bring him to justice, for the sake of our children and grandchildren, for the sake of our nation. We find the truth. We stop the killing."

He rolled his eyes.

"And don't let me talk of Inspector Colonna and his men. No, I'll say nothing. My lips are shut tight, lips that would never blame an overworked police force for starting the rumor that Don Tigro and his thugs killed Rosa's women. Now, no more talk of the who, not yet. Let's look at the what and the how."

"Why did I start with her?"

"And God doesn't agree with you, either," she added, rubbing her forehead and walking over to the window. Looking out, she saw Gusti's body lying on the stones, Scarpo guarding it.

Alone before the sea Rosa stood, clothed in a dress of black bombazine, the wind whipping her skirts. Hearing the crunch of gravel behind her, she turned. She held a handkerchief to her unpainted face.

Serafina walked up to her, arms outstretched. They hugged. They cried. Serafina gave her a double kiss. "Remember Carlo?"

"Look at him now," Rosa said. "Madonna, what a fine young man. This high," she said, chopping the air close to her stomach, "last time I saw you. He's got Carmela's coloring, but with dark curls, and the eyes of a god born in the sea."

"Studies medicine at the University of Palermo now. Home this weekend for *Li Morti*. Comes with me today to take a look at poor, dead Gusti."

Rosa dried her eyes. "Visit us when you're home again, and after your mother solves this vileness, when things are better. A visit on the house, a glorious toss, I promise—"

"Rosa! I, the mother, stand next to you. On your other side is Gusti's corpse, not yet cold, and you invite my son to visit your house?"

Carlo's eyes brightened. "Accepted with pleasure."

"Don't be silly. She thinks she jokes."

Rosa opened her mouth, but snapped it shut when Serafina pointed to the body. "That's where you found her?"

Rosa nodded.

Serafina put an arm around her shoulders. *Not the same as Bella.* "Beppe should be arriving any moment with Colonna."

"Thank you, both of you. Colonna is a useless goose, but we need him now." The rims of her eyes were red, and Serafina noticed dark circles beneath them. Rosa began to cry again. "My fault, I should have listened to her last night."

"Gusti?"

Rosa nodded.

"Tell me."

"Through with my bath—powdered, perfumed, trussed—when I heard a knock on my door. Gusti. And what did she say to me? Oh Madonna, I thought she was only talking."

"A rambler, Gusti. In the end she gave me some interesting information when I interviewed her the other evening, but I interrupt," Serafina said.

"'I know who did it,' she said. 'Are you sure?' I asked. She thought a moment. 'Well, almost sure.' She wanted to send for you;

she said you told her to come to you if she had any information, but I told her it could wait, it being Friday night, and all I could think of was—" Rosa began crying. "Told her to think it over while she worked, that her Friday clients were important, and she agreed. Now she's dead. My poor girl, my poor dear girl. All my fault."

Serafina reached into her pocket and handed Rosa a fresh handkerchief. "You got up early?"

She nodded. "Middle of the night, I heard a sound, like a creature from the netherworld had me in chains and was dragging me away. At first I thought I was having a bad dream. But, no, I wasn't sleeping. I got up, lit the lamp. The noise continued. Then I thought it must be a rowdy customer. The sound grew louder. Coming from inside? Outside? Couldn't tell. Awake by this time, I got that feeling again, that terrible crawling at the back of my neck." She blew her nose.

Serafina said, "Take a moment." But she felt it, too, an indescribable weirdness.

"I felt the spider crawling up my neck and knew something bad had happened. Oh, such a fool, I thought, if I dress, the dream and the spider will go away. By this time, it was first light, the world, fuzzy and still. I opened the door, held up my lamp. Looked to the right, saw the creep of dawn, and reassuring myself that it was only a nightmare or a swallow of bad wine, I walked outside, looked to the left, and, oh, Madonna, I saw her. I screamed. Arcangelo and Scarpo came running—"

"They were here?" Carlo asked.

"They heard me yell. I asked Arcangelo to get you." Rosa blew her nose. "Let's go to my office. I need food. My head throbs, and there's nothing I can do for her now. I could have last night, I could have saved her." She sobbed.

"Rosa, you didn't kill Gusti."

The madam closed her eyes, held up her palm. "Nothing more you can say." ❧

The Fourth Victim

erafina told Rosa to go inside while she and Carlo took a closer look at the body. It lay in back of Rosa's house, a few meters from her office, in full view of the lawn and the rocks and the sea.

"Looks like asphyxiation," Carlo said. He and Serafina knelt by the victim. "Been dead for a while, six or seven hours at least."

Serafina rubbed one knee, then the other. "This killing is not the same as the others." The wind lifted her skirt, revealing a lace petticoat. "They died of a single stab wound to the heart. And there's no image carved into Gusti's forehead, either. Not the same killer."

Carlo said, "We don't know that for sure. Just like we don't know the cause of death. Remember, I'm not the—"

"I know, you're not the doctor." She didn't want to argue with him. She didn't want to argue with anyone ever again. Four of Rosa's prostitutes were murdered, one by one, in less than four months, and gazing into the dead face of poor Gusti, Serafina's mind was numb. Despite her speech to Carlo a few minutes ago, she had no inkling of this killer's identity. Could it be the don? Bandits? If that were the case, what would she do? She'd prove it, but she'd need the help of Colonna's men, and the thought of that turned her stomach. She shivered.

Of all the women she'd interviewed, she had liked Gusti the most, and there she lay—well, not Gusti, exactly, but a grotesquery, as if some vengeful god created her effigy, then set about destroying it. What could any human have done to deserve a death like this?

The body lay on its side, head twisted and slightly upturned as if to view its startled audience. The face was swollen, mottled in caput mortuum. The eyes were bloodshot, wild with the knowledge of imminent death. Knotted around the neck, a scarf—probably the instrument used to strangle.

Gusti was clothed in a fringed evening gown with matching bag. The straps on the dress were thinner than the legs of a spider. Stuffed into her mouth was a purple slipper, and on her left foot, its mate. She wore no jewelry. Strange. Hadn't Gusti been wearing a cartload of gems the other night?—pearls, strands of gold, earrings, rings, bracelets.

Serafina opened the bag and found one handkerchief and a twenty lire gold piece stamped with the king's likeness. "Vittorio Emanuele Due," she said, holding them in her fingers for Carlo to see. "Look at her hands. Anything?"

"The right one's clenched. Don't want to touch the body. Let Loffredo see it first. Might give him a better idea of the time of death. Won't he be the one to examine her?"

She nodded.

Carlo continued. "The left hand, let's see, looks like a clump of hair or material of some sort caught on one of her fingernails. Without touching the corpse, he tugged at the strands of caught hair. "Oops, broke the nail."

"Take it, take them both, the fingernail and the hair. Give them to me."

"I don't think—"

"Do it." She gave him half a smile.

He passed them over, not looking at her.

She examined the hair. Fair, she'd call it. Curled. Falco's? She laid the strand and the piece of fingernail on a blank page of her notebook. Serafina was about to close her bag when a glint of metal near Gusti's head caught her eye. She grabbed it.

"What?"

"An earring. Into my reticule it goes."

Carlo took another look at the body. "No other wounds that I can see. No other marks, except for facial bruising caused by the slipper being forced into the mouth." Carlo stood up and brushed dust from his pants and frock coat. A few black curls slipped over his forehead and he pushed them back with splayed fingers.

"Anything strike you as odd?" she asked as she rose.

"You're joking."

"No, well, I mean where's her coat or shawl or cape? If she met her killer outside, she'd be wearing one, no?" She faced him, held out her palms. "Let's take a peek in Gusti's room. We'd better hurry before the police come and traipse through Rosa's house, messing up the evidence."

He raised an eyebrow. "And far be it from you to leave anything behind for them to find."

"Except, of course, for the body."

"Oh, please."

"Four bodies in less than four months. No leads, no theories—"

"Not true. There's a theory, and you know what it is. Besides, the police have their hands full. Protests, bandits, prisoners being set free, wave after wave of cholera, the September uprising, the curfew. They're up to their eyeballs in work, and I must say, you're not very trusting."

"Not very trusting? Cautious, that's all. But as for trust, I trust my family and Rosa."

"Carmela too?"

She swiveled from him, looked beyond the rocks to a ragged sky, and spoke into the wind, "I'll catch this killer. I swear I will." She held a hand over her mouth and blinked her eyes dry before turning back to him. "I think Gusti was killed inside this house, right under everyone's noses and her body dumped here. And what's more, I think whoever killed Gusti knows who killed the other three. Tessa stays with us until we catch him."

Rosa had a large tray on her desk with cups, plates, napkins, utensils, two pots of fresh tea and steaming milk. She motioned for them to sit and pulled the cord.

"In Gusti's bag," Serafina said, handing her the two gold coins.

The domestic entered holding another tray with a large cassata. "Cook made your favorite cake," she said.

"Formusa knows how to cheer me up." Looking at her guests, she said, "Eat. You'll feel better." Rosa cut pieces for Serafina and Carlo. He began eating his portion, forking down large mouthfuls and asking for seconds while Rosa beamed. Serafina declined the cake but drank her tea and asked for more. "This time with more milk."

"Your Carlo has appetites, and we can fill them, am I right, Mr. Carlo? Salute to you."

Carlo reddened and wiped the corners of his mouth.

Serafina rolled her eyes. "First, we need to look in Gusti's room. It won't take long."

Later, as they ascended the stairs, Rosa said, "Follow me, but, shhh, the others are still asleep. They know nothing yet."

Serafina looked at her watch pin. "Shouldn't some of them be up?"

"They worked hard last night. Noon or one before they'll rise," she said.

"We'll need to wake them before that," Serafina said, "and I want to interview all the women who were here last night."

Rosa shrugged and led them to Gusti's room, climbing the three flights without breathing, it seemed to Serafina.

Rosa turned the key, and the three of them entered.

"Gusti not make the bed? Not like her. Neat as a pin, that one," Rosa said. Twisted bedclothes lay in a heap on the floor, the mattress at angles to the posts. Dresser drawers were open, as were the two cabinet doors, their contents jumbled together and strewn over the floor.

"Signs of a fight," Serafina said.

"Shhh!" Rosa put a finger to her lips.

"Let's get on with this. We're wasting time."

Carlo said, "No bickering, you two. And show some respect for the dead."

"Respect the living first. The dead are dead and need nothing," Rosa said, signing herself.

They looked through Gusti's clothes, on the floor of the cabinet, behind it, underneath the bed, in all the dresser drawers. They found nothing except clothes: no jewelry, no money, no letters, no clues, no nothing.

They were about to leave when Serafina noticed an etching of the Duomo askew on the wall. She looked behind it and saw a hole covered by an ill-fitted piece of plaster.

"We need light," Carlo whispered. He found some matchsticks next to an oil lamp on the nightstand, lit the wick, and held the lamp up to the hole.

Serafina peered inside. "I see something over there." Reaching in, she retrieved a leather case. Locked. She shook the case. "Sounds like jewels to me."

Rosa nodded.

They untangled the bed clothes and looked through them.

Serafina ran her hand over the surface of the mattress. "Turn it over."

Carlo frowned, but heaved the mattress up and over, Rosa and Serafina catching it before it hit the springs.

Serafina found a small square of rough stitching, similar to the one in Bella's room—Rosa's women must learn from one another. Carlo cut around them with his pocket knife, stuck his hand into the opening, and pulled out a key and some paper—documents or letters.

Serafina held her hand out for the key. "Necklaces and bracelets, gobs of them." She bit into one. "Gold."

"I wonder what she did for this strand?" Rosa's eyes sparked in the dim light.

"Give the jewels and key to Rosa. Put the papers in your pocket. No time to read them now," Serafina said. "Let's clean up this mess and get out."

While Serafina and Rosa folded the sheets, Carlo refitted the piece of plaster and picture. He looked at the documents and thrust them into his pocket. When he thought Serafina wasn't looking, he whispered something in Rosa's ear.

"Face it, this is an inside job," Serafina said.

Rosa's eyes were like spoiled fruit. "None of my girls did this. None. Properly screened, or they don't get in. Gusti's killer must be a customer. My fault, all my fault." She shook her head. "Business not so good, especially around *Li Morti* and I was too soft and let some salty characters into the house."

"Falco?" Serafina asked.

Rosa's eyes moistened.

Serafina hugged her. "No more blame."

"Besides, we don't have the time," Carlo added.

Serafina turned to him. "She was strangled in here. The killer must have been looking for something."

"But left the jewels?" Carlo held up both hands.

"Not any of my girls—"

"He wasn't looking for money or jewels," Serafina said. "Admit it, Rosa. The killer had to have knowledge that only an insider could give him. Perhaps we'll find out when we talk to the women."

"If she was strangled here, how would the killer get rid of the body?" Carlo asked.

Rosa said, "Couldn't carry Gusti down the main staircase, not past the guards."

"Even after midnight?" Serafina asked.

"Since Gemma's murder, there's a guard at the door, always. Another makes the rounds. Guards are easy to find after the war— all the leftovers—but many of them are dim."

"That's what they get for killing. Leftovers?" Serafina asked.

"Redshirts. Scarpo hired them to work the off-hour shifts. Turi used them to ride behind the carriage. Don't you remember them on our trip to Palermo?"

Serafina nodded.

The madam continued. "Scarpo himself watched during our peak hours. Or Arcangelo." She brushed the air with both hands and shook her head. "An inside job?—impossible! Murdered outside, Gusti."

"Then why wasn't she wearing a cape?"

Rosa chewed on her thumbnail. "Dragged her body down the back stairs, then. But there's a bolt on the outside and it's always fastened."

"Must've had the key, or something wrong with the lock. Let's find out."

"This way." Rosa turned to Carlo. "Take that lamp." She looked at Serafina and put a forefinger to her lips. "And you, shhh, like an aging *strega*, the pitch of your voice."

Serafina rolled her eyes, but said nothing. No more fighting, not even a harmless skirmish. Rosa led them down the hall to a door and opened it.

Carlo held his lamp high. They saw freshly-made footprints in the layer of dust on the top landing, too many to count, and a dust-free path down the middle of the stairs.

"Must have dragged the body," Carlo said. "Dead weight was too heavy for the killer."

As he led the way, the lantern cast globes of dim light on walls and ceiling. Dark, winding, cavernous, the staircase, with air that smelled like the exhalation of old ghosts.

Halfway down, Rosa pointed to something glinting.

Carlo picked it up.

"The other earring," Serafina said.

"Other?" Rosa asked.

"Found one outside, near the body."

"Let's see what Colonna does with it," Rosa said, turning up one corner of her mouth.

"He won't find it. I took it."

When he reached the bottom of the staircase, Carlo opened the door with ease, a few meters from where Scarpo stood next to Gusti's body.

Surprised, Scarpo asked, "You took the key, Signura?"

"It was unlocked," Carlo said.

Serafina looked at the bolt. "No lock. Gone. No sign of force."

Rosa froze, staring at Serafina. "The spider crawls again."

Turning to her, Serafina said, "Gusti's killer had inside help, face it."

"Or Don Tigro. His men work magic, guards or no guards," Carlo added.

"But his men would have taken Gusti's jewels. If not her jewels, then for sure the twenty lire gold piece in her purse."

They were back in Rosa's office by nine.

"So we've established that Gusti was killed in her own room, her body dragged down the back stairs. Who'd know about that staircase, or have the key to the outside lock?" Serafina asked.

Rosa was about to reply when they heard the crunch of wooden wheels on stone, the low tones of male voices, and one had an unmistakable pitch.

Serafina said, "We'd better go out."

Carlo looked at Rosa. "My trusting Mama."

Rosa rocked her head back and forth, eyes closed, both forefingers ticking back and forth. "Watch Colonna operate—you'll get a big lesson on how to do nothing."

Colonna wore a long overcoat and fedora hat. He moved from side to side. "You again?"

"I sent for her, Inspector," Rosa said. She managed a smile, and took his arm. "Forgive me, I was distraught, but now that you're here, I feel better." She pressed her front into his forearm. "But you see, you and your men, you've been so busy, so much violence, so many crimes. I say to myself, that Inspector, how does he do it? So I asked my friend, Fina, here, to help me." She patted his hand.

Smiling, he tipped his hat. "Hard for you, Signura, I know, and you keep such a, such a clean and distinguished establishment." He couldn't help his eyes from roaming over Rosa's bosomy vastness.

The madam smiled and looked into his eyes. "Too kind, Pirricù."

"And your friend—Fina, you say?" He looked at Serafina. "Found out what, so far?"

Serafina interrupted. "And we sent for you, as soon as we heard. We didn't know if you'd be here or in Catania. We're told there's been another uprising. The peasants are—"

"Well, I'm here but leaving shortly. Troops sent to Catania, most of my men with them. Only Colonna here!" He thumped his chest "And two others to help me keep the peace." He gestured to the two uniformed men who accompanied him and continued. "But we'll manage. Loffredo should arrive any minute." He turned to his men. "Get the artist."

"Already sketching the body," someone said.

"When he finishes, and Loffredo finishes," Colonna said, gesturing to indicate the meaning of 'finishes,' "take the body away." Another flourish. "In the meantime, La Signura and I will be in her office."

Serafina saw the artist kneeling by the body. Several meters away, two hospital workers in black cassocks bearing a stretcher stood in silence, their eyes cast to the ground, hoods donned, waiting alongside a draped cart and mule in mourning headgear.

They reminded her of that first Sunday in October and a death so different. How Rosa had grieved, still does, for Bella. She must find this killer.

Serafina smelled neroli oil and heard Loffredo's distinctive step but continued talking to her son, feeling her cheeks burn despite the sea wind.

The doctor removed his gloves and kissed Serafina's hand. "Upsetting for you. And poor Rosa, a fourth victim."

"Otto, you remember my son, Carlo. He goes to University. Home for *Li Morti*."

"Doubt I would have recognized you. A man now, and the last time we met, you were a child. I hear good things about you from Professor Libertate. 'Excellent doctor he'll make,' he tells me. Said you're an exacting dissector." He paused, looking closer at Carlo's face. "You have your mother's looks, her gift of persistence, your father's scholarly bent, and your parents' intelligence. If you're not busy Monday morning, I could use your help at the morgue What I do here is preliminary."

Suspects and Jugglers

"Pirricù, is it?" Serafina lifted an eyebrow. She sat across the desk from Rosa.

"Good riddance to that insolent goose of an inspector. One small look at the body, two big glasses of grappa, and in three minutes he was gone."

"Loffredo is here now, doing the preliminary examination with Carlo. They'll continue in the morgue Monday morning. Strangled with her own scarf."

Rosa shuddered. "Marsala?"

"Too early for me, but I could use another cup of tea or a caffè."

Rosa pulled the cord. In a few minutes, the domestic came in with a tray and two cups of espresso.

"Too old for this business."

Serafina said nothing. She took a cup and drank. In the past when she'd suggested that Rosa close the house, the idea was met with a sudden storm.

"I miss Tessa, but she'll be home this evening," Rosa said, downing her espresso.

"Don't you think Tessa should stay with us, in light of Gusti's murder, just until we find the killer?"

Rosa opened her mouth to protest.

Serafina held up her hand. "Think about it. And after Loffredo leaves, you must wake the women. We need to talk to them."

Rosa opened her mouth again.

"We interview the women, you and I together, in this room. Today. The killer has an accomplice, someone who knows the house well, the ins and outs, the front, the back, the comings, the goings. Is there a customer who knows the layout of this house so well?

Consider the question before you answer," Serafina said.

Rosa shook her head. "Then it has to be someone in the house, one of the girls. Unless it's Falco or a maid."

"Any record of his being here recently with his usual women? Would Scarpo or the guards know?"

Rosa bowed her head and ran a finger back and forth on the desk. "Had the run of the house, I'm afraid."

"All the more reason to speak to the women. Gioconda will tell me. Proud of being one of Falco's favorites. But what about the guards. Could it be one of them?"

Rosa shook her head. "Guards aren't allowed inside of the house."

"So it's one of your women, Falco, Scarpo or Turi."

"Turi, no. Scarpo, never!"

"And I'm sure Gusti knew the accomplice, perhaps even the identity of the killer. Anyway, she knew too much, so she had to be killed."

"Should have given her more time last night. Oh, if I could only take it back!"

"And Gusti fought her killer," Serafina said. "One of her nails broke, and clutched in her hand, I found a strand or two of hair, probably from the scalp of her killer. While we talk to the women, we'll look for a scar somewhere on the face near the hairline or on the neck or behind the ear. or neck."

"I'll wake them one by one. Who first?"

Serafina reached for her notebook and put it on the desk. "Her friends. They'll be able to give us the most information about her."

Rosa's eyes were wet. "Gusti was an outsider, and the only friend she had was Carmela. We must tell her."

Serafina slid her cup onto the tray. It teetered with a metallic sound, like the distant clang of swords.

"Did you hear me?" Rosa asked.

She tried to speak, but a devouring sadness lay between her and the rest of the world. She felt her heart quicken, the pulse like a thousand drums in her ears, and a memory overwhelmed her, compressing the years and painting the event in vibrant colors. Serafina was in the nursery with her mother and the twins—Carlo, black-curled, Carmela, with her ginger locks and iridescent skin. Maddalena, wrinkling her nose, was teaching her granddaughter how to walk while Carlo made running circles round the pair. "Yes. We must speak to Carmela," Serafina whispered.

They women learned nothing more from interviewing the prostitutes.

"A special customer last night occupied all my time. Voracious, the appetites of some men," Gioconda said and yawned.

"And you didn't see Falco in the parlor?"

She shook her head.

Lola's story was different. Shivering, dabbing at her eyes with a lace handkerchief and clutching her robe around her, she claimed at first not to have seen Falco, then changed her mind. "Now that you mention his name, well, earlier in the evening I might have done. Yes, as a matter of fact, I think I did, but you understand, mine was a fleeting glance. Busy last night so I whisked through the parlors. We're supposed to show up, you know, if just to parade through, but Falco was not here to see me. These days I'm booked in advance. Last night, among others I entertained—"

She stopped when she saw the madam's glower.

No one else heard anything unusual, no shouting, no strange noises.

Neither Serafina nor Rosa noticed any sores or bruising on the women's faces, no neck scratches, nothing behind the ears or at the base of the scalp, except for Lola, nursing her hand because of a spider bite, Rosa having tended the wound herself the other day. And Rosalia, too, had a scratch on her neck, from an unruly customer, she claimed. But she shook during the interview like a frightened goat, and Serafina ruled her out. She offered nothing, except an observation that, if anything, Gusti had been more secretive of late.

The three of them—Carlo, Serafina and Scarpo—were seated in front of Rosa in her office. Carlo, his long legs crossed, glanced at his watch, and Serafina ran a hand through her hair, searching for a passage in her notebook.

"Another log for the fire before we begin," Rosa said, pulling the cord.

When the domestic entered, she said, "Caffè and some hot milk, Gesuzza. We are four. And remind the laundress to fetch the sheets in Gusti's room."

Scarpo returned with the log. When he bent to throw it on the fire, shards of light from the flames bounced from his knife handle straight into Serafina's eyes. He sat back down on the edge of his chair.

"So," Serafina began, blinking, "Not much time, and we must go over what we know about Gusti's death, discuss any evidence that may shed light on the other murders, and we must review our list of suspects, and—"

Rosa said, "Not so fast. Are you forgetting your request for information from Scarpo about Eugenia and the smith?"

"Just getting to that. Scarpo?"

"What's this about?" Carlo asked.

"I asked Scarpo to find out two things—the whereabouts of Eugenia, and from the blacksmith, whether anyone had rented mules or carts from him beginning in early August through early October."

"Eugenia?" Carlo asked.

"A woman who worked here for a time. Others in the house accused her of stealing, and she left."

"I kicked her out," Rosa corrected.

Scarpo snapped his braces. "Hard to find, Eugenia, but yesterday, I was successful. Secunda told me, or at least—"

"Secunda?" Carlo asked.

"My name for her. She runs a house in Palermo, second in glory to mine."

Serafina rubbed her forehead. "Continue, Scarpo." Remembering the introspective turn Rosa's grieving took after Bella's body was found, she was glad for the madam's spikes today. Best to ignore them, or this would take all day.

"Secunda told me the story of Eugenia, and there was another in the room, a woman, beautiful, tall, with large—"

"The daughter," Rosa said.

"Let him finish!"

Rosa pursed her lips.

"The daughter and Secunda both said Eugenia was working in an unsavory house."

"Unsavory?"

"Secunda's word—a house in a rough area on outskirts of Palermo. You know the kind?" Scarpo asked.

Carlo nodded.

Rosa said, "Continue, Scarpo."

"Eugenia shared a bed with a *puttana* who worked days, and she, Eugenia, worked nights until some weeks ago, they said, when ..." He paused.

"When what?"

Scarpo looked at the floor. "When they found Eugenia's body."

"Where?" Serafina asked.

"Hanging from the rafters."

Rosa reached for her handkerchief.

Serafina asked, "Was there a letter or note? A piece of paper written in Eugenia's hand?"

Scarpo shook his head. "No note, and Secunda said it was as if all her belongings were stirred with a stick—blouses, undergarments, skirts, mixed into the bed clothes and thrown into a heap on top of the mattress. A mess. Her death closed that house of filth, Secunda told me."

"Good. Houses like that give us a bad name."

"And something else—a carving on Eugenia's face, Secunda said. Officials told her it looked like the sign of Charybdis."

Serafina and Rosa exchanged glances. Carlo regarded the cupids dancing in the ceiling's dome. No one spoke.

Serafina broke the silence. "So, possibly Eugenia's killer was the same one who kills Rosa's women."

They nodded and there was a pause while Rosa looked for a clean handkerchief.

Serafina continued, trying for a conclusion. "We know that Eugenia, who may or may not have been involved in the murders of Rosa's women, is dead. We also know that she could not have killed Gusti or had any part in her death, because she herself was dead. And, it's occurred to me that we don't know, really, if she was the one who stole items from *your* women," Serafina said, looking at Rosa. "So our killer is alive and may very well kill again soon."

Rosa looked like she'd seen a ghost, and she seemed to have shrunk in her chair. Except for two spots of color on her cheeks, her face was pale and Serafina thought she detected a slight tick close to the madam's right eye, but she did not refute Serafina's suggestion. Poor Rosa, she had held up so well throughout this grizzly ordeal, but she could tell that the madam was beginning to feel the weight of four deaths, and, perhaps, the ignominious and unnecessary decline of a prostitute's career after being accused, wrongly, of theft.

Serafina finished writing. "And what did the smith say about space in his stable or carts for hire?"

Scarpo summarized his conversation with the blacksmith: he had no free stalls for hire, because they were all taken by regular customers. Hadn't had an empty pen for years.

Carlo wound his watch.

"But one thing," Scarpo said, "I saw an old cart sitting in the corner. I asked the blacksmith whether it might be for rent. He said, no, belongs to a man, a poor one. The man collects from the rich, sells in the rough areas. That's his cart, he told me, and that's his stall."

"A ragpicker," Serafina said.

"That's what the smith called him," Scarpo said. "And I said, that's not a stall. And the smith said, big enough for the ragpicker. Couldn't rent it otherwise."

"What does he collect?" Serafina asked.

"Old clothes, broken furniture, rope, nets, things like that. His cart is always full, the blacksmith said. He sells goods in the rough neighborhoods, and he sharpens knives there, too."

"Why would he rent to a man who cuts into his business, so to speak?"

Scarpo shrugged. "Yes, I asked, too. The smith told me the ragpicker only sharpens knives in the rough neighborhoods, where the smith doesn't care to go."

While they were talking about the blacksmith and his knives, Serafina was half-listening. Her mind was wrapped around the swaybacked mule and the weather-beaten cart, remembering the number of times she'd seen that forlorn pair. "I've seen the ragpicker, I know I have, in the piazza and in the forlorn neighborhoods, as well," Serafina said. She told them about the commotion she'd seen when driving with Minerva. "Her hearing makes up for her lack of sight, and she sensed the altercation long before I did."

Again, Carlo looked at his watch. "Doctor Loffredo confirmed what I thought caused Gusti's death. Asphyxiation. Strangled by the scarf she wore. He's sure she was killed elsewhere, found some bruising on her back indicating her body was dragged to the spot where Rosa found it. Wants to perform an autopsy, but he's busy at the moment. Other autopsies come before Gusti's, and he has his practice. He wants to do it Monday morning and he asked me to assist."

Serafina filled Scarpo in on what they'd discovered this morning in Gusti's room, the scuffle and marks on the back stairs, the earrings, the box of jewels. "We believe Gusti was killed inside, probably in her room where we saw evidence of a struggle, bedclothes all knotted, coming off the mattress. Then her body was dragged down the back stairs where we found an earring. It matched what we found outside near her body. And we also know that Gusti struggled with her killer. We found a strand of hair in one of her fingernails."

Rosa said, "The girls are frightened. No help to us when we interviewed them, and now they're huddled about the kitchen table where Formusa feeds them *biancomangiari* and toasted bread. Which reminds me, where's our caffè?" She pulled the cord several times.

"Gusti's and Eugenia's deaths are related to the other three, but different," Serafina said. "The killer is cleaning up after himself, removing obstacles and clues."

"Cleaning up? Obstacles? You're not making much sense, not to me," Rosa said.

"The killer gets rid of threats to himself. Gusti knew too much, perhaps Eugenia, too."

Scarpo shook his head and Carlo squirmed in his seat and looked at the door.

Serafina said, "The more we know, the more I realize we are in danger."

There was a moment of hushed silence until Rosa broke it by telling Scarpo about her last conversation with Gusti who thought she knew something about the killer and wanted to speak with Serafina.

"We don't know much about Gusti, nothing about her family or where she was born, but she was bright, Gusti, and the smart customers all went for her," Rosa said.

"So she may have discovered the killer's accomplice," Serafina said. "We know that she kept to herself, except of course for her customers and her friends, and we know one of her good friends was Carmela."

Carlo's eyes widened at the sound of his twin's name in his mother's mouth. He reached inside his coat pocket, and told Scarpo, "We found two letters from Carmela hidden in Gusti's mattress." He handed both to Rosa.

After putting on her spectacles, Rosa began to read, using a finger to follow the words, mouthing them in a whisper, then summarizing the contents aloud. "Dated a year ago October, before any of this sorry business. She told Gusti about Achille, her lover. Life was good, she said. She missed their talks, told her to guard her valuables."

She passed the letter to Serafina who looked at the writing. "Yes, that's Carmela's hand, the letters so rounded, just like a child's." Her eyes filled, and she handed the letter to Carlo.

"And the second one?"

"Dated March 15, this year."

Dearest Gusti,

My apologies for not writing sooner, but for the last few months, my life has been in sorry disarray.

Achille left to join Garibaldi and his men, promising him extra coins, but since he never was paid for his service in 1862, so I am doubtful that this will be the case. In any event, I doubt I'll ever see him again. No

*matter, I say good riddance. Yes, we were happy, but
he's chosen a life without me, and as soon as he did so, I
cared no more for him.*

And now for the special news: I carry his child!

*Coins were scarce so after Achille departed, I walked
until I came to the orphanage. As you know Mother
Concetta is a good friend of Nonna and has made a
place for me. I care for the young children. My days are
full, and I am happy. One of the little ones reminds me
so much of Maria. How I do miss my family: Nonna,
my father, my brothers, sisters, and even, if you can
believe it, my mother, although I never could live in my
home again, not with her in residence. And of course I
long for our talks and laughs.*

*In answer to your question, take great care. Do not
become friends with her. We know her to be like the
weather, fair one moment, foul the next.*

Ever your friend,

Carmela

Serafina grabbed the letter. When she finished reading, she stared
into the distance, lost in thought.

"We know *who* to be like the weather?" Rosa asked, running a
finger up and down a page in her ledger.

Serafina shrugged. "Her letter raises questions, answers nothing."

"Oh, Gusti, you and your closed mouth," Rosa said.

Gesuzza returned, bringing a cart of food. Serafina smelled dark
mocha, coffee, ricotta, orange sauce and heavy cream. She tasted
bile.

"From cook," the domestic said. The bottom shelf held trays
of pastry—*sfinci, cannulicchi, cassateddi, minni della Vergine,
pagnuttella*; and on the top shelf, large cups with caffè latté, the
milk frothy, the drink steaming and topped with bits of chocolate
and powdered sugar.

"Couldn't eat," Serafina said. "My stomach and head are rocks.

"Nor I," Carlo said.

"Scarpo?" Rosa asked.

He held up his hand.

Rosa said, "Tell cook, she's such a comfort in our hour of need, but perhaps later. We'll take the latté. Close the door on your way out."

Serafina accepted a cup. "I want to bring up what's on everyone's minds. You may have heard it in the street, too, Scarpo. We need to face it."

"Stop talking like a professor of the unknown." Rosa sipped her caffè.

"The rumor in town is that Don Tigro is behind these murders." Serafina took a few sips of her caffè. "They say he wants Rosa's business. The deaths of Gemma, Nelli, Bella do not bear the mark of the don, and we know from Scarpo that you pay faithfully."

"Each month," Rosa said, wiping foam from her mouth.

"But these last killings smack of his style—the slipper stuffed into Gusti's mouth, a body hanging from the rafters of a cheap bordello." As she spoke, she saw Gusti's bloated face, Eugenia's bare feet hanging overhead, dirty and with toenails chipped.

Scarpo and Rosa shook their heads. "We'd know," Scarpo insisted. "La Signura pays. Every month I give him the money. His thugs come around for it. And before the don strikes, there's a warning—he likes the world to know—that's his way." He took off his bandanna, swiped at his forehead, and finished his caffè. "The rumor must have been created to comfort the crowd because the officials do nothing about these deaths, and no one can explain them. They are the work of someone sick in the head because of a woman or the work of the devil, such like that, but not the work of the don."

Carlo downed his coffee, looked at Serafina. "Ask him yourself. You're going there this afternoon to see Elisabetta. Put it to him then."

She nodded. "I intend to do just that, but before we continue, there's the matter of the lock. It's missing from the back door. Where are the keys?"

Rosa said, "I have a set and so does Scarpo. Only two were made by the smith."

"Show me your keys."

Scarpo pulled his from a chain attached to his breeches, and found the key to the lock.

"Rosa?"

Rosa had been searching in her desk. Her arm was into the drawer up to the elbow, and a not-so-delicate color washed up her face. "Missing," she said. "My keys are gone! You're right—there's an accomplice within these walls." Just as quickly as it had filled with it, her face drained of color.

Serafina turned to Scarpo. "This afternoon, go to the smith and have him change all locks on the doors. For now, have him make one set of keys."

He nodded.

She turned her notebook to the first page. "Our best lead is the monk." She read from the list they had made what, a week, ten days ago, quoting Scarpo, "There is one who keeps coming back, Signura, a stranger, he has a funny smell, not from around here. Pigheaded, too. Returns many times. Wears a brown cloak and hat."

Scarpo nodded and set his cup on the desk.

"And we found strands of hair in Gusti's hand," Carlo said. "Where are they?"

Serafina opened her book to the page where the strand was coiled and the fingernail dug into the paper. She turned up the wick on Rosa's lamp. The four stared at them.

Getting up for a better look, Scarpo put his head very close and nodded, gawping at the hair now gleaming in the light from the oil lamp. He picked it up, smelled it. "Has your smell, Donna Fina, now that it's wedged into your book." He sniffed again. "It could be the monk's, but it's hard to tell."

"Have you seen him recently?" Serafina asked.

Scarpo sat down, adjusted himself. "Last time I saw him, he was begging near the fountain."

"That's where I saw him," Serafina said. "Tessa's seen him there, too—"

"—talking to Gemma and Bella near the fountain," Rosa said.

"Right. Carlo and Vicenzu are riding with us to see Elisabetta this afternoon. They'll drive our carriage, and while we visit, they can snoop in the don's stables."

"Could be Falco's hair, too," Serafina said.

"Will you stop it with Falco! Like a dog and a bone you are with that man."

"Who is this Falco, anyway?" Carlo asked.

Rosa and Serafina glared at each other until, laughing, Rosa looked at Carlo and winked. "Falco is an old friend of your mother."

Serafina cut in. "An acquaintance from school. Now one of Rosa's frequent visitors."

Rosa waved a hand. "What do you know about my customers? He's harmless, adds a little sparkle to the evening."

Serafina was amazed at the twists and turns of the madam's mind, her inability to hold onto the truth when it came to her women and customers—those whom she liked, that is—and while she may have been convinced the other day of their culpability, her conviction did not last, and she reverted to her former belief, unable it seemed, to grasp for long that the charming could be dangerous. "He's the brother of Bella's father. He handed over his business to Falco after Bella died."

"Not to his sons?" Carlo asked.

"All killed in the war on the same day, I understand," Rosa said.

"All on the same day? Impossible," Carlo said.

"Battle of Milazzo," Scarpo said. "Hundreds killed."

"Falco gains the most because of Bella's death," Serafina said. "That puts him on our list of suspects."

"But what about the two other women killed before Bella? Why would Falco murder them?" Scarpo asked.

Carlo said, "He could have done. Could have started out with them in order to practice before he attempted the important kill, like dissecting frogs before tackling a cadaver."

Scarpo flicked a piece of dirt from his suspenders.

"Just what I said to you on the train, remember?" Rosa asked.

She flipped again.

Rosa rubbed her hands together. "But behind the story of Falco lurks the truth: in the end, murder is about money."

"If the murders continue, and Falco is behind them, you'll be ruined, and he'll have control of the house," Serafina said. "What we said on the train, remember?"

Rosa's eyes widened, and she nodded. "The wizard is right."

Serafina rubbed her forehead. "For now, let's say Falco is a strong suspect. We must be like jugglers. First, Falco costumed as a monk. Don't forget, he's an actor, and he's handy with a knife. I saw the carved figures in his shop last week."

"Anyone can dress as a monk. There are so many of them."

Serafina rolled her eyes.

"In Palermo we see them all the time," Carlo said.

"And while I think these murders are the work of one man, Gusti's murder could not have been committed without an accomplice, either living right here under Rosa's roof, or someone who knows the house well—well enough to steal Rosa's keys. And that points to one of the women."

"Or to me or Formusa or the laundress or Gesuzza," Scarpo said.

"But, I must admit, Rosa's right, anyone can dress up as a monk," Serafina said. "It means we must catch the killer in the act."

Silence.

Carlo said, "Forget the ragpicker, a false turn."

"No, I cannot. I must find out more about him," Serafina said.

Carlo gave her an elaborate shrug.

"We have guards, Signura, old Redshirts I trust," Scarpo said. "They're thick and plodding in the head, but good with the feet. For show, mostly, to scare away bandits on the road, but maybe they can help."

"Ask them to follow this ragpicker. Ferret out what they can," Serafina said.

Scarpo nodded.

"If you plan to catch him just before he kills his next victim, why follow anyone?" Carlo asked.

Serafina said, "You're forgetting about forewarned and forearmed. We need to find out as much as we can about these suspects. What if the monk is two or three people in a league? Or a gang of killers?"

Rosa clutched her chest.

Carlo threw up his hands. "Something else: I have an important test Tuesday morning and haven't studied. I was hoping to take the train Monday afternoon after the autopsy."

"You must. Don't forget your father's hopes for you. The three of us, Rosa, me, Scarpo, in Rosa's office tomorrow afternoon. We haven't much time. Today's the third. Gusti's and Eugenia's deaths don't change my mind about the monk's schedule: he kills on the sixth or seventh."

"There's a horror in my bones," Rosa said. "It sneaks into my soul, and a large latté doesn't take it away. Fina is right. The killer will strike again with reckless purpose, uncanny focus, madness eating his mind. He is the one we call the monk, but the monk could be anyone—Falco, say, who has a history of acting. But whoever he is, the wild one must have help from someone inside, the *strega* who wore those earrings when Gusti was killed. Where are they?"

Serafina dug into her purse and put them on the desk beside the book. They gleamed in the light of the lamp.

On the ride home, Serafina was silent. Beppe swung the gates open.

"This Falco?" Carlo winked.

"None of your business," she said and stepped from the carriage, surprising herself with the venom of her anger. She'd done it again, smashed another platter of porcelain.

No speaking until they reached the path to the front door when Serafina forced herself to look at her son, and her eyes moistened. "Carlo, forgive me, I know you were teasing. Usually I love it, but something's wrong with me today."

"No apologies. Hard morning." He looked at the ground, brushed lint from his coat.

"Are you visiting Carmela again?"

He nodded.

"Ask her about these." She handed him the earrings, kissed him on the cheek. "Tell her."

"Tell her what?" Carlo asked.

"Tell her how much we—"

"Need her?" he asked. His smile was crooked.

"Tell her how much I miss her," Serafina said.

Tessa and the Monk

Serafina looked up at a grey and curdled sky. A bougainvillea stood by the side of the house, one or two withered leaves hanging from its branches, and a few pansies bloomed. In another month they'd be gone. She heard a Scarlatti sonata coming from the parlor and glanced at the stone angel. "You're the only one smiling."

Serafina kissed Renata who stood by the oven stirring the sauce. She blew a kiss to Giulia who sat by the fire working in her book on a pattern of some sort. Were he alive, Giorgio would be there to kiss her and hang up her cape. She felt his presence by her side, usually reassuring, but today, inscrutable.

Totò ran to greet her. "Assunta took us to the gardens. I saw the white birds."

"Your favorites, my precious little man." Serafina kissed him. She reached over to kiss Tessa, who stood solemn-faced. "And Tessa, did you like the gardens?"

Tessa hung her head, arms hugging her waist. "I'm ready to go home now," she said, looking up at Serafina.

"You miss your mother."

She nodded.

"Of course you do. You miss your bed and your doll. You can go home just as soon as we, just as soon as everything is settled and—"

"You mean as soon as you catch the killer."

"Well, yes, that's it, precisely. And it's going to happen very soon." Serafina brushed a wayward strand off the child's face with her hands. "But today you want to be home. I know how you feel. Do you know how she feels, Totò?" Serafina's forehead raged.

He shook his head.

"No, he wouldn't, would he? He's not as wise as you."

"But he didn't see him."

"Him?"

"The monk. The one who talked to Gemma and Bella, the one I told you about. I don't like him."

"Let's sit down over there." Her heart raced as she walked with the children, taking each one by the hand to the sofa on the far side of the room. Its cushions were deep, and a brisk fire crackled in the hearth. "Now, tell me, about this monk. Where did you see him?"

"In the piazza. He wore a brown coat, and he smelled." She held her nose with thumb and forefinger and made a face.

Totò laughed.

"Gusti hates the monk. Carmela, too. Once I heard them arguing with Nelli and Gemma. He talked to Bella, too, I saw them together near the Duomo."

"Yes, you told me that on the train. I remember."

"Bella told me he was a special monk, but I didn't believe her. He smells like a shepherd. One night I heard Bella tell Gusti that the monk has marvels. I heard them shouting about him. Bella wanted Gusti to go with her to get the marvels, but Gusti wouldn't go. She just laughed. She said he was a snake and not a monk and no one can do marvels anymore, not since the olden days. Now they're all tricksters, but Bella said she was going to meet him anyway. I saw her going out."

"What did Bella say about him when she returned?"

"Bella died."

"I'm thirsty, can I have something to drink?" Totò asked.

"That's a marvelous idea. Tessa, what about you, would you like something?" Telling herself to stop the trembling, Serafina straightened the ribbon on the top of Tessa's head.

Tessa folded her hands, wiggling one row of fingers, then switching movement to the fingers on the other side. She looked at Totò. He watched her fingers, looked into her eyes, laughed. The ghost of a smile crossed the girl's lips.

"It's a snake," Totò said.

"It's not a snake. It's a spider."

"No. It's a snake, like in your story about the smelly monk,"

Totò said.

Serafina's head spun. "How about some hot cocoa?"

"Good!"

"And you, Tessa?"

She shrugged, nodded.

"Renata," she called, "make us some nice hot milk, the kind that makes mustaches. And a few cookies, too."

"But dinner will be ready in a few—"

Serafina put a finger to her lips.

"Cookies, too," Totò said. "Lots. I'm hungry."

"Me too," Tessa said and followed.

Renata rolled her eyes. She said something about spoiling.

Swinging her legs below the chair, Tessa hunched over the table and blew on the hot liquid. Serafina stood over her, ready to sprinkle more sugar and chocolate flecks into the froth. Totò blew on his foam. It spilled onto the table cloth. Giggles from both children.

"You are five now, or six?" Serafina asked.

Without looking up, Tessa took another sip of milk and spread the fingers and thumb of one hand in the air. Renata brought a plate of cookies, set it on the table in front of Totò.

Totò took a handful, shoved them into his face and gulped his drink. He looked over at Tessa. They laughed. Crumbs flew out of his mouth. Tessa reached out tentatively and took a cookie.

"Soon you'll go to school." Serafina smoothed the child's collar.

Tessa shrugged. She set the cup down, wiped her mouth with the back of one hand.

Renata sprinkled more chocolate flakes and powdered sugar into each cup.

"More story," Totò said, cookie crumbs now sticking to the drying foam around his mouth.

Tessa skated her eyes around the room and took another sip. "I saw him today near the birds."

Serafina bit her lip.

Pointing to Assunta, she said, "She brought bread for us and gave it to Totò, and when Totò went up to the water and bent down to feed the birds, I was alone. The birds flew away when Totò tried to feed them."

"Did not."

"Did too."

"Not. When I tried to feed them, they stayed, but when you ran over to me, you scared the birds and they flew away. I whispered, shhh, stay there, but you ran to me, anyway."

"Because of the monk, that's why. He came too close. His hand reached for me." She hung her head.

"Big wings, Mama. Big wings those birds have." Totò made flapping wings with his arms.

Tessa laughed at him and licked her milk mustache.

Serafina's breath was shallow. She knew she must calm down.

Totò said, "Tessa has to play with me now. I want to show her how to feed Octavia."

"Who's she?"

"Our goat, silly."

Tessa laughed.

"Be careful," Serafina said to their disappearing backs. "I don't want Octavia to get sick like the last time."

A soft knock. The door opened a crack, and Carlo's foot wedged itself into the space between floor and jamb. "Should we go away?" he asked.

"Of course not. Come in. Sit down on the chaise, both of you." Serafina wore her good watered silk, the dress Giulia made for her last month. She kissed them, went back to her dressing table where she sat and struggled with her hair. "Can never get it right, but Assunta is needed downstairs."

"Let Assunta help with the hair." Renata pulled the cord. "We've got to leave soon. Vicenzu and Giulia can watch the children while you finish, and Arcangelo stays here with Beppe, too. All fine."

Serafina told them about Tessa and the monk in the public gardens this morning. "We must keep a close watch." Adjusting the lace around her collar, she said, "Tell me about Carmela, now—I'm anxious to hear." She pinned on Maddalena's brooch.

"This is a week for crying," Carlo said. "First Carmela for her father and grandmother, next, Rosa for Gusti, and then Carmela for Gusti and for ... many things." He sat on the edge of the chaise, looking at Renata.

"Carmela cries for many things?" She turned to them. "So much emotion in one so young. Of course, it is because she is with child, and because she doesn't know her own mind. Oh, Carmela, my poor lost Carmela." Serafina rose, plowed around the room, whirling. She sat back down at her dressing table and willed the tears to disappear.

Carlo said, "She asked about you."

"The plain truth, no sugar. Last week she wouldn't speak or look at me."

"I heard. It's all too complex for my understanding. When I told her I had harsh news, she said 'Oh, no, not Mama!' The first words out of her mouth, I swear to you. I was amazed."

Serafina twisted her hands. "And how is she, Carlo? Inside, I mean. Her heart?"

He shrugged. "Don't know what to say."

"Would you say Carmela's confused, angry, hurt, frightened?" Renata asked.

Carlo said, "All of that. Plus, she's, well, slow, wobbly."

"Wobbly?" Renata and Serafina asked in unison.

"You mean weepy?" Renata asked.

He nodded. "Must be miserable in that dump."

"We begged her to come home," Serafina said. Twice. Does that mean she wants to come home now?"

Carlo shrugged. "Like Renata said, she's confused. Doesn't know what she wants. After all, her man left her to fight with Garibaldi."

"Left her with child, you mean. You call him a man?" Serafina began taking the pins out of her hair and throwing them on the table, brushing her curls. Terrible behavior in front of her children, she knew it, but could not, did not want to stop. Tears rolled down the cheeks. "My poor sweet child falls in love with a ... a rotter." The faster she brushed, the harder she cried. She ripped out some of her scalp along with springy bits of frizz. Finally she threw the brush on the floor, buried her head, and sobbed while her children looked on, helpless.

She felt their confusion, but they didn't move. From somewhere in her mind, she remembered Giorgio on a similar occasion, twisting his fingers in the air and taking out his watch. "We must give La Donna *Cinque Minuti.*" Giorgio, always the jester, but he knew her so well, and somehow tantrums were more fun when he was alive.

The memory did not lessen her emotion. She pounded her fist on the top of the dressing table. "Why, why, why, Carmela? And you, why did you have to die? Why?"

Out of the corner of her vision, she watched as brother and sister looked at each other, peeked as Carlo picked up the brush and set it ever so gently on the table, saw Renata restraining him from going to Serafina. Renata whispered something to him. The two, brother and sister, stood there unheeding Serafina's words.

Nothing for it but to lift her head. Her crying subsided. Carlo looked up from his watch and nodded to his sister. Renata tiptoed over to the dressing table and handed Serafina a linen. She looked at her daughter and gave her a bleak smile.

A knock.

Carlo sprang to open the door.

"Just in time, my sweet Assunta," Serafina said, her voice thick. "Do something please with this tangled mane of mine."

The Ride to Villa Subiaco

*S*erafina wished she had not arranged to visit Elisabetta today, but when she discussed the possibility of canceling the trip with her older children, they told her that the drive would do them all good, even in this afternoon's wet weather. Carlo seemed almost glad to be going, saying, "Good for us to get out, see the country, even in this foul weather. Help our heads." Strange, even Vicenzu looked forward to the ride. "We'll stay, Carlo and I, in the stables. I want to see their system of tending to the beasts."

And Serafina? Except for the day of Giorgio's sudden death, she couldn't remember a time when life has been so full of misery. It was a devastation, seeing Gusti's body, the violated form so foreign from the woman bursting with life just a few days ago. So far she, Serafina, had failed Rosa, her oldest, dearest friend, who was now faced with losing her business, one prostitute at a time.

As the coach made its way to Don Tigro's estate, a rolling fog crept over the land, shrouding the hills as if they were ghosts. Serafina and Maria sat on one side, facing Renata and Giulia. Vicenzu and Carlo rode outside—Carlo holding the reins, Vicenzu, a shotgun. Enough protection; after all they were on the road to visit the don's wife. What could happen to them?

Serafina tapped on her bag containing herbs and special drinks for Elisabetta. Her toes were frozen. She felt each rut in the road as the mules strained upward pulling their load. She compared their carriage—old and patched in places—with Rosa's, and the brisk, cushiony ride they'd had to Palermo last month.

She smeared fog off the window, stared at the dripping almond branches, and tried to imagine how they would look in spring, heavy with blossoms against a backdrop of lush fields. But today, most of the crimson and gold leaves that gave the landscape such mighty color a few weeks ago lay in soaking heaps upon the rocky ground, or hung in ones and twos from twigs, dripping and desolate. Did the soul of Gusti hover over them as she made her solitary way to eternity?

Renata clutched the basket of *dolci* she'd packed for Elisabetta. "Horrible, the weather," she said, her face as dismal as the day.

Serafina patted her knee. "You miss your routine, I know you, my sweetest girl. You like to stay at home, cooking our meals. Your kitchen keeps us healthy and together."

"Not all of us," Renata said.

"Carmela may be home soon. I feel it. Carlo saw her today, and I begin my plan, but it's too early to talk about it. Shhh, not a word to—" She pointed upward.

Renata and Giulia shared wide-eyed looks.

Maria pushed up her glasses, and rolling with the movement of the coach, studied a score. "Carmela? She wouldn't even look at you the other day. What makes you think she'll come home?"

"Study your score, precious. The ways of the heart are complicated."

They stopped for sheep blocking the way. As they started up again, Serafina said, "Giulia, the day dress Elisabetta wore on Friday when I saw her—the fabric was stunning, but the stitching, not so well finished as ours. Two more years to wear this black."

Maria said, "Some women wear it all their lives. Others, for six months."

"How would you know? You're only eight," Giulia said. "Some of the widows in Rome don't wear black at all, not even the first year. The baroness told me."

"First time we're wearing colors in public. Doesn't feel right with Papa not even six months in his grave," Renata said.

"Nothing feels right to you today, sweetness, but your father would want you to wear colors. You look splendid."

Serafina took Giulia to Palermo last month to buy the silk for the outfits they wore today. She created dresses for each of them with skirts not too full, trimmed in lace and thin satin ribbon;

Renata's in French blue, Giulia's in muted green, both gathered slightly at the waist and pulled to the back, giving them a touch of padding. In addition to a loose-fitting dress with long sleeves in midnight blue for Maria, she made a smock for her to wear over it. And when they were buying shoes for the season, the cobbler found a piece of cordovan that Maria fancied, the leather fine and light, large enough to make a pair of boots in her size, but at a cost well over Serafina's budget.

Giulia noticed the costumes of aristocratic women, especially the wardrobe of Lady Lanza, a fancy baroness and friend ever since Serafina delivered her children. The baroness told Giulia about Worth & Bobergh in Paris. "Last time I was there, I saw the Empress Eugénie disappear into a fitting room, and now everyone—I mean just everyone—goes to Worth's." Lady Lanza talked too much, Serafina had told Rosa, filling Giulia's head with ideas of Paris, telling her about Sarah Bernhardt, "that expensive tart who calls herself an actress. The French idolize her. Well, they would." All this bother of Bernhardt and Paris and poor Giulia would be doomed. But it wouldn't hurt for her to see Elisabetta's French gowns today. She could copy them, perhaps make a dress for Carmela, something remarkable with an indefinite waist.

"Glad I wore my cape today," Giulia said.

"Me too," said Renata.

Serafina held out the front of her cape, looking at her gold braids. Just like Queen Marie Sophie's. Her gloved hand brushed off a piece of lint.

Maria said nothing.

Renata elbowed Giulia. They giggled.

Maria looked at them, frowned, reached up, and knocked on the ceiling. "Carlo, stop this carriage," she yelled.

Of all her children, Maria surprised Serafina the most. She played Aunt Giuseppina's piano at two, the marvel of it vivid in Serafina's memory. The child asked unpredictable questions, had adult responses, and all her life, all she wanted was her piano. So serious, not at all like the rest of the family. For instance, Maria asked Giulia to embroider the bodice of her new dress. "Make gold and silver stars in the night sky: it will help my audience remember me," she had said. Serafina pictured her youngest daughter at the keyboard, alone, without her or the rest of the family, in a strange part of the world, wearing her midnight blue dress, reaching for the pedals with feet clad in soft cordovan.

The carriage stopped, and Carlo opened the door.

"Why aren't we there yet?" Maria asked.

"You stopped the carriage for that?" he asked. "Who made you the reigning queen?"

They laughed.

"But since you want to know, little sister, the road is not very good today. It's damp and soft. The wheels dig into the earth more than on a dry day, and the mules have a heavy load. In addition, Villa Subiaco is in the mountains, and we're going up a steep hill to reach it. The journey home will be faster." He made a sled with his hand and drove it downward, whistling to show her how fast they'd travel on the return trip.

Maria listened, holding her lower lip with her teeth. She nodded her head while Renata and Giulia snickered.

"What's so funny? I'm sitting here trying to catch the killer of Rosa's women," Serafina pointed at Maria, "and you ask your brother to stop the carriage while you two prickly pears laugh. As if we were watching the clowns at *Li Morti.*" Her remarks made Renata and Giulia laugh even harder. They slapped their skirts and held their stomachs.

Carlo shook his head, kissed Maria, and pushed her hat down so that it covered her face. "Time to get going. It won't be long now."

The mules strained and the wheels slowly started to roll.

Giulia said to Maria, "If you play in New York, I'd come to the concert, and I might stay and open a dressmaker's shop, or a fine house of fashion, like Worth's in Paris."

"Such dreams we have! Giulia, how old are you now, my honey lamb, sixteen?"

She nodded. "Almost a woman, and—"

Serafina stopped listening. She didn't understand her children. Their humor today, their dreams for tomorrow—wild. Most of all, she didn't understand the strength of her own feelings. Had she lost her focus? Had her wizardry vanished?

She felt like weeping for Rosa and her dead women and their dead dreams, for the poor dead Gusti, and for Eugenia whom she never met, but who, in Serafina's mind, hung unknown, slowly spinning from a rope attached to the rafters of a cheap bordello with the mark of the brazen serpent on her forehead. She felt like crying for spending too much on Maria's boots while their savings dwindled and their prospects dimmed. Her ears were plugged. Her curls, frizzed with moisture, made her scalp so tight it burned. She wished Giorgio were here because she needed to understand what was happening. He'd tell her in words that would make the world clear and well-ordered once again.

"Look!" Maria said. She pointed to movement in the fields. "An orange animal with a bushy tail."

They all moved to one side, and the coach tipped slightly. Silently they watched the animal's sleek movements, the stretch, the dazzle of him against the sodden earth.

"It's a red fox, my sweetest girls. Without effort he glides, how supple, how fleeting!"

They watched, silent for a moment.

"Oh, my! Look at that sweeping arc he makes against the grey sky, like the finger of God stroking the earth. How rare! Where did he go?"

"There!" Maria pointed to a tawny flash skimming over the wheat.

The field trembled in its wake. Then Serafina stared at emptiness.

"Blue patches in the heavens," Maria said, her finger marking a hole in the clouds.

The four of them sat back in their seats, not speaking, calm in the changing light, jostled by ungiving wheels on a dirt road.

At the entrance they stopped at an iron gate with a guardhouse. Vicenzu jumped down and, dragging his damaged leg behind, lumbered over, and gave his name to the armed guard who told them to pass.

When they turned onto the long gravel drive leading to the villa, Renata, Giulia, Maria, even Serafina, were without words. Men were everywhere, some in the palm trees lining the drive, removing fruit and withered seed pods, pruning dead fronds or raking the road several meters ahead. Others cleaned statues and fountains, pushed wheelbarrows, swept debris with pointed brooms.

With his veneer of culture, his love of theater, learning, and especially his knowledge of music, Don Tigro was an anomaly, not at all like the other mafia leaders in and around Palermo. This didn't lessen his violence—Serafina knew it could be quick and devastating—it only helped him prosper. It spread his sphere of influence among the cultured. He was a friend to the powerful, including, it was rumored, titled landholders, the subprefect, the leading clerics. Most, of course, held him in disdain. Others were puzzled by him, but he was worshipped by the men who served him. And in the countryside around Oltramari, this included all of the peasants who cultivated his soil, planted and harvested his wheat, tended his olive and almond groves. He hired the desperate who would do anything for him.

In her mind, Serafina was visiting the orphanage as a child with her mother, seeing Betta and Tigro, two of the orphans standing side by side. Inseparable the two, her mother told her.

Tigro was dressed in hand-me downs like the rest, but in bearing, he was straight and proud, muscular for a boy; his hands at his side, and so still, except for his thumb and forefinger, rubbing them together slowly, deliberately, back and forth. Then he was gone, banished by Mother Concetta, Betta told her, but didn't elaborate. She was on the edge of telling Serafina once, much later, as she midwifed the birth of her twins, but Betta never finished the story.

Early in Serafina's marriage, before the children started coming, she and Giorgio met Elisabetta and Tigro in town one evening, the four of them sitting together in the public gardens under the eucalyptus in early spring, with the doves cooing and the breeze soft and Elisabetta's stomach swollen. They sat, two young couples, talking of this and that. "Hasn't the weather been fine, oh, fine, quite ... the oranges bigger than the moon this year ... the peasants happy for once ... but now the papers talk of revolution, another uprising in Palermo ..." and out of nowhere, Tigro interrupted. "Betta carries my child, needs a midwife, will you—?" Giorgio's elbow found Serafina's side, but not before she had said, "Of course."

So long ago now, it seemed another life. Giorgio was dead, and poor Elisabetta, surrounded by ill-gotten goods, was a prisoner. How she had loved Tigro as a child in the orphanage, loved him even now, Serafina was sure.

And if Maddalena's story was true? Serafina shivered. ❧

Maria's Piano

The sun shone in earnest as the carriage pulled in front of the villa. Two liveried footmen appeared. Vicenzu jumped from the seat, probably ticking off in his head the cost of all this opulence. He limped over to one of the men who showed him and Carlo the way to the stables. The other footman helped the women out of the coach. They lifted their skirts and followed him up the marble steps to the entrance, where a somber man in formal attire opened the doors leading into the foyer.

Elisabetta, wearing a loose-fitting day dress in rose watered silk, greeted them. She was flanked by two servants. "This is Madama Mercurio, the housekeeper. She's married to our butler, Nello."

A familiar-looking face.

As if reading her thoughts, Elisabetta added, "When not attending to his duties here, Nello helps Tigro with his work."

"Enchanted," Serafina said to Madama Mercurio who, attired in black silk with a white lace collar, inclined her head and smiled.

Inside, Serafina's eyes were drawn to a vaulted ceiling with frescoed angels banded by egg-and-dart molding. Two young women dressed as maids stood to one side, curtsying when she passed.

Elisabetta gave them a tour of the house and led them to one of the parlors. "My favorite room," she told them.

It surprised Serafina, this space—an oasis in the midst of overstatement, shaped in an airy hexagon and decorated in cool colors. The furniture was light, oriental looking, most of it upholstered in floral prints, except for a small gilded writing desk and red plush chair in the corner. The windows were draped with batiste. Oriental carpets in patterns of blues, greens, and reds muffled the parquet floors. On the outside wall, floor to ceiling windows faced a sea of grass interrupted by a small garden. In the middle distance were groves of cypress and almond trees. Beyond these sat the Madonie mountains.

But the center of the room held its magic, a grand piano. Suspended from the ceiling and slightly to one side, so that its light rimmed the pianist, was a four-tiered crystal chandelier.

"Perhaps your daughters would like to stay here while the three of us go somewhere and talk." Elisabetta turned to Renata. "We won't be long."

Serafina looked at the piano, then at Maria.

Serafina watched as Maria's eyes riveted on the piano. She whispered in her ear. "Count the candles in that chandelier, and tell me how many there are when I return."

"A concert grand, a Steinway. If I had this room, I'd never leave." Maria began walking toward the keyboard. Serafina reached out, but Giulia stopped Maria first, grabbing the back of her smock.

Just then a sharp movement caught Serafina's attention. Looking out at the park and the hills beyond, she saw a man gallop into view. He dismounted, limped over to the head gardener. They exchanged a few words, and the gardener walked toward the house, wiping his hands on his apron. While the man in black led his horse to the stable, Serafina stood at the window; she recognized him, but couldn't remember at first where she'd seen him. Of course—in town with Betta the other day, helping her into the carriage. He had the same hobbled gait, the same cobra eyes. Was he the man Rosa and Scarpo called "the limping cobra?" She swallowed, feeling her heart race, and had to be brought back to the present by her daughter who looked at her with puckered brows. "Nothing, dear," she muttered. Quitting the room with a backward glance, Serafina saw Maria perched on the edge of her chair with a forefinger pointed toward the chandelier, counting candles.

Elisabetta directed Serafina to a parlor on the other side of the house.

"Let's sit here. The light from that window will let me have a good look at you," Serafina said. "I don't like the color of your skin, Elisabetta, and I see dark circles underneath the eyes. Are you resting, eating abundant meat, cheese, pasta, drinking goat's milk, or are you watching your figure and trying to do too much work?" From the corner of her eye Serafina saw Madama Mercurio nodding her head. "Ah, too much work, I thought so. This is true, Madama, no?" she asked.

"I'm between lady's maids right now, so Agata has taken on that duty as well as remaining my housekeeper, and she has her hands full. But in my condition, I feel lucky to have such a dear by my side."

A competent, self-effacing servant, Serafina could tell. She liked the woman.

"Lately I've had certain obligations—more entertaining, more engagements, Tigro and I. I have, perhaps, overdone?" She scrutinized Serafina's face. "Yes, you're right; I need to slow down."

"Make an appearance, excuse yourself, and retire by ten. For the sake of the unborn, tell him. He'll understand. I'll say something to him myself before I leave, and I can tell that Agata will make certain you do as I suggest." Serafina glanced at Madama Mercurio who smiled.

She continued. "May we talk with your cook? There may be some essential foods that you're forgetting to eat. Rest at least once a day, twice, if you'll be entertaining that evening. And I brought you this." Serafina reached down and opened her bag, pulling out several bottles. "The juice of medicinal herbs in a special mix, Mama's secret recipes. Two spoonfuls a day from each bottle— simple. Perhaps have a talk with your physician. Who knows? He might have a good idea, men sometimes do. But don't worry, all will be well if you follow my advice and Agata watches over you. I want to see you again the week before Christmas. Should we arrange it now? Say, Tuesday the 18th?"

Elisabetta teared up. "Serafina, I knew you'd make everything right. I thought, maybe I'm too old—"

"Too old? Nonsense! If Giorgio were alive, we'd be working at it morning, noon and night. Plenty of time for you to have another child, not to worry, and I see a touch of color returning to your cheeks already. Crying and laughing? Like the clouds and sun today." She took Elisabetta's pulse, patted her hand. Pulling out her stethoscope, she listened to Elisabetta's chest and stomach. "Heart strong like an ox, and the baby's, too."

Elisabetta kissed her on both cheeks, and Serafina saw the color bloom on the woman's cheeks. Arm in arm, the three walked down to the kitchen to speak with cook, who was preparing afternoon tea and laying out Renata's pastries.

If Serafina had this kitchen, she might even take a turn planning menus, perhaps even preparing a meal. But no, she must remain focused on solving murders. She must ignore this great domed room with kitchen hearth and spit, the double-oven newly blackened; covet not the cook's staff of six, the tiled walls and floor, the gleaming copper hanging from a central rack, the porcelain, the stemware, the silver.

A crash of chords. The crystal vibrated in response, and music filled the house. The kitchen staff looked up. Serafina cringed. "Brahms," she said, and turned to Elisabetta. "Maria's agog over him. Perhaps because he's young? I'll go up and stop her."

Elisabetta touched her shoulder. "Please don't. Let's go upstairs and enjoy it."

Maria was beginning the second movement when Serafina and Elisabetta walked in, followed by Madama Mercurio and two maids carrying in the tea service. After setting down their drays, they stood at the edge of the room.

Serafina motioned to Giulia who walked over to Maria and said something in her ear. Maria stopped. The audience groaned.

"What talent, Maria, my dear. Your mother told me, but I had no idea," Elisabetta said. Maria pushed up her spectacles, looking solemn.

The door opened and a voice boomed. "What happened to the piano?"

Maria faced Don Tigro.

"Continue, please," he said.

She looked at Serafina who nodded.

As Maria played, Elisabetta whispered something to Madama Mercurio who tiptoed out of the room, and in a few minutes, the housekeeper returned, followed by the other servants. They lined the walls—downstairs maids, kitchen staff, footmen, gardeners in their blue aprons clutching straw hats. The group was silent for the rest of the performance.

When Maria finished, Don Tigro showed his teeth and clapped. The rest followed. When they stopped, he spoke. "How old are you?"

"Eight."

"Well, thank you for the gift of Brahms. He fills my house today in a way I thought impossible. Third piano sonata, I believe?"

"In F-minor."

He nodded. "Written one year before this Steinway was made. I want to hear more from you very soon. One day you'll play your piano all over the world. And to think we have a prodigy in Oltramari." He lifted his head, closed his eyes. "Tea, my Betta?"

Elisabetta poured, and two maids passed out cups of tea, offering platters of sweets, orange, and almond sauces.

"Delicious pastries. My compliments to cook."

"Renata made them," Elisabetta said. "She was *Monzù* Alonzo's pastry chef last summer at Prince Zazzo's."

"Hit of the party. The marzipan centerpiece, memorable. I salute you, Signurina." He turned to Serafina. "After you've finished, I'll see you in my office." He walked over to his wife, said something in her ear, straightened his vest, and disappeared. "Agata will take you."

Serafina took a bite of pastry, sipped her tea, considered. Her melancholy had vanished. In its place, fire. ✐

Serafina and the Don

Two men dressed in ill-fitting suits stood outside Don Tigro's office. They held rifles pointed at the ceiling. Agata knocked and Nello opened the door, motioning for Serafina to enter.

Heavy with furniture, his office, not at all Elisabetta's taste. Three of the walls held books bound in tooled leather. Serafina ran a finger along one shelf. Felt for dust and found none. A footman began lighting gas lamps in wall sconces, oil lamps on desk and tables.

In a far corner, two young men slouched in velvet chairs around a table. They were expensively suited, reading the newspaper, and drinking caffè from china cups.

She walked over to them. "You must be Elisabetta's children."

They stood.

"Nineteen years ago, I delivered you, my first set of twins."

Shifting from side to side, they smiled and looked bored.

Nello, who caught up with her, introduced them. "Yes, these are the sons of Don Tigro. Franco, with black hair, Vito, red like his father."

The two young men bowed. Vito stared at her hair, then at his father's. Franco gave her a lopsided smile.

"Your mother has told me about your studies. *Bravi.*" She turned and walked toward the desk, not waiting for their reply.

Windows lined the outside wall. Through them Serafina glimpsed laborers packing up their tools for the day and wheeling carts out of sight. Afternoon light splashed orange onto violet hills, a winter sunset. In the sky, hawks circled high above the land, and Serafina thought of the fox arcing through the fields, swift and sure, breathtaking, deadly. One day, perhaps soon, he would be carrion.

Not short, not tall, Don Tigro sat at his desk in frock coat, grey vest, and a silk cravat held in place by a diamond stud. He breathed in, doubtless just enough air, his chest almost immobile, the rest of his body still. With a slight movement of his eyes, he beckoned to Nello who placed a wing chair in front of the desk and helped Serafina to sit. He and Agata quit the room, along with Don Tigro's sons.

The don raised his head and regarded her through half-closed lids, waved a hand back and forth, ever so slightly, to shadowy figures standing in dark corners. "Leave us now, Bruto, Iago."

The door closed after them.

He was still, not looking at her or at anything, it seemed. "Congratulations on the hard-won reputation you've earned as midwife. The people revere you. And now you embark on yet another adventure." His desk was empty, save for a single paper, an oil lamp, and a bowl of cut flowers: red geraniums.

"For the sake of my friend, Rosa, I sleuth," she said.

"Ah, yes. Friends since childhood, I believe. Like the three of us—you, me and Betta."

"I wouldn't call ours a friendship."

He ignored her remark. "Your mother, a wonderful woman. Knew her quite well, quite well." He stared at his desk. "But you know that." His eyes met hers.

"Everyone who knew her loved her," Serafina said, unflinching.

He nodded slowly.

"Why did you want to see me?" she asked.

He brought the corners of his mouth up a fraction. "Haven't changed, have you, Serafina? Born with a quick retort, the sting of a viper." He paused, waiting, perhaps, for her to speak, but she wouldn't dream of it, not now—bad timing.

"The killing of young women, that's what I want to talk about. You know these murders have nothing to do with our cause. Unthinkable. An indelible stain upon our honor to kill a woman, even a fallen one. Some are too quick to point the finger at us, the ones who look but do not see."

"Personally, I don't think you are responsible. The killings don't bear your gruesome mark, but people are saying that, whether responsible or not, you profit by their deaths. They say the murders weaken Rosa, force her to ask for your aid. Such a request would hand over control and profit to you, and Rosa's is a profitable business—make no mistake—but I tell you nothing you don't know."

"My business to know everything, often before it happens." He cocked his head and she could see the family resemblance in that movement, saw her mother in the angle of his head, and in the way shadows crossed his face.

He added, "Would I soil my hands for such little gain? Please. Rosa's business doesn't interest me."

"But you have—"

"Other houses. True. But they don't pay, not well. Their acquisition?—the misadventure of a fledgling businessman." He rubbed his thumb and forefinger back and forth. "When I was a young man, two or three asked for my help. Gave it to them in return for a larger cut. But the take?—a pinch of profit, not worth my effort. And I have simpler methods of watching men in high places."

He forced air through tight lips. "What interests me? The new world. Not this silly *centesimo* here, fifty lire there. Winning in my business is attainable only through expansion to other lands—the Americas, South Africa, where this gem comes from." He touched the diamond stick in his cravat. "Export, import. Doing business in a primitive land, raw with need, where desolate immigrants yearn for someone with power who speaks their language. My people."

Gazing at some inner vision, he said, "The times are bad for the peasants. They'll become worse. Europe's banks are about to fail, and when they do, whole villages will disappear overnight. Rosa's house? Not worth my trouble. In ten years, what is now the envy of every madam in Italy will be a deserted hulk. Lend me your support, declare your friendship—"

"Not interested."

"A pity. Then I cannot help you overcome the financial ruin which awaits you and your family. Soon you won't be able to support your children. You'll lose them. What about Maria? It takes money to build the career of a prodigy. And, no, I cannot help you find the killer. Three murders—too much for Rosa's reputation to absorb in three months, unless of course you want me—"

"Never." She leaned forward. "I'd be a fool to tackle your organization. Factions in the government, despite what they say, support you and your so-called honor, and if I made the slightest accusation against you, they would destroy me. But perhaps you could clarify for me what your interests are. And don't tell me 'diamonds in South Africa' or 'immigrants to the Americas.' You think me a fool? Your interests are here and now. Just to make sure we understand each other."

His eyes were shadowed. "You know what my organization does."

She rose from her chair and stood in front of his desk, her voice strong. "Oh yes, I know what you say it does: it protects. Protects whom from what? Rosa pays you each month, and what protection has she received? We come to an understanding for now. I don't believe you're involved in the killings at Rosa's house, but if I discover otherwise ..." She stopped, not for emphasis, but because she realized he didn't know yet about Gusti's murder. She swallowed to hide her surprise. She continued. "... I won't hesitate to lend my voice to those who whisper your guilt. But my voice won't have the meekness of a lamb, the decorum of a woman of my class. No, my voice will proclaim your guilt for the deaths of these violated women in the accents of a *strega*—shrill and unafraid. Do we understand each other?"

He looked up at her and flashed his extraordinary teeth.

Sitting on the edge of her chair, she leaned toward him. "Betta needs your help. Her skin coloring's not good, and she's got circles under her eyes. Her heart seems strong, so I'm not alarmed, but she's doing too much. If she needs to make social appearances, she'll have to leave early. Your guests will understand."

He nodded and something in his face shifted. "You have my word."

"I return to see her in three weeks. If her health hasn't improved, I'll recommend that she move closer to town."

He frowned. "We have an important dinner to attend in Prizzi on the ..." He hesitated, looked at his desk calendar. "This coming

Saturday, on the 10th. After dinner, she and Agata will be excused."

"You stay overnight?"

"Of course."

"In that case, I don't see a problem."

"How are you preparing for Maria's career?" he asked.

She was surprised by the question. "Only eight. She needs her family, her school, her music, and that's all. Far too young to play in public now. My aunt—"

"—is first harpist of the Palermo Symphony," he said.

"On her advice, Maria has two teachers in Oltramari, both respected by the musicians in Palermo, Giuseppina tells me."

"She's right," he said.

"One teaches Maria theory and composition, the other listens to her piano. When she's older, I'll reassess my plans for her musical instruction, but for now I want her to have a normal childhood. Too many prodigies don't. Too many children don't. That's all I wish to say about Maria."

Don Tigro was still. "Such plans you mothers have. My mother?—she never talked to me about what I should or shouldn't do. She understood my work, but she loved me. Never judged, never planned. Of course, I met her late in life."

Hard to breathe, as if the powerful forces whirling around Scylla and Charybdis engulfed her, squeezing the air from her lungs while she navigated treacherous straits. She felt dizzy and looked down at his desk, searching for a still point until her steadiness returned, and found it in the bowl of geraniums. Her eyes clung to it, as if to a lifeline when, suddenly, she saw the blooms as if for the first time, remembering finding the flowers on her mother's grave, and knew for certain that she and Tigro shared the same mother. Had he told Betta? No, of course not, Tigro held the secret close to his chest, a deadly weapon, waiting for the right time to wield it, when it would do the greatest harm. Her children must never know.

She rubbed her forehead. "Being a mother is impossible at times. We act, knowing even as we do so that we're wrong."

"You speak in riddles. In the realm of motherhood, I would think there is no right or wrong—only love."

Serafina rose. "And now we've finished." ✍

A Near Miss

The hills burned with light. Hoping for another glimpse of the red fox, Serafina held up a gloved hand, shielding her eyes from the strength of the setting sun.

"I think they liked my performance," Maria said.

"Who wouldn't love it, my precious? Keep up your Brahms."

"What?"

"Brahms, good for the fingers, Papa would say."

Renata and Giulia exchanged smirks.

"How does Don Tigro know Brahms?" Maria asked.

"Betta told me he spent some time at the Naples Conservatory and got to know many musicians. And musicians talk."

"What instrument does he play?"

Serafina laughed. "He doesn't play, my precious. I don't think he studied at the conservatory at all. Who knows what he did in Naples?"

"Papa told me that Don Tigro is a bad man."

"Your papa was right." She crossed herself. "Don Tigro does bad things to good people in order to make money, and he takes money from everyone, even from our store. If you don't pay him monthly, bad things happen to you or to your family or your store."

"Pay him monthly? You mean, he's like a bank?" Maria asked.

"Worse," she said.

"Then why do you talk to him? Why did we go to his home today?"

Serafina opened her eyes. "First of all, Elisabetta is my friend. I've known her since I was your age. She asked me to deliver her baby and wanted to see me today to make sure she was on the right regimen. I gave her *Nonna's* recipe for a healthy pregnancy. Second, Don Tigro, who happens to be her husband, asked to see me after the Brahms. And the way to deal with bad people is to meet them head on, not to pretend they don't exist."

"Like you do with Carmela?"

Silence except for the mules blowing air through their nostrils and Renata's elbow hitting Giulia's side.

"Honey lamb, that is a deep question, very deep." Her eyes moistened. She thought a moment. "We all need to find our specialness. That's my difference with Carmela."

"Because she never found it?"

"No. Because she never looked for it," Serafina said.

"Don't cry, not again. Where's your linen, Mama? When we get home, I'll play Scarlatti. You'll feel better."

"Play whatever you want. All beautiful from your fingers."

Another rustle of silk from Giulia or Renata, one of them.

"But today, as your brother Carlo said earlier, is a day for tears." She kissed Maria. "Now, Giulia, tell me about the dresses. Any ideas?"

They hit a bump. Maria laughed. "I like it better when we go downhill." She tapped the ceiling. "Faster!" she yelled.

An answering tap from above, and the scenery blurred. Swaying, Serafina hung onto her seat.

Renata said, "Elisabetta took us to see her wardrobe while you were talking to Don Tigro, and—"

"You should see it—a huge room on the top floor, windows on one side, mirrors on the other. Two closets in the room," Giulia said.

"And the closets are rooms, too," Maria said. "Full of gowns and day dresses, suits, capes, furs."

"The colors and the fabrics, her style, all so different," said Renata.

"From Paris, the House of Worth & Bobergh," said Giulia. "All that gathering in the back. Too much, I don't like it. How do they sit?"

"Elisabetta does for most of the day, my darlings. You saw her servants running."

Giulia said, "The stitching, the finishing, even the lining is magnificent. But my designs are more interesting."

"Good for you, my darling seamstress. Finally you see your own talent."

"Only the fabric is so fine, so beautiful, the colors so alive, the wools, plaids, silks, such texture. We don't have that selection in Oltramari."

"Then we must go to Palermo. To the finest of shops. You pick out the fabric and improve on the design of Worth and Whatever by making your own. For once in her life, Aunt Giuseppina made a good choice, sending you the subscription to *Godey's*."

Renata rolled her eyes.

Serafina heard a ping. The carriage swayed. They rocked back and forth.

"What was that?" Renata asked.

"Nothing, my genius. A stone hitting the side of the coach."

"I counted her gowns—one hundred and forty-seven. Why does she need so many?" Giulia asked.

A shot rang out. Serafina's eyes popped, but her daughters seem unconcerned. "They entertain, my cherub. And they are invited. That's all they do, give dinners and go to dinners." Serafina grabbed the blanket behind her seat bench and steadied her breathing. Turning to Renata, she said, "Why the frown?"

"I was just thinking. All that splendor, and look at the peasants. See them?" She nodded to a group walking by the side of the road. "Shoeless," Renata said.

Except the one who rides in the weather-beaten cart, Serafina realized, but kept it to herself, hoping her hunch about the ragpicker was wrong, hoping he would be intimidated by the rifle Vicenzu held. *Why didn't I ask to borrow the guards?* "Yes, our shame. For thousands of years, they've been used." Her eyes followed the cart, twisting her neck to watch through the rear window as it shrank slowly, now partially hidden by dust.

More shots. The coach sped, swayed.

"Quick. On the floor. Now!"

Serafina covered her daughters with the blanket. "Not a peep," she said, trying to still the trembling in her hands.

Then she saw someone on a black steed speeding toward them. She thought it might be ... yes, it was the man she saw in Betta's park today. Her throat swelled. Blood pounded in her ears. Maria popped her head up. "Down, Maria," Serafina said.

"But I'm suffocating under this horsehair," Maria said.

Gunshots, too many to count.

A silvery ping, a scream from Vicenzu.

Largo in the lead gave a hee-haw bray. The carriage halted.

Sound of hooves growing louder.

She looked back to see the rider very close now. Coming to kill us all. Must divert him. Opening the door, she said to the moving blanket, "Stay here, all of you. Don't move a muscle until I say it's safe to come out. That means you, Maria!" The blanket stilled. Grabbing the rail, she searched for the footplate, her boot almost sliding off it, took a deep breath and jumped down.

Shaking her skirt and holding a linen to her nose, she peered up, saw Carlo bending over Vicenzu. Untying his bandana, the limping man slowed alongside their coach, his horse kicking clods of dirt into Serafina's face. He grabbed the rail, pulled himself up to the driver's seat, and bent over Vicenzu.

"You! Off now!" she said.

Cobra eyes looked at her, continuing to hold Vicenzu.

"Off!" she yelled. She grabbed the rail, started to climb.

"It's Carmine from the don's stable. He's helping!" Carlo shouted.

Vicenzu lifted a pale face to her and managed a smile. "Lucky for us he rides to Oltramari to visit his parents this evening."

"Bullet ricocheted, nicked his upper arm. Bad aim, the bandit," Carmine said. He gestured to a moving cloud of dust in a distant field. The cart, she was sure. The peasants had gone. They must have scattered with the first shot.

On the rest of the ride, they were quiet. Dusk mantled the fields, and Serafina felt the chill of early evening. Fingering gold braids, Serafina was glad for the warmth of her cape. She dozed, and had a vision. She saw her husband's face in the casket, but his body had become Vicenzu's lifeless form. Waking with a start, she told herself that her son had nearly killed, thanks to her, an innocent, beautiful son. Not enough that his leg had been maimed by a galloping horse and left for dead in the streets, oh, no, and such a genius with numbers which she seldom stopped to appreciate or to praise, but once again, she had disregarded him, just like her other quiet children, not caring enough to consider the precariousness of allowing him to ride next to Carlo. She hit the side of her thigh and swayed with the coach, presently falling into a deep sleep.

When she awoke, it was almost dark, but they were on the edge of town and should be home before curfew. If not and they were stopped, Serafina would talk to the roadside guards. For her family and to find the killer of Rosa's women, she'd do anything. Anything. She gazed out the window, not at the passing scenery, but at the plan she was forming. It was spread out before her, shining, a rough sketch right now. Today she had eliminated two suspects—Don Tigro and the limping cobra. Time to catch the monk.

A Lair in the Rocks

Sunday, November 4, 1866

*S*erafina tossed. The Duomo's bells chimed midnight, half-past. She turned, tangled up in sheets. Slept, woke, worried about the safety of her children. Then she worried about coins. When the bells gonged two o'clock, she pounded out of bed, and opening the shutters, breathed in the night air, gazing for a time at the moon.

Since she couldn't sleep, she might as well go over her notes. Sitting at Giorgio's desk in far corner of the bedroom, she scrabbled about in her notebook, sure that she'd forgotten something. With care she read again her impressions of everyone she'd interviewed, reviewing the list of suspects she and Rosa had made, now whittled down to two—Falco and the monk. Then she made another list. She labeled it 'Sitings of the Cart': 1) Outside the shoemaker's, spewing feathers and old clothes; 2) On Via Saturnalia with Minerva; 3) Near the rope seller's shop; 4) On the highway (the wounding of Vicenzu). The last one, she circled. Serafina rubbed her eyes. Something, a ragged bit of information she failed to understand, tossed about her mind. It was important, she was sure.

Scrambling to her feet, she gave one last look outside. Leaning against the sash, she pictured Giorgio, his body lean, his curls dripping neroli oil. The image vanished. Beyond the chestnut tree in the front garden, she could pick out shapes in the piazza next to the statue. A cart near the fountain? Her breath caught in her throat. Was it the ragpicker? The begging monk?

She shut the window, sat on the edge of the bed and thought, trying to quiet the pounding of her blood. In a while, when her eyelids felt like splintered shells in sand, she snuggled into the covers and fell into a sound sleep.

Serafina watched the sun melt the mist. Deserted the shore, as usual, at this hour. She stared out at the Tyrrhenian Sea, telling herself to be watchful. From now on her movements must be deliberate: she had two more days to catch the killer.

For the past several mornings, she had combed the beach close to where she found Bella's reticule, but so far, the tall grass yielded nothing more than bits of old newspaper and cloth, the shells of sea urchins, the sticky remnants of a spider's web. Had Bella been killed elsewhere, her purse washed here by chance?

Yesterday she noticed a boulder and some smaller rocks partially covering what looked like an opening in a massive outcrop that stood below the orphanage. She was able to squeeze through the fissure into a small space, but the darkness prevented further exploration.

Before she set out this morning, she shoved her notebook, a lantern, some candles and match sticks inside Giorgio's old knapsack, and slinging the bag over her back, started off on her usual trek down to the lower part of town, determined to uncover as much as she could before leaving for Palermo to keep her appointment this afternoon with the contessa.

Serafina consulted her watch. Seven o'clock, still plenty of time before there'd be others on the shore. She squeezed past the boulder, its sides slick with dew, and stood for a moment. After mopping her brow with a linen, she lit the lantern and peered inside at a long narrow hall of stone leading into blackness. She was interrupted by a voice behind her.

"What are you doing here?" 🙟

Part Three

November 4 – 12, 1866

Biancomangiare

*S*urprised, Serafina swiveled, slipped on wet stone, catching herself for a moment on the boulder before tumbling to the ground. The lantern, by some miracle, landed upright.

The figure rushed to her. "Hurt?"

"Fine, I think." Serafina brushed sand from her skirt. Her hand flew to her chest. "I might ask the same of you. I mean, why are *you* here?" *Mind your tongue, let her lead the way.*

"I've been watching you snoop around these rocks for a couple of days. Orphanage above us. See? Why are you up so early?"

"Investigating the murders of Rosa's women. Police do nothing. I found Bella's reticule here, and I'm looking for more evidence. Why aren't you with the orphans?" She bit her lip. *No more questions.* She gave her daughter the ghost of a smile, only one corner of her mouth upturned.

"My day off. You'd better rest."

They leaned on the rocks and looked at the sea.

"Carlo told me about Gusti." Carmela looked down. "And Mother Concetta gave me a mighty lecture."

"Don't pay attention to that old nun."

"No, she was right. Always is. Hate to admit it, but—" Carmela's eyes were wet. "I should have said, I shouldn't have said—"

My poor girl. "Enough words. No need for more." Serafina held her daughter, not for the first time, and she vowed, not for the last. No more separation. Never again, never. She'd cling to her children like urchins on the floor of the sea.

They sat. Then Serafina told Carmela what she'd learned so far about the murdered women, the suspects, Rosa's other prostitutes, the guards, the maids, Formusa, Scarpo, Falco. She summarized the meaning of the marks on the victims' foreheads, the significance of the six and seven. Retrieving her notebook from the knapsack, she went through the pages, making sure she'd left nothing out. "The killer strikes on the sixth day of the month, kills on the seventh. We have two days to create a foolproof plan."

"Turn up the wick and let's go," Carmela said.

Serafina looked back at the outcrop—the rocks steep and wet, treacherous, it seemed from their vantage. "Not in your condition."

"What would *Nonna* say?"

Serafina chewed her cheek. "She'd say, 'Baby the baby, not the mother.'"

Serafina consulted her watch pin: only eight o'clock, they still had a few hours.

After climbing the rocks and squeezing through the opening again, they walked through a long winding hall, the ceiling at least five meters above them, and heard the sound of dripping water, of slithering creatures. Serafina smelled must and dead animals and human waste. Her curls tightened. She held up the lantern, lit a candle for Carmela.

Stepping slowly forward, Serafina slipping a few times, their wicks guttered as they entered another cavernous space. Water dripped from the ceiling, beaded on the walls, and pooled on the floor. In the middle was a long table with a few chairs scattered about. One was overturned. In the corner were piles of rags and papers, a matted brown cape, gloves, a skein of rope.

"Look at this." Carmela pointed to a red spot on the table.

"The mark of the serpent," Serafina said.

"Freakish, this lair."

"The den of a madman, I'm afraid." Serafina lowered her voice to a whisper and pressed her fingers against the table top, ashamed of her trembling. "Doubtless the place where he executed Rosa's women." Serafina looked at her daughter. "Let's get out of here before he returns. We've no weapons."

Their flames were nearly extinguished when they clambered out of the cave.

"Go back and rest, my sweet girl."

"Not a chance. Let me help. I've got to. Gusti was my friend, Bella, too. I owe it to them. I know so much about the women and the life at Rosa's."

Serafina held her breath.

"And right now I have a hunger for Renata's *biancomangiare*."

"Rosa picks me up soon to visit the contessa, and when I return, we'll plan. Until then, you can rest and eat." Serafina cuffed her tears and followed her daughter home.

Tears. Kisses. Hugs.

"Carmela's home!" Vicenzu yelled up the stairs.

"At least for today. My day off. I haven't told Mother Concetta—"

"We'll tell her," Vicenzu said.

"Renata, some food for Carmela. And get your poor sister something to drink. Assunta, change the linen on her bed. Giulia, Carmela's clothes need pressing. What can we get you, my sweet girl? Oh, where's the food for this poor child, Assunta? And do we have—"

Carlo came into the room with the children. Rubbing her eyes, Tessa wanted to know if it was Christmas. Totò, hiding in Maria's robe, pointed to Carmela. Maria was silent.

"You see?" Serafina held out her arms like Cicero addressing the senate after one of his fat orations. "My daughter, she knows. She knows how much I've missed her. She knows how much this family needs her. Suffered too much. No more loss. No more words."

"You? No more words? Not a chance!" Carlo said.

"Now we are whole. When I return, we'll plan."

"Return from where? No, don't tell me, it's too early."

"Where's my food?" Carmela asked. ✍

The Contessa

On the way, Serafina told Rosa that Carmela was home. "The news of Gusti, I think, brought her to her senses, and she insists on helping us."

After the tears, the hugs, the madam telling her how glad she was that Carmela was home, Serafina summarized her meeting with Don Tigro yesterday afternoon. "Can you imagine? He didn't know about Gusti's death, or even about Eugenia's body swinging from the rafters."

Rosa laughed. "Don Tigro's got his spies everywhere, scuttling back and forth to him with their stories. Worthless crabs—they should have told him all about Eugenia. A prostitute who steals can signal a dangerous business, and he should have known about the likes of her. But far worse, he hadn't heard about Gusti's death? How stale the air he breathes."

Serafina said, "Proves he's not the one killing your women—he's got his ear to another ground."

"Good. Then I'll forget to pay his—"

"No!" Serafina said. "And we can forget about the limping cobra, too." Serafina told her about the shooting incident on the road late Saturday. "If it weren't for Carmine's help, I shudder to think—"

"You take too many chances." Rosa crossed herself.

"Can't sit at home, afraid of my own shadow." The carriage swayed, but it was Rosa's coach, so the wheels hummed. "I've a family to feed, but I should have asked you for the loan of two guards. Vicenzu was shot. A graze, thank the Madonna."

"Fina," said the madam, clutching her chest, no more rides on the road without the guards."

When they arrived at the contessa's, a maid greeted them. Rosa sat next to a plate of sweets while Serafina feasted on the bold design of the room. Each corner was decorated with contrasting furniture—a red lacquered Chinese cabinet next to a zebra-striped chaise lounge, carved walnut tables paired with plush chairs. Near the hearth, a sofa upholstered in green velvet faced a pair of wing chairs, one in red and green plaid, the other in deep rose damask, the footstool in chrome yellow sailcloth. A chestnut desk stood in front of shelves holding books in no apparent order, some with cracked spines suggesting that the contessa was a reader. Paintings hung on ochred walls. Oriental carpets lay on black and white-tiled floors, and drawing the eye upward, angels twisted into a vaulted ceiling. None of the usual shabbiness of the nobility here.

Serafina roamed around, stopping at a gilded table. She lifted up a terra cotta cherub sitting on its top and discovered the inlaid profile of Dante, his gaze 'unblinking into the future,' Giorgio would have said. Wishing she had Dante's vision, she stepped over to the desk, and her eyes caught the miniature of a man in formal attire, a medal pinned to his sash. According to the gold inscription in the lower left-hand corner, the picture was taken several years ago by a well-known Palermitan photographer. Next to it, she noticed a piece of paper lying on the desk, folded and held in place by a brass weight. She opened it, a draft for five hundred lire dated Friday, August 3, 1866. Drawn on account from the *Banco di Sicilia*, it was made out to Francesca Grinaldi and signed by Bella Maria Baldassare. It confirmed Nittù Baldassare's story and the truth of what Bella told her father, that the prostitute's departure from Rosa's had begun two months before she was killed. Bella was shedding her old life for a new one, like a snake does its skin. Serafina returned the note.

She walked to the outside wall and gazed at the palms and domes and parapets of Palermo. In the distance, Monte Pellegrino brooded over the city. While Rosa sat on the sofa coveting *dolci*, Serafina turned this way and that, picking up a book, plumping a pillow, until she heard footsteps in the hall, when she busied herself by studying a group of drawings on a nearby wall.

"Rosa, darling, you look wonderful!"

"Francesca—beautiful, even in grief," Rosa said.

The two women kissed, and handkerchiefs sallied forth.

"Since the last time I saw you, how the world has changed, like this: presto!" The contessa snapped her fingers.

Rosa cried.

The two women hugged each other again.

"How will I go on, Rosa, dearest? But I forget myself. Here is your old friend, Serafina. Saw her at the wake, didn't I, but we haven't met." Francesca stirred the air with an encompassing gesture. "Doubtless she's not comfortable in this unfamiliar setting." Arm in arm they walked over to the wall of prints where Serafina stood examining one.

Indicating the drawings, Francesca said, "By Serpotta, studies for *La Carita*. Fun, aren't they?" She pointed a finger at the bare backside of the Christ child, the drawing in foreshortened perspective. "No doubt you've seen his work in the Oratory of San Lorenzo?"

"But of course," Serafina lied.

Rosa stepped in. "How to introduce my Fina? She's my oldest, my dearest friend. And, 'Cesca, you know the police do nothing, so I've asked her to investigate the deaths of the women in my house. She thought that you, being Bella's closest friend, could answer one or two questions."

As Rosa talked, Francesca and Serafina looked each other up and down, the contessa lifting her chin to peck the air above Serafina's cheeks.

"Yes, I'd like to hear about Bella," Serafina said.

Francesca nodded, but at the mention of Bella's name, both she and Rosa teared up again. Beneath the contessa's heavy makeup, Serafina saw the pale transparency of skin below her eyes, the drawn look on her face, and, yes, the wrinkles.

Standing before her was a woman in her late forties or early fifties, considerably older than Serafina, a fading blonde, her hair held in place with a snood. Arresting eyes, dark green with flecks of orange. Tall, even taller than Giuseppina, and with those same long bony fingers. Unfortunate breasts, though, a pity.

Like the décor, her dress was a surprise, showing no signs of mourning. She wore a full skirt of honeyed maroon in watered silk that, when she sat, revealed the antique lace of her petticoat. A short wool jacket with ruckled sleeves in brown and yellow plaid with alizarin crimson stripes covered a low-cut linen blouse. Her black slippers had gold clasps, her stockings of heavy rose silk. A strand of pearls and a long chiffon scarf gave her a flowing look. Except for the tape measure draped around her neck, she could have emerged from a plate in *Godey's*. On the spot Serafina decided she liked this woman, despite her melodrama.

"Chilly in here, even with the sun. Warmer near the fire." Francesca motioned for them to be seated.

The contessa settled herself in the rose wing chair facing her guests. "Please call me Francesca," she said to Serafina. "My late husband, Federico d'Alco, gave me a title but no children. He followed Garibaldi and what was his reward? An early grave. Now that Bella's dead, I am so alone." Chiffon floated in the air. "Oh, I feel too much for my own good," she said, flapping her arms like damaged wings, "when all around me is chaos, the peasants starve, the bandits kill, madmen rule the world, and I, not content with my crust of bread, pursue impossible dreams, impossible now that Bella Maria ... why did she have to die?"

"I need to know more about her life, especially in her last few days. That's why we've come to you. We're hoping you can shed some light," Serafina said.

The domestic entered carrying a tray with coffee and pastries. Surrounded by silver and china pieces, a cassata caught Rosa's eye.

"It's early and you have a long journey back to your little village, Oltramari, but do have some refreshment while we talk."

"You are too kind," Serafina said.

"I've heard so much about you. Bella told me that you saved Tessa's life."

Accepting a large slice of cake from the domestic, Rosa thanked her and said, "Enjoys full life my girl, Tessa." She took a large bite, swallowed her caffè, and, chewing, said, "Fina is a wizard. If anyone can find the killer of my girls, she will."

"Please, if there is anything at all I can tell you, anything." The contessa's eyes filled with water. She dabbed at her eyes, drank her caffè, and leaned over to take a cookie.

Serafina sipped her caffè and reached for her notebook. "Do you know any reason why someone would want to kill Bella? My best guess is that she and the other prostitutes were murdered by the same person, a madman, a killer acting alone."

The contessa nodded. "I read an article in the *Giornale di Sicilia* about the first two killings. Bella Maria was alive then, and showed it to me, and I remember telling Bella it was time to leave." The contessa blotted her lips with the napkin. "Bella was afraid, but for the others, not for herself, no, never for herself. 'I am old. He'd never choose me,' she told me. Oh, bitter words." Francesca sniffed. "We never had a disagreement and, let me see, we've been working together, had been working together—" Francesca looked out, lost now, like a bird felled in mid-air.

"My deepest sympathies, Francesca. How did you and Bella meet?"

"Childhood friends, like you and Rosa. Our families are both costumers, have been for centuries. We'd get together for feast days." Francesca, with an empty look, gazed into the room. Minutes passed.

Serafina felt the rawness of Francesca's grief.

Still peering into middle distance, the contessa said, "Brave, even as a girl, Bella Maria. I often wonder what her last thoughts were and if she ... if she cried out in the end."

Silence except for the ticking of a clock somewhere, and the muffled sounds of the city.

"Bella told me she was leaving in November, this month," Rosa said.

Still writing, Serafina asked, "Did Bella have enemies?"

Francesca shook her head. "Sweet-tongued, Bella. Not like me. Mine is like a serpent's by comparison." She gave the room a half-smile.

"And you planned to go into business together?"

"We were in business together. She gave notice to Rosa, I think, or at least meant to, after the Princess Rosso asked us to design her wardrobe for next season—day dresses, gowns for at least six balls, outerwear, even a coat for her dog. Oh, I rushed to Bella Maria to tell her, had my driver take me, didn't bother with my hair, brought material for Bella Maria to see, samples the princess picked out from our scraps."

"And this was when?"

"In July. I'll remember the day on my deathbed. Third Wednesday, July 19. My domestic rushed in. 'Contessa,' she called, 'it's the Princess Rosso and her French dog.' Bella Maria was so happy when I told her."

Serafina wrote down the date. Rosa helped herself to a few cookies.

"The first large order. Our dream appeared before our eyes." The contessa blew her nose. "I don't know how much you understand of high fashion." Her smile was withering. "A man from London established one of the first houses. Worth is his name. I met him through friends of my husband when he first came to Paris. He designed a wardrobe for the Queen. Sissi wore one of his gowns for her royal portrait. The court talked of nothing else, and that gave him his start. But you see, wars have changed us, especially women. Now high fashion is not exclusively for the court, but spreads to anyone with a title and money. Or if only money, no matter—the title will follow. Bella and I wanted to be a part of this. She was the creative force; I have the contacts."

"Designed our gowns, and gave our house a look." Rosa patted her curls. Turning to Serafina, she said, "Must you make so much noise when you write?"

"Scratch away, I'm used to being around all sorts of people." The contessa lifted her beak and smiled. "As a child, Bella designed our dresses. Always sewing, unhappy at school until the nuns gave her the job of making the vestments and whatnots. She loved to sew for the priests. Had that awe of the church and its clergy which I never had, never, but Bella did. You might say, she had a craving for such things." Francesca brushed crumbs off her skirt. "I'm the one who knows people and, being from a family of tailors, I know how to sew a little, but more important, I know the language of the trade."

Patting her lips with the napkin, Francesca examined her watch pin, rang the bell, and stood. "Bella and I knew it would be hard to plant our feet in this business, so we had this room decorated. Bella's design, no expenses spared." Flinging her arm upward, she said, "Hired a painter for the ceiling. Needed to have a room suitable for greeting our clients." Her voice faded. Serafina could see the woman clutching at the back of her dream.

The domestic entered. "Finished, La Grinaldi?"

"Kindly take away the tray." She pulled at her watch pin and turned to Rosa. "Two o'clock. You have only thirty minutes before you must leave, and I want to show you Bella's work." She teared up again.

"Get up the stairs, La Grinaldi. Move now. Make Bella proud," the domestic said, and left, casting a glance over her shoulder.

With a toss of her head and a remark about the insolence of servants, Francesca led them up a winding staircase, her scarf trailing behind.

The workroom was high-ceilinged, surrounded by windows, the view of Palermo and the sea, captivating. There were at least six sewing machines, five or six cutting tables, scissors, tape measures, mannequins. Shelves on one wall held bolts of material, large spools of thread. In the middle of the room stood an iron figure draped in a satin gown of emerald green with gossamer sleeves and high collar.

"Princess Rosso's favorite color is green. How she loves all the shades—green of the sea, tender leafy greens, greens of the forest deep, viridians, oxides, adores them all mixed together. She expects a fitting in a month, and I don't know what to do."

"When was the last time you saw Bella?"

She closed her eyes, remembering. "Saturday, October 6. She came on Thursday to spend the weekend. How busy we were, discussing our client and her wardrobe. The princess wanted two new gowns right away, wanted them ready for the Christmas season, wanted to see sketches for a complete wardrobe for the new season—dresses, skirts, coats, evening wear, leisure—everything. Bella designed two frocks, dashing the drawings off like a crazed woman. We pinned fabric together," she said, indicating the mannequin robed in green, "both of us leaning over the drawing table, laughing, poring over the sketches, the domestic bringing us caffè and *caponata*. Ate standing up while we worked. On Friday, Bella told me that she must leave the next day for Oltramari, that she was to meet her confessor in the Duomo, in front of the

Madonna's Chapel at dusk. 'Permanent absolution he'd grant her; she'd earned it, no matter what,' she told me."

Serafina felt her skin prickle. That was it, the information she needed.

On the way home, Rosa stared out the window, grappling with some demon or other. "Still must do the ledgers," Rosa said. "Stayed in the parlor too late last night."

"Good. Drop me off. Tessa stays with us tonight. I'll bring her home tomorrow after Carmela and I have done our planning. Then we can discuss and make our final plans to catch the beast."

The Plan

Monday morning, November 5, 1866

Vicenzu had already gone to the shop, Maria and Giulia to school, Carlo to the morgue.

Serafina ran down the stars, stopped at the newel, and kissed Renata good morning. "Carmela's door is closed. I don't want to disturb her. She and Carlo stayed up late last night talking. It'll probably take her a while to get her strength back, fall into our routine," Serafina said. "Always a late sleeper, Carmela. Takes after me." They walked into the kitchen.

"Carmela's been up for hours. She helped me with the breakfast, walked Maria and Giulia to school, paid a visit to Mother Concetta, and helped Assunta and me feed Tessa and Totò. They're outside now with her—she's showing them how to milk the goat, and she's been giving the gardener directions about creating something interesting around the chestnut tree."

Serafina looked out the window and saw Carmela holding Octavia's leash.

"Totò, don't!" Tessa yelled.

"Big squirt, Tessa, big, big squirt," Totò said.

"Carlo left the paper for you. It's on the table," Renata said. "Sit down. Eat."

Serafina leafed through the pages. "A lot to do." Assunta brought her breakfast, *biancomangiare*, roll, and coffee. Serafina sensed a certain quiet about the house. Peace, she might call it. Yes, that was it. She took a bite of breakfast.

Later she asked her daughter, "More food?"

She shook her head. "Full."

Serafina gave Carmela more background on Falco. "He gained from Bella's death. He was a regular at Rosa's, apparently had his choice of women. Do you remember him? Tall, light brown curls, slippery—an actor."

Carmela shook her head. "Don't think so."

"I think, especially after yesterday, that someone acts the part of a monk, someone familiar with Rosa's, and who, better than Falco?" But Serafina stressed her conviction that the killer must have an accomplice within Rosa's walls, someone on whom he relied for his information, someone without whom the killings could not have happened.

"It must be someone with access to the inside of the house, couldn't be the guards, the driver, the gardeners," Carmela said.

Serafina shook her head. "They don't have trusted relationships with the other prostitutes or freedom of access inside the house."

Carmela agreed.

"I believe the quickest way to find this killer is to work through this accomplice." Serafina swiped the corners of her mouth. "From what you know about Rosa's women, who could be assisting the killer?"

"Could be a few—Eugenia for instance—she was at Rosa's when I was. Kicked out before the killings, but she could have supplied the killer with information. Makes sense that he would kill her when he no longer needed her, or he'd gotten another one to do his bidding, someone within the walls."

Serafina looked at the moisture forming on the front windows. "So who do you think is his current helper?"

"Scarpo?" Carmela asked.

Serafina shook her head. "At first he topped my list of suspects, but after I talked to him, my intuition tells me, no. Too devoted to Rosa, and his son is a work of art with a sophistication beyond his years—saved my life through wit and courage. No, it has to be another prostitute."

They were silent a moment.

"You're sure about Scarpo?" Carmela asked. "Sometimes we're blind to the people we know."

Serafina felt her toes growing cold. Could he be helping the killer all along? He had opportunity and means, and was present for each of the murders, but motive? Why was she so sure he wasn't the accomplice? Her temples began to throb, and she shook her head, feeling the pull of her knotted hair. "As sure as I am of anyone, Scarpo is not helping the killer. But you've got a point … I suppose. Before I knew him, I suspected Scarpo, but now that … oh, I don't know." She chewed a little on her lip. "It's so hard to know the truth about someone you like, especially those who are close to us, but in the end, we've got to trust our intuition. I'll say this: as sure as I am of anything, Scarpo is not the accomplice." Without thinking, she went over to the barrel and swiped a few olives, chewing them slowly, lost in her thoughts.

Carmela smiled. "Me, too. I think he's a dear, and his son is magnificent. Rosa is lucky to have them, but our plan and Rosa's business depends on our gut." Carmela held the sides of her belly, now considerable, with both hands. All at once, she stood. "He kicked! I swear he did!"

"A sure sign," Serafina said and swallowed, wiping her hands on the tablecloth, but the lump in her throat did not go away.

Carmela told Serafina what she knew from Gusti's letters and from Carlo's visit yesterday afternoon. Serafina wrote as Carmela described at length the personalities—Rosa's favorites, the different cliques, the names of all the women who frequented the Madonna's Chapel, much of which Rosa had told her or she learned from the interviews.

"Understand, I was long gone when the murders occurred, but there was one in particular who, at times, became crazed with her desire for salvation. 'The serpent save me,' she'd implore. Oh, and one time she said, 'But for the serpent we are damned, damned I tell you,' screaming this like a jumped-up *strega*. She could be in the murderer's thrall."

"Bella, I know was interested in—"

"Not Bella," Carmela said and ran fingers through her curls.

"No, of course, not Bella. She was interested in the embroidery of vestments, costume, design."

Carmela nodded.

"And speaking of the longing for salvation, Bella's was a gift, a grace from on high, not a frenzied desire. Hers was purposeful, an understandable wish to be saved." Serafina saw raindrops sliding down the panes. "But there was one who struck me as too young to be in Rosa's house."

Carmela nodded.

"And yet," Serafina said, looking at something indistinct, "she seemed so innocent, so young when I met her, not at all interested in salvation and told me so."

"Looks can be deceiving, as can words. And mark me, she was a good actress." Carmela straightened on the chair. "In a way, I don't blame her—no father, unstable mother who pushed her out the door, the whole family hungry. Struck me as unbalanced and easily led."

Serafina said, "She longed for a true friend, one she could trust, who would never desert her, never be finished with her—this need of hers had no bottom."

Carmela said, "You've just described all of us."

Serafina could hear the spatter of rain on the window.

"She must be handsomely rewarded by the killer."

"Or perhaps she believes in the monk and the brazen serpent, and passes him information or obtains recruits and isn't compensated: a blind follower, like you say, a thrall. We just don't know. He may use her until he no longer needs her, like Eugenia, or she learns too much, like Gusti."

"Poor Gusti. Can't believe she's dead," Carmela said.

"Which reminds me: we found two of your letters in Gusti's room, last one dated March 1866. What did you mean by, 'We know her to be like the weather, fair one moment, foul the next'? Was she referring to the accomplice?"

Carmela nodded.

Serafina stared at the wall, tangled up in her thoughts. "I'm beginning to get a clear picture of this killer." She pulled at a loose thread on her sleeve. "But I need to be sure. It's time to think."

"What if there are two accomplices?" Carmela asked.

Serafina shook her head. "Don't think so. I think this killer works with one confidante at a time. But I need to step back, and so do you. In our recent past, we've not agreed on much, but now we must. We must take the time to be sure."

"And if we disagree on the accomplice?" Carmela asked.

Serafina said, "We've got to convince each other."

"Until we are of one mind?"

Serafina nodded. "Rest. You were up early. Then we'll talk."

As Serafina ascended the stairs to her mother's room, she smelled the scent of orange peel and lavender, and when she opened the door, she saw Maddalena sitting in her favorite chair, her skin luminous, gowned in her velvet dress, but no longer carrying her midwife's satchel. Instead, she peered into Serafina's eyes. "Took you long enough."

"Long enough? But Carmela wasn't speaking to me."

"Typical, you misunderstand my meaning. It took you far too long to let her into your heart. If it weren't for Concetta, Carmela would still be foundering."

Serafina had to agree. "Your friend gave her a roof over her head and a job."

"Much more. She showed her the way to remorse and love. But now that she's here, you dally again. Get a move on. Time lopes away."

"If you're immortal, just tell me what you know. Better yet, catch the killer and present him to me."

"Why should I tell you what you can discern for yourself?" Maddalena asked. "Robs you of your greatest happiness."

"But I need all the facts. There are unknowns—"

"Trust your instincts: you know the killer."

"I know his accomplice."

Maddalena laughed. "The time is ripe to strike, but demands your highest concentration. What you do in the next two days determines the fate of your oldest friend, Rosa, her house, and your family. A misstep will cause tragedy that will tumble down the generations, so tread with care but step decisively."

"Too dramatic as usual."

Maddalena wrinkled her nose. "Above all, don't ruin it by thinking you know everything, because you don't. Life is a mystery, even for immortals like me. Savor it. Agonize over it. But know you are in the thickest part of the puzzle, a web woven by the mad—wild with evil, sick from the sickness of others, crazed with the lust for coins and revenge. Arcangelo is quick and cunning, a good choice to guard Carmela, but he is still a child. This time don't let her out of your sight. Ask Mother Concetta for help."

"Now you talk in riddles. How can that old nun—"

"Throw away your attitudes, girl. They make your mind so muzzy!"

"I don't understand you at times, Mama. Why would I ask for Mother Concetta's help? And Carmela's back at last. We're mother and daughter once more."

Maddalena wrinkled her nose and disappeared in a burst of light.

Serafina lingered in the chair her mother vacated, deep into her thoughts.

Carmela sat at the table, scrunched down in the chair, fanning herself with the newspaper.

Serafina said, "Rosalia."

Carmela nodded her agreement at once. "The accomplice."

"But somehow—"

"Believe it. She's changeable, an actress."

They were silent. Serafina frowned. She was cold, remembering how she held Rosalia as she cried, a vulnerable child, really. Had she been able to deceive Serafina so easily? And if Rosalia, what about the others? She shook herself. "We know that Bella had an appointment to meet a monk in front of the Madonna's Chapel the evening before she died."

"How?"

"Her contessa friend told me."

"In business, together?"

Serafina nodded. "I believe this was the assignation with her killer."

"I have a plan to catch him," Carmela said, "using Rosalia to arrange a meeting for me with the monk. It's rough, and you and I must refine it, but basically, we say that I long for salvation, I need the monk. She arranges for me to meet with him at the Madonna's Chapel. You, Rosa, her guards, Scarpo lurk about—behind the chapel, in the piazza, somewhere close by. We may be able to get help from Colonna. The monk will probably take me to his cave. You follow and we capture him."

"A meeting with Rosalia for you? Never. Won't work."

"Why not?"

"Because they know who you are. Falco does, but surely Rosalia does, Rosa's other women, too. They don't trust you."

Carlo opened the door, stomped into the room. "Still here?"

"Leave your sister alone, Mr. Smarts. Better yet, tell me about the autopsy. Loffredo found?"

"Nothing more of interest. Gusti was not abused, and she was not with child. Asphyxiated," Carlo said, batting the newspaper Carmela held in front of her. He sat. "More breakfast, Assunta."

"The glorious son returns, and all the world runs to do his bidding," Carmela said, shaking her paper.

A plate appeared with *biancomangiare*, pork, bread, caffè, and eggs, just the way he liked them. He began to eat, shoving the food into his mouth and gulping hot caffè.

Carmela peered around the side of her paper and grabbed a piece of bread from his plate.

"So we know as much today as we did yesterday. But enough, you don't want to miss the train. Good luck with your exam tomorrow, my handsome boy. A thousand thanks for your help."

"Should stay until this business with Rosa is over, but—" He grabbed the paper from Carmela as she bit into the bread. The twins shouted at each other, laughing as they lurched from their seats, and the chase around the table began.

Assunta entered with Totò and Tessa. The children shed their outer garments and joined in the chase, both of them running after what, laughing for what, they did not know. The domestic shambled away, untouched by the riot, her pace inexorable, like the slow drip of time.

"Watch the oven for me, Assunta," Renata said, untying her apron and running after her siblings. Soon the laughter grew louder.

Serafina heard their shrieks, the galloping overhead, their

stampede down the stairs. The line sped through the kitchen. "No, Carlo, don't worry about me," Serafina said to his blurred form as he stretched for the paper in her hand. "Watch it, you two, Carmela's delicate—"

"Nothing delicate about her," he said. "She stole my paper. I had it first, give it over, need something to read on the train."

"His paper, Carmela, big train!" Totò yelled, running. Tessa, laughing, ran after him.

The line snaked out of the room, up the stairs, Carmela in the lead, flapping the newsprint, Carlo in pursuit, Renata holding onto the ends of his frock coat.

"I have all the help I need. Just pass your test, or no more Gloria," Serafina said to the empty kitchen. *About time laughter returned to this house.*

"Back to our plan, my precious. It's dangerous, and depends on secrecy and timing." She blew her nose.

"Must be me, not you," Carmela said.

"Cannot be. Rosa's women know you too well."

"But they trust me, they know I've been absent, fallen on bad times."

She shook her head. "You're too precious to lose. If something were to happen to you, I'd walk into the sea. Your brothers and sisters would be orphans."

"But using you to meet wouldn't work. They call you 'the snoop,' Gusti told me."

Serafina shook her head. "If I were to dress as someone else—"

"A terrible idea. Even *Nonna* said you weren't an actress—she told me she knew each time when you lied to her. What you really believe is written all over your face. No, it's got to be me. I'll take Papa's stiletto if it will make you feel better."

Serafina rolled her eyes. "You've never used one."

"Achille taught me."

She swallowed. Considered. She had to admit, it made sense to use Carmela, but she couldn't hold with it. She couldn't imagine the horror if something happened to her."

Serafina paced around the room, popped a few olives into her mouth. "If something happened to you ... What if you lost your child?" She couldn't stop her voice from shaking.

Carmela shook her head. "What would Nonna say? Time and time again, I heard it from her lips—Baby the baby, not the mother'—and she almost never lost a mother under her care. She was a marvelous midwife."

"Trained by the best in France," Serafina agreed. She was silent for a few moments. "Oh, all right, but you must keep me informed, or I'll go mad."

Serafina and her daughter filled in the details of their plan. "Arcangelo must shadow you at all times. You'll need to return to the orphanage for a few days, Arcangelo too. He must be armed, remain within calling distance. Tell Mother Concetta that you'll need rooms."

"I won't need to tell her anything—she'll be two steps ahead of us," Carmela said.

Serafina shrugged. "I'm sure she'll find plenty of work for both of you to do while you're there."

Carmela rubbed her palms together. "Can hardly wait. I'll rip him apart."

"Too much like me," Serafina muttered.

Carmela smiled.

Serafina continued. "I fear the killer has his spies in the center of town as well as within Rosa's walls." She told Carmela about the shooting on the way home Saturday, the incident with Tessa and the monk in the park. "Maybe I'm reading too much into daily occurrences. After all, there are monks galore on the streets of Oltramari, have been for centuries, but I don't think so. I've got to go with my hunches, and I think the monks we see, some of them in unusual habits, are his spies, or the killer himself. If he discovers that we work together, he'll be forewarned, and we'll be in mortal danger, you, most of all."

"Mortal danger? Please, Mama, don't exaggerate. This is a child's game."

"Listen to me. Dr. Loffredo told me that the killer is an expert with a knife. Each woman was killed by one fling of the blade to the heart—he doesn't miss—and after he killed his victims, he carved the sign of the brazen serpent into their flesh."

Carmela blew curls from her forehead and listened, unblinking, as if she and Serafina were planning a meal. She spelled out the rest—how Carmela would go to Rosa's and ask for a meeting with the monk who promises salvation.

"The timing depends on you. Send me word as soon as you've made contact with her."

"Mother C. can help me look tattered," Carmela said. "And I'll have her send costumes for all of you, too. She's a wonder with them. You'll need to be disguised."

"Except for Arcangelo. I want him in his own clothes. Nothing must hamper his movements. But are you sure about the costumes? Concetta is a nun."

"When Concetta needs money from the archbishop, she dresses some of the orphans in torn clothes saved for such occasions, puts a little makeup on their faces to make them look forlorn, and takes them with her."

Serafina nodded slowly.

Carmela continued. "So sharp, so theatrical. She and *Nonna* worked together at a theater in Palermo. That's how they met, didn't you know?"

"My mother? Acting? She'd never stoop so low," Serafina said. "Would she?"

"Believe it."

"I'll write to her this morning—"

"No need. I'll ask when I see her today." Carmela rose from her chair. "Better get ready. We haven't much time."

"Sit. There's more," Serafina said. "I've no idea if our plan to draw out the monk will be successful and, if so, where you'll meet him. If what we know is true, and if his pattern holds, it will be the Madonna's Chapel, but wherever the meeting is, we'll be as close to you as possible. Arcangelo will get word to us of any changes. It bothers me that you'll be—"

"That I'll be the star?"

She shook her head. "I fear for your life. I cannot lose you again. You don't seem to understand. This plan is dangerous, especially for you."

Silence. As she gazed at her, Serafina realized that despite being with child, Carmela still had the fearlessness that marked her youth, a characteristic that her mother found so, what to call it, so enticing. For her part, she envied it—her heart was pounding just thinking about carrying out the venture. "Still willing?" Serafina asked.

Carmela's eyes sparkled. "This gets better and better!"

Serafina shook her head. "Tessa and I will bring Rosa back here to stay with us. It won't be easy to pry the madam away from her precious house, but it's no longer safe for her there, even with all her guards, not until we catch the monk and do something with his accomplice."

"Rosa visits an aunt in Trabia," Carmela said.

"Good, that's where we'll say she's going. We must also request help from Colonna, if only to see him squirm."

"Can't I help with your plan?" Renata asked, walking into the kitchen, her eyes pleading.

"Where are the children?" Carmela asked.

"Outside with the goat."

Serafina bit her lip, realizing she'd left Renata out of the planning. Was it because she, Renata, was undemanding? "Of course I need your help. With Papa gone, absolutely you must stay here. You're the one with the cool head. I need you to watch the children, and I'll see if Rosa can spare a guard. He can sleep in the stable. My greatest fear is that the monk, sensing danger, will use Totò and Tessa as his pawns." She told Carmela about Tessa's sighting of the monk in the public gardens on Saturday. She turned to Renata. "No telling what he'll do, so you have an important role—they must be ever in your sight. And we'll have extra mouths to feed until this business is over. You'll need to make sure everyone eats well, the way you always do. Carmela returns to the orphanage, just for one day. Vicenzu will help you when he's not at the store. Rosa, Scarpo, and I will keep Beppe and Arcangelo very busy." ✎

Torrone

Monday afternoon, November 5, 1866

Serafina and Tessa approached the piazza as bells clanged the end of something or other in church. The Duomo's copper doors opened, discharging the stillness of white-haired women, bent, in black, squinting into the light. Outside they found voice, cackling with one another or calling to their men who sat waiting for them underneath the eucalyptus. Gesticulating hands punctured the air.

Serafina looked around. The usual knot of Don Tigro's thugs blighted the far side of the piazza, and near the fountain in the middle, a flower seller parked her cart crammed with ivy and wild scrub. On the other side of the kneeling statue, a peasant leaned on his dilapidated cart, legs crossed, a straw dangling from his mouth, his cap pulled over his eyes. Familiar, his shape. Stones rumbled in Serafina's stomach.

"Let's walk another way. We'll buy that present for your mother," she said to Tessa. They turned away from the piazza and walked down a side street, stopping at the sweet shop.

"Take a deep breath. Smell the cocoa, the almonds, the orange. Delicious, don't you think?"

Tessa slipped her eyes around the counter, walking back and forth to survey the display, at home in a world she understood, of marzipans in all shapes and sizes, painted saints and ghosts, fruits and vegetables and red-shirted soldiers, trapeze artists and circus bears, bars of *torrone*, dark brown, creamy, white, sugar-coated chocolate bites and large bars of deep chocolate. Serafina watched her finger pointing to each one until she decided. "That one." She pressed her hand to the glass, indicating a bar of *torrone*.

"Your favorite?" the clerk asked.

She shook her head. "My mother's."

Serafina bought several, asking the clerk to cut two small pieces and wrap the rest.

On the way Tessa sucked the samples, one in each cheek. At Rosa's, she ran up the steps and into the office.

Although she was at her sacred ledger, Rosa picked up her daughter, hugging her. "What a loud voice, Tessa, my girl, like an army." The madam reached into her front and pulled out a linen.

Serafina handed her the package. "Tessa picked it out."

"For you, Mama."

"A delicious treat, my darling girl." She put her nose close to one of the bars, inhaled, closed her eyes, and with steeple-fingered hands, gestured toward Tessa. "She knows her mama's favorite. Let's have cook cut one of the bars into pieces, shall we? Take the *torrone* to her. We'll have it after dinner. Now, off you go, my beauty, while Fina and I talk."

After Tessa left, Rosa said, "She loves your family."

"Wonderful place for her to be, with children her age, thinking of school—"

Rosa rolled her eyes and went back to counting her money. "Not right," she said, more to herself than to Serafina. Her spectacles slipped down her nose. "This whole week we've been busy, except for that *festa*. The take should be bigger." She pointed a finger at the pile of notes, the stacks of coins separated into gold and silver and muttered to herself.

"Can I help?" Serafina asked.

"Numbers and you don't mix. Besides, it's nothing. An oversight. Happened before," she said, pulling the cord. "Someone forgot to give Scarpo her tips, that's all … maybe."

After Scarpo joined them, Serafina told him that Carmela was home and was helping her plan.

Scarpo turned to Serafina. "You asked me to find out more about the ragpicker. Had one of my guards follow him. Spent most of his time in the rough neighborhoods sharpening knives, just like the smith said."

"Did he get a good look at the fellow?" Serafina asked.

Scarpo said, "Disappeared like a snake down a hole."

"You mean the guard lost him?"

Scarpo nodded.

Rosa shrugged. "Running out of time. Carlo was right—a false turn, the picker."

Serafina scratched her nose. She told them about finding the killer's lair, filled them in on what Carmela learned from Gusti's letters—that all of the murdered women had appointments to meet the monk at the Madonna's Chapel."

"Why didn't we hear about this sooner?" Rosa asked, her face paling.

Serafina said, "Some of us keep our secrets buried deep."

"Speak for yourself," Rosa said.

She let the barb drop. Instead, she detailed everyone's role in the plan she and Carmela devised. "And I want two guards posted near the monk's cave."

Scarpo nodded. "Where is it?"

She gave him directions. "A filthy place. Tell them not to go inside, but they should conceal themselves behind the tall grass, and ask them not to wear their red shirts."

"We're very close to catching the mad monk." Rosa squirmed in her chair, and wiped her forehead with the linen. "I feel it."

"Beginning tonight, you and Tessa stay with us until this business is over." Before the madam could reply, Serafina added, "It wasn't a bandit who attacked us on Saturday."

"You mean it was the killer?" the madam asked.

"He feels our breath close upon him." She watched Rosa's eyes blacken, her hands twist. "You're not safe here. Scarpo knows it."

He nodded.

"Come home with me. Bring your maid if you like. You and Tessa can stay on the third floor in Mama's old room, Gesuzza in Papa's study. You'll have plenty of privacy."

"But who will be hostess in my house tonight?"

"What about Gioconda? Has a certain flair."

"Bah, wouldn't do."

"All right, stay here, and I'll cry over your corpse in the morning."

Rosa rubbed a spot off her sleeve. "Business is slow on a Monday. All right."

"The excuse for your leaving?—you visit an aunt in Trabia. Let it be known that I go with you."

"Long dead, my aunt, but it will do."

Serafina turned to Scarpo. "Expect a visit from Carmela tomorrow. She'll be costumed as a desolate one. Not to worry, she's an actress."

"We knew that," Scarpo said, smiling.

Serafina continued. "She'll ask to see Rosalia. She's the monk's accomplice." ✒

The Meeting

Monday evening, November 5, 1866

Rosalia sat in the parlor, her arm around Carmela. "I felt the same as you before I was saved by the monk. Soon I'll return to my family and begin a life devoted to prayer and to helping others."

Hair matted, face smudged with dirt, Carmela hunched into herself, scrubbed at her eyes with fingerless gloves. "When will you know? I must see him as soon as possible, before my child is born. This morning I felt a powerful cramping."

The thief picked at a spot on her chin. "Difficult to say. There's one, a ragpicker, the monk's friend, who tells me his whereabouts. Haven't seen him in recent weeks. I need to find him, so he can summon the monk."

Carmela began. "Please. My mother has abandoned me. The old nun beats me, and I can barely stand to dress myself before waking the children in the cold, in the dark." Carmela shivered. "So hungry, not enough food. My back aches from bathing and feeding the orphans. I'm sick, tired, and I have a thirst that comes from I know not where. Help me."

Rosalia shrugged.

Carmela swiped a hand through matted hair and hugged her stomach. "The fetus kicks! Don't you see it? I can't return to this life of sin. My child must be born from a pure vessel." Carmela opened her purse.

Rosalia's eyes sparked.

"And if I die in childbirth, I won't be—"

The accomplice held up a palm. "Because we're friends, I'll see what I can do. But you must tell no one you've come here. Permanent absolution is reserved for a select few. If word spreads, there will be a stampede looking for the monk."

"No one will know." Carmela crossed herself.

Rosalia said, "And the cost, five hundred lire."

"Not to worry," Carmela said, inwardly gulping.

"In that case, give me a few coins to cover expenses. Two hundred lire will do for now."

Carmela handed her the coins.

"At first light by the old eucalyptus you will see a man with an unpainted cart. Don't look into his face. Do not speak to him. Take the note he gives you and leave."

The Adder's Bite

Monday night, November 5, 1866

She held out the money. "She's desperate for the brazen serpent," Rosalia said. "And she's got abundant coins. I impressed on her the need for secrecy, but she must have your absolution tomorrow, she told me."

"The time is perfect," the monk said, grabbing the coins.

"La Signura visits her aunt in Trabia, and the snoop has gone with her."

"Even better. You quoted her a price?"

"Five hundred lire."

"For you, a great reward in heaven, my child."

"I've done your bidding, but I can help you no longer. My family is hungry. I don't ask for much, but one hundred lire will feed them and keep them together for at least five years."

The monk hesitated. "Come here tomorrow after the angelus has rung. Your wish will be granted." He smiled.

Rosalia nodded. She felt a sudden sting, an adder's bite. The knife had hit its mark. 🖋

Strength

Tuesday morning, November 6, 1866

*M*orning mist had not yet disappeared as Carmela, clad in black, hunched on the stone bench underneath the eucalyptus. She appeared not to notice the approaching cart and driver, but quickly snatched the note he dropped at her feet and read, "Madonna's Chapel. Eighteen hundred hours, you will meet the monk. Give him the rest of the coins, and permanent absolution will be yours." When she lifted her eyes, the cart and driver had vanished.

Carmela ranged through narrow passageways, casting about with anxious eyes. No one. She glanced over her shoulder at intervals, stopping only when she saw a figure on one knee, tying his boot. In the half-light she hugged the wall of a dilapidated building, her heart racing. When she saw a niche big enough for both of them, she motioned him forward. "Take this to Donna Fina. Wait for her reply."

When it arrived, Serafina folded Carmela's message, turning to Arcangelo. "Rosa needs to read this and open her coffers, but she's not yet awake. Some breakfast while you wait?"

He shook his head.

"Nonsense, you'll need your strength today. Tonight, too. Renata, some *biancomangiare*, omelet, pork, brioche, ricotta, caffè. Pile this young man's plate. Assunta, ask Rosa to come down here right now. Tell her we have news from Carmela, and Arcangelo, take your time. You know how slow the madam can be in the morning—it's long before her usual waking hour." She winked.

"Long before yours, too," Renata said, setting a large breakfast in front of Arcangelo.

While he ate, Serafina said, "Better when the whole family is here and the house shakes."

"Totò and Tessa are outside with Octavia and the guard. Vicenzu's at the shop, Maria and Giulia at school, Carlo studying, we hope. And Carmela—"

"I know, my precious," Serafina said and gave Renata a hug.

A thousand thoughts raced through her brain, all of them mashed together. For something to do, she fetched pen and paper, but half a minute later, too excited to sit, she glided to the window and looked out at Totò and Tessa feeding the goat. When she heard the first tremor on the stairs, she rushed into the hall and saw Rosa descending, scarlet slippered, purple robed.

Serafina handed her Carmela's note.

The madam donned her spectacles, her lips pushing in and out as she read. "She'll not get more coins from me!"

"Carmela's life is at stake," Serafina said.

Rosa hesitated. "Where is Arcangelo? Fetch me a quill and vellum." Rosa scratched out some words and signed.

Arcangelo appeared, cheeks stuffed.

"Run to your father. Give him this." Rosa handed him her note. "Tell him to take five hundred lire from the safe, and bring the coins to Carmela. She waits for you where?"

He swallowed. "The orphanage."

"And tell Scarpo to meet us here at five o'clock this afternoon," Serafina said.

"Why?" Rosa asked.

"Didn't you read Carmela's message? Because at six o'clock she's meeting the monk in front of the Madonna's Chapel."

Rosa read it again, a red line of color ascending her neck. "I didn't see it the first time. Must have been the shock of having to sign away five hundred lire—ten years worth of wages for a cook—a devastation." She twisted her hands and looked at Serafina. "I bury what I'd rather not know."

Mid-morning the package from Mother Concetta arrived,

containing four habits in homespun, a large latchkey, and a note.

> *The enclosed opens the screened grille to the chancel behind the Madonna's Chapel.*
> *Viewed from outside, the room's objects appear as dim shadows, nothing more. But its occupants are able to see through the screen to the chapel and hear every word uttered on the altar.*
> *Lock the door upon leaving. Return the key to me when finished. Burn the garments.*

> *Mother Concetta Maria, OP*

Serafina handed it to Rosa.

This time the madam read sitting down and with her finger moving underneath the words. "We don't need a disguise, not to walk the few meters from here to the Duomo."

Serafina had already donned the homespun over her dress, marveling at the size of the pockets in nuns' habits, and making a mental note to tell Giulia.

Straightening the scapula, she said, "And when the monk leads Carmela to his lair, what if he turns around and sees us following him? What if he's a customer who recognizes you or Scarpo? What then? We are unmasked, our plan in tatters, and Carmela's life in danger if not lost."

"You have a point," the madam said, trying on a habit.

"We'll wear them to request Colonna's help as well. The monk may have his spies in the piazza, and don't forget, we are supposed to be in Trabia."

"Time for sweets," Serafina said, removing the homespun. "Renata, call the children."

Totò opened the door, tugging on a long rope. "C'mon, move! Push, Tessa!"

"Don't you dare bring that goat in here!" Renata yelled. "Oh, where is Carmela when we need her?"

Later, when Rosa was resting, Serafina asked Renata, "Who delivered the parcel from Mother Concetta?"

"The little girl we met at the orphanage last month. You remember her, the one missing a few front teeth."

"But she's a child, about six or seven, I should think. How can one so slight carry something so heavy?"

Renata threw her a look as if she, Serafina, had gone round the twist. "She wheeled it here in a small wagon."

Serafina nodded. "Of course." She stood a moment, rubbing her arms and looking at nothing in particular. "It all falls into place now. Why did it take me so long?"

"I've sent word to Carmela," Renata said.

"Word?"

"That you'll be in the chancel when she talks to the monk, just like she and Mother Concetta hoped you'd be."

"You see? I couldn't manage without you," Serafina said.

Shaking her head, Renata went back to stirring the sauce.

Clothed in nuns' habits, Serafina and Rosa set out in the afternoon to talk with the inspector. A sharp wind whipped their skirts. Puddles from the morning's rain glittered. The center of town began filling with people pushing about, men holding onto their caps, shawled women leaning into the blowing force like ships pitching in a gale.

When they arrived at the Municipal Building, they asked to speak with Colonna and were ushered into his office.

Colonna's jaw dropped.

Serafina explained the need for their disguises, and summarized the deaths to date, including the victims' longing for redemption. Rosa told him their primary suspect was a man disguised as a begging monk who appeared in the piazza offering eternal salvation. Serafina described the accomplice, someone within Rosa's walls who fed the killer information and procured his victims. Emphasizing the significance of timing, given the importance of the numbers six and seven in the crazed mind of the killer, Serafina reminded him that all three women were murdered sometime between the sixth and seventh day of the month. She ended by detailing their plan for catching the killer.

"But there was a fourth death, different from the other three, no?" the inspector asked.

"Pirricù, my handsome inspector," Rosa said, adjusting her habit, "we talked about that on Sunday, remember? Gusti knew too much, was in the way. That's why she was murdered." The madam looked at Serafina and, without words, the two decided not to tell him about Eugenia.

Serafina continued. "The timing of Gusti's death falls outside the pattern he established with his first three murders, a scheme he is sure to follow with the timing of his next killing."

"Today is the sixth day of the month. We must act now. Give us several of your men to help carry out our plan. You won't regret it." Serafina stopped speaking and stared at the baffled inspector whose brain, she was sure, was back on his question, unable to fathom their answer.

He smiled at both women, raised his eyebrows, and pulled the cord.

A functionary appeared.

"Look in the record book and tell me if we issued any permits to mendicants during the last month. And bring me names and dates," Colonna ordered. He said, "And, now, we shall see what we shall see." Folding his hands and placing them on the desk, he smiled, waiting.

Serafina furrowed her brows. "Could you please explain that last remark? I am unclear as to the meaning of the first 'see' in your previous sentence. Is it the same as the second 'see'?"

Colonna was lost. "My dear, best you leave police business to the professionals."

In a few moments the functionary returned. "None in the last six months, Inspector."

Colonna turned to the women, and with an elaborate shrug said, "So, dear ladies, you see? There is no proof that the monk exists. But that doesn't mean I don't believe you." He cleared his throat. "The monk may well have been begging and you may well have seen him, or thought you had seen him. But, new rules, desperate times, and I must justify my every move. Does the monk exist? If I have no permit, I have no proof, so there. How can I send a man or two to chase after a fantasy?"

Rosa's face reddened, and Serafina was at a loss for words.

Colonna's face reddened. "Your plan is ingenious." He stroked his mustache.

She held up Carmela's note. "But Inspector, the monk meets my daughter this evening in front of the Madonna's Chapel. The last victim had a similar rendezvous with him. Surely you can spare a—"

"Save your time. Call off your plan. Ah, yes, you have concocted a nice plot, for a ... woman. Might even work with some modification and with luck. But it is based on intuition and on information from a—how can I put it—your daughter is what, a fallen woman, no? Doubtless this monk exists, but is he the one who killed?" He closed his eyes, shook his head. "The rioting continues in Catania and I still have most of my men tied up in that chaos. A thousand apologies, but with the increase in crime, I have no one to spare." He lifted his palms in a placatory gesture. "Can your plan wait five or ten days, perhaps a month or two? Then of course we will take a look at it." He beamed.

Rosa looked like Etna erupting.

"Time we do not have, Inspector," Serafina said. "In less than twenty-four hours, another woman will be dead if we don't intervene. In another month, another of Rosa's women will follow. Rosa, her women, perhaps even the child, Tessa, are in jeopardy. We must act now."

He straightened the pile of papers on his desk while he spoke. "All right, you convince me. Come back tomorrow, or soon after tomorrow, say, in a week or two, and I might be able to spare you a man."

Outside Rosa sputtered. "He cannot wait until siesta when he will sink his teeth into food and, afterward, take a nice long nap. He sees nothing. He knows nothing. He does nothing. Useless, our visit."

Serafina fought to control herself. "No matter, Rosa. No time for anger. If we are to catch the killer ourselves, we must remain calm. I know our plan will work, and I'm sure the monk acts alone—except, of course, for his accomplice—so we outnumber him. There will be five of us—four in the chancel, and Arcangelo somewhere in the shadows near Carmela."

"And don't forget the guards." Rosa said.

They were crossing the piazza on their way home, hands folded into copious sleeves. Passing the fountain and the statue, Serafina saw the ragpicker leaning against a weather-beaten cart crammed with old cloth, his cap pulled down low against the wind, his one-eyed mule swishing its tail. In his line of sight were the Duomo's copper doors. She welcomed his presence, a fearful confirmation, like the fleeting glimpse of death.

All her deliberation for the rest of the afternoon must be focused on their plan for this evening. Nothing must be left to chance. And afterward, Arcangelo could rescue the mule. She hung onto this thought, a strand of mercy in a skein of madness and death.

Capture

Tuesday late afternoon, November 6, 1866

he wind was a knife at their backs as the wimpled group blew across the street to the Duomo's side entrance. Nodding to the guards who sat, as prearranged, on a nearby stone bench, they climbed a flight of stairs and filed through the sacristy to the main altar.

Serafina led the way. With downcast eyes, she snaked through the sanctuary toward the Madonna's Chapel, genuflected, kissed her beads, and cast an outward glance. No shadows moved in the darkness beyond the communion rail. Turning around, she saw the madam scowling to herself, red-faced in her tight-fitting headpiece. She spied Beppe frowning and Scarpo, his face strange looking without his mustache. They followed her in single file to the rear of the chapel. Serafina fit the key into the chancel's lock, wincing as the tumblers fell and echoed throughout the cathedral. Slowly she opened the heavy, grilled doors, and the four slipped inside.

Cold, damp, dark, the room contained nothing of comfort. Simple wooden furniture was scattered throughout, a few straight-backed chairs with seats of straw, several unforgiving prie-dieus sat in a row. A small altar jutted out from one wall. After her eyes adjusted to the dimness, Serafina glanced at Rosa. Kneeling, and with head bowed, the madam grasped the crucifix of her beads as if it were a pistol. She knelt beside her. Sensing Serafina's gaze, Rosa turned to her and smiled. Beppe and Scarpo stood against the stone wall, Scarpo with one hand on the knife wedged into his belt.

Looking out, she could see nothing at first, no shadows, no

movement, but soon Carmela's form emerged. Facing Serafina, several meters beyond reach, she sat in the first pew waiting for the monk's arrival. Serafina's heart raced as she whispered the words to a half-remembered prayer.

Where is he, this monk? Had he gotten wind of their plan? Perhaps, after conferring with his accomplice, he saw through Carmela's ruse, devised a surprise of his own. For all Serafina knew, the cunning monster had them in his sights and would appear in fury, whipping steel blades into their hearts. She stopped her hands from trembling. No chance, then, to save her child. She started from her prie-dieu, but forced herself to kneel again, wiping her forehead.

Minutes seemed like hours. Finally she heard footsteps, felt the vibrations of a heavy object on stone. *Tap-step-step-tap. Tap-step-step-tap.* An iron rod rammed the floor. It shook her skull, and she pulled out a handkerchief from her sleeve, wiping her brow. *Tap-step-step-tap.*

From out of the shrouded gloom a silhouette appeared, faint at first, becoming more distinct as it approached. She blinked, took a deep breath, reached over, and clasped Rosa's arm. Perhaps their plan would work.

Wearing a cowl and what looked like dark sackcloth covering his head, face, and neck, the monk walked toward the front. As he drew closer to her daughter, Serafina gasped for air, lightheaded, overwhelmed by the enormity of their task. Cold eyes peered out from behind two slits. In one gloved hand, he held a staff. At its top, a piece of metal coiled around a cross, and Serafina recognized the same spiraling snake she'd seen over and over again in Bella's magazine—the symbol of the brazen serpent. The monk stopped alongside Carmela, unmoving and speechless.

The old nun was right. Despite the headdress Serafina wore, its starched cotton muffling sound, she heard everything, even the tremor in her daughter's voice as she began to speak.

"Do you know where I can find the monk?" she asked, her voice growing stronger. "The one who gives absolution to a few of the chosen? I have sinned, and no ordinary priest has the power to forgive me. What's worse, I probably will sin again."

My girl. Serafina looked at Rosa and smiled.

There was a long pause before the monk replied. "I am the only path to the one you seek. You must follow me and kiss the brazen serpent." He pointed to the coiling snake on his staff. "It is the serpent, not I, who offers absolution."

"Give me this absolution, monk," Carmela said. "I can pay." She opened her reticule and held out gold coins. They gleamed in the light from nearby candles.

Serafina turned and saw a veiled Beppe, his brow furrowed, his cheeks working in and out. Looking down the main aisle to the vestibule, she could pick out, in a sliver of light from the rose window, a figure walking softly toward Carmela and the monk, but keeping well behind them.

"No gold can buy you absolution, lady," the monk said, grabbing the coins in his gloved hands. "A few are chosen. You are one of the lucky ones, but first you must feel the viper's sting." He rapped his staff on the floor and the vaulted ceiling seemed to shake. "I will sign you with his mark, and you will be absolved in his blood. For this you must go with me to my chapel."

Carmela nodded. "Where is it, this chapel of yours?"

"Follow me."

Serafina's heart pounded. The monk was leading Carmela up the steps to the rear of the chapel, pointing beyond the main altar to a hall leading to the sacristy. They were nearing the chancel. Serafina crouched down as far as possible, and the others did the same. She felt the air move as Carmela and the monk passed so close to them that Serafina could have reached out and grabbed his sleeve. As if anticipating her move, Rosa shook her head, restraining Serafina's arm.

"My chapel is not far from here, in the rocks by the sea, but hurry, I must hear your confession before the bell tolls midnight. We haven't much time. Walk faster."

"Why, monk? Why before midnight? And why not here?"

He turned to her, rapped the marble floor with his staff. "Quiet!" he hissed.

Careful, Carmela. Serafina wanted to pull her daughter inside to safety and rip apart this mad monk, but with one who had shown such quick and deadly power, and her daughter's life at stake, she was too afraid to try and overtake him now. Oh, Madonna, help us, she whispered.

"Keep your head down. Speak to no one, and hurry!" the monk said.

Arcangelo bounded up the aisle, past the chancel and the altar. Serafina opened the grille and the four exited. She led them through the hallway to the sacristy and down the stairs in time to see the door at the bottom closing. They ran down the stairs.

At the bottom, Rosa caught Arcangelo's elbow. "Stalk this monk, but as we rehearsed, as quietly as possible, staying a few meters behind us, keeping close to the walls. Careful: his knife never misses the heart."

"Everyone, stay close to the walls!" Serafina said softly.

Arcangelo nodded, grabbed his revolver and, like a cat, slipped out the door.

Outside Serafina looked around. She saw the glint from Arcangelo's revolver several blocks behind them, followed by the two lolloping figures of the guards. Otherwise the piazza and surrounding streets were empty. The wind swirled around them, blowing their veils, knocking stones against their shoes, burning Serafina's eyes, but the time for fear was over. Her mind was a beacon focused only on the two moving silhouettes she saw in the near distance. So far, the plan was working. They must capture this killer monk—they would not, could not fail.

"Where are they?" Scarpo asked.

Rosa pointed to the monk's cross glimmering with light from early evening stars.

"Can't we remove these habits?" Rosa asked.

Serafina shook her head.

They walked toward the lower city, hugging the walls. Buildings closed in on them. Serafina felt light-headed, squinting into the wind, watching the outlines of the monk's swaying robe. As they passed a tavern, she heard drunken shouts from within, the sudden roar of laughter, pounding fists on wooden tables. The stench of urine gagged her. Rosa held a handkerchief to her nose. They followed the monk and Carmela as they descended through twisting alleys and garbage-strewn passageways.

Soon Serafina smelled seaweed, heard pounding waves in the distance. Her curls tightened. Her wimple bit into her face. She saw Rosa's veiled form thrashing in the blowing force, but could not see the guards.

"Where did they go?" she asked Rosa.

The madam looked around. "With Arcangelo!"

Suddenly Arcangelo yelled, "Stop!" as a large wooden crate thundered from an upper-story window, crashing onto the cobbles, missing Serafina by a hair's-breadth, and hurtling debris into them. In a flash, Serafina saw the monk stop and turn toward them, his attention snagged by the commotion. Shielding her face, Serafina stumbled. Rosa gasped, holding Serafina upright, together with Scarpo and Beppe, who steadied her before she catapulted into the splintered wood and flying garbage.

"Get back!" she said to Rosa, Scarpo, and Beppe. "Keep to the walls."

Serafina stood in full view, ready to meet the monk as he approached.

"Give her up, monk!" she yelled.

Ahead, the gleaming cross stopped. With a jerk of his free hand, the dark specter pointed to Serafina. He yanked Carmela in front of him, holding her neck in the crook of his arm, and pushing her forward. Struggling up the sharp incline and dragging the brazen serpent behind him, he plodded toward Serafina.

Knee-deep in offal from the fallen crate, Serafina stood ramrod straight, staring at the approaching monk. Arcangelo and the guards hugged the walls behind them.

"Back here!" Arcangelo yelled.

Serafina turned, saw him pointing to an opening in a building a few meters behind them. She motioned to Rosa, Scarpo, Beppe.

"In here, quick!" Arcangelo shouted.

They scurried into an alcove and flattened themselves against the wall. Taking in every detail, Serafina saw Beppe fumbling with something underneath his scapula. Arcangelo whispered to the guards who drew their pistols and retreated several paces.

Serafina brushed garbage off her sleeves. She looked at the dull shine of Scarpo's shepherd's knife, the beads of sweat on Rosa's face. Serafina squeezed her friend's hand. "Almost over now. A slight change in plans, but if this works, we won't have to fight him in his cave," she said.

The alcove was crammed with the five of them squeezed together and Serafina heard the dull thud of the monk's staff growing louder, heard Scarpo's habit scraping on the stucco wall. As her eyes adjusted to the half-light, she pointed to a door at the end of a small corridor. Scarpo pounded his fist on the wood.

Serafina listened for movement inside, but all she heard was the beating of her heart.

"I count to three, we push," Scarpo said.

They nodded.

Counted.

Pushed.

Door creaked, but held.

"Harder," Serafina whispered.

They compressed against one another, a determined wedge.

Serafina ground her heels into the earth. Her stomach lurched, her blood thundered. *Oh God and all you angels, where are you when my poor Carmela needs you?*

She heard footfalls and brass clanging on stone, felt him coming closer.

Tap-step-step-tap.

Louder.

Tap-step-step-tap.

"Won't budge," Arcangelo whispered.

"Must," Rosa said. She stepped back, and with a mighty heave from her massive haunches, slammed her elbow into the back of Beppe who retched in surprise.

The force of her blow buckled the door and its hinges gave way, sending them all careening into a small room like rocks cascading into the abyss.

Scarpo straightened the hinges. Serafina heard the click, felt the whoosh of air as the door shut behind them.

Inside, an old woman with surprised eyes sat in the far corner, her candle guttering, one hand covering her mouth. Scarpo tore off his headdress and turned to the woman, mouthing one word, "Bandits!" and she, nodding at a truth she understood, crossed herself. He drew his revolver with one hand, clutched his knife in the other, and waited by the door.

Beppe crouched down in front of the keyhole.

Serafina stood next to Scarpo, ready to seize her daughter.

She turned and saw the madam tiptoe to the stove, grab an iron pan sitting on its top. Listing from side to side, Rosa headed over to where the granny sat and whispered something in her ear. The woman hunched her shoulders, nodded. Rosa picked up a ladder-back chair and returned to the entryway, placing the chair near the door, opposite Scarpo.

Arcangelo joined Beppe and they took turns peering through the keyhole.

"The guards?" Serafina asked.

"Across the street, in case something goes wrong," he said. "Shhh! The monk's coming." He and Beppe stepped aside.

No one moved.

"Let go of me!" Serafina heard Carmela say from outside as the monk and her daughter approached the alcove.

A second of silence. Then a wail, unearthly.

They waited for what seemed like hours for the monk to enter. Serafina reached for the door. Scarpo restrained her. Sweat streamed from his scalp as he motioned for the young men to stand alongside Serafina.

In one graceful arc, Rosa jumped up and stood on top of the chair's seat, skillet held aloft, while Scarpo waited by her side. Serafina saw motes of dust churn in the madam's wake.

Loud kicks. Door rattled.

Scarpo yanked it open, causing the monk to teeter off balance and stumble inside. His staff clattered to the ground.

Carmela broke free and lost her balance.

After the monk regained his footing, he pointed to Serafina, reached inside his sleeve, and pulled out a knife.

"Now you die!"

"Out of the way!" Beppe shoved Serafina aside as the monk flung his knife.

Even now she can hear it hum through the air, can see the blade meant for her body find a home in Beppe's chest.

She stared at Beppe's frozen face as he fell freely through the air, his body landing on the floor, the knife sticking up from his chest.

"Carmela!" Serafina grabbed her daughter and held her. Both women watched as Arcangelo dragged Beppe's body away from the struggle.

Scarpo lifted the monk up by his cape and held him out to Rosa.

She slammed the top of the cleric's head with her skillet.

Sandaled feet kicked the air.

Squeezing the monk's cape, Scarpo shook him hard, shook him until his teeth rattled and his sandals fell off.

The monk continued to squirm.

Rosa struck him again with the skillet.

This time his masked head drooped.

Scarpo released his hold, and the figure dropped into a corner, deflated, folding in on itself like a rag doll.

Unmasked

"**W**hat have I done?" Serafina knelt, cradling Beppe's body as the others looked on, silent. Arcangelo reached for the knife sticking into the fallen man's chest.

"Leave it," Scarpo said.

"Heartless, I'm so wanton. Look what I've done! Oh, Madonna, plead for me!" *Turn back the clock.* But it couldn't be. How thoughtless she'd been, disregarding the life of her servant. How cruel, fickle, despicable, worse than the monk. Beppe, an orphan who never had a chance, gave his life for her. Blood pounded in her ears as she held him, and her gorge rose.

Rosa knelt beside her. "No blood?" she asked. "Eyelids closed? Cheeks red? Nostrils going in and out, chest working up and down?"

She shook Serafina's shoulder. "What's wrong with you—lost your wizardry?"

Beppe opened his eyes, peered down his nose at the knife sticking out of his chest. Smiling, he yanked it out.

"Losing his touch, the monk," Rosa said.

"Misjudged the thickness of the cloth," Scarpo said.

"And this," Beppe said. He fumbled under his scapula and pulled out a thick pouch. "I heard Donna Fina say that the monk never misses, so I tied this around my chest."

Serafina undid the pouch and retrieved a book. "*Natural History, Volume Two, Pliny the Elder.* But Beppe, you can't possibly read this. Where did you get it?"

"Giulia," he said, sitting up. "You said, 'Ask Giulia about the polar star.' So I did, and she gave me this book to read. Her father's book, she said—it's about the heavens."

The monk began to stir. With a yank, Arcangelo and Scarpo grabbed his arms, stood him up. Beppe removed his hood.

Serafina heard silk rubbing against hair, a soft sucking sound, as golden locks lifted up, broke free, and tumbled about the monk's shoulders.

For a moment no one moved. They were a tableau without words.

"Lola!" Rosa said.

Serafina unwound the rope she had tied around her waist earlier.

"You think of everything!" Scarpo said, flashing a smile and taking the rope from her. He tied Lola's hands and feet. Lola stood motionless, her eyes fixed on something beyond their ken. 🪶

Another Body

While Scarpo, Beppe, and the guards took Lola to the municipal building, Arcangelo walked back to town with Rosa and Serafina.

Before they separated, Serafina told Scarpo, "Renata prepared a late supper. Come to our home afterward."

"I'm famished—no food for days," the madam said.

"At least not since the noon meal." Serafina looked at Carmela. "We'll grab a bite before tending to Rosalia."

As they crossed the piazza, she spotted the ragpicker's mule and cart tied to a post near the fountain.

"Poor mule," Arcangelo said. "Who would leave a beast tied up like that?"

"After we eat, you and Beppe see to him."

"If he's still here," Arcangelo said.

"He'll be here. Take him to our barn. We'll need to search the cart."

"The wizard speaks in riddles," Rosa said, slow in her gait. The weight of the evening was taking its toll.

"Lola's the ragpicker."

"I still can't believe it. Lola, the killer? Why?" Carmela asked.

"*You* can't believe it. What about me?" Rosa asked. "I took her in, trusted her, regarded her as the best of my girls."

"So full of life, Lola. Bossy, conniving, two-faced, but not a killer," Carmela said.

Serafina said, "Quite mad, Lola. She should be locked up in hospital, not jail. She suffered as a child, poor lost soul."

"Poor lost soul? She killed my girls and took my coins. Would have taken my house, if it weren't for you. That's how poor and

283

lost she is."

"That's her mule and cart, her means of transporting bodies and costumes from the monk's lair to your house to the Duomo," Serafina said. "And the reason *rigor mortis* was broken?—Lola killed her victims in the monk's lair by the sea, then went back to work, entertaining her customers. She returned to retrieve the body, using the cart to transport the dead one to your stoop," Serafina said, opening her front gate. "What's more, Lola was the ruffled mourner at Gemma's wake."

Carmela stopped. "How do you know all this?"

"She's a wizard," Rosa said.

Serafina gestured to her temple with a forefinger. "Couldn't sleep the other night. Conjured the truth from the facts, the many times I'd run into the ragpicker and his cart when he tried to shoot me or had an altercation in town or wounded my son on the road."

Rosa and Carmela looked at each other and shook their heads.

"Lola, the actress," Serafina said. "She costumed herself as a monk, as a mourner, as a ragpicker, shifting her shape to suit the situation."

Serafina turned back and saw Arcangelo untying the mule. "All right, Arcangelo, we can't stand to see the beast suffer any longer, either. Take him now to our stable, but be sure to return for supper."

By the time Serafina and the madam reached Villa Rosa, it was after midnight, and mist was rising from the sea.

"Not in her room, Rosalia," Rosa said. They checked with the laundress and the cook, the upstairs maids, the downstairs maids. They spoke with the other prostitutes, those who were free.

"Haven't seen her all evening," one of the women said.

In Scarpo's absence, Rosa and Serafina went outside to speak with one of the guards. No sound, except for the waves and the wind.

"And you say she just disappeared?" Serafina asked.

A torch lit his face. He nodded. "Late morning it was. Out the front door she goes, the girl, all dressed up. Takes a side path, doubles back along the grass and down to the rocks. We follow, Orazio and I, sneaking so she doesn't see. Scrambles down the rocks, she does. Walks on the shore a ways and, *presto*, disappears into a hole between two big rocks. So we wait for her to come out."

"And you didn't follow her inside?"

"Never. We don't go inside nowheres. Work only the outside. Scarpo's orders. So we wait. Hasn't come out, the girl. Take turns, we do, keeping a safe watch. Orazio, he's there now."

"Did you see anyone else?"

The guard shook his head. "Only a beggar with his mule tripping on the rocks near the old house sitting high overhead. Late this afternoon it was."

"A beggar?" Serafina asked.

The guard said, "Cart worn, mule, too."

Serafina turned to the madam. "We can't navigate those rocks tonight. Tomorrow morning's soon enough, after I search the rooms of the two prostitutes. In the meantime, the guards should continue watching the cove."

Lost Souls

Wednesday November 7, 1866

So peaceful here, as if nothing had happened, Serafina thought, riding through the length of Rosa's park. The sun streamed through palm fronds. Men cut and raked and readied the earth for winter. Beppe took Largo's reins, and helped Serafina down.

Sitting in front of the madam who was busy counting coins, she said, "I'd like to see Lola's room."

She followed her to the bedrooms on the second level where Rosa unlocked the first door to the right of the staircase.

"Stuffy in here," she said, lifting the sash and opening the shutters. Sunlight and a sea breeze flooded the room.

Serafina prowled around the room, large and rococo, similar to Bella's, but without the sewing machine. Decorated in blues and greens, somehow soft but at the same time opulent, not what she expected to see. "So neat."

"Surprised?" Rosa asked.

"Everything about Lola surprises me."

Serafina lifted the spread. No bedding. She felt the cold grip her stomach.

Serafina walked around, opening desk drawers. Empty. One was stuck.

She opened the closets. They were filled with dresses, neatly arranged, matching shoes and bags underneath. In the bureau drawers, Lola's linen was folded and well-ordered.

Lifting the chair cushion, Serafina felt with her hands for

anything, a scrap of paper, a note or letter. Nothing.

Returning to the desk, she pried the stuck drawer. Wedged in the back between the desk and the wall, was a leather-bound book. Serafina riffled the blank pages until she came to one with writing—scribbles, really. The hand was small and cramped, the pages scrawled with words that made no sense.

While the madam sat fanning herself with a linen and staring into space, Serafina lifted the bedspread, peered underneath the bed, and saw a box. She tried to pull it toward her, but it wouldn't move. "Help me with this will you?"

They pulled on it together. At first it wouldn't move—the box seemed to be packed with iron—but slowly the box began to move, and they slid it out from under the bed.

Rosa opened it. "Gold!" She began to count, but shrugged.

"We'll carry it to your desk," Serafina said.

"Leave it. A job for Scarpo."

Serafina held her lower lip. "This room tells me nothing. Difficult to understand how a person can inhabit a space and not leave it impressed with her presence."

"Which presence? Many people, our Lola. Sometimes a *strega*, sometimes a lost soul, a snake, a clown, a friend, a killer. My enemy."

Later Serafina sat in the office, watching Rosa count her coins when here was a knock.

"We've found Rosalia," Scarpo said. "You'd better come."

The sea wind blew up sand in swirls. It stung her face as Serafina, her skirt tucked beneath her, swayed on the back of a mule, led by a guard. The group moved slowly, picking their way down the face of steep rocks. Ahead Scarpo led the madam, astride another beast. Three guards followed, pulling a mule and cart. Waves crashed the shore, their sound unceasing. The wind continued its howl.

Inside the monk's cave Serafina saw Rosa, a linen to her nose, shaking her head.

Rosalia lay on the ground near a heap of clothes. The dead prostitute was fully clothed for the evening, a knife stuck in her heart, her face cold to the touch, the mark of the serpent on her forehead. ⚒

In Prison

Thursday, November 8, 1866

Serafina wound down the stairwell leading to the dungeon's lower level, her toes like yellow pods stuck into the frozen earth. The flame on her torch fouled the air. Moisture tightened her curls, seeped into her armpits. A dark form scurried past, perhaps the shade of some dead innocent, here to exact its revenge.

As she entered the visitors' room, Lola, shackled, stared ahead. Her lips were cracked, her nails bleeding, her clothes rent. Serafina smelled a strong, ferrous stench. She handed her torch to a guard and sat.

"There," one of her keepers barked to the inmate, indicating the stool opposite Serafina. Lola seemed not to comprehend, but stood motionless, until he pawed the prisoner's shoulders, forcing her to sit. Then, as if waking from a dream, Lola's eyes began to focus. "Good of you to visit," she said, licking her lips.

"Brought cigarettes." Serafina set them on the table in front of Lola.

"Here, none of that," a guard said, reaching for the box.

"It's all right. The inspector gave permission," Serafina lied.

The guard opened the box and examined the cigarettes. He looked at his companion who shrugged and flipped them back on the table.

Without removing her gaze from Serafina, Lola grabbed a cigarette, struck a match, and breathed in the weed. When she exhaled, yellow smoke encircled her, catching the light from the wall torches.

Serafina waited for Lola to finish the cigarette. *She looks like a violated Madonna, chipped and spent.*

Lola sucked in and puffed out. Crushing the ember, she reached for another. Several more minutes passed in silence while the room filled with smoke. One guard shuffled his feet.

"How did you come to know of the brazen serpent?" Serafina asked.

"I told you about the child. I left. Taken in by a family. I went to school with the daughter. The nuns taught us, but it didn't work out."

"How so?"

She bit a nail, concentrated on chewing, as a dog would a bone. "I left. You would have, too."

Serafina nodded, remembering Rosa telling her about the whip marks on Lola's back.

Lola wiped her bleeding nails on her skirt. "Ran away. Came to a church. The nuns took me in. Hard life, cold."

"In the north, you told me."

Lola stared at the wall. Her speech became clipped, her voice, almost a whisper. "Lombardy. People hard to understand. Work. Prayers. Mass every morning. But good food, a soft bed. I met the man I told you about."

"And he told you about the brazen serpent?"

She nodded. "Yes, it was there that the voices had pity on me. They came to me after they took my child away. They said the brazen serpent had chosen me."

"The inspector said you confessed to the murders of five women."

Lola's eyes had an inward look. "I was given the work of the brazen serpent at the appointed time to rid the world of sinners. The harlots chose to leave this life for a better one. I sent them to that life. I'm proud of it."

"But it's six, isn't it—six murdered women?"

Lola said nothing. She chewed on her lip.

"You had help."

Lola shook her head again and again. "No help. No help! None. Only these." With sudden fury, her hands, like claws, clutched for

Serafina, but she was restrained by her manacles before the guards could pull her back.

"You, I could not rid the earth of you. I tried, oh, the brazen serpent gave me the strength and the grace, gave me the means—a perfect night, a perfect number, a perfect feast. Yes, the voices helped me, save me even now. And I could have succeeded, if it hadn't been for Scarpo's child in Satan's grip."

Serafina felt a coldness from within.

No longer smiling, Lola rubbed her hands together and, for the first time, her eyes searched the room. She began pulling her hair, hanging now in thick, clotted strands. "No help, no help," she said. "Except for the voices. They wait for the turning. When I take over the reins, the world will suffer no more." She flung the empty cigarette box on the floor.

A guard called time.

Lola lifted her head and stared.

"May I visit again?" Serafina asked.

"I promise them a soft sleep, the voices. Their work is almost over." 🖎

A Fitting Reward

Monday, November 12, 1866

She entered Rosa's office. The sea was a wrinkled blanket underneath a sodden sky, and like a mystic mumbling prayers, the madam sat at her desk whispering numbers and entering them into her ledger. Serafina sat in the chair facing her. Flexing her frozen toes, she heard the whir of the abacus, the hiss of the fire, the ping of sleet hitting the window.

Rubbing her hands together, Rosa said, "I tell you, counting coins is endless work. Wouldn't be so bad if I could go to my bed at a decent hour, but I was up until three this morning."

"Cut down on your hours."

"You have no mind for business. Not the same without me in the parlor, joking, offering drinks, praising the customers for their handsome manliness. And business is brisk, I tell you. In the morning I count the money, make sure the house is clean, the sheets laundered, direct the cooking. Now Colonna tells me my girls must pass a health test once a month." She shook her head. "More papers to fill out, more money under the table."

"I brought you these." Serafina handed her a tray covered with linen. "They are a bribe. I have a favor to ask."

"It is I who owe you. Ask away." She scooped up the coins, the notes and the ledger, shoving them all into the middle drawer, and looked at the tray.

"Hear me out before you say no. I need to borrow Tessa if she—"

"Never. Tessa stays with me."

"Why are you afraid?" Serafina didn't wait for an answer. "Totò has been moping ever since our next door neighbors left. One day they're here, and the next moment, the whole family vanishes— parents, both grandmothers, the children. Here for generations, gone in a heartbeat. They left after sunset, no goodbyes. We learned last week that they took the night train, boarded a steamer in Palermo for South America. Now my Totò stares out the window looking at the emptiness next door, and I can't stand it. Assunta takes him out for sweets and ices, but it doesn't lift his spirits. We read to him, talk to him, and the other children try to comfort him. But he has lost his playmates and misses Tessa. I can't bear to see him suffer—my youngest, you know."

Rosa threw her an inscrutable look. She snuggled her nose up to the sweets and breathed in. "Oh Madonna, exquisite!" Lifting her head toward the ceiling and steepling her hands in prayer, she uncovered the tray and offered one to Serafina who shook her head.

Rosa helped herself. "Mmmm, Renata made these? Divine." Helped herself to another. "Best *cannoli* I've ever eaten. The shell is paper thin, crackles like Christmas candy, and melts in the mouth. The taste of the filling is … heaven." She ate another, closed her eyes, rolled her hands back and forth. "Even the nuns in Palermo do no better." She bit into a fourth. "You know," she said, with a full mouth, "we need to celebrate. I could borrow Renata just to show Formusa the recipe and—"

"No one borrows Renata. Better to be married to that dunce of an inspector than to lend out Renata."

Rosa wiped her face with her handkerchief. At the edge of vision, Serafina saw an oblong with a mustache standing in the doorway, fedora in hand. He carried a large envelope.

Colonna nodded to Serafina. "Your domestic said I'd find you here. Good day to you both, dear ladies."

"*Cannolo*, Inspector?" Rosa asked.

He shook his head. "Thanks, but my wife, you know, she watches my stomach."

"Something to drink then? Please, sit down." Rosa pulled the cord.

When Gesuzza arrived, Rosa said, "Caffè."

Colonna began, "Some distressing news first. They found Lola's body this morning hanging from the rafters of her cell. How she obtained the rope she used, who knows?" He played with one end of his mustache. His eyes were without glimmer.

Rosa bowed her head and drummed her fist on her chest.

Serafina's eyes swam. "How did she tie the rope to the rafters?" she asked. "The ceiling in her cell is what, almost five meters from the floor—she couldn't have reached the rafters."

It was Colonna's turn to be surprised. Surprised, because a woman had knowledge enough to ask such a question. Surprised because a woman had the nerve to ask such a question. And surprised because Serafina knew the structure of their keep. In reply, he held up both palms to the ceiling and shrugged.

Rosa's eyes darted between Serafina and Colonna.

Serafina asked, "Did she leave a note?"

Colonna shook his head. "We told her family."

"What family?" Rosa asked.

Silence while Gesuzza entered, carrying a tray with glasses of espresso.

Colonna drank his espresso in one gulp and eyed Rosa's bottle of grappa. "From her identity card and the ministry's records, we located an uncle or some such living in the province of Enna. They said one day Lola vanished and never contacted them again. Didn't know what had happened to her until my men showed up. We sent her remains to Sperlinga this morning."

Serafina wondered how Colonna had unlimited help from police all of a sudden. "The other day I visited her. What a horrible dungeon you have. Even the visitor's room is dank—lizards crawling up the walls, spiders creeping on the ground—you must be ashamed of it, no? My clothes were soaked. I had to change them when I came home."

She continued. "Quite mad, Lola, a lost soul, and wearing the same dress she wore underneath her monk's costume. She hadn't been washed or given a comb for her hair, not even prisoner's garb. How could the state be so cruel?"

Rosa wiped her eyes.

The inspector shrugged and handed Serafina an envelope. "This came by messenger from the prefect's office yesterday. Addressed to you."

Serafina put down her espresso, looked at the envelope penned in formal script, and broke the seal. As she read the contents, she jerked a hand to her heart, feeling the heat sear up her face.

"Typical," Rosa said. "She keeps us in suspense until we stand it no longer. Tell us!"

Serafina summarized its contents. "For my invaluable help in apprehending the Ambrosi murderer, I am awarded one hundred lire." Serafina brushed back curls and pushed the vellum across the desk to Rosa.

"And he doubles your stipend? Bah. Nothing times two is still nothing. Had you been a man, he would have awarded you the Civilian Medal of *Risorgimento*."

Colonna played with his mustache.

"A pittance. She deserves much more." Following the line of words with painted nails, Rosa moved her lips while she read. When finished, she looked at Colonna. "I'll go at once to Palermo and tell the prefect myself. Perhaps you'll go with me, Pirricù?" She poured him a grappa. "But why does he refer to the 'Ambrosi murderer,' not that I'd want him to mention my house."

Serafina said, "No doubt an editor at the *Giornale di Sicilia* crafted the epithet."

Colonna drank. He said, "Me, I don't understand its meaning, but the phrase has been taken up by the people."

Serafina told them what she knew about the Ambrosian rite practiced in Milan and their use of serpent-like imagery. "In her disturbed way, Lola was fascinated with everything that the brazen serpent represents—the concepts of grace and power, of death and new life, of expiation and redemption. She took the meaning and the trappings of the rite and bent them to suit her mad ends, dwelling too much on the sting of the serpent and not enough on redemption."

Rosa said, "Dwelling too much on my coins, you mean, but tell me one thing, oh wizard. You weren't surprised when her disguise slipped away and Lola stood unmasked before us?"

Serafina shook her head. "All along I thought it was either Falco or Lola. But since yesterday, I was convinced the monk was someone in your house. Had to be Lola."

"How did you know?" Rosa asked.

Serafina said, "She had the means. She had the motive. She had the opportunity."

Colonna was having trouble following the conversation, and Rosa looked bored.

"Stop sounding like a tax collector," she said. "Tell us, but don't use too many words."

Serafina said, "First the means. You told me last month she carved your sign."

Rosa nodded.

"So Lola knew how to handle a knife, and we knew that the ragpicker sharpened knives in the rough neighborhood—Scarpo told us, remember?"

Rosa nodded. "But how did your mind jump from Lola to the ragpicker?"

Serafina said, "This ragpicker, he gnawed at my head. Ran into him everywhere. Kept seeing him in the piazza. I saw him in an altercation with the rope seller and again in a collision with the mattress maker, and other times, I saw him in and around the piazza, staring at the Duomo. I saw him on the road between Oltramari and the Madonie when we returned from Elisabetta's home—he was the one who shot Vicenzu."

"An altercation with the rope seller, you say?" Rosa asked.

"He has a shop on the piazza across from the shoemaker—you know the one I mean."

"Why would I?"

Serafina continued. "No matter. The rope seller dealt the picker a handy blow or two, drew blood from his nose, and that was the end. Hadn't a clue how to fight, the ragpicker. What man doesn't know how to fight, I asked myself."

Rosa chuckled. "They learn how in the womb." She poured Colonna another grappa. "But how did you know that the ragpicker was Lola?"

"I didn't at first, but my mind leapt."

"We know, like a gazelle," Rosa said.

Serafina rubbed her forehead. "Lola was fascinated by artifice."

"Wily, that one."

"And a shapeshifter, inventing, reinventing," Serafina said. "Poor, lost Lola."

"Better get to the motive part before we put Colonna to sleep." Rosa poured the inspector another grappa.

He gulped his drink, wiping his mustache with his hand.

"Motive. That's a bit tricky. She's mad, Lola."

"Tricky? Stole my coins, the *strega*. What's so tricky about that?" The two women were silent. Colonna's eyelids were heavy.

"Never went to church as far as I knew—well, except disguised as a monk. She'll always be a mystery to me. Too happy, too sad, our Lola, and all at once."

"She should have been put away, not imprisoned," Serafina said. Rosa asked, "This 'opportunity.' What do you mean?"

"We've touched on it."

"Well, touch on it again." Rosa said.

Serafina drank the last of her caffè. "Ave Maria's wagon made it all fall into place. The ragpicker's cart gave her opportunity to be here, to be there, to fetch, to carry, to costume."

The madam shook her head. "Too much. We'll be here all morning."

Colonna appeared dumbfounded and shifted in his chair. "The people are proud of you, Donna Fina," he said. "And you too, Rosa. A writer from *Giornale di Sicilia* called on the mayor the other day asking for your addresses. He said he wants to interview you both."

Serafina asked, "So I take it the case is closed, the killings solved as far as you are concerned, even though there are still unknowns, especially surrounding Lola's death? No note and you still say it's a suicide?"

Again the inspector shrugged. Beads of sweat were forming on his forehead. "No need for you ladies to be present at the hearing. Before she took her life, Lola signed a confession. She admitted killing five women."

"It was six, that I know of," Serafina said. "Gemma, Nelli, Bella, Eugenia, Gusti, Rosalia."

After he left, the madam said, "Why couldn't I see it? She had moods you know, my Lola, terrible and deep, and yet she was an angel sometimes, so loving, so droll. But she wanted to take over my house, a devil disguised as a monk."

"What about me? I'm the wizard, remember? You handed me the truth about her from the very beginning." Serafina reached into her reticule, brought out the notebook, flipped to the right page and read, "'My Lola, she can do anything when she wants.' I should have asked you what you meant by 'when she wants.' I should have taken more time questioning the women. I knew they were hiding something from me, probably from themselves. It took me too long to discover."

"Took me long enough to see, and it took you long enough to decide, slow and pokey as usual, but you found the killer in less than three weeks. Your plan was brilliant. Shimmering fantasy. And you have your daughter back. Time to move on." Serafina made baroque circles in the air. "This house, the whole thing, it's too much for you. We are women of a certain age now."

"Speak for yourself."

"And I have a plan," Serafina said. "You sell the business to Scarpo. Buy the villa next to ours."

Rosa opened her mouth, but Serafina continued. "Picture it. A sunny day. You sleep till noon, waking to Maria's Brahms wafting through the window. Renata runs over with a tray of pastries for your breakfast. Vicenzu's medicinal recipes settle your stomach. In the afternoon, you have a fitting for a new wardrobe created to your specifications by the House of Giulia while your gardens are primped by Carmela. Totò helps Tessa milk your goat. Dr. Carlo fixes your every pain. And the best of all, I promise to invent intrigue upon intrigue for us to solve. See what happens when you give Tessa a proper life?"

For a moment Rosa sat like a buddha, perhaps ex"You haven't seen the carts passing in and out of the gate next to your door? The carpenters? The stone masons? The gardeners? And you call yourself a wizard? Tessa and I move in tomorrow."

About the Author

Susan Russo Anderson is a writer, a mother, a grandmother, a widow, a member of Sisters In Crime, a graduate of Marquette University. She has taught language arts and creative writing, worked for a publisher, an airline, an opera company. Like Faulkner's Dilsey, she's seen the best and the worst, the first and the last. Through it all, and to understand it somewhat, she writes.

DEATH OF A SERPENT, the first in the Serafina Florio series, published in ebook format in January 2012. It began as a painting of the Lower East Side, the landmark immigrant neighborhood in Manhattan, and wound up as a mystery story set in nineteenth-century Sicily.

NO MORE BROTHERS, a novella, published May 2012, the second in the series. The third book, DEATH IN BAGHERIA, published in December 2012. You can read excerpts of all her books on Amazon and on her website, susanrussoanderson.com.